ALISTAIR MACLEAN

Alistair MacLean, the son of a Scots minister, was brought up in the Scottish Highlands. In 1941, at the age of eighteen, he joined the Royal Navy. After the war he read English at Glasgow University and became a school-master. The two and a half years he spent aboard a wartime cruiser were to give him the background for *HMS Ulysses*, his remarkably successful first novel, published in 1955. He is now recognized as one of the outstanding popular writers of the 20th century, the author of twenty-nine worldwide bestsellers, many of which have been filmed, including *The Guns of Navarone*, *Where Eagles Dare*, *Fear is the Key* and *Ice Station Zebra*. In 1983, he was awarded a D.Litt. from Glasgow University. Alistair MacLean died in 1987.

By Alistair MacLean

ALISTAIR MACLEAN

Santorini

HarperCollins*Publishers*

HarperCollins*Publishers*
1 London Bridge Street,
London SE1 9GF

www.harpercollins.co.uk

HarperCollins*Publishers*
1st Floor, Watermarque Building, Ringsend Road
Dublin 4, Ireland

This paperback edition 2021
1

Previously published in paperback by HarperCollins 2009
and by Fontana 1987

First published in Great Britain by
Collins 1986

ISBN: 978-0-00-833670-7

Printed and bound in Great Britain by
CPI Group (UK) Ltd, Croydon CR0 4YY

MIX
Paper from
responsible sources
FSC www.fsc.org **FSC™ C007454**

This book is produced from independently certified FSC™ paper
to ensure responsible forest management.

For more information visit: www.harpercollins.co.uk/green

To Tom and Rena

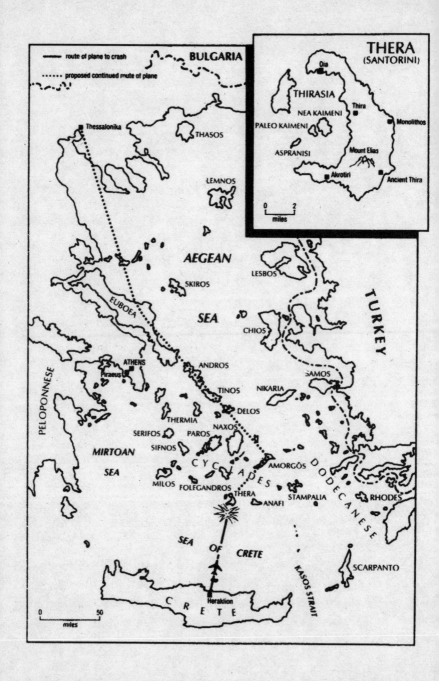

route of plane to crash
proposed continued route of plane

BULGARIA

THERA (SANTORINI)

THIRASIA

Oia

NEA KAIMENI

PALEO KAIMENI

Thira

Monolithos

ASPRANISI

Mount Elias

Akrotiri

Ancient Thira

0   2
miles

THASOS

Thessalonika

LEMNOS

AEGEAN

SEA

LESBOS

SKIROS

EUBOEA

CHIOS

TURKEY

ATHENS

ANDROS

Piraeus

SAMOS

TINOS

NIKARIA

PELOPONNESE

THERMIA

DELOS

SERIFOS

PAROS

NAXOS

SIFNOS

MIRTOAN

CYCLADES

SEA

AMORGOS

DODECANESE

MILOS

FOLEGANDROS

THERA

STAMPALIA

RHODES

ANAFI

SEA   OF   CRETE

KASOS STRAIT

SCARPANTO

CRETE

Heraklion

0   50
miles

1

An overhead broadcaster on the bridge of the frigate *Ariadne* crackled into life, a bell rang twice and then O'Rourke's voice came through, calm, modulated, precise and unmistakably Irish. O'Rourke was commonly referred to as the weatherman, which he wasn't at all.

'Just picked up an odd-looking customer. Forty miles out, bearing 222.'

Talbot pressed the reply button. 'The skies above us, Chief, are hotching with odd-looking customers. At least six airlines criss-cross this patch of the Aegean. NATO planes, as you know better than all of us, are all around us. And those pesky fighter-bombers and fighters from the pesky Sixth Fleet bloweth where the wind listeth. Me, I think they're lost half the time.'

'Ah! But this is a very odd odd-looking lad.' O'Rourke's voice was unruffled as ever, unmoved by the less than flattering reference to the Sixth Fleet, from which he was on temporary loan. 'No trans-Aegean airline uses the flight path this plane is on. There are no NATO planes in this particular sector on my display screen. And the Americans would have let us know. A very courteous lot, Captain. The Sixth Fleet, I mean.'

'True, true.' The Sixth Fleet, Talbot was aware, would have informed him of the presence of any of their aircraft in his vicinity, not from courtesy but because regulations demanded it, a fact of which O'Rourke was as well aware as he was. O'Rourke was a doughty defender of his home fleet. 'That all you have on this lad?'

'No. Two things. This plane is on a due south-west to north-east course. I have no record, no information of any plane that could be following this course. Secondly, I'm pretty sure it's a big plane. We should see in about four minutes – his course is on a direct intersection with ours.'

'The size is important, Chief? Lots of big planes around.'

'Not at 43,000 feet, sir, which is what this one is. Only a Concorde does that and we know there are no Concordes about. Military job, I would guess.'

'Of unknown origin. A bandit? Could be. Keep an eye on him.' Talbot looked around and caught the eye of his second-in-command, Lieutenant-Commander Van Gelder. Van Gelder was short, very broad, deeply tanned, flaxen-haired and seemed to find life a source of constant amusement. He was smiling now as he approached the captain.

2

'Consider it done, sir. The spy-glass and a photo for your family album?'

'That's it. Thank you.' The *Ariadne* carried an immense and, to the uninitiated, quite bewildering variety of looking and listening instruments that may well have been unmatched by any naval ship afloat. Among those instruments were what Van Gelder had referred to as the spy-glass. This was a combined telescope and camera, invented and built by the French, of the type used by spy satellites in orbit and which was capable, under ideal atmospheric circumstances, of locating and photographing a white plate from an altitude of 250 miles. The focal length of the telescope was almost infinitely adjustable: in this case Van Gelder would probably use a one in a hundred resolution, which would have the optical effect of bringing the intruder – if intruder it was – to an apparent altitude of four hundred feet. In the cloudless July skies of the Cyclades this presented no problem at all.

Van Gelder had just left the bridge when another loudspeaker came to life, the repeated double buzzer identifying it as the radio-room. The helmsman, Leading Seaman Harrison, leaned forward and made the appropriate switch.

'I have an SOS. I think – repeat think – vessel's position is just south of Thera. All I have. Very garbled, certainly not a trained operator. Just keeps repeating "Mayday, Mayday, Mayday".' Myers, the radio operator on duty, sounded annoyed:

every radio operator, the tone of his voice said, should be as expert and efficient as he was. 'Wait a minute, though.' There was a pause, then Myers came on again. 'Sinking, he says. Four times he said he was sinking.'

Talbot said: 'That all?'

'That's all, sir. He's gone off the air.'

'Well, just keep listening on the distress frequency, Harrison, 090 or near enough. Can't be more than ten, twelve miles away.' He reached for the engine control and turned it up to full power. The *Ariadne*, in the modern fashion, had dual engine-room and bridge controls. The engine-room had customarily only one rating, a leading stoker, on watch, and this only because custom dictated it, not because necessity demanded it. The lone watchman might, just possibly, be wandering around with an oil-can in hand but more probably was immersed in one of the lurid magazines with which what was called the engine-room library was so liberally stocked. The *Ariadne*'s chief engineer, Lieutenant McCafferty, rarely ventured near his own domain. A first-class engineer, McCafferty claimed he was allergic to diesel fumes and treated with a knowing disdain the frequently repeated observation that, because of the engine-room's highly efficient extractor fans, it was virtually impossible for anyone to detect the smell of diesel. He was to be found that afternoon, as he was most afternoons, seated in a deckchair aft and immersed in his

4

favourite form of relaxation, the reading of detective novels heavily laced with romance of the more dubious kind.

The distant sound of the diesels deepened – the *Ariadne* was capable of a very respectable 35 knots – and the bridge began to vibrate quite noticeably. Talbot reached for a phone and got through to Van Gelder.

'We've picked up a distress signal. Ten, twelve miles away. Let me know when you locate this bandit and I'll cut the engines.' The spy-glass, though splendidly gimballed to deal with the worst vagaries of pitching and rolling, was quite incapable of coping with even the mildest vibration which, more often than not, produced a very fuzzy photograph indeed.

Talbot moved out on to the port wing to join the lieutenant who stood there, a tall, thin young man with fair hair, thick pebbled glasses and a permanently lugubrious expression.

'Well, Jimmy, how do you fancy this? A maybe bandit and a sinking vessel at the same time. Should relieve the tedium of a long hot summer's afternoon, don't you think?'

The lieutenant looked at him without enthusiasm. Lieutenant the Lord James Denholm – Talbot called him 'Jimmy' for brevity's sake – seldom waxed enthusiastic about anything.

'I don't fancy it at all, Captain.' Denholm waved a languid hand. 'Disturbs the even tenor of my ways.'

Talbot smiled. Denholm was surrounded by an almost palpable aura of aristocratic exhaustion that had disturbed and irritated Talbot in the early stage of their acquaintanceship, a feeling that had lasted for no more than half an hour. Denholm was totally unfitted to be a naval officer of any kind and his highly defective eyesight should have led to his automatic disbarment from any navy in the world. But Denholm was aboard the *Ariadne* not because of his many connections with the highest echelons of society – heir to an earldom, his blood was indisputably the bluest of the blue – but because, without question, he was the right man in the right place. The holder of three scientific degrees – from Oxford, UCLA and MIT, all *summa cum laude* – in electrical engineering and electronics, Denholm was as close to being an electronics wizard as any man could ever hope to be. Not that Denholm would have claimed to be anything of what he would have said to be the ridiculous kind. Despite his lineage and academic qualifications, Denholm was modest and retiring to a fault. This reticence extended even to the making of protests which was why, despite his feeble objections – he had been under no compulsion to go – he had been dragooned into the Navy in the first place.

He said to Talbot: 'This bandit, Captain – if it is a bandit – what do you intend to do about it?'

'I don't intend to do anything about it.'

6

'But if he *is* a bandit – well, then, he's spying, isn't he?'

'Of course.'

'Well, then –'

'What do you expect me to do, Jimmy? Bring him down? Or are you itching to try out this experimental laser gun you have with you?'

'Heaven forfend.' Denholm was genuinely horrified. 'I've never fired a gun in anger in my life. Correction. I've never even fired a gun.'

'If I wanted to bring him down a teeny-weeny heat-seeking missile would do the job very effectively. But we don't do things like that. We're civilized. Besides, we don't provoke international incidents. An unwritten law.'

'Sounds a very funny law to me.'

'Not at all. When the United States or NATO play war games, as we are doing now, the Soviets track us very closely indeed, whether on land, sea or air. We don't complain. We can't. When they're playing their game we do exactly the same to them. Can, admittedly, have its awkward moments. Not so long ago, when the US Navy were carrying out exercises in the Sea of Japan an American destroyer banged into, and quite severely damaged, a Russian submarine which was monitoring things a little too closely.'

'And *that* didn't cause what you've just called an international incident?'

'Certainly not. Nobody's fault. Mutual apologies between the two captains and the Russian was towed to a safe port by another Russian warship. Vladivostok, I believe it was.' Talbot turned his head. 'Excuse me. That's the radio-room call-up.'

'Myers again,' the speaker said. '*Delos*. Name of the sinking vessel. Very brief message – explosion, on fire, sinking fast.'

'Keep listening,' Talbot said. He looked at the helmsman who already had a pair of binoculars to his eyes. 'You have it, Harrison?'

'Yes, sir.' Harrison handed over the binoculars and twitched the wheel to port. 'Fire off the port bow.'

Talbot picked it up immediately, a thin black column of smoke rising vertically, unwaveringly, into the blue and windless sky. He was just lowering his glasses when the bell rang twice again. It was O'Rourke, the weatherman, or, more officially, the senior long-range radar operator.

'Lost him, I'm afraid. The bandit, I mean. I was looking at the vectors on either side of him to see if he had any friends and when I came back he was gone.'

'Any ideas, Chief?'

'Well . . .' O'Rourke sounded doubtful. 'He *could* have exploded but I doubt it.'

'So do I. We've had the spy-glass trained on his approach bearing and they'd have picked up an explosion for sure.'

'Then he must have gone into a steep dive. A very steep dive. God knows why. I'll find him.' The speaker clicked off.

Almost at once a telephone rang again. It was Van Gelder.

'222, sir. Smoke. Plane. Could be the bandit.'

'Almost certainly is. The weatherman's just lost it off the long-range radar screen. Probably a waste of time but try to get that photograph anyway.'

He moved out on to the starboard wing and trained his glasses over the starboard quarter. He picked it up immediately, a heavy dark plume of smoke with, he thought, a glow of red at its centre. It was still quite high, at an altitude of four or five thousand feet. He didn't pause to check how deeply the plane was diving or whether or not it actually was on fire. He moved quickly back into the bridge and picked up a phone.

'Sub-Lieutenant Cousteau. Quickly.' A brief pause. 'Henri? Captain. Emergency. Have the launch and the lifeboat slung outboard. Crews to stand by to lower. Then report to the bridge.' He rang down to the engine-room for Slow Ahead then said to Harrison: 'Hard a-port. Steer north.'

Denholm, who had moved out on to the starboard wing, returned, lowering his binoculars.

'Well, even I can see that plane. Not a plane, rather a huge streamer of smoke. Could that have been the bandit, sir – if it was a bandit?'

'Must have been.'

Denholm said, tentatively: 'I don't care much for his line of approach, sir.'

'I don't care much for it myself, Lieutenant, especially if it's a military plane and even more especially if it's carrying bombs of any sort. If you look, you'll see that we're getting out of its way.'

'Ah. Evasive action.' Denholm hesitated, then said doubtfully: 'Well, as long as he doesn't alter course.'

'Dead men don't alter courses.'

'That they don't.' Van Gelder had just returned to the bridge. 'And the man or the men behind the controls of that plane are surely dead. No point in my staying there, sir – Gibson's better with the spy-glass camera than I am and he's very busy with it. We'll have plenty of photographs to show you but I doubt whether we'll be able to learn very much from them.'

'As bad as that? You weren't able to establish anything?'

'Very little, I'm afraid. I did see the outer engine on the port wing. So it's a four-engined jet. Civil or military, I've no idea.'

'A moment, please.' Talbot moved out on the port wing, looked aft, saw that the blazing plane – there was no mistaking the flames now – was due astern, at less than half the height and distance than when he had first seen it, returned to the bridge, told Harrison to steer due north, then turned again to Van Gelder.

'That was all you could establish?'

'About. Except that the fire is definitely located in the nose cone, which would rule out any engine explosion. It couldn't have been hit by a missile because we know there are no missile-carrying planes around – even if there were, a heat-seeking missile, the only type that could nail it at that altitude, would have gone for the engines, not the nose cone. It could only have been an up-front internal explosion.'

Talbot nodded, reached for a phone, asked the exchange for the sick bay and was through immediately.

'Doctor? Would you detail an SBA – with first-aid kit – to stand by the lifeboat.' He paused for a moment. 'Sorry, no time to explain. Come on up to the bridge.' He looked aft through the starboard wing doorway, turned and took the wheel from the helmsman. 'Take a look, Harrison. A good look.'

Harrison moved out on the starboard wing, had his good look – it took him only a few seconds – returned and took the wheel again.

'Awful.' He shook his head. 'They're finished, sir, aren't they?'

'So I would have thought.'

'They're going to miss us by at least a quarter mile. Maybe a half.' Harrison took another quick look through the doorway. 'This angle of descent – they should land – rather, hit the sea – a mile, mile and a half ahead. Unless by some fluke they carry on and hit the island. That would be curtains, sir.'

'It would indeed.' Talbot looked ahead through the for'ard screens. Thera Island was some four miles distant with Cape Akrotiri lying directly to the north and Mount Elias, the highest point of the

11

island – it was close on 2000 feet – to the north-east. Between them, but about five miles further distant, a tenuous column of bluish smoke, hardly visible against a cloudless sky, hung lazily in the air. This marked the site of Thira Village, the only settlement of any size on the island. 'But the damage would be limited to the plane. The south-west of the island is barren. I don't think anyone lives there.'

'What are we going to do, sir? Stop over the point where it goes down?'

'Something like that. You can handle it yourself. Or maybe another quarter or half mile further on along the line he was taking. Have to wait and see. Fact is, Harrison, I know no more about it than you do. It may disintegrate on impact or, if it survives that, it may carry on some distance under water. Not for far, I should think – not if its nose has gone. Number One –' this to Van Gelder '– what depths do we have here?'

'I know the five fathom mark is about half a mile offshore along the south of the island. Beyond that, it shelves pretty steeply. I'll have to check in the chart-room. At the moment I'd guess we're in two to three hundred fathoms. A sonar check, sir?'

'Please.' Van Gelder left, brushing by Sub-Lieutenant Cousteau as he did. Cousteau, barely in his twenties, was a happy-go-lucky youngster, always eager and willing and a more than competent seaman. Talbot beckoned him out on to the starboard wing.

'Have you seen it, Henri?'

'Yes, sir.' Cousteau's normal cheerfulness was in marked abeyance. He gazed in unwilling fascination at the blazing, smoking plane, now directly abeam and at an altitude of under a thousand feet. 'What a damnable, awful thing.'

'Aye, it's not nice.' They had been joined by Surgeon Lieutenant-Commander Andrew Grierson. Grierson was dressed in white shorts and a flowing multi-coloured Hawaiian shirt which he doubtless regarded as the correct dress of the day for the summer Aegean. 'So this is why you wanted Moss and his first-aid box.' Moss was the Leading Sick Bay Attendant. 'I'm thinking maybe I should be going myself.' Grierson was a West Highland Scot, as was immediately evident from his accent, an accent which he never attempted to conceal for the excellent reason that he saw no earthly reason why he ever should. 'If there are any survivors, which I consider bloody unlikely, I know something about decompression problems which Moss doesn't.'

Talbot was conscious of the increased vibration beneath his feet. Harrison had increased speed and was edging a little to the east. Talbot didn't even give it a second thought: his faith in his senior quartermaster was complete.

'Sorry, Doctor, but I have more important things for you to do.' He pointed to the east. 'Look under the trail of smoke to the plane's left.'

'I see it. I should have seen it before. Somebody sinking, for a fiver.'

'Indeed. Something called the *Delos*, a private yacht, I should imagine, and, as you say, sinking. Explosion and on fire. Pretty heavily on fire, too, I would think. Burns, injuries.'

'We live in troubled times,' Grierson said. Grierson, in fact, lived a singularly carefree and untroubled existence but Talbot thought it was hardly the time to point this out to him.

'The plane's silent, sir,' Cousteau said. 'The engines have been shut off.'

'Survivors, you think? I'm afraid not. The explosion may have destroyed the controls in which case, I imagine, the engines shut off automatically.'

'Disintegrate or dive?' Grierson said. 'Daft question. We'll know all too soon.'

Van Gelder joined them. 'I make it eighty fathoms here, sir. Sonar says seventy. They're probably right. Doesn't matter, it's shallowing anyway.'

Talbot nodded and said nothing. Nobody said anything, nobody felt like saying anything. The plane, or the source of the dense column of smoke, was now less than a hundred feet above the water. Suddenly, the source of the smoke and flame dipped and then was abruptly extinguished. Even then they failed to catch a glimpse of the plane, it had been immediately engulfed in a fifty-foot-high curtain of water and spray. There was no sound of impact and certainly no disintegration for when the water and the spray cleared away there was only the empty sea and curiously small waves, little more than ripples, radiating outwards from the point of impact.

Talbot touched Cousteau on the arm. 'Your cue, Henri. How's the whaler's radio?'

'Tested yesterday, sir. Okay.'

'If you find anything, anybody, let us know. I have a feeling you won't need that radio. When we stop, lower away then keep circling around. We should be back in half an hour or so.' Cousteau left and Talbot turned to Van Gelder. 'When we stop, tell sonar I want the exact depth.'

Five minutes later the whaler was in the water and moving away from the side of the *Ariadne*, Talbot rang for full power and headed east.

Van Gelder hung up a phone. 'Thirty fathoms, sonar says. Give or take a fathom.'

'Thanks. Doctor?'

'Hundred and eighty feet,' Grierson said. 'I don't even have to rub my chin over that one. The answer is no. Even if anyone could escape from the fuselage – which I think would be impossible in the first place – they'd die soon after surfacing. Diver's bends. Burst lungs. They wouldn't know that they'd have to breathe out all the way up. A trained, fit submariner, possibly with breathing apparatus, might do it. There would be no fit, trained submariners aboard that plane. Question's academic, anyway. I agree with you, Captain. The only men aboard that plane are dead men.'

Talbot nodded and reached for a phone.

'Myers? Signal to General Carson. Unidentified four-engined plane crashed in sea two miles south of Cape Akrotiri, Thera Island. 1415 hours. Impossible to determine whether military or civilian. First located altitude 43,000 feet. Apparent cause internal explosion. No further details available at present. No NATO planes reported in vicinity. Have you any information? Sylvester. Send Code B.'

'Wilco, sir. Where do I send it?'

'Rome. Wherever he is he'll have it two minutes later.'

Grierson said: 'Well, yes, if anyone knows he should.' Carson was the C-in-C Southern European NATO. He lifted his binoculars and looked at the vertical column of smoke, now no more than four miles to the east. 'A yacht, as you say, and making quite a bonfire. If there's anyone still aboard, they're going to be very warm indeed. Are you going alongside, Captain?'

'Alongside.' Talbot looked at Denholm. 'What's your estimate of the value of the electronic gear we have aboard?'

'Twenty million. Maybe twenty-five. A lot, anyway.'

'There's your answer, Doctor. That thing's gone bang once already. It can go bang once again. I am not going alongside. *You* are. In the launch. That's expendable. The *Ariadne*'s not.'

'Well, thank you very much. And what intrepid soul –'

'I'm sure Number One here will be delighted to ferry you across.'

'Ah. Number One, have your men wear over-alls, gloves and flash-masks. Injuries from burning diesel can be very unpleasant indeed. And you. I go to prepare myself for self-immolation.'

'And don't forget your lifebelts.'

Grierson didn't deign to answer.

They had halved the remaining distance to the burning yacht when Talbot got through to the radio-room again.

'Message dispatched?'

'Dispatched and acknowledged.'

'Anything more from the *Delos*?'

'Nothing.'

'Delos,' Denholm said. 'That's about eighty miles north of here. Alas, the Cyclades will never be the same for me again.' Denholm sighed. Electronics specialist or not, he regarded himself primarily as a classicist and, indeed, he was totally fluent in reading and writing both Latin and Greek. He was deeply immersed in their ancient cultures as the considerable library in his cabin bore testimony. He was also much given to quotations and he quoted now.

> 'The isles of Greece, the isles of Greece!
> Where burning Sappho loved and sung,
> Where grew the arts of war and peace,

Where Delos rose, and Phoebus sprung,
Eternal summer –'

'Your point is taken, Lieutenant,' Talbot said. 'We'll cry tomorrow. In the meantime, let us address ourselves to the problem of those poor souls on the fo'c's'le. I count five of them.'

'So do I.' Denholm lowered his glasses. 'What's all the frantic waving for? Surely to God they can't imagine we haven't seen them?'

'They've seen us all right. Relief, Lieutenant. Expectation of rescue. But there's more to it than that. A certain urgency in their waving. A primitive form of semaphoring. What they're saying is "get us the hell out of here and be quick about it".'

'Maybe they're expecting another explosion?'

'Could be that. Harrison, I want to come to a stop on their starboard beam. At, you understand, a prudent distance.'

'A hundred yards, sir?'

'Fine.'

The *Delos* was – or had been – a rather splendid yacht. A streamlined eighty-footer, it was obvious that it had been, until very, very recently, a dazzling white. Now, because of a combination of smoke and diesel oil, it was mainly black. A rather elaborate superstructure consisted of a bridge, saloon, a dining-room and what may or may not have been a galley. The still dense smoke and flames rising six feet above the poop deck indicated

18

the source of the fire – almost certainly the engine-room. Just aft of the fire a small motorboat was still secured to its davits: it wasn't difficult to guess that either the explosion or the fire had rendered it inoperable.

Talbot said: 'Rather odd, don't you think, Lieutenant?'

'Odd?' Denholm said carefully.

'Yes. You can see that the flames are dying away. One would have thought that would reduce the danger of further explosion.' Talbot moved out on the port wing. 'And you will have observed that the water level is almost up to the deck.'

'I can see she's sinking.'

'Indeed. If you were aboard a vessel that was either going to go up or drag you down when it sank, what would your natural reaction be?'

'To be elsewhere, sir. But I can see that their motorboat has been damaged.'

'Agreed. But a craft that size would carry alternative life-saving equipment. If not a Carley float, then certainly an inflatable rubber dinghy. And any prudent owner would carry a sufficiency of lifebelts and life-jackets for the passengers and crew. I can even see two lifebelts in front of the bridge. But they haven't done the obvious thing and abandoned ship. I wonder why.'

'I've no idea, sir. But it is damned odd.'

'When we've rescued those distressed mariners and brought them aboard, you, Jimmy, will have forgotten how to speak Greek.'

'But I will not have forgotten how to listen in Greek?'

'Precisely.'

'Commander Talbot, you have a devious and suspicious mind.'

'It goes with the job, Jimmy. It goes with the job.'

Harrison brought the *Ariadne* to a stop off the starboard beam of the *Delos* at the agreed hundred yards distance. Van Gelder was away at once and was very quickly alongside the fo'c's'le of the *Delos*. Two boat-hooks around the guard-rail stanchions held them in position. As the launch and the bows of the sinking yacht were now almost level it took only a few seconds to transfer the six survivors – another had joined the group of five that Talbot had seen – aboard the launch. They were, indeed, a sorry and sadly bedraggled lot, so covered in diesel and smoke that it was quite impossible to discriminate among them on the basis of age, sex or nationality.

Van Gelder said: 'Any of you here speak English?'

'We all do.' The speaker was short and stocky and that was all that could be said of him in the way of description. 'Some of us just a little. But enough.' The voice was heavily accented but readily understood. Van Gelder looked at Grierson.

'Any of you injured, any of you burnt?' Grierson said. All shook their heads or mumbled a negative. 'Nothing here for me, Number One. Hot showers, detergents, soap. Not to mention a change of clothing.'

'Who's in charge here?' Van Gelder asked.

'I am.' It was the same man.

'Anybody left aboard?'

'Three men, I'm afraid. They won't be coming with us.'

'You mean they're dead?' The man nodded. 'I'll check.'

'No, no!' His oil-soaked hand gripped Van Gelder's arm. 'It is too dangerous, far too dangerous. I forbid it.'

'You forbid me nothing.' When Van Gelder wasn't smiling, which wasn't often, he could assume a very discouraging expression indeed. The man withdrew his hand. 'Where are those men?'

'In the passageway between the engine-room and the stateroom aft. We got them out after the explosion but before the fire began.'

'Riley.' This to a Leading Seaman. 'Come aboard with me. If you think the yacht's going, give me a call.' He picked up a torch and was about to board the *Delos* when a hand holding a pair of goggles reached out and stopped him. Van Gelder smiled. 'Thank you, Doctor. I hadn't thought of that.'

Once aboard he made his way aft and descended the after companionway. There was smoke down there but not too much and with the aid of his torch he had no difficulty in locating the three missing men, all huddled shapelessly in a corner. To his right was the engine-room door, slightly buckled from the force of the explosion. Not without some difficulty, he forced the door open and at once began coughing as the foul-smelling smoke caught his throat and eyes. He pulled on the goggles but still there was nothing to see except for the red embers of a dying fire emanating from some unknown source. He pulled the door to behind him – he was reasonably certain there was nothing for him to see in the engine-room anyway – and stooped to examine the three dead men. They were far from being a pretty sight but he forced himself to carry out as thorough an investigation as he could. He spent some quite considerable time bent over the third man – in the circumstances thirty seconds was a long time – and when he straightened he looked both puzzled and thoughtful.

The door to the after stateroom opened easily. There was some smoke there but not so much that he required to use his goggles. The cabin was luxuriously furnished and immaculately tidy, a condition which Van Gelder very rapidly altered. He pulled a sheet from one of the beds, spread it on the floor, opened up wardrobes and drawers, scooped up armfuls of clothes – there was no time to make any kind of selection and even if there had been he would have been unable to pick and choose, they were all women's clothing – dumped them on the sheet, tied up the four corners, lugged the bundle up the companionway and handed it over to Riley.

'Put this in the launch. I'm going to have a quick look at the for'ard cabins. I think the steps will be at the for'ard end of the saloon under the bridge.'

'I think you should hurry, sir.'

Van Gelder didn't answer. He didn't have to be told why he should hurry – the sea was already beginning to trickle over on to the upper deck. He passed into the saloon, found the companionway at once and descended to a central passage.

He switched on his torch – there was, of course, no electrical power left. There were doors on both sides and one at the end. The first door to port opened up into a food store, the corresponding door to starboard was locked. Van Gelder didn't bother with it: the *Delos* didn't look like the kind of craft that would lack a commodious liquor store. Behind the other doors lay four cabins and two bathrooms. All were empty. As he had done before, Van Gelder spread out a sheet – in the passageway, this time – threw some more armfuls of clothes on to it, secured the corners and hurried up on deck.

The launch was no more than thirty yards away when the *Delos*, still on even keel, slid gently under the surface of the sea. There was nothing dramatic to mark its going – just a stream of air bubbles that became gradually smaller and ceased altogether after about twenty seconds.

Talbot was on deck when the launch brought back the six survivors. He looked in concern at the woebegone and bedraggled figures before him.

'My goodness, what a state you people are in. This the lot, Number One?'

'Those that survived, sir. Three died. Impossible to get their bodies out in time.' He indicated the figure nearest him. 'This is the owner.'

'Andropulos,' the man said. 'Spyros Andropulos. You are the officer in charge?'

'Commander Talbot. My commiserations, Mr Andropulos.'

'And my thanks, Commander. We are very deeply grateful –'

'With respect, sir, that can wait. First things first, and the very first thing is to get yourselves cleaned up immediately. Ah. And changed. A problem. Clothes. We'll find some.'

'Clothing we have,' Van Gelder said. He pointed at the two sheet-wrapped packages. 'Ladies. Gentlemen.'

'A mention in dispatches for that, Number One. You said "ladies"?'

'Two, Commander,' Andropulos said. He looked at the two people standing by him. 'My niece and her friend.'

'Ah. Well, should apologize, I suppose, but difficult to tell in the circumstances.'

'My name is Charial.' The voice was unmistakably feminine. 'Irene Charial. This is my friend Eugenia.'

'We could have met under happier circumstances. Lieutenant Denholm here will take you to my cabin. The bathroom is small but adequate. By the time you bring them back, Lieutenant, I trust they are recognizable for what they are.' He turned to a burly, dark-haired figure who, like most of the crew, wore no insignia of rank. 'Chief Petty Officer McKenzie.' McKenzie was the senior NCO on the *Ariadne*. 'The four gentlemen here, Chief. You know what to do.'

'Right away, sir. If you will come with me, gentlemen.'

Grierson also left and Van Gelder and Talbot were left alone. 'We can find this place again?' Van Gelder asked.

'No trouble.' Talbot looked at him speculatively and pointed towards the north-west. 'I've taken a bearing on the monastery and radar station on Mount Elias there. Sonar says that we're in eighteen fathoms. Just to make sure, we'll drop a marker buoy.'

General Carson laid down the slip of paper he had been studying and looked at the colonel seated across the table from him.

'What do you make of this, Charles?'

'Could be nothing. Could be important. Sorry, that doesn't help. I have a feeling I don't like it. It would help a bit if we had a sailor around.'

Carson smiled and pressed a button. 'Do you know if Vice-Admiral Hawkins is in the building?'

'He is, sir.' A girl's voice. 'Do you wish to speak to him or see him?'

'See him, Jean. Ask him if he would be kind enough to stop by.'

Vice-Admiral Hawkins was very young for one of his rank. He was short, a little overweight, more than a little rubicund as to his features and exuded an aura of cheerful bonhomie. He didn't look very bright, which he was. He was widely regarded as having one of the most brilliant minds in the Royal Navy. He took the seat to which Carson had gestured him and glanced at the message slip.

'I see, I see.' He laid the message down. 'But you didn't ask me here to comment on a perfectly straightforward signal. The Sylvester is one of the code names for the frigate HMS *Ariadne*. One of the vessels under your command, sir.'

'Don't rub it in, David. I know it, of course – more accurately I know of it. Don't forget I'm just a simple landlubber. Odd name, isn't it? Royal Naval ship with a Greek name.'

'Courtesy gesture to the Greeks, sir. We're carrying out a joint hydrographic survey with them.'

'Is that so?' General Carson ran a hand through his grizzled hair. 'I was not aware that I was in the hydrographic business, David.'

'You're not, sir, although I have no doubt it could carry out such a survey if it were called for. The *Ariadne* has a radio system that can transmit to, and receive transmissions from, any quarter of the globe. It has telescopes and optical instruments that can pick out the salient features of, say, any passing satellite, even those in geosynchronous orbit – and that's 22,000 miles up. It carries long-range and surface radar that is as advanced as any in the world. And it has a sonar location and detection system that can pick up a sunken object at the bottom of the ocean just as easily as it can pinpoint a lurking submarine. The *Ariadne*, sir, is the eyes and the ears and the voice of your fleet.'

'That's nice to know, I must say. Very reassuring. The ability of the commanding officer of the *Ariadne* is – ah – commensurate with this extraordinary array of devices he controls?'

'Indeed, sir. For an exceptionally complex task an exceptionally qualified man. Commander Talbot is an outstanding officer. Hand-picked for the job.'

'Who picked him?'

'I did.'

'I see. That terminates this line of conversation very abruptly.' Carson pondered briefly. 'I think, Colonel, that we should ask General Simpson about this one.' Simpson, the over-all commander of NATO, was the only man who outranked Carson in Europe.

'Don't see what else we can do, sir.'

'You would agree, David?'

'No, General. I think you'd be wasting your time. If you don't know anything about this, then

I'm damned sure General Simpson doesn't know anything either. This is not an educated guess, call it a completely uneducated guess, but I have an odd feeling that this is one of your planes, sir – an American plane. A bomber, almost certainly, perhaps not yet off the secret lists – it was, after all, flying at an uncommon height.'

'The *Ariadne* could have been in error.'

'The *Ariadne* does not make mistakes. My job and my life on it.' The flat, unemotional voice carried complete conviction. 'Commander Talbot is not the only uniquely qualified man aboard. There are at least thirty others in the same category. We have, for example, an electronics officer so unbelievably advanced in his speciality that none of your much-vaunted high-technology whizzkids in Silicon Valley would even begin to know what he's talking about.'

Carson raised a hand. 'Point taken, David, point taken. So an American bomber. A very special bomber because it must be carrying a very special cargo. What would you guess that to be?'

Hawkins smiled faintly. 'I am not yet in the ESP business, sir. People or goods. Very secret, very important goods or very secret and very important people. There's only one source that can give you the answer and it might be pointed out that their refusal to divulge this information might put the whole future of NATO at risk and that the individual ultimately responsible for the negative decision would be answerable directly to the president of the United States. One does not imagine that the individual concerned would remain in a position of responsibility for very much longer.'

Carson sighed. 'If I may speak in a spirit of complaint, David, I might point out that it's easy for you to talk and even easier to talk tough. You're a British officer. I'm an American.'

'I appreciate that, sir.'

Carson looked at the colonel, who remained silent for a couple of moments, then nodded, slowly, twice. Carson reached for the button on his desk.

'Jean?'

'Sir?'

'Get me the Pentagon. Immediately.'

2

'You are unhappy, Vincent?' Vincent was Van Gelder's first name. There were three of them seated in the wardroom, Talbot, Van Gelder and Grierson.

'Puzzled, you might say, sir. I don't understand why Andropulos and the others didn't abandon ship earlier. I saw two inflatable dinghies aboard. Rolled up, admittedly, but those things can be opened and inflated from their gas cylinders in seconds. There were also lifebelts and life-jackets. There was no need for this the-boy-stood-on-the-burning-deck act. They could have left at any time. I'm not saying they'd have been sucked down with the yacht but they might have had a rather uncomfortable time.'

'Same thought had occurred to me. Mentioned it to Andrew here. Odd. Maybe Andropulos had a reason. Anything else?'

'The owner tried to stop me from boarding the yacht. Maybe he was concerned with my health. I have the feeling he wasn't. Then I would much like to know what caused that explosion in the engine-room. A luxurious yacht like that must have carried an engineer – we can find that out easily enough – and it's a fair guess that the engines would have been maintained in an immaculate condition. I don't see how they could have caused an explosion. We'll have to ask McCafferty about that one.'

'That, of course, is why you were so anxious that we pinpoint the spot where the *Delos* went down. You think an expert on the effects of explosives could identify and locate the cause of the explosion? I'm sure he could, especially if he were an expert at determining the causes of aircraft lost through explosions – those people are much better at that sort of thing than the Navy is. Explosives experts we have aboard but no experts on the effects of explosives. Even if we did, we have no divers aboard – well, you and myself apart – trained to work at levels below a hundred feet. We could borrow one easily enough from a lifting vessel or salvage tug but the chances are high that he'd know nothing about explosives. But there's really no problem. It would be a simple matter for any lifting vessel to raise an aircraft fuselage to the surface.' Talbot regarded Van Gelder thoughtfully. 'But there's something else worrying you, isn't there?'

'Yes, sir. The three dead men aboard the *Delos* – well, to be specific, just one of them. That's why I asked the doctor here to come along. The three of them were so smoke begrimed and blackened that it was difficult to tell what they were wearing but two of them appeared to be dressed in white while the third was in a navy blue overall. An engineer wouldn't wear whites. Well, I admit our engineer Lieutenant McCafferty is a dazzling exception; but he's a one-off case, he never goes near his engines anyway. In any event I assumed the man in the overalls was the engineer and he was the one who caught my attention. He had a vicious gash on the back of his head as if he had been blown backwards against a very hard, very sharp object.'

Grierson said: 'Or been struck by a very hard, sharp object?'

'Either way, I suppose. I wouldn't know. I'm afraid I'm a bit weak on the forensic side.'

'Had his occiput been crushed?'

'Back of his head? No. At least I'm reasonably certain it hadn't been. I mean, it would have given, wouldn't it, or been squashy. It wasn't like that.'

'A blow like that should have caused massive bruising. Did you see any?'

'Difficult to say. He had fairly thick hair. But it was fair. No, I don't think there was any.'

'Had it bled a lot?'

'He hadn't bled at all. I'm quite sure of that.'

'You didn't notice any holes in his clothing?'

'Not that I could see. He hadn't been shot, if that is what you're asking and that is what I think you are asking. Who would want to shoot a dead man? His neck was broken.'

'Indeed?' Grierson seemed unsurprised. 'Poor man was through the wars, wasn't he?'

Talbot said: 'What do you think, Andrew?'

'I don't know what to think. The inflicting of the wound on the head and the snapping of the vertebra could well have been simultaneous. If the two weren't simultaneous, then it could equally well have been – as Vincent clearly seems to think – a case of murder.'

'Would an examination of the corpse help at all?'

'It might. I very much doubt it. But an examination of engine-room bulkheads would.'

'To see if there were any sharp edges or protrusions that could have caused such a head wound?' Grierson nodded. 'Well, when – and if – we ever raise that hull, we should be able to kill two birds with one stone: to determine the causes of both the explosions and this man's death.'

'Maybe three birds,' Van Gelder said. 'It would be interesting to know the number and layout of the fuel tanks in the engine-room. There are, I believe, two common layouts – in one case there is just one main fuel tank, athwartships and attached to the for'ard bulkhead, with a generator or generators on one side of the engine and batteries on the other, plus a water-tank to port and another to starboard: or there could be a fuel tank on either side with the water-tank up front. In that case the two fuel tanks are interconnected to keep the fuel levels equal and maintain equilibrium.'

'A suspicious mind, Number One,' Talbot said. 'Very suspicious. What you would like to find, of course, is just one fuel tank because you think Andropulos is going to claim that he didn't abandon ship because he thought another fuel tank was about to go and he didn't want his precious passengers splashing about in a sea of blazing fuel oil which would, of course, also have destroyed the rubber dinghies.'

'I'm grieved, sir. I thought I'd thought of that first.'

'You did, in fact. When the passengers are cleaned up see if you can get this young lady, Irene Charial, alone and find out if she knows anything about the layout of the engine-room. The casual approach, Vincent, the innocent and cherubic expression, although I doubt the last is beyond you. Anyway it's possible she's never been there and may possibly know nothing about it.'

'It's equally possible, sir, that she knows all about it and may well choose to tell me something. Miss Charial is Andropulos's niece.'

'The thought had occurred. However, if Andropulos is not all he might be, then the chances are high that there is some other member of his ship's company in his confidence and I would have thought that would be a man. I don't say that that's because you know what the Greeks are like because I don't know what the Greeks are like. And we mustn't forget that Andropulos may be as innocent as the driven snow and that there is a perfectly rational explanation for all that has happened. Anyway, it would do no harm to try and you never can tell, Vincent – she might turn out to be a classic Greek beauty.'

From the fact that the whaler was lying stopped in the water and that Cousteau, his hand resting idly on the tiller, appeared to be expressing no great degree of interest in anything, it was obvious that his wait had been a vain one, a fact he confirmed on his arrival on the bridge.

Talbot called the sonar room. 'You have pinpointed the location of the plane?'

'Yes, sir. We're sitting exactly above it. Depth registered is eighteen fathoms. That's the echo from the top of the fuselage. Probably lying in about twenty fathoms. It's lying in the same direction as it was flying when it came down – northeast to south-west. Picking up some rather odd noises down here, sir. Would you care to come down?'

'Yes, I will.' For reasons best known to himself Halzman, the senior sonar operator, preferred not to discuss it over an open line. 'A minute or two.' He turned to Van Gelder. 'Have McKenzie put down a marker buoy, about midships. Tell him to lower the weight gently. I don't want to bump too hard against the plane's fuselage in case we do actually come into contact with it. When that's been done, I want to anchor. Two anchors. A stern anchor to the north-west, about a hundred yards distant from the buoy, then a bow anchor a similar distance to the south-east.'

'Yes, sir. May I suggest the other way around?'

'Of course, you're right. I'd forgotten about our old friend. Taking a holiday today, isn't it? The other way around, of course.' The 'old friend' to which he referred and which Van Gelder clearly had in mind, was the Meltemi wind, referred to as the 'Etesian' in the British sailing directions. In the Cyclades, in the summer months – and indeed in most of the Aegean – it blew steadily, but usually only in the afternoon and early evening, from the north-west. If it did start up, the *Ariadne* would ride more comfortably if it were bows on to it.

Talbot went to the sonar room which was only one deck down and slightly aft. The sonar room was heavily insulated against all outside noise and dimly lit by subdued yellow lighting. There were three display screens, two sets of control panels and, over and above all, a considerable number of heavily padded earphones. Halzman caught sight of him in an overhead mirror – there were a number of such mirrors around, speaking as well as any other kind of sound was kept to a minimum in the sonar room – removed his earphones and gestured to the seat beside him.

'Those earphones, sir. I thought you might be interested in listening for a minute.'

Talbot sat and clamped the earphones on. After about fifteen seconds he removed them and turned to Halzman, who had also removed his.

'I can't hear a damned thing.'

'With respect, sir, when I said a minute, I meant just that. A minute. First of all you have to listen until you hear the silence, then you'll hear it.'

'Whatever that means, I'll try it.' Talbot listened again, and just before the allotted minute was up, he leaned forward and creased his brow. After another thirty seconds he removed the head-set.

'A ticking sound. Strange, Halzman, you were right. First you hear the silence and then you hear it. Tick . . . tick . . . tick, once every two to three seconds. Very regular. Very faint. You're certain that comes from the plane?'

'I have no doubt, sir.'

'Have you ever heard anything like it before?'

'No, sir. I've spent hundreds of hours, more likely thousands, listening to sonar, asdics, hydrophones, but this is something quite new on me.'

'I've got pretty good hearing but I had to wait almost a moment before I could imagine I could hear anything. It's very, very faint, isn't it?'

'It is. I had to turn the hearing capacity up to maximum before I stumbled on it – not a practice I would normally follow or recommend – in the wrong circumstances you can get your eardrums blasted off. Why is it so faint? Well, the source of the sound may be very faint to begin with. I've been thinking about this, sir – well, I've had nothing else to think about. It's either a mechanical or electrical device. In either case it has to be inside a sealed or waterproof casing. A mechanical device could, of course, operate in water even if it was totally submerged, but operating in water would dampen out the sound almost completely. An electrical device would have to be totally sealed against sea-water. The plane's own electrical system, of course, has ceased to function, so it would have to have its own supply system, almost certainly battery-powered. In either event, mechanical or electrical, the sound impulses would have to pass through the waterproof casing, after which they must pass through the fuselage of the plane.'

'Have you *any* idea as to what it might be?'

'None whatsoever. It's a two and a half second sequence – I've timed it. I know of no watch or clock movement that follows that sequence. Do you, sir?'

'No, I don't. You think it could be some sort of timing device?'

'I thought about that too, sir, but I put it out of my mind.' Halzman smiled. 'Maybe I'm prejudiced against that idea because of all those cheap and awful video film cassettes we have aboard, with all their special effects and pseudo science. All I know for sure, sir, is that we have a mysterious plane lying on the sea-bed there. Lord only knows what mysterious kind of cargo it was carrying.'

'Agreed. I think we'd better leave it at that for the moment. Have one of your boys monitor it, once, say, in every fifteen minutes.'

When Talbot returned to the bridge he could see the marker buoy just astern, bobbing gently in the very small wake Van Gelder was creating as he edged the *Ariadne* gently to the north-west. Very soon he stopped, juggled the engines to and fro until he reckoned the bows were a hundred yards distant from the buoy, had the anchor dropped, then moved just as slowly astern, the anchor chain being paid out as he went. Soon the stern anchor had been paid out and the *Ariadne* was back to where she had started, the buoy nudging the midships port side.

'Neatly done,' Talbot said. 'Tell me, Number One, how are you on puzzles?'

'Useless. Even the simplest crossword baffles me.'

'No matter. We're picking up a strange noise on the sonar. Maybe you'd like to take a turn along there, perhaps even identify it. Baffles me.'

'Consider it done. Back in two or three minutes.'

Twenty minutes elapsed before he returned to the bridge where Talbot was now alone: as the ship was no longer under way, Harrison had retired to his Mess.

'That was a long couple of minutes, Vincent, and what are you looking so pleased about?'

'I really don't know how you do it, sir. Incredible. I don't suppose you have any Scottish blood?'

'Not a drop, as far as I'm aware. Am I supposed to be following you, Number One?'

'I thought maybe the second sight. You were right. A classic Greek beauty. Irene. Miss Charial, that is. Odd, mind you, blonde as they come. I thought all those warm-blooded young Latin ladies had hair as black as a raven's wing.'

'It's the sheltered life you lead, Vincent. You should go to Andalucia some day. Seville. On one street corner a dusky Moorish maiden, the next a Nordic blonde. We'll discuss pigmentation some other time. What did you learn?'

'Enough, I hope. It's an art, sir, this casual and inconsequential approach. The questioning, I mean. She seems honest and open enough, not ingenuous, if you know what I mean, but quite straightforward. Certainly didn't give the impression of having anything to hide. Says she doesn't know the engine-room well but has been there a couple of times. We came to the question of fuel oil – I was just wondering out loud, natural curiosity, I hope she thought – as to what could have caused the explosion. Seems I was wrong when I said there were just two common ways of arranging fuel and water tanks. Seems there's a third. Two big tanks on either side of the engine, one fuel, one water. How big, I don't know, she was a bit vague about that – no reason why she should

40

know – but at least thousands of litres, she says. If there was a spare fuel tank she didn't know about it. I look forward, sir, to hearing Mr Andropulos justifying his decision not to abandon ship.'

'So do I. Should be interesting. Anyway, congratulations. A good job.'

'No hardship, sir.' Van Gelder scanned the sea around. 'Odd, don't you think, sir? I mean, are we the only ones who heard the SOS? I would have thought the horizon would have been black with converging vessels by this time.'

'Not so strange, really. Nearly all the vessels around at this time of year are private yachts and fishermen. Lots of them don't carry any radio at all and even those who do almost certainly wouldn't be permanently tuned to the distress frequency.'

'But we are.'

'This time I'm ahead of you. The *Delos* – or at least Andropulos – *knew* that we would be permanently tuned to the distress frequency, that we are automatically alerted by bell or buzzer whenever the distress frequency is energized. This presupposes two things. He knew we were a naval vessel and he also knew that we were in the vicinity.'

'You realize what you are saying, sir? Sorry, I didn't mean it to sound that way. But the implications, sir. I must say I really don't like those at all.'

'Neither do I. Opens up all sorts of avenues of interesting speculation, doesn't it?' He turned as McKenzie came on to the bridge: 'And how are our oil-stained survivors, Chief?'

41

'Clean, sir. And in dry clothes. I don't think any of them will make the list of the ten best-dressed men.' He looked at Van Gelder. 'I gather you didn't have too much time, sir, for the selection and careful matching up of clothes. They're a bit of an odd sight, I must say, but respectable enough. I knew you would want to see them, Captain – Mr Andropulos seems very anxious to see you – and I know you don't like unauthorized people on the bridge so I took the liberty of putting the four gentlemen and the two young ladies in the wardroom. I hope that's all right, sir.'

'Fine. You might ask the Surgeon Commander and Lieutenant Denholm to join us there. And send a couple of your boys up here to keep a look-out. Who knows, our radar might have a day off.'

The six survivors from the *Delos* were standing around rather awkwardly, not talking, when Talbot and Van Gelder reached the wardroom. The four men, as McKenzie had suggested, did present rather an odd spectacle. They looked rather as if they had just raided an old clothes shop, few of the items of their clothing being a match, and for the most part, fitting only where they touched. In striking contrast, both girls were immaculately clad: dressed in white blouses and white skirts, they could have stepped straight from the pages of *Vogue*.

'Please,' Talbot said. 'All of you be seated. Before we talk, I suggest we get our priorities right. First things first. You've had a harrowing experience and a lucky escape. I suggest you will not take amiss the suggestion of a suitable restorative.' He pressed a bell and a steward entered. 'Jenkins. Refreshments. Find out what they would like.' Jenkins did so and left.

'I'm the captain,' Talbot said. 'Talbot. This is Lieutenant-Commander Ven Gelder. Ah!' The door had opened. 'And this is Surgeon-Commander Grierson, whom you have met and whose services you fortunately didn't require, and Lieutenant Denholm.' He looked at the short stocky man seated before him. 'I take it that you, sir, are Mr Andropulos, the owner.'

'I am, Commander, I am.' Andropulos had black hair, black eyes, white teeth and a deeply tanned complexion. He looked as if he hadn't shaved that morning but then, he would always look as if he hadn't shaved that morning. He leapt to his feet, took Talbot's hand, and shook it vigorously. He positively radiated a combined aura of benevolence and bonhomie. 'Words cannot express our gratitude. A close-run thing, Commander, a very close-run thing. We owe you our lives.'

'I wouldn't go as far as to say that but I'll admit you were in a rather nasty pickle.'

'Pickle? Pickle?'

'Dangerous circumstances. I deeply regret both your loss of the members of your crew and your yacht.'

'The yacht is nothing. I can always buy another. Well, Lloyd's of London can buy it for me. Still sadder to lose an old friend like the *Delos* but sadder still, much sadder, to lose the three members of my crew. Been with me for many years. I treasured them all.'

'Who were they, sir?'

'My engineer, chef and steward. With me for many years.' Andropulos shook his head. 'They will be sadly missed.'

'Wasn't it odd for a chef and steward to be in the engine-room?'

Andropulos smiled sadly. 'Not aboard the *Delos*, Commander. It was not exactly run along the lines of a ship of the Royal Navy. They were in the habit of having an after-lunch drink there with the engineer. They had my permission, of course, but they preferred to be discreet about it – and what more discreet place than the engine-room? Alas, their discretion cost them their lives.'

'That is ironic. May I be introduced to the others?'

'Of course, of course. This is my very dear friend Alexander.' Alexander was a tall man with a thin, unsmiling face and black, cold eyes who didn't look as if he could possibly be anybody's very dear friend. 'This is Aristotle, my captain.' Andropulos didn't say whether Aristotle was the first or last name: he had watchful eyes and a serious expression but looked as if he might, unlike Alexander, be capable of smiling occasionally. 'And this is Achmed.' He didn't say what occupation Achmed held. He was young, pleasant-faced and smiled

44

readily. Talbot couldn't even begin to guess at his nationality except that he wasn't Greek.

'But I forget myself. Deplorable, deplorable. I forget myself. Such manners. Should have been ladies first, of course. This is my niece, Irene.' Van Gelder hadn't made any mistakes about her, Talbot thought, except that he'd missed out on the wide green eyes and a rather bewitching smile. 'And this is Eugenia.' This one, Talbot reflected, was much closer to Van Gelder's concept of a warm-blooded young Latin lady. She had a slightly dusky skin, black hair and warm brown eyes. And she also, no doubt, was quite beautiful. It seemed to Talbot that Van Gelder was going to find himself in something of a quandary.

'I congratulate you, Mr Andropulos,' Talbot said gallantly, 'and ourselves. Certainly the loveliest passengers we've ever had aboard the *Ariadne*. Ah. The steward.'

Andropulos took his glass – a scotch and not a small one, and disposed of half the contents in one gulp.

'My goodness, I needed that. Thank you, Commander, thank you. Not as young as I was nor as tough, either. Age cometh to us all.' He quaffed the rest of his drink and sighed.

Talbot said: 'Jenkins, another for Mr Andropulos. A slightly larger measure this time.' Jenkins looked at him expressionlessly, closed his eyes momentarily and left.

'The *Ariadne*,' Andropulos said. 'Rather odd, is it not. Greek name, British vessel.'

'Courtesy gesture to your Government, sir. We are carrying out a hydrographic charting exercise with your people.' Talbot saw no point in mentioning that the *Ariadne* had never carried out a hydrographic exercise in its life and that the ship had been called *Ariadne* to remind the Greeks that it was a multi-national vessel and to persuade a wavering Greek government that perhaps NATO wasn't such a bad thing after all.

'Hydrographic, you say. Is that why we're moored fore and aft – a fixed platform for taking bearings.'

'A fixed platform, yes, but in this instance the purpose is not hydrographic. We've had quite a busy afternoon, Mr Andropulos, and at the moment we're anchored over a plane that crashed into the sea just about the time we were receiving your SOS.'

'A plane? Crashed? Good God! What – what kind of plane?'

'We have no idea. It was so wreathed in smoke that it was impossible to distinguish any important features.'

'But surely – well, don't you think it was a big plane?'

'It may have been.'

'But it could have been a big jet. Maybe *hundreds* of passengers.' If Andropulos knew it wasn't

46

a jet carrying hundreds of passengers, his face wasn't saying so.

'It's always possible.' Talbot saw no point in telling Andropulos that it was almost certainly a bomber and equally certainly not carrying hundreds of passengers.

'You – you mean to tell me that you left the area to come to our aid?'

'A reasonable enough decision, I think. We were pretty certain that there were people alive aboard the *Delos* and we were also pretty certain that there was no one alive aboard that plane.'

'There could have been survivors aboard that plane. I mean, you weren't there to see.'

'Mr Andropulos.' Talbot allowed a certain coldness to creep into his voice. 'We are, I hope, neither callous nor stupid. Before leaving, we lowered one of our motorboats to circle the area. There were no survivors.'

'Oh dear,' Irene Charial said, 'Isn't it awful? All those people dead and there we were, busy doing nothing except feeling sorry for ourselves. I'm not being inquisitive, Captain, and I know it's none of my business, but why do you remain anchored here? I mean, there can't possibly be any hope now that some survivors may surface.'

'There is no hope, Miss Charial. We're remaining here as a marker until the diving ship arrives.' He didn't like lying to her but thought it inadvisable to tell her that there was no rescue ship hurrying to the scene and that, as far as he knew, the only other people who knew of the disaster were the NATO HQ in Italy. More especially, he didn't want any person or persons in her company to know.

'But – but it will be too late to save anyone.'

'It's already too late, young lady. But they'll send divers down to investigate, to find out whether it's a passenger-carrying jet or not and to try to ascertain the cause of the accident.' He was looking, without seeming to look, at Andropulos as he said the last words and felt almost certain that he saw a flicker of expression cross his face.

Andropulos's captain, Aristotle, spoke for the first time. 'How deep is this plane, Commander?'

'Seventeen, eighteen fathoms. Just over thirty metres or so.'

'Thirty metres,' Andropulos said. 'Even if they do get inside – and there's no guarantee that they will be able to do so – won't it be difficult to move around and see anything?'

'I can guarantee they'll get inside. There are such things as oxyacetylene torches, you know. And they'll have powerful underwater torches. But they won't bother with either of those things. The divers will carry down a couple of slings with them. A diving ship will have no difficulty at all in bringing the fuselage to the surface. Then they'll be able to examine the plane at their leisure.' This time there was no trace of expression in Andropulos's face: Talbot wondered if he, Andropulos, had become aware that such changes in expression were being sought for.

Jenkins entered and handed Talbot a sealed envelope. 'From the radio-room, sir. Myers said it was urgent.'

Talbot nodded, opened the envelope, extracted and read the slip of paper it had held. He slipped it in his pocket and stood.

'My apologies, ladies and gentlemen. I have to go to the bridge. Come along with me, Number One. I'll join you at seven o'clock for dinner.'

Once outside, Van Gelder said: 'You really are a fearful liar, sir. A fearfully good liar, I mean.'

'Andropulos isn't half bad, either.'

'He's had practice. Between the two of you – well, in his own phrase, it's a close-run thing. Ah, thank you.' He unfolded the slip of paper Talbot had handed him. ' "Vitally urgent you remain in closest contact with downed plane Stop will join you earliest in the morning Stop Hawkins". Isn't that the Vice-Admiral, sir?'

'None other. Vitally urgent and flying down to see us. What do you make of that?'

'I make it that he knows something that we don't.'

'Indeed. Incidentally, you've kind of forgotten to tell me about your visit to sonar.'

'Sorry about that, sir. I had something else on my mind.'

'Somebody, not something. Having seen her I can understand. Well?'

49

'The noise from the plane? Tick . . . tick . . . tick. Could be anything. Halzman half suggested it might be some sort of timing device. Could be that he's right. I don't want to sound alarmist, sir, but I don't think I like it very much.'

'I don't particularly care for it myself. Well, then, the radio-room.'

'I thought you said you were going to the bridge?'

'That was for Andropulos's benefit. The less that character knows about anything the better. I think he's cunning, astute and alert for the slightest nuances.'

'Is that why you didn't make any reference to the engine-room explosion?'

'Yes. I may, of course, be doing him a massive injustice. For all I know he may be as fresh and innocent as the dawn's early dew.'

'You don't really believe that, sir.'

'No.'

Myers was alone in the radio-room. 'Another message to Rome,' Talbot said. 'Again Code B. To Vice-Admiral Hawkins. Message received. Strongly advise that you come soonest. Tonight. Report repeated two and a half second ticking sounds from plane. Could be timing device. Please phone immediately.'

'A ticking sound, possibly a timing device, Talbot says.' Vice-Admiral Hawkins was standing by Carson's chair as the general read and reread the slip of paper Hawkins had just handed him.

'A timing device. We don't have to discuss the implications of this.' From his high-rise office Carson looked out over the roofs of Rome, then at the colonel across the desk, then finally up at Hawkins. He pressed a button on his desk.

'Get me the Pentagon.'

The Chairman of the Joint Chiefs of Staff was also standing as the man behind the desk read the slip of paper he had just been handed. He read it three times, laid it down carefully on the desk, smoothed it out and looked across at the Chairman. His face looked drawn and tired and old.

'We know what this means, or what it could mean. If anything goes wrong the international repercussions will be enormous, General.'

'I'm afraid I'm fully aware of that, sir. Apart from the universal condemnation, we will become the pariah dog, the outcasts of the world.'

'And no hint of any Soviet involvement.'

'None whatsoever. No proof, direct or indirect. As far as the world is concerned, they are blameless. My first reaction is that they are indeed blameless. My second thoughts are exactly the same. I can see no way they are linked with this. We bear the burden, sir.'

'We bear the burden. And will stand condemned before the court of mankind.' The General made no reply. 'The Chiefs have no suggestions?'

'None that I regard as very useful. In short, bluntly, none. We have to rely on our people out there. *Carte blanche*, sir?'

'We have no option. How good are your men in the Mediterranean?'

'The very best. No rhetoric, sir. I mean it.'

'And this British vessel on the spot?'

'The frigate *Ariadne*? A very special vessel indeed, I am given to understand. Whether or not it can cope with this, no one can say. There are too many imponderables.'

'Do we pull it out?'

'That's not for my decision, sir.'

'I know it's not.' He was silent for a long moment then said: 'It may be our only hope. It stays.'

'Yes, Mr President.'

Talbot was alone with Van Gelder on the bridge when the radio-room called.

'I have voice contact with Rome, sir. Where will you take it?'

'Here.' He gestured to Van Gelder to take up a listening phone. 'Talbot here.'

'Hawkins. I'm leaving shortly with two civilians for Athens. You'll have a phone call from there letting you know our estimated time of arrival. We'll be landing on Thera Island. Have a launch standing by to meet us.'

'Yes, sir. Take a taxi down to Athinio – there's a new quay about two miles south of the Thira Village anchorage.'

'My map shows that the Thira anchorage is nearer.'

'What your map may not show is that the only way down to Thira anchorage is by mule-track down a precipitous cliff. A seven-hundred-foot cliff, to be precise.'

'Thank you, Talbot. A life saved. You have not forgotten my twin *bêtes noires*, my fatal flaws. Till this evening, then.'

'What *bêtes noires*?' Van Gelder said. 'What flaws?'

'He hates horses. I would imagine the detestation extends to mules. And he suffers from acrophobia.'

'That sounds a very nasty thing to suffer from. And what might that be?'

'Vertigo. A fear of heights. Almost got him disbarred from entry to the Navy. He had a powerful aversion to climbing up rigging.'

'You know him well, then?'

'Pretty well. Now, this evening. I'd normally send young Henri to pick anybody up but Vice-Admiral Hawkins and the two no doubt equally distinguished civilians who are with him are not anybody. So we do it in style. A Lieutenant-Commander, I thought.'

'My pleasure, sir.'

'And tell them all you know about the plane, the *Delos* and the survivors. Also our suspicions about the survivors. Saves the time when they get here.'

'I'll do that. Speaking about the survivors, when I go ashore do you want me to take them along and dump them?'

'You are unwell, Number One?'

'I'm fine. Didn't for a moment think you'd want them out of your sight. And we couldn't very well abandon the two young ladies on that barren rock there.'

'It's as well the islanders can't hear you. There's fourteen hundred people in the Thira township and there's a fair amount of tourist accommodation. And speaking again of the survivors, not to mention our three other visitors, we'll have to find sleeping accommodation for them. The Admiral can have the admiral's cabin – it'll be the first time an admiral has slept there. There are three empty cabins. You can have mine, I'll sleep here or in the chart-room. The rest, well, you fix it.'

'Five minutes,' said he confidently.

He was back in forty-five.

'Took me a little longer than I thought. Ticklish problems.'

'Who's got my cabin?'

'Irene. Eugenia has mine.'

'It took you three-quarters of an hour to arrange that?'

'Decisions, decisions. Calls for a little delicacy and a modicum of finesse.'

'My word, you do do yourselves well, Commander,' Andropulos said. He sipped some claret. 'Or is this a special treat for us?'

'Standard fare, I assure you.' Andropulos, whom Grierson had reported as having a remarkable

54

affinity for scotch, seemed relaxed to the point of garrulity. Talbot would have taken long odds that he was cold sober. He talked freely about quite a number of subjects, but had not once broached the question of being sent ashore. It was clear that he and Talbot had at least one thing in common – the wish that he remain aboard the *Ariadne*.

Jenkins came in and spoke softly to Van Gelder, who looked at Talbot.

'Call from the radio-room. Shall I take it?' Talbot nodded. Van Gelder left and returned within half a minute.

'Call was delayed, sir. Difficulty in contacting us. They will be there in less than half an hour. I'd better go now.'

'I'm expecting visitors later this evening,' Talbot said, 'I shall have to ask you not to come to the wardroom for some time after they come. Not for too long. Twenty minutes at the most.'

'Visitors?' Andropulos said. 'At this time of the evening. Who on earth are they?'

'I'm sorry, Mr Andropulos. This is a naval vessel. There are certain things I can't discuss with civilians.'

3

Vice-Admiral Hawkins was the first up the gangway. He shook Talbot's hand warmly. The Admiral didn't go in much for saluting.

'Delighted to see you again, John. Or I would be if it weren't for the circumstances. And how are you, my boy?'

'Fine, sir. Again, considering the circumstances.'

'And the children? Little Fiona and Jimmy?'

'In the best, thank you, sir. You've come a long way in a short time.'

'Needs must when the devil drives. And he's sitting on my tail right now.' He turned to the two men who had followed him up the gangway. 'Professor Benson. Dr Wickram. Gentlemen, Commander Talbot, the captain of the *Ariadne*.'

'If you will come with me, gentlemen. I'll have your gear taken to your quarters.' Talbot led them to the wardroom and gestured them to their seats. 'You want me to get my priorities right?'

'Certainly.' Talbot pressed a bell and Jenkins came in. 'A large gin and tonic for those two gentlemen,' Hawkins said. 'Lots of ice. They're Americans. Large scotch and water for me. Quarters, you said. What quarters?'

'You haven't been aboard since before commissioning but you won't have forgotten. For an admiral, an admiral's quarters. Never been used.'

'How perfectly splendid. Honoured, I'm sure. And for my two friends here?'

'A cabin apiece. Also never been used. I think they'll find them quite comfortable. I'd like to bring along some of my officers, sir.'

'But of course. Whom did you have in mind?'

'Surgeon-Commander Grierson.'

'Know him,' Hawkins said. 'Very wise bird.'

'Lieutenant Denholm. Our electronic *Wunderkind*. I know you've met him, sir.'

'That I have.' He looked at his two friends, smiling broadly. 'You'll have to mind your p's and q's here. Lieutenant Denholm is the heir to an earldom. The genuine article. Fearfully languid and aristocratic. Don't be deceived for an instant. Mind like a knife. As I told General Carson, he's so incredibly advanced in his electronic speciality that your high-tech whizzkids in Silicon Valley wouldn't even begin to understand what he's talking about.'

'Then there's Lieutenant McCafferty, our senior engineer, and, of course, Lieutenant-Commander Van Gelder whom you've already met.'

'For the first time. Favourably impressed. Very. Struck me as an able lad indeed.'

'He's all that. More. If I were laid low tomorrow you wouldn't have to worry. He could take over the *Ariadne* at any moment and you wouldn't notice the difference.'

'From you, that's worth any half-dozen testimonials. I'll bear it in mind.'

Introductions completed, Hawkins looked at Talbot and his four officers and said: 'The first question in your minds, of course, gentlemen, is why I have brought two civilians with me. First I will tell you who they are and then, when I have explained the purpose of our coming, you will understand why they are here. In passing, I might say how extraordinarily lucky I am to have them here with me. They seldom leave their home state of California: it just so happened that both were attending an international conference in Rome.

'Professor Alec Benson here.' Benson was a large, calm man in his early sixties, grey of hair, cherubic and cheerful of countenance, and wearing a sports jacket, flannels and polo jersey, all of varying shades of grey and all so lived in, comfortable and crumpled that he could well have inherited them from his grandfather. 'The Professor is the director of the seismological department of the California Institute of Technology in Pasadena. He's also a geologist and vulcanologist. Anything that makes the earth bang or shake or move is his field. Regarded by everybody in that line as the world's leading expert – he chaired, or was chairing until I so rudely interrupted him, an international conference in seismology in Rome. You all know, of course, what seismology is.'

'A rough idea,' Talbot said. 'A kind of science – I think "study" would be a better word for it – of the causes and effects of earthquakes.'

'A kind of science?' Hawkins said. 'I am distressed. It *is* a science.'

'No offence meant, I'm sure, and none taken,' Benson said equably. 'The Commander is perfectly correct. Far from being a science, we're still only dabbling on the periphery of the subject.'

'Ah, well. Dr Wickram is a physicist, as well known in his own field as Professor Benson is in his. He specializes in nuclear physics.'

Talbot looked at Dr Wickram who, in startling contrast to Benson, was thin, dark and immaculately dressed in a blue suit, white button-down collar and a black tie, the funereal hue of which went rather well with the habitual severity of his expression, and said: 'Does your interest in nuclear physics extend to nuclear weaponry, Dr Wickram?'

'Well, yes, it does rather.'

'You and the Professor are to be congratulated. There should be some kind of civilian medal for this. Vice-Admiral Hawkins, of course, is acting in the line of duty. I would have thought you two gentlemen should have stayed in Rome. I mean, isn't it safer there?'

Hawkins cleared his throat. 'You wouldn't dream of stealing a superior officer's thunder, would you?'

'I wouldn't dream of it, sir.'

'Well, to the point. Your two signals duly received. The first gave rise to some concern, the second was profoundly disturbing.'

'The "tick . . . tick . . . tick" bit, sir?'

'The "tick . . . tick . . . tick" bit. Both signals were sent to the Pentagon, the second one also going to the White House. I should imagine that the word consternation would suitably describe their reaction. Guessing, of course, but I think the speed of the reply to the second message showed how badly shaken they were. Normally, it can take forever – well, even months at times – to extract just a nugget of information from the Pentagon, but this time minutes only. When I read their reply, I could understand all too well.' Hawkins paused, possibly for suitable dramatic effect.

'So can I,' Talbot said.

'What do you mean?'

'If I were the Pentagon or the White House I'd be upset too if a US Air Force bomber or cargo plane, carrying a load of bombs, suddenly disappeared into the sea. Especially if the bombs – or missiles – that plane was carrying were of the nuclear variety. Even more especially if they were hydrogen bombs.'

'Well, damn your eyes, Talbot, you do deprive ageing vice-admirals of the simpler pleasures of life. There goes my thunder.'

'It wasn't all that difficult, sir. We had already guessed it was a bomber. Civilian planes, with the exception of Concorde, don't fly at the height at which we picked it up. We'd have had to be pretty stupid not to assume what we did. Bombers usually carry bombs. American reaction made it inevitable that it was an American plane. And you wouldn't have come down here in such a tearing hurry, and be accompanied by an expert in nuclear weaponry, unless the bombs were of a rather nasty variety. I can't imagine anything nastier than hydrogen bombs.'

'Nor can anyone. When you put it the way you put it, I suppose I should have guessed that you had guessed. Even the Pentagon don't know or won't divulge what type of plane it was. They suggest an advanced design of the C.141 Starlifter cargo plane. It was refuelled in the Azores and heading for Greece. From your first message we gathered you saw the plane crash into the sea but couldn't identify it. Why not?'

'Number One, show the Admiral why not.'

Van Gelder produced a sheaf of photographs and handed them to Hawkins who flipped through them quickly, and then, more slowly, a second time. He sighed and looked up.

'Intriguing, I suppose, if you're a connoisseur of the pattern effects of smoke and flame. I'm not.

All I can make out is what I take to be the outer port engine and that's no help at all. And it gives no indication as to the source or cause of the fire.'

'I think Van Gelder would disagree with you, sir,' Talbot said. 'He's of the opinion that the fire originated in the nose cone and was caused by an internal explosion. I agree with him. It certainly wasn't brought down by ship-based anti-aircraft fire. We would have known. The only alternative is a heat-seeking missile. Two objections to that. Such a missile would have targeted on the engines, not the fuselage and, more importantly, there are no vessels in the area. Our radar would have picked them up. As a corollary to that, the missile didn't come from an aircraft, either. The Admiral will not need reminding that the radar aboard the *Ariadne* is as advanced as any in the world.'

'That may no longer be true, sir.' Denholm's tone was deferential but not hesitant. 'And if it is true, then we can't discount missiles just like that. This is not a dissenting opinion, I'm just exploring another possibility.'

'Explore away, Lieutenant,' Hawkins said. 'Any light that can illumine the darkness of our ignorance, etcetera, etcetera.'

'I'm not sure I'm all that good as a beacon, sir. I do know that I don't go along with the belief that the Soviets always trail the West in technological advancement. Whether this belief is carefully and officially nurtured I do not know. I admit that the Soviets spend a certain amount of time and trouble in extracting military secrets from the West. I say "certain" because they don't have to try all that hard: there appears to be a steady supply of scientists, both American and British, who, along with associates not necessarily involved in direct research at all, are perfectly willing to sell the Soviets anything they want – provided, that is, the price is right. I believe this to be true in the case of computers where they do lag behind the West: I do not believe it in the case of radar.

'In this field, Plessey, of Britain, probably leads the West. They have developed a revolutionary new radar system, the Type 966, which is fitted, or about to be fitted, to Invincible-class aircraft-carriers, the Type 42 Sheffield-class destroyers and the new Type 23 Norfolk-class frigates. This new radar is designed not only to detect and track aircraft and sea-skimming missiles, but it also –'

Hawkins cleared his throat. 'Sorry to interrupt, Denholm. You may know this but surely it comes under the heading of classified information?'

'If it did, I wouldn't talk about it even in this company, sir. It's in the public domain. As I was about to say, it's also able to control Sea Dart and Seawolf missiles in flight and home them in on their targets with great accuracy. I also understand they're virtually immune to jamming and radar decoys. If Plessey have done this, the Soviets may well have also. They're not much given to advertising such things. But I believe they have the know-how.'

Hawkins said: 'And you also believe, in this case, that a missile was the culprit?'

'Not at all, sir. I'm only suggesting a possibility. The Captain and Lieutenant-Commander Van Gelder may well be right. Trouble is, I know nothing about explosives. Maybe there are missiles with such a limited charge that they cause only limited damage. I would have thought that a standard missile would have ensured that a plane it brought down would not have struck the sea with its fuselage relatively intact but in a thousand pieces. Again, I simply don't know. I just wonder what the security was like at the base from which that plane took off in the States.'

'Security? In the case of a super-sensitive plane such as this? Total.'

'Does the Admiral really believe there is such a thing as total security?' The Admiral didn't say what he believed, he just sipped his scotch in silence. 'There were four major air disasters last year, all four planes involved having taken off from airports which were regarded as having maximum security. In all four cases terrorists found the most stringent airport checks childishly easy to circumvent.'

'Those were civilian airports. This would be a top-secret US Air Force base, manned exclusively by US Air Force personnel, specially chosen for their position, rigidly screened, backgrounds exhaustively researched, and all subjected to lie-detector tests.'

'With respect to the Vice-Admiral, and our American friends, lie-detector tests – more accurately, polygraph tests – are rubbish. Any moderately intelligent person can be trained to beat the polygraph test, which, after all, depends on crudely primitive measurements of pulse rate, blood pressure and perspiration. You can be trained to give right answers, wrong answers or merely confusing ones and the scrutineer can't tell the difference.'

'Doesn't measure up to your idea of electronics, eh?'

'Nothing to do with electronics, sir. Polygraphs belong to the horse-and-buggy era. You've just used the word supersensitive, sir. The *Ariadne*, if I may put it that way, is a hotbed of super-sensitivity. How many members of this crew have ever been subjected to a polygraph test? None.'

Hawkins considered his glass for a few moments, then looked up at Talbot. 'Should the need arise, Captain, how long would it take you to contact the Pentagon?'

'Immediately. Well, half a minute. Now?'

'No. Wait. Have to think about it. Trouble is, even the Pentagon is having difficulty in extracting information from this Air Force base which is, I believe, somewhere in Georgia. The Pentagon's own fault, really, although you can't expect them to admit this. They've so inculcated this passion for absolute secrecy into the senior officers of all four services that no one is prepared to reveal anything without the permission of the commanding officer of the Air Force base or ship or whatever. In this particular case, the commanding officer who, to the Pentagon's distress, would appear to have a human side to his nature, has elected to take twenty-four hours off. No one appears to know where he is.'

Van Gelder said: 'Makes it a bit awkward, sir, doesn't it, if war breaks out in the next half-hour?'

'No. Base remains in full operational readiness. But there's still no relaxation of the iron-bound rules concerning the release of classified information.'

Talbot said: 'You wouldn't be sitting here unless they'd released *some* information.'

'Naturally not. The news they've released is vague and incomplete but all very, very bad. One report says there were twelve nuclear weapons aboard, another fifteen. Whether they were missiles or bombs was not disclosed: what was disclosed was that they were hydrogen devices, each one in the monster megaton range, twelve to fifteen megatons. The plane was also understood to be carrying two of the more conventional atom bombs.'

'I think I'll break a self-imposed regulation and have a scotch myself,' Talbot said. A half-minute passed in silence, then he said quietly: 'This is worse than I ever dreamed.'

'Dream?' Grierson said. 'Nightmare.'

'Dream or nightmare, it won't matter to us,' Lieutenant Denholm said. 'Not when we're drifting through the stratosphere in vaporized orbit.'

'A hydrogen bomb, Dr Wickram,' Talbot said. 'Let's call it that. Is there any way it can spontaneously detonate?'

'In itself, impossible. The President of the United States has to press one button, the man on the spot another: the radio frequencies are so wildly different that the chances of anyone happening on the right combination are billions to one.'

'Is there a chance – say a billion to one – that the Soviets might have this combination?'

'None.'

'You say it's impossible to detonate in itself. Is there any other way, some external means, whereby it could be detonated?'

'I don't know.'

'Does that mean you're not saying or that you're not sure? I don't think, Dr Wickram, that this is the time to dwell on such verbal niceties.'

'I'm not sure. If there were a sufficiently powerful explosion close by it might go up by sympathetic detonation. We simply don't know.'

'The possibility has never been explored? I mean, no experiments?'

'I should hope not,' Lieutenant Denholm said. 'If such an experiment were successful, I wouldn't care to be within thirty or forty miles at the time.'

'That is one point.' For the first time, Dr Wickram essayed a smile, but it was a pretty wintry one. 'In the second place, quite frankly, we have never envisaged a situation where such a possibility might arise. We could, I suppose, have carried out such an experiment without the drastic consequences the Lieutenant has suggested. We could detonate a very small atom bomb in the vicinity of another. Even a charge of conventional explosive in the vicinity of a small atom bomb would suffice. If the small atom bomb went up, so then would the hydrogen bomb. Everybody knows that it's the fissioning of an atom bomb that triggers off the fusion of a hydrogen bomb.'

Talbot said: 'Is there any timing device, specifically a delayed one, fitted in a hydrogen bomb?'

'None.' The flat finality in the voice left no room for argument.

'According to Vice-Admiral Hawkins, there may be a couple of conventional atom bombs aboard the sunken plane. Could they be fitted with timing devices?'

'Again, I don't know. Not my field. But I see no reason why they couldn't be.'

'For what purpose?'

'Search me. Realms of speculation, Captain, where your guess is as good as mine. The only thing that occurs to me is a mine, a marine mine. Neatly dispose of any passing aircraft carrier, I should think.'

'That's thinking small,' Van Gelder said. 'A hydrogen mine would neatly dispose of any passing battle fleet.'

'Whose passing fleet? One of ours? In wartime as in peacetime, the seas are open to all.'

'Not the Black Sea. Not in wartime. But a bit far-fetched. How would this mine be activated?'

'My continued ignorance must be a great disappointment. I know nothing about mines.'

'Well, time was when mines were either magnetic or acoustic. Degaussing has made magnetic mines *passé*. So, acoustic. Triggered by a passing ship's engines. Interesting, isn't it? I mean, we've passed over it several times since we first heard the ticking and we've triggered nothing. So far. So maybe that ticking doesn't mean that the mine is set to go off any time. Maybe it's not activated – by which I mean ready to go off when a vessel passes over it – until the ticking stops. Or maybe it's just set to go up whenever the ticking stops. Trouble is, we've no idea what started the ticking in the first place. I can't see any way it could have been deliberate. Must have been caused by the explosion that brought down the plane or by the impact of striking the water.'

'You're a source of great comfort, Van Gelder,' Hawkins said heavily.

'I admit, sir, that the alternatives aren't all that attractive. My own conclusions, which in this case are probably completely worthless, are that this ticking represents a period of grace – I mean that it cannot explode – as long as the ticking lasts and that it's not designed to explode when the ticking stops but is then activated and ready to explode when triggered by passing engines. A guess, sir, but not necessarily a wild one. I'm going on the assumption that this mine could well be dropped by a surface vessel as well as a plane. In that case, the ship would want to be a large number of miles away before the mine was activated. So it would start the timing mechanism running at the moment it dropped it over the side. I am sure, sir, that the Pentagon could provide some illumination on this subject.'

'I'm sure it could,' Hawkins said. 'And your conclusions are far from worthless, they make a good deal of sense to me. Well, Captain, what do you propose to do about all this?'

'I rather thought, sir, that your purpose in coming down here was to tell *me* what to do.'

'Not at all. I just came to make myself *au fait* with the situation and to garner some information in return for some I give you.'

'Does this mean, Admiral – I say this carefully, you understand – that I have a hand in making the decisions?'

'You don't have a hand. You damn well make them. I'll endorse them.'

'Thank you. Then my first decision – or, if you like, a suggestion respectfully made – is that you and your two friends depart for Rome immediately. It's not going to help anyone, and will be a considerable

70

loss to both the scientific and naval communities, if you three gentlemen elect for self-immolation. Besides, by asking me to make the decisions, you have implied that there's nothing you can do here that my crew and I can't. Lieutenant-Commander Van Gelder is at your immediate service.'

'The Lieutenant-Commander will have to wait. For me, at least. Your logic is sound but I'm not feeling very logical at the moment. But I do agree as far as my two friends are concerned. They could be back at their international conference in Rome tomorrow, without anyone having noticed their absence. We have no right to put the lives of civilians, not to mention two such eminent civilians, at risk.'

'You've just put your finger on it, Admiral.' Benson puffed comfortably on a sadly blackened pipe. 'Eminent or not, we are civilians. Civilians don't take orders from the military. I prefer the Aegean to Rome.'

'Agreed,' Wickram said. 'Ludicrous. Preposterous.'

'You don't seem to have any more clout with your two friends than I have with the three of you.' Talbot produced two slips of paper from his inner pocket, 'I suggest you sign those, sir.'

Hawkins took them, looked thoughtfully at Talbot, scanned the two sheets, then read from one of them.

' "Request urgent immediate dispatch of nearest salvage or diving vessel to 36.21N, 25.22E due

71

south Cape Akrotiri, Thera Island, to recover one sunken plane, one sunken yacht. Further request immediate dispatch by plane to Thera Island two deep-sea divers with diving equipment for four, repeat four. Priority one double A. Signed Vice-Admiral Hawkins." ' Hawkins looked at Benson and Wickram. 'This message is directed to Rear-Admiral Blyth, HMS *Apollo*. Rear-Admiral Blyth is the operational commander of European section of NATO sea forces in the Eastern Mediterranean. Priority one double A means drop everything else, this has absolute priority. Admiral Hawkins is, I take it, my good self. Why, Captain, the request for four diving suits?'

'Van Gelder and I are trained divers, sir. Ex-submariners.'

'I see. Second signal directed to Defence Minister, Athens. "Urgent contact Air Control Athens airport for information re aircraft, thought American, that crashed 1415 today south of Thera Island. Did it ask permission for flight path to, and landing in, Athens or other Greek airfield? Further request you enlist immediate aid of police and Intelligence re anything known about one Spyros Andropulos, owner of yacht *Delos*." This message is also, I'm flattered to observe, signed by me. Well, well, well, Captain, I nearly did you a great injustice a minute or two ago, I thought you had not perhaps addressed yourself to the problem on hand. But you have, and in some style and quite some time before I arrived. Two questions.'

'The aircraft and Andropulos?' Hawkins nodded. 'At 43,000 feet, the pilot didn't have to bother to notify anyone about his presence. He knew he was alone in the sky. But once he started descending, it was a different matter entirely. He wouldn't be too keen on bumping into anyone, especially not with the cargo he had on board. And, of course, he would require permission to land.'

'But why Greece?'

'Because the flight path he was following when we first located him would have taken him to Ankara in Turkey, or some place pretty close by. Now, even although Turkey is – nominally, at least – a member of NATO, I'm sure the Americans have no air bases at, or near, Ankara. I don't even know if they have any air bases at all in Turkey. I'm certain they have no missile launching bases. In Greece, the Americans have both. So, Greece. As for Andropulos, several of my officers and I think he's a leery customer and a suspicious one. Not one thing that could be proved in a court of law, of course. We suspect that he may know something about the downing of this plane that we don't *know* he knows, if you follow me. He says the *Delos* was sunk as the result of an explosion. But it's the old question of did he fall or was he pushed? In other words, was the explosion accidental or deliberate? If we could hoist the *Delos* to the surface we might well find out.'

'We might well indeed. Still, first things first.' Hawkins looked briefly at the signals again. 'Seem to fit the task admirably. I'll gladly sign.' Hawkins produced a pen, signed and handed the papers to Talbot. 'As you had all this figured out quite some time, I suspect, before I left Rome, why didn't you send those signals yourself?'

'Lowly commanders don't give the instructions to Rear-Admiral Blyth. I haven't the authority. You have. That's why I asked you to join us as soon as was possible. Thanks for the signing, sir. That was the easy part. Now comes the difficult part.'

'Difficult part?' Hawkins said warily. 'What difficult part?'

'Have we the moral right to ask the crew of the salvage vessel or lifting vessel, not to mention the divers, to join us, in Lieutenant Denholm's elegant phrase, in drifting through the stratosphere in vaporized orbit?'

'Ah. Yes. A point, of course. What do *you* think?'

'Again, not a decision for lowly commanders. Admirals only.'

'Dear, oh dear. Then, if things go wrong, you'll have nothing on your conscience and everything in the world to reproach me with.'

'If anything goes wrong, sir, I don't think we'll be having too much to say to each other when we're in vaporized orbit.'

'True. Mine was an unworthy remark. No one likes to bear the responsibility for such decisions. Send the signals.'

'Very good, sir. Lieutenant Denholm, ask Myers to come here.'

Hawkins said: 'I understand – I'm not making comparisons – that the President of the United States was faced with a problem similar to the one you've just confronted me with. He asked the Chairman of the Joint Chiefs of Staff if he should pull out the *Ariadne* which they knew, of course, was sitting over the crashed plane. The Chairman said, quite rightly, that that wasn't his responsibility, the old and honoured American tradition of passing the buck. The President decided that the *Ariadne* should stay.'

'Well, I could come all over bitter and say that's very noble and gallant of the President, especially as there's no chance of his being blown out of his seat in the Oval Office when this little lot goes up, but I won't. It's not a decision I would care to have to make. I assume he gave a reason for his decision?'

'Yes. The greatest good of the greatest number.'

Myers came in. Talbot handed him the two messages.

'Get these off at once. Code B in both cases. To both messages add "Immediate, repeat Immediate, confirmation is requested."' Myers left and Talbot said: 'It is my understanding, Admiral, that in your capacity as officer commanding the naval forces in the Eastern Mediterranean you have the power to overrule the President's instructions.'

'Yes.'

'Have you done so?'

'No. You will ask why. Same reason as the President. The greatest good of the greatest number. Why the questioning, Captain? You wouldn't leave here even if I gave a direct order.'

'I'm just a bit puzzled about the reason given – the greatest good of the greatest number. Bringing a rescue vessel, which admittedly is my idea, will only increase the greatest danger to a greater number.'

'I don't think you quite appreciate just how great the greatest number is in this case. I think Professor Benson here can enlighten you. Enlighten all of us, for I'm rather vague about it. That's why Professor Benson is here.'

'The good Professor is not at his best,' Benson said. 'He's hungry.'

'Most remiss of us,' Talbot said. 'Of course you haven't eaten. Dinner, say, in twenty minutes?'

'I'd settle for a sandwich.' Talbot looked at Hawkins and Wickram, both of whom nodded. He pressed a bell.

'I'm a bit vague about it myself,' Benson said. 'Certain facts are beyond dispute. What we're sitting on top of at this moment is one of them. According to which estimate of the Pentagon's you choose to believe, there's something like a total of between 144 and 225 megatons of high explosive lying down there. Not that the difference between the lowest and highest estimate is of any significance. The explosion of a pound of high explosive in this wardroom would kill us all. What we are talking about is the explosive power of, let me see, yes, four and a half billion pounds. The human mind cannot comprehend, differences in estimates become irrelevant. All we can say with certainty is that it would be the biggest man-made explosion in history, which doesn't sound so bad when you say it quickly as I'm saying it now.

'The results of such an explosion are quite unknown but stupefyingly horrendous however optimistic your guess might be, if optimistic is the word I'm looking for, which it isn't. It might fracture the earth's crust, with cataclysmic results. It might destroy part of the ozone layer, which would permit the sun's ultra-violet radiation either to tan us or fry us, depending upon how large a hole had been blasted in the stratosphere: it might equally well cause the onset of a nuclear winter, which is so popular a topic among both scientists and laymen these days. And lastly, but by no means least, are the *tsunami* effects, vast tidal waves usually generated by undersea earthquakes: those *tsunami* have been responsible for the deaths of tens of thousands of people at a time when they struck low-lying coastal areas.'

Benson reached out a grateful hand for a glass that Jenkins had brought. Talbot said: 'If you're trying to be encouraging, Professor, you're not doing too well at it.'

'Ah, better, much better.' Benson lowered his glass and sighed, 'I needed that. There are times

77

when I'm quite capable of terrifying even myself. Encouraging? That's only the half of it. Santorini's the other half. In fact, Santorini is the major part of it. Gifted though mankind is in creating sheer wanton destruction, nature has him whacked every time.'

'Santorini?' Wickram said. 'Who or what is Santorini?'

'Ignorance, George, ignorance. You and your fellow physicists should look out from your ivory towers from time to time. Santorini is less than a couple of miles from where you're sitting. Had that name for many centuries. Today it's officially known, as it was five thousand years ago at the height of its civilization, as Thera Island.

'The island, by whatever name, has had a very turbulent seismic and volcanic history. Don't worry, George, I'm not about to sally forth on my old hobby-horse, not for long anyway, just long enough to try to explain what the greatest number means in the term the greatest good of the greatest number.

'It is commonly enough imagined that earthquakes and volcanic eruptions are two faces of the same coin. This is not necessarily so. The venerable Oxford English Dictionary states that an earthquake is specifically a convulsion of the earth's surface caused by volcanic forces. The dictionary is specifically wrong: it should have used the word "rarely" instead. Earthquakes, especially the big ones, are caused when two tectonic plates –

segments of the earth's crust that float freely on the molten magma beneath – come into contact with one another and one plate bangs into another or rubs alongside it or dives under it. The only two recorded and monitored giant earthquakes in history were of this type – in Ecuador in 1906 and Japan in 1933. Similarly, but on a lesser scale – although still very big – the Californian earthquakes of San Francisco and Owens Valley were due to crustal movement and not to volcanoes.

'It is true that practically all the world's 500–600 active volcanoes – someone may have bothered to count them, I haven't – are located along convergent plate boundaries. It is equally true that they are rarely associated with earthquakes. There have been three large volcanic eruptions along such boundaries in very recent years: Mt St Helens in the state of Washington, El Chichón in Mexico and one just north-west of Bogotá in Columbia. The last one – it happened only last year – was particularly nasty. A 17,000-foot volcano called Nevada del Ruiz, which seems to have been slumbering off and on for the past four hundred years, erupted and melted the snow and ice which covered most of its upper reaches, giving rise to an estimated seventy-five million cubic yards' mudslide. The town of Armero stood in its way. 25,000 people died there. The point is that none of those was accompanied by an earthquake. Even volcanoes in areas where there are no established tectonic frontiers are guiltless in this respect: Vesuvius, despite the fact that it buried Pompeii and Herculaneum, Stromboli, Mt Etna and the twin volcanoes of the island of Hawaii have not produced, and do not produce, earthquakes.

'But the really bad apples in the seismic barrel, and a very sinister lot those are, too, are the so-called thermal hotspots, plumes or upswellings of molten lava that reach up to or through the earth's crust, giving rise to volcanoes or earthquakes or both. We talk a lot about those thermal plumes but we really don't know much about them. We don't know whether they're localized or whether they spread out and lubricate the movements of the tectonic plates. What we do know is that they can have extremely unpleasant effects. One of those was responsible for the biggest earthquake of this century.'

'You have me confused, Professor,' Hawkins said. 'You've just mentioned the really big ones, the ones in Japan and Ecuador. Ah! But those were monitored and recorded. This one wasn't?'

'Certainly it was. But countries like Russia and China are rather coy about releasing such details. They have the weird notion that natural disasters reflect upon their political systems.'

'Is it in order to ask how you know?'

'Of course. Governments may elect not to talk to governments but we scientists are an incurably gabby lot. This quake happened in Tangshan province in north-east China and is the only one ever known to have occurred in a really densely populated area, in this case involving the major cities of Peking and Tientsin. The primary cause was undoubtedly a thermal plume. There are no known tectonic plate boundaries in the area but a very ancient boundary may be lurking in the area. The date was July 27, 1976.'

'Yesterday,' Hawkins said. 'Just yesterday. Casualties?'

'Two-thirds of a million dead, three-quarters of a million injured. Give or take a hundred thousand in each case. If that sounds flippant or heartless, it's not meant to be. After a certain arbitrary figure – a hundred thousand, ten thousand, even a thousand, it all depends upon how much your heart and mind can take – any increase in numbers becomes meaningless. And there's also the factor, of course, that we're referring to faceless unknowns in a far-off land.'

'I suppose,' Hawkins said, 'that that would be what one might call the grand-daddy of them all?'

'In terms of lives lost, it probably is. We can't be sure. What we can be sure of is that Tangshan rates as no more than third in the cataclysmic league. Just over a century ago the island of Krakatoa in Indonesia blew itself out of existence. That was quite a bang, literally – the sound of the explosion was heard thousands of miles away. So much volcanic material was blasted into the stratosphere that the world was still being treated to a series of spectacular sunsets more than three years afterwards. No one knows the height of the *tsunami* caused by this eruption. What we do know is that much of the three great islands bordering the Java Sea – Sumatra, Java and Borneo – and nearly all of the smaller islands inside the sea itself lie below an altitude of 200 feet. No tally of the dead has ever been made. It is better, perhaps, that we don't know.'

'And perhaps it's also better that we don't know what you're going to say next,' Talbot said. 'I don't much care for the road you're leading us along.'

'I don't much care for it myself.' Benson sighed and sipped some more gin. 'Anyone ever heard of the word "*kalliste*"?'

'Certainly,' Denholm said. 'Means most beautiful. Very ancient. Goes back to Homeric times.'

'My goodness.' Benson peered at him through his pipe smoke. 'I thought you were the electronics officer?'

'Lieutenant Denholm is primarily a classicist,' Talbot said. 'Electronics is one of his hobbies.'

'Ah!' Benson gestured with his thumb. 'Kalliste was the name given to this little lady before it became either Thera or Santorini, and a more singularly inapt name I cannot imagine. It was this beautiful lady that blew her top in 1450 BC with four times the explosively destructive power of Krakatoa. What had been the cone of a volcano became a circular depression – we call it a caldera – some thirty square miles in area into which the sea poured. Stirring times, gentlemen, stirring times.

'Unfortunately those stirring times are still with us. Santorini has had, and continues to have, a very turbulent seismic history. Incidentally, mythology has it that there was an even bigger eruption about 2500 BC. However it hasn't done too badly since 1450 BC. In 236 BC another eruption separated Therasia from north-west Thera. Forty years later the islet of old Jaimeni appeared. There have been bangs and explosions, the appearances and disappearances of islands and volcanoes ever since. In the late sixteenth century the south coast of Thera, together with the port of Eleusis, vanished under the sea and stayed there. Even as late as 1956 a considerable earthquake destroyed half the buildings on the west coast of the island. Santorini, one fears, rests on very shaky foundations.'

Talbot said: 'What happened in 1450 BC?'

'Regrettably, our ancestors of some thirty-five centuries back don't seem to have given too much thought to posterity, by which I mean they left no records to satisfy their descendants' intellectual curiosity. One can hardly blame them, they had too many urgent and pressing matters on hand at the time to worry about such things. According to one account, the explosion caused a tidal wave 165 feet high. I don't know who worked this out. I don't believe it. It is true that water levels on the Alaskan coast, caused by *tsunami*, earthquake-related tidal waves, have risen over three hundred feet but this only happens when the sea-bed shallows close inshore: in the deep sea, although the *tsunami* can travel tremendously fast, two, perhaps three, hundred miles an hour, it's rarely more than a ripple on the surface of the water.

'The experts – an expert may be loosely defined as any person who claims he knows what he's talking about – are deeply divided as to what happened. Loggerheads would be too mild a term. It's an archæological minefield. The explosion *may* have destroyed the Cyclades. It *may* have wiped out the Minoan civilization in Crete. It *may* have swamped the Aegean isles and the coastal lowlands of Greece and Turkey. It may have inundated lower Egypt, flooded the Nile and swept back the Red Sea waters to permit the escape of the Israelites fleeing from the Pharaoh. That's one view. In 1950 a scientist by the name of Immanuel Velikovsky caused a considerable furore in the historical, religious and astronomical worlds by stating unequivocally that the flooding was caused by Venus which had been wrenched free from Jupiter and made an uncomfortably close encounter with earth. A very scholarly and erudite work, widely acclaimed at the time but since much maligned. Professional jealousy? Upsetting the scientific apple-cart? A charlatan? Unlikely – man was a friend and colleague of Albert Einstein. Then, of course, there was Edmund Halley, he of comet fame – he was equally certain that the flooding had been caused by a passing comet.

'There's no doubt there was a huge natural disaster all those millennia ago. As to its cause, take your pick – your guess is as good as mine. Reverting to the situation we find ourselves in at this moment, there are four facts that can be regarded as certainties or near-certainties. Santorini is about as stable as the proverbial blanc-mange. It's sitting on top of a thermal plume. Thirdly, the chances are high that it is sitting atop an ancient tectonic boundary that runs east-west under the Mediterranean – this is where the African and Eurasian plates are in contention. Lastly, and indisputably, *we* are sitting atop the equivalent of roughly 200 million tons of TNT. If that goes up I would say it is highly probable – in fact I think I should use the word inevitable – that both the thermal plume and the temporarily qui-escent earthquake zone along the tectonic fault would be reactivated. I leave the rest to your imagination.' Benson drained his glass and looked around hopefully. Talbot pressed a bell.

Hawkins said: 'I don't have that kind of imagi-nation.'

'None of us has. Fortunately. We're talking about the combined and simultaneous effect of a massive thermonuclear detonation, a volcanic eruption and an earthquake. This lies outwith the experience of mankind so we can't visualize those things except to guess, and it's a safe guess, that the reality will be worse than any nightmare. The only consolation, of course, is that we wouldn't be around to experience anything, nightmare or reality.

'The extent of potential annihilation beggars belief. By "annihilation" I mean the total extinction of life, except possibly some subterranean or aquatic forms. What lava, volcanic cinders, dust and ashes don't get, the blast, air percussion waves, fire and *tsunami* will. If there are any survivors – and this could be in an area of thousands of square miles – the massive radio-active fall-out will attend to them. It hardly seems necessary to talk about such things as nuclear winters and being fried by ultra-violet radiation.

'So you can see, Commander Talbot, what we mean when we talk about the greatest good of the greatest number. What does it matter if we have two ships or ten out here, two hundred men or two thousand? Every extra man, every extra ship may, just may, be of a tiny percentage more help in neutralizing this damn thing on the sea-floor. What's even two thousand compared to the unimaginable numbers who might perish if that device does detonate sooner or later – almost certainly sooner – if we don't do something about it?'

'You put things very nicely, Professor, and you make things very clear. Not that the *Ariadne* had any intention of going anywhere but it's nice to have a solid reason to stay put.' Talbot thought briefly. 'Solves one little problem, anyway. I have six survivors from the yacht *Delos* aboard and had thought to put three of the innocent parties among them ashore but that seems a little point-less now.'

'Alas, yes. Whether they are aboard here or on Santorini it will be all one to them when they join us in what Lieutenant Denholm is pleased to call vaporized orbit.'

Talbot lifted a phone, asked for a number, listened briefly and hung up.

'The sonar room. Still tick . . . tick . . . tick.'

'Ah,' Benson said. 'Tick . . . tick . . . tick.'

4

'You had an enjoyable tête-à-tête with Mr Andropulos, sir?' Vice-Admiral Hawkins, together with his two scientist friends, had just come to the bridge in response to Talbot's invitation that they join him.

'Enjoyable? Ha! Thank you, incidentally, for rescuing us. Enjoyable? Depends what you mean, John.'

'I mean were you suitably impressed.'

'I was suitably unimpressed. Interested, mind you, but deeply unimpressed. Man's character, I mean, not his quite extraordinary affinity for strong spirits. He comes across as whiter than the driven snow. A man of such transparent honesty has to have something to hide.'

'And he got his slurring wrong, too,' Benson said.

'Slurring, sir?'

'Just that, Commander. Thickened his voice in the wrong places to try and convince us that he was under the influence. Maybe he could have got away with it in his native Greek but not in English. Cold sober, I believe. And clever. Anyway he's clever enough to hoodwink those two charming young ladies he has with him. I *think* they're being hoodwinked.'

'And his bosom friend, Alexander,' Hawkins said. 'He's not so clever. He comes over as what he might well be – a paid-up member, if not a capo, in the Mafia. He was quite unmoved when I sympathized with them about the loss of the three members of their crew. Andropulos said he was desolated by the deaths of his treasured friends. Van Gelder had already told us that. Maybe he was overcome by grief, maybe not. In view of the fact that, like you, I regard him as a fluent liar and consummate actor, I think not. Maybe he is conscience-stricken at having arranged their deaths. Again, I think not. By that I don't mean he couldn't have been responsible for their deaths, I just mean that I don't think he's on speaking terms with his conscience. Only information I gathered from him is that he abandoned his yacht because he thought his spare fuel tank was going to blow up. A man of mystery, your new-found friend.'

'He's all that. Very mysterious. He's a multi-millionaire. Maybe a multi-multi-millionaire. Not in the usual Greek line of tankers – bottom's fallen out of that market anyway. He's an international businessman with contacts in many countries.'

Hawkins said: 'Van Gelder told me nothing of this.'

'Of course he didn't. He didn't know. Your name attached to a message, Admiral, is a guarantee of remarkably quick service. Reply received to our query to the Greek Defence Ministry received twenty-five minutes ago.'

'A businessman. What kind of business?'

'They didn't say. I knew that would be your question so I immediately radioed a request for that information.'

'Signed by me, of course.'

'Naturally, sir. Had it been a different matter I would of course have asked your permission. But this was the same matter. The reply came in a few minutes ago listing ten different countries with which he does business.'

'Again, what kind of business?'

'Again, they didn't say.'

'Extraordinarily odd. What do you make of it?'

'The Foreign Minister must have authorized this reply. Maybe censored it a little. He is, of course, a member of the government. I would assume that the mysterious Mr Andropulos has friends in the government.'

'The mysterious Mr Andropulos gets more mysterious by the moment.'

'Maybe, sir. Maybe not – not when you consider the list of ten foreign trading partners he has. Four of them are in cities of what you might regard as being of particular interest – Tripoli, Beirut, Damascus and Baghdad.'

'Indeed.' Hawkins thought briefly. 'Gun-running?'

'But of course, sir. Nothing illegal about being gun-runners – Britain and America are hotching with them. But all governments are holier-than-thou in this respect and never publicly associate themselves with them. Never do to be classified as a merchant of death. Could well explain why the Greek government is being so cagey.'

'Indeed it could.'

'One thing strikes me as odd: why is Tehran missing from the list?'

'True, true. The Iranians – with the possible exception of the Afghans, are more desperate for arms than any other place around. But gun-runners don't specialize in blowing up planes in flight.'

'I don't know what we're talking about, sir. The Hampton Court maze has nothing on this lot. I have the feeling that it's going to take us quite some time to figure this out. Fortunately we have more immediate problems to occupy our minds.'

'Fortunately?' Hawkins lifted his eyes heavenwards. 'Did you say fortunately?'

'Yes, sir. Vincent?' This to Van Gelder. 'I should think Jenkins knows the requirements of the Vice-Admiral and his two friends by this time.'

'You are not joining us?' Benson said.

'Better not. We expect to be quite busy later on tonight.' He turned to Van Gelder again. 'And give orders for our six shipwrecked mariners to return to their cabins. They are to remain there until further orders. Post guards to see that those instructions are obeyed.'

'I think I'd better go and do this myself, sir.'

'Fine. I'm all out of tact at the moment.'

Hawkins said: 'Do you think they'll take kindly to this – ah – incarceration?'

'Incarceration? Let's call it protective custody. Fact is, I don't want them to see what's going on in the next few hours. I'll explain why in a moment.

'The Ministry of Defence had another item of information for us. About the bomber. It *had* been in touch with air control in Athens and had been instructed to alter course over the island of Amorgós – that's about forty miles north-east of here – and proceed on a roughly north-north-west course. Two fighter planes – US Air Force F15s – went up to meet it and escort it in.'

'Did you see any such planes in the vicinity?'

'No, sir. Wouldn't have expected to. Rendezvous point was to be over the island of Euboea. The destination was not Athens but Thessalonika. I assume the Americans have a missile base in that area. I wouldn't know.

'Admiral Blyth on the *Apollo* has also come through. We've had luck here – two pieces of luck. A recovery ship en route to Piraeus has been diverted to Santorini. Diving crews, recovery gear, the lot. You'll know it, sir. The *Kilcharran*.'

'I know it. Auxiliary Fleet vessel. Nominally under my command. I say "nominally" because I also have the misfortune to know its captain. Lad called Montgomery. A very crusty Irishman with a low opinion of Royal Navy regulations. Not that that matters. He's brilliant at his job. Couldn't ask to have a better man around. Your other item of good news?'

'There's a plane en route to Santorini at this moment with a couple of divers and diving equipment for four aboard. Very experienced men, I'm told, a Chief Petty Officer and a Petty Officer. I've sent Sub-Lieutenant Cousteau ashore to pick them up. They should be here in half an hour or so.'

'Excellent, excellent. And when do you expect the *Kilcharran*?'

'About five in the morning, sir.'

'By Jove, things are looking up. You have something in mind?'

'I have. With your permission, sir.'

'Oh, do shut up.'

'Yes, sir. It will also answer your two questions – why Van Gelder and I are on the wagon and why the six survivors have been – well, locked up out of harm's way. When Cousteau comes back with the divers and equipment, Van Gelder and I are going down with them to have a look at this plane. I'm pretty sure we won't be able to accomplish much. But we'll be able to assess the extent of the damage to the plane, with luck locate this ticking monster and with even greater luck try to free it. I know in advance that we're not going to have that kind of luck but it's worth a try. You'd be the first to agree, sir, that in the circumstances, *anything* is worth a try.'

'Yes, yes, but, well, you'll excuse me if I frown a bit but you and Van Gelder are the two most important people on this ship.'

'No, we're not. If anything should happen to us personally, and I don't see what can happen, you are, in your spare time, so to speak, accustomed to commanding a battle fleet. I can hardly see that a mere frigate is going to inconvenience you to all that extent. And if anything should happen on a catastrophic scale, nobody's going to be worrying too much about anything.'

Wickram said: 'You are a cold-blooded so-and-so, Commander.'

Hawkins sighed. 'Not cold blood, Dr Wickram. Cold logic, I'm afraid. And when and if you come back up, what then?'

'Then we're off to have a look at the *Delos*. Should be very interesting. Andropulos may have made a mistake, Admiral, in telling you that he was scared that his spare fuel tank might blow up. But then, he could have had no idea that we were going to have a look at the *Delos*. That's why he's locked up. I don't want him to know we've got divers aboard and I especially don't want him to see me taking off with divers in the general direction of the *Delos*. If we find that there *was* no spare tank, we shall have to keep an even closer eye on him. And, for good measure, on his dear friend Alexander and his captain, Aristotle. I can't believe that that young seaman, Achmed or whatever his name is, or either of the two girls can have anything to do with this. I think they're along for the purpose of camouflage, respectability, if you will. In any event we should be back long before the *Kilcharran* arrives.' He turned to look at Denholm who had just arrived on the bridge. 'Well, Jimmy, what drags you away from the fleshpots?'

'If I may say so with some dignity, sir, I'm trying to set them an example. I've just had a thought, sir. If you will excuse me, Admiral?'

'I think that any thought you might have could be well worth listening to, young man. Not Greek literature this time, I'll be bound. This – ah – hobby of yours. Electronics, is it not?'

'Well, yes, it is, sir.' Denholm seemed faintly surprised. He looked at Talbot. 'That atom bomb down there, the one that goes tick . . . tick . . . tick. The intention is, or the hope, anyway, to detach it from the other explosives?'

'If it can be done.'

'And then, sir?'

'One thing at a time, Jimmy. That's as far as my thinking has got so far.'

'Would we try to de-activate it?' Denholm looked at Wickram. 'Do you think it could be de-activated, sir?'

'I honestly don't know, Lieutenant. I have powerful suspicions, but I just don't know. I should have imagined that this lay more in your field than mine. Electronics, I mean. I know how to build those damned weapons but I know nothing about those fancy triggering devices.'

'Neither do I. Not without knowing how they work. For that I'd have to see the blueprint, a diagramatic layout. You said you had powerful suspicions. What suspicions, sir?'

'I suspect that it can't be de-activated. In fact, I'm certain the process is irreversible. The second suspicion is also a certainty. I'm damn sure that I'm not going to be the one to try.'

'That makes two of us. So what other options are open to us?'

Benson said: 'May a total ignoramus venture an opinion? Why don't we take it to some safe place a hundred miles away and dump it at the bottom of the deep blue sea?'

'A tempting thought, Professor,' Denholm said, 'but not a very practicable one. It is, of course, a hundred per cent certain that this triggering device is battery-powered. The latest generation of Nife cells can lie dormant for months, even years, and still spring smartly to attention when called on to do their duty. You can't declare a whole area of the Mediterranean off-limits to all shipping for years to come.'

'I prefaced my suggestion by saying that I was an ignoramus. Well, in for a penny, in for a pound.

Another doubtlessly ludicrous suggestion. We take it to the self-same spot and detonate it.'

Denholm shook his head, 'I'm afraid that still leaves us with a couple of problems. The first is, how are we going to get it there?'

'We take it there.'

'Yes. We take it there. Or we set out to take it there. Then somewhere en route the ticking stops. Then the triggering device cocks its ear and says, "Aha! What's this I hear? Ship's engines," and detonates. There wouldn't even be a second's warning.'

'Hadn't thought of that. We could – I say this hopefully – tow it there.'

'Our little friend is still listening and we don't know and have no means of knowing how sensitive its hearing is. Engines, of course, would set it off. So would a generator. A derrick winch, even a coffee-grinder in the galley might provide all the impulse it requires.'

Talbot said: 'You came all the way up to the bridge, Jimmy, just to spread sweetness and light, your own special brand of Job's comfort?'

'Not quite, sir. It's just that a couple of ideas occurred to me, one of which will have occurred to you and one which you probably don't know about. Getting the bomb to its destination would be easy enough. We use a sailing craft. Lots of them hereabouts. Aegean luggers.'

Talbot looked at Hawkins. 'One can't think of everything. I forgot to mention, sir, that in addition to being a student of ancient Greek language and literature Lieutenant Denholm is also a connoisseur of the small craft of the Aegean. Used to spend all his summers here – well, until we nabbed him, that is.'

'I wouldn't begin to know how to sail those luggers or caïques, in fact I couldn't even sail a dinghy if you paid me. But I've studied them, yes. Most of them come from the island of Samos or Bodrum in Turkey. Before the war – the First World War, that is – they were all sailing craft. Nowadays, they're nearly all engined, most of them with steadying sails. But there's quite a few both with engines and a full set of sails. Those are the Trehandiri and Perama types and I know there are some in the Cyclades. One of those would be ideal for our purposes. Because they have shallow keels, a minimum draught and no ballast they are almost useless performers to windward but that wouldn't matter in this case. The prevailing wind here is north-west and the open sea lies to the south-east.'

'Useful information to have,' Talbot said. 'Very useful indeed. Um – you wouldn't happen to know anyone with such a craft?'

'As a matter of fact I do.'

'Good God! You're as useful as your information.' Talbot broke off as Van Gelder entered the bridge. 'Duty done, Number One?'

'Yes, sir. Andropulos was a bit reluctant to go. So were Alexander and Aristotle. In fact, they point-blank refused to go. Infringement of their liberties as Greek civilians or some tosh to that effect. Demanded to know on whose orders. I said yours. Demanded to see you. I said in the morning. More outrage. I didn't argue with them, just called up McKenzie and some of his merry men, who removed them forcibly. I told McKenzie not to post any guards, just lock the doors and pocket the keys. You're going to hear from the Greek government about this, sir.'

'Excellent. Wish I'd been there. And the girls?'

'Sweet reason. No problem.'

'Fine. Now, Jimmy, you said a couple of ideas had occurred to you. What was the second one?'

'It's about the second problem that the Professor raised. The detonation. We could, of course, try sympathetic detonation by dropping a depth charge on it but as we would be in the immediate vicinity at the time I don't think that would be a very good idea.'

'Neither do I. So?'

'The Pentagon could have the answer. Despite feeble denials to the contrary, everyone knows that the Pentagon controls NASA – the National Aeronautics and Space Administration. NASA, in turn, is supposed to administer the Kennedy Space Center. "Supposed" is the operative word. They don't. The centre is operated by EG & G, a major defence contractor. EG & G – Dr Wickram will know much more about this than I do – oversees such things as nuclear-weapons tests and the so-called Star Wars. More importantly, they are developing, or have developed, what they call the krytron, a remote-controlled electronic impulse trigger that can detonate nuclear weapons. A word from the Admiral in the ear of the Pentagon might work wonders.'

Hawkins cleared his throat. 'This little titbit of information, Lieutenant. It will, of course, like your other titbits, be in the public domain?'

'It is, sir.'

'You astonish me. Most interesting, most. Could be a big part of the answer to our problem, don't you agree, Commander?' Talbot nodded. 'I think we should act immediately on this one. Ah! The very man himself.'

Myers had just entered, carrying a piece of paper which he handed to Talbot. 'Reply to your latest query to the Pentagon, sir.'

'Thank you. No, don't go. We'll have another message to send them in a minute.' Talbot handed the paper to Hawkins.

' "Security at bomber base",' Hawkins read, ' "believed to be 99.9% effective. But cards on the table. However unlikely, there may be one chance in ten thousand that security has been penetrated. This could have been that one chance". Well, isn't that nice. Absolutely useless piece of information, of course.

' "Plane carried fifteen H-bombs of fifteen megatons each and three atom bombs, all three equipped with timing devices". Well, that's just fine. So now we have three of those ticking monsters to contend with.'

'With any luck, just one,' Talbot said. 'Sonar picks up only one. Extremely unlikely that all three would be ticking in perfect unison. Point's academic, anyway. One or a hundred, the big boys would still go up.'

'Identified by size, they say,' Hawkins went on. 'Sixty inches by six. Pretty small for an atom bomb, I would have thought. 4000 kilotons. That's a lot, Dr Wickram?'

'By today's standards, peanuts. Less than half the size of the Hiroshima bomb. If the bomb is the dimensions they say, then it's very large for such a small explosive value.'

'It goes on to say that they're designated for marine use. I suppose that's a fancy way of saying that they are mines. So your guess was right, Dr Wickram.'

'Also explains the size of the bomb. Quite a bit of space will be taken up by the timing mechanism and, of course, it will have to be weighted to give it negative buoyancy.'

'The real sting comes in the tail,' Hawkins said. ' "When the ticking stops the timing clock has run out and the firing mechanism is activated and ready to be triggered by mechanical stimulation", by which I take it they mean ship's engines. So it looks as if you were right about that one, Van Gelder. Then, by way of cheerful farewell, they say that enquiries so far confirm that the timing mechanism, once in operation, cannot be neutralized and appears to be irreversible.'

The last words were met with silence. No one had any comment to make for the excellent reason that everyone had already been convinced of the fact.

'A message to the Pentagon, Myers. "Urgently require to know state of development of the EG & G krytron" – that's k-r-y-t-r-o-n, isn't it, Lieutenant? – "nuclear detonation device." ' Talbot paused. 'Add: "If operating model exists essential dispatch immediately with instructions." That do, Admiral?' Hawkins nodded. 'Sign it Admiral Hawkins.'

'We must be giving them quite some headaches in the Pentagon,' Hawkins said in some satisfaction. 'This should call for still more aspirin.'

'Aspirins are not enough,' Van Gelder said. 'Sleepless nights are what are called for.'

'You have something in mind, Van Gelder?'

'Yes, sir. They can have no idea of the really horrendous potential of the situation here in Santorini – the combination of all those megatons of hydrogen bombs, thermal plumes and volcanoes and earthquakes along the tectonic plate boundaries and the possibly cataclysmic results. If Professor Benson here were to make a very brief précis of the lecture he gave us in the wardroom this evening it might give them something more to think about.'

'You have an evil mind, Van Gelder. What a perfectly splendid suggestion. Uneasy will lie the heads along the Potomac this night. What do you think, Professor?'

'It will be a pleasure.'

When Sub-Lieutenant Cousteau, together with the two divers and their equipment, returned from Santorini, they found the *Ariadne* in virtual darkness. With the thought of the malevolent listening bug on the sea-floor dominating every other in his mind, Talbot had sought Lieutenant Denholm's advice on the question of noise suppression: Denholm had not been half-hearted in his recommendations, with the result that the use of all mechanical devices on the ship, from generators to electric shavers, had been banned. Only essential lighting, radar, sonar and radio were functioning normally: all these could function equally well, as they had been designed to do, on battery power. The sonar watch on the ticking device in the crashed bomber was now continuous.

The two divers, Chief Petty Officer Carrington and Petty Officer Grant, were curiously alike, both aged about thirty, of medium height and compact build: both were much given to smiling, a cheerfulness that in no way detracted from their almost daunting aura of competence. They were with Talbot and Van Gelder in the wardroom.

'That's all I know about the situation down there,' Talbot said, 'and heaven knows it's little enough. I just want to know those three things – the extent of the damage, the location of this ticking noise and to see if it's possible to remove this atom bomb or whatever, which I'm convinced in advance is impossible. You are aware of the dangers and you are aware that I cannot order you to do this. How does the prospect appeal, Chief?'

'It doesn't appeal at all, sir.' Carrington was imperturbable. 'Neither Bill Grant nor I is cast in the heroic mould. We'll walk very softly down there. You shouldn't be worrying about us, you should be worrying about what your crew is thinking. If we slip up they'll all join us in the wide blue yonder or whatever. I know you want to come down, sir, but is it really necessary? We're pretty experienced in moving around inside wrecks without banging into things and we're both Torpedo Gunner Mates and explosives, you might say, are our business. Not, I admit, the kind of explosives you have down there but we know enough not to trigger a bomb by accident.'

'And we might?' Talbot smiled. 'You're very tactful, Chief. What you mean is that we might bang into things or kick a detonator on the nose or something of the kind. When you say "necessary", do you mean "wise"? I refer to our diving experience or lack of it.'

'We know about your diving experience, sir. You will understand that when we knew what we were coming into we made some discreet enquiries. We know that you have commanded a

104

submarine and the Lieutenant-Commander was your first lieutenant. We know you've both been through the HMS *Dolphin* Submarine Escape Tower and that you've done more than a fair bit of free diving. No, we don't think you'll be getting in our way or banging things around.' Carrington turned up palms in acceptance. 'What's your battery capacity, sir?'

'For essential and non-mechanical purposes, ample. Several days.'

'We'll put down three weighted floodlights and suspend them about twenty feet above the bottom. That should illuminate the plane nicely. We'll have a powerful hand-flash each. We have a small bag of tools for cutting, sawing and snipping. We also have an oxyacetylene torch, which is rather more difficult to use under water than most people imagine, but as this is just a reconnaissance trip we won't be taking it along. The closed-circuit breathing is of the type we prefer, fifty-fifty oxygen and nitrogen with a carbon dioxide scrubber. At the depth of a hundred feet, which is what we will be at, we could easily remain underwater for an hour without any risk of either oxygen poisoning or decompression illness. That's academic, of course. Provided there's access to the plane and the fuselage is not crushed a few minutes should tell us all we want to know.

'Two points about the helmet. There's a rotary chin switch which you depress to activate an amplifier that lets us talk, visor to visor. A second press cuts it off. It also has a couple of sockets over the ears where you can plug in what is to all effects a stethoscope.'

'That's all?'

'All.'

'We can go now?'

'A last check, sir?' Carrington didn't have to specify what check.

Talbot lifted a phone, spoke briefly and replaced it.

'Our friend is still at work.'

The water was warm and still and so very clear that they could see the lights of the suspended arc-lamps even before they dipped below the surface of the darkened Aegean. With Carrington in the lead and using the marker buoy anchor rope as a guide they slid down fifty feet and stopped.

The three arc-lamps had come to rest athwart the sunken bomber, sharply illuminating the fuselage and the two wings. The left wing, though still attached to the fuselage, had been almost completely sheared off between the inner engine and the fuselage and was angled back about thirty degrees from normal. The tail unit had been almost completely destroyed. The fuselage, or that part of it that could be seen from above, appeared to be relatively intact. The nose cone of the plane was shrouded in shadow.

They continued their descent until their feet touched the top of the fuselage, half-walked, half-swam until they reached the front of the plane, switched on their flash-lights and looked through the completely shattered windows of the cockpit. The pilot and the co-pilot were still trapped in their seats. They were no longer men, just the vestigial remains of what had once been human beings. Death must have been instantaneous. Carrington looked at Talbot and shook his head, then dropped down to the sea-bed in front of the nose cone.

The hole that had been blasted there was roughly circular with buckled and jagged edges projecting outwards, conclusive proof that the blast had been internal: the diameter of the whole was approximately five feet. Moving slowly and cautiously so as not to rip any of the rubber components of their diving suits, they passed in file into a compartment not more than four feet in height but almost twenty feet in length, extending from the nose cone, under the flight deck and then several feet beyond. Both sides of the compartment were lined with machinery and metal boxes so crushed and mangled that their original function was incomprehensible.

Two-thirds of the way along the compartment a hatch had been blasted upwards. The opening led to a space directly behind the seats of the two pilots. Aft of this was what was left of a small radio-room with a man who appeared to be peacefully sleeping leaning forward on folded arms, the fingers of one hand still on a transmitting key.

Beyond this, four short steps led down to an oval door let into a solid steel bulkhead. The door was secured by eight clamps, some of which had been jammed into position by the impact of the blast. A hammer carried by Carrington in his canvas bag of tools soon tapped them into a loosened position.

Beyond the door lay the cargo compartment, bare, bleak, functional and obviously designed for one purpose only, the transport of missiles. These were secured by heavy steel clamps which were in turn bolted to longitudinal reinforced steel beams let into the floor and sides of the fuselage. There was oil mixed with the water in the compartment but even in the weird, swirling, yellowish light they looked neither particularly menacing nor sinister. Slender, graceful, with either end encased in a rectangular metal box they looked perfectly innocuous. Each contained fifteen megatons of high explosive.

There were six of those in the first section of the compartment. As a formality, and not because of any expectations, Talbot and Carrington applied their stethoscopes to each cylinder in turn. The results were negative as they had known they would be: Dr Wickram had been positive that they contained no timing devices.

There were also six missiles in the central compartment. Three of these were of the same size as those in the front compartment: the other three were no more than five feet in length. Those had to be the atom bombs. It was when he was testing the third of those with his stethoscope that Carrington beckoned to Talbot, who came and listened in turn. He didn't have to listen long. The two and a half second ticking sequence sounded exactly as it had done in the sonar room.

In the aft compartment they went through the routine exercise of listening to the remaining six missiles and found what they had expected, nothing. Carrington put his visor close to Talbot's.

'Enough?'

'Enough.'

'That didn't take you long,' Hawkins said.

'Long enough to find out what we needed. Missiles are there, all present and correct as listed by the Pentagon. Only one bomb has been activated. Three dead men. That's all, except for the most important fact of all. The bomber crashed because of an internal explosion. Some kindly soul had concealed a bomb under the flight deck. The Pentagon must be glad that they added the faint possibility that there was one chance in ten thousand that security might be breached. The faint possibility came true. Raises some fascinating questions, doesn't it, sir? Who? What? Why? When? We don't have to ask "where" because we already know that.'

'I don't want to sound grim or vindictive,' Hawkins said, 'because I'm not. Well, maybe a little. Should cut the gentlemen on Foggy Bottom, or wherever, down to size and make them a mite more civil and cooperative in future. Not only is it an American plane that is responsible for the dreadful situation in which we find ourselves, but it was someone in America who was ultimately responsible. If they ever do discover who was responsible, and it's not without the bounds of possibility, it's going to cause an awful lot of red faces and I'm not just referring to the villain himself. I'd lay odds that the person responsible is an insider, a pretty high-up insider with free access to secret information, such as closely guarded secrets as to the composition of the cargo, the destination and the time of take-off and arrival. Wouldn't you agree, Commander?'

'I don't see how it can be otherwise. Not a problem I'd care to have on my hands. However, that's *their* problem. *We* have an even bigger problem on our hands.'

'True, true.' Hawkins sighed. 'What's the next step, then? In recovering this damn bomb, I mean?'

'I think you should ask Chief Petty Officer Carrington, sir, not me. He and Petty Officer Grant are the experts.'

'It's a tricky one, sir,' Carrington said. 'Cutting away a fuselage section large enough to lift the bomb through is straightforward enough. But before we could lift the bomb out we would have to free it from its clamps and this is where the great difficulty lies. Those clamps are made of high-tensile steel fitted with a locking device. For that we need a key and we don't know where the key is.'

'It could be,' Hawkins said, 'that the key is held at the missile base where the bombs were due to be delivered.'

'With respect, sir, I think that unlikely. Those clamps had to be locked at the Air Force base where they were loaded. So they would have to have a key there. I think it would be much easier and more logical if they just took the key with them. Trouble is, a key is a very small thing and that's a very big bomber indeed.

'If there's no key there are two ways we can remove that clamp. One is chemical, using either a metal softener or corrosive. The metal softener is used by stage magicians who go in for spoon-bending and such-like.'

'Magicians?' Hawkins said. 'Charlatans, you mean.'

'Whatever. The principle is the same. They use a colourless paste which has no effect on the skin but has the peculiar property of altering the molecular structure of a metal and making it malleable. A corrosive is simply a powerful acid that eats through steel. Lots of them on the market. But in this case, both softeners and corrosives have one impossible drawback: you can't use them underwater.'

Hawkins said: 'You mentioned two ways of removing the clamp. What's the other?'

'Oxyacetylene torch, sir. Make short work of any clamp. It would also, I imagine, make even shorter work of the operator. Those torches generate tremendous heat and I should also imagine that anyone who even contemplates using an oxyacetylene torch on an atom bomb is an obvious candidate for the loony-bin.'

Hawkins looked at Wickram. 'Comment?'

'No comment. Not on the unthinkable.'

'I speak in no spirit of complaint, Carrington,' Hawkins said, 'but you're not very encouraging. What you are about to suggest, of course, is that we wait for the *Kilcharran* to come along and hoist the damn thing to the surface.'

'Yes, sir.' Carrington hesitated. 'But there's a snag even to that.'

'A snag?' Talbot said. 'You are referring, of course, to the distinct and unpleasant possibility that the ticking might stop while the *Kilcharran*'s winch engine is working overtime at hauling the bomber to the surface?'

'I mean just that, sir.'

'A trifle. There are no trifles that the combined brain-power aboard the *Ariadne* can't solve.' He turned to Denholm. 'You can fix that, Lieutenant?'

'Yes, sir.'

'How, sir?' There was a pardonable note of doubt if not outright disbelief in Carrington's voice: Lieutenant Denholm didn't look like the type of person who could fix anything.

Talbot smiled. 'If I may say this gently, Chief, one does not question Lieutenant Denholm on those matters. He knows more about electrics and electronics than any man in the Mediterranean.'

'It's quite simple, Chief,' Denholm said. 'We just couple up the combined battery powers of the *Ariadne* and the *Kilcharran*. The *Kilcharran*'s winches are probably diesel-powered. We may or may not be able to convert them to electrical use. If we can't, it doesn't matter. We have excellent electric anchor windlasses on the *Ariadne*.'

'Yes, but – well, with one of your two anchors out of commission you'd start drifting, wouldn't you?'

'We wouldn't drift. A diving ship normally carries four splayed anchors to moor it precisely over any given spot on the ocean floor. We just tie up to the *Kilcharran*, that's all.'

'I'm not doing too well, am I? One last objection, sir. Probably a feeble one. An anchor is only an anchor. This bomber and its cargo probably weighs over a hundred tons. I mean, it's quite a lift.'

'Diving ships also carry flotation bags. We strap them to the plane's fuselage and pump them full of compressed air until we achieve neutral buoyancy.'

'I give up,' Carrington said. 'From now on, I stick to diving.'

'So we twiddle our thumbs until the *Kilcharran* arrives,' Hawkins said. 'But not you, I take it, Commander?'

'I think we'll have a look at the *Delos*, sir.'

They had rowed about a mile when Talbot called up the *Ariadne*. He spoke briefly, listened briefly, then turned to McKenzie who was at the tiller.

'Ship oars. The timing device is still at it so I think we'll start the engine. Gently, at first. At this distance I hardly think we'd trigger anything even if the bomb was activated, but no chances. Course 095.'

There were nine of them in the whaler – Talbot, Van Gelder, the two divers, McKenzie and the four seamen who had rowed them so far. Those last would not be required again until they reached the last mile of the return trip.

After about forty minutes Van Gelder moved up into the bows with a portable six-inch searchlight which, on such a clear night, had an effective range of over a mile. The searchlight was probably superfluous for there was a three-quarter moon and Talbot, with his night-glasses, had a clear bearing on the monastery and the radar station on

Mount Elias. Van Gelder returned within minutes and handed the searchlight to McKenzie.

'Fine off the port bow, Chief.'

'I have it,' McKenzie said. The yellow buoy, in the light of both the moon and the searchlight, was clearly visible. 'Do I anchor?'

'Not necessary,' Talbot said. 'No current that's worth speaking of, no wind, a heavy anchor weight and a stout anchor rope. Just make fast to the buoy.'

In course of time McKenzie did just that and the four divers slipped over the side, touching down on the deck of the *Delos* just over an hour after leaving the *Ariadne*. Carrington and Grant disappeared down the for'ard companionway while Talbot and Van Gelder took the after one.

Talbot didn't bother entering the after stateroom. The two girls had stayed there and he knew it would hold nothing of interest for him. He looked at the dead engineer, or the man whom Van Gelder had taken to be the engineer because of his blue overalls, and examined the back of his head carefully. The occiput had not been crushed and there were no signs of either bruising or blood in the vicinity of the deep gash in the skin of the skull. He rejoined Van Gelder who had already moved into the engine-room.

There was, of course, no smoke there now and very little traces of oil. In the light of their two powerful flashlights visibility was all that could be wished for and it took them only two minutes to carry out their examination: unless one is looking for some obscure mechanical fault there is very little to look for in an engine-room. On their way out they opened up a tool-box and took out a long slender chisel apiece.

They found the bridge, when they arrived there, to be all that they would have expected a bridge on such a yacht to be, with a plethora of expensive and largely unnecessary navigational aids, but in all respects perfectly innocuous. Only one thing took Talbot's attention, a wooden cupboard on the after bulkhead. It was locked, but on the understandable assumption that Andropulos wouldn't be having any further use for it Talbot wrenched it open with a chisel. It contained the ship's papers and ship's log, nothing more.

A door on the port side of the same bulkhead led to a combined radio-room and chart-room. The chart-room section held nothing that a chart-room should not have had, including a locked cupboard which Talbot opened in the same cavalier fashion he had used on the bridge: it held only pilot books and sailing directions. Andropulos, it seemed, just liked locking cupboards. The radio was a standard RCA. They left.

They found Carrington and Grant waiting for them in the saloon. Carrington was carrying what appeared to be a portable radio: Grant had a black metallic box slightly larger than a sheet of foolscap paper and less than three inches thick. Carrington put his visor close to Talbot's.

'All we could find. Of interest, I mean.'

'We have enough.'

'Dispatch would appear to be the keynote of your investigations, Commander,' Hawkins said. Glass in hand, he was seated across the wardroom table from Talbot, 'I mean, you seem to spend singularly little time on your – um – aquatic investigation.'

'You can find out interesting things in a very short space of time, sir. Too much, for some people.'

'You refer to our shipwrecked friends?'

'Who else? Five things, sir. Van Gelder was right, there were no signs of bruising or blood where the engineer had been gashed on the head. An examination of the engine-room turned up no signs of protrusions, angle-beams or sharp metallic corners that could have caused the injury. Circumstantial evidence, I know, but evidence that strongly suggests that the engineer was clobbered by a heavy metallic instrument. No shortage of those in an engine-room. We have, of course, no clue as to the identity of the assailant.

'Secondly, I'm afraid the owner of the *Delos* has been guilty of telling you fibs, Admiral. He said he abandoned the *Delos* because he was afraid that the reserve fuel tank might blow up. There is no such tank.'

'Isn't that interesting. Does make things look a little black for Andropulos.'

'It does a bit. He could always claim of course that he knew nothing of the layout of the engine-room and had always assumed that there had to be a reserve tank or that in a panic-stricken concern for the welfare of his beloved niece he had quite forgotten that there was no such tank. He's undoubtedly intelligent, we know he's a thespian of some note and could put up a spirited and convincing defence in court. But he'd have no defence against a further charge that the explosion was not due to natural causes, unless you regard the detonation of a bomb, almost certainly a plastic explosive, under the main fuel tank as being a natural cause.'

'Well, well, well. One wonders how he'll talk his way out of this one. You're quite certain, of course?'

'We are wounded, sir,' Van Gelder said. 'The Captain and I are developing quite some expertise on the effects of explosives on metal. In the bomber, the metal of the fuselage was blown outwards: in this case the metal of the fuel tank was blown inwards.'

'We are not explosives experts, sir,' Talbot said. 'But it would seem that Andropulos wasn't either.' He nodded towards Carrington and Grant. 'But those two gentlemen *are* experts. We were talking about it on the way back. They reckon that Andropulos – if it was Andropulos, it could have been Alexander or Aristotle – made an amateurish blunder. They say the villain, whoever he was, should have used what they call an inverted bee-hive plastic explosive attached to the underside of the tank by a magnetic clamp, in which case more than ninety per cent of the explosive charge would have been directed upwards. It would seem that they didn't use such a device.'

Hawkins looked at Carrington. 'You can be sure of this, Chief?'

'As sure as can be, sir. We do know that he couldn't have used a beehive. The explosive charge would have been either flat, circular or cylindrical and in any of those cases the disruptive explosive power would have been uniformly distributed in all directions. Grant and I think he didn't deliberately sink the yacht but that he just, through ignorance, kind of accidentally blew a hole through the bottom.'

'If it weren't for the three dead men, this could be almost amusing. As it is, one has to admit that life is full of its little ironies. What's that you've got in front of you there, Carrington?'

'Some sort of radio, sir. Took it from the captain's cabin.'

'Why did you take it?'

'Struck me as odd, sir, unusual, out of place, you might say. Every cabin is fitted with its own bulkhead radio – all probably fed from the central radio in the saloon. So why should he require this additional radio, especially when he had access to – and was probably the only user of – the much superior radio in his radio-room?'

119

Talbot looked at Denholm. 'Just a standard radio, is it?'

'Not quite.' Denholm took the radio and examined it briefly. 'A transceiver, which means it can transmit as well as receive. Hundreds of them around, thousands, most commonly as ship-to-shore radios in private yachts. Also used in geological and seismological work and construction building. Remote control detonation.' He paused and looked around myopically. 'I don't want to sound sinister, but it could equally well be used to trigger off the detonator in an explosive device being carried by an American Air Force bomber.'

There was a brief silence, then Hawkins said: 'I don't want to complain, Denholm, but you do rather tend to complicate matters.'

'I used the word "could", sir, not "did". On the whole, given the mysterious and inexplicable circumstances, I rather think I prefer the word "did". If that is the case it leads, of course, to even more mysteries. How did Andropulos or whoever know when, and from where, that bomber was leaving? How did he know its cargo? How did he know an explosive device was being smuggled aboard? How did he know the radio wavelength to set it off? And, of course, there's the why, why, why.'

The silence was considerably longer this time. Finally, Hawkins said: 'Maybe we're doing Andropulos an injustice. Maybe Alexander is the mastermind.'

120

'Not a chance, sir.' Van Gelder was definite. 'Andropulos lied about the spare tank. He has connections with main centres of known gun-running activities. The fact that Alexander, who unquestionably plays the role of assistant villain, had the radio in his cabin is of no significance. I should imagine that Irene Charial might be in the habit of dropping in on her uncle occasionally and he wouldn't want her saying, "Whatever are you doing with a spare radio in your cabin, Uncle?" I can hardly imagine her dropping in on Alexander at any time, far less occasionally. So, Alexander kept the radio.'

'You mentioned the possibility of an insider at this Air Force base in America, sir,' Talbot said, 'I think we should be thinking in terms of a whole platoon of insiders. You will be composing messages for the Pentagon, Air Force Intelligence and the CIA? Suitably etched in acid. I think by this time they must be dreading the thought of another signal from the *Ariadne*. I don't see much point in your going to Washington and entering a popularity stakes contest.'

'The slings and arrows – well, we're accustomed to injustices. What do you have in that box?'

'Petty Officer Grant picked this up in Andropulos's cabin. Haven't opened it yet.' Not without difficulty he undid two spring clips and lifted the lid. 'Waterproof, by Jove.' He looked at the contents. 'Means nothing to me.'

Hawkins took the box from him, lifted out some sheets of paper and a paperback book, examined them briefly and shook his head. 'Means nothing to me, either. Denholm?'

Denholm shuffled through the papers. 'In Greek, naturally. Looks like a list of names, addresses and telephone numbers to me. But I can't make sense of it.'

'I thought you understood Greek?'

'I do. But I don't understand Grecian code. And this is what it's written in – a code.'

'Code! Damn it to hell.' Hawkins spoke with considerable feeling. 'This could be urgent. Vital.'

'It's more than likely, sir.' Denholm looked at the paperback. 'Homer's *Odyssey*. I don't suppose it's here just by coincidence. If we knew the connection between the poem and what's written on those sheets, then cracking the code would be child's play. But we don't have the key. That's locked away inside Andropulos's mind. Anagrams and word puzzles are not in my line of country, sir. I'm no cryptologist.'

Hawkins looked moodily at Talbot. 'You don't have a code-cracker among this motley crew you have aboard?'

'To the best of my knowledge, no. And certainly not a Greek code-cracker. Shouldn't be too difficult to find one, I should imagine. The Greek Defence Ministry and their Secret Service are bound to have some cryptologists on their staffs. Just a radio call and a half-hour's flight away, sir.'

Hawkins glanced at his watch. 'Two a.m. All God-fearing cryptologists are tucked up in their beds by this time.'

'So are all God-fearing admirals,' Denholm said. 'Besides, my friend Wotherspoon didn't mind being rousted out of bed an hour ago. Positively cheerful about it, in fact.'

Talbot said: 'Who, may I ask warily, is Wotherspoon?'

'Professor Wotherspoon. My friend with the Aegean lugger. You asked me to contact him, remember? Lives in Naxos, seven or eight hours' sail from here. He's on his way with the *Angelina*.'

'Very civil of him, I must say. *Angelina*? Odd name.'

'Better not let him hear you say that, sir. Name of his lugger. Ancient and honoured Grecian name, some sort of classical goddess, I believe. Also the name of his wife. Charming lady.'

'Is he – what shall we say? – slightly eccentric?'

'All depends upon what you mean by eccentric. He regards the rest of the world as being slightly eccentric.'

'A professor? What does he profess?'

'Archæology. Used to. He's retired now.'

'Retired? Oh dear. I mean, have we any right to bring an elderly archæologist into this?'

'Don't let him hear you say that either, sir. He's not elderly. Old man left him a fortune.'

'You warned him of the perils, of course?'

'As directly as I could. Seemed amused. Said his ancestors fought at Agincourt and Crécy. Something to that effect.'

'What's good enough for a retired archæologist should be good enough for a Greek cryptologist,' Hawkins said. 'Not that I follow the logic of that. If you would be so good, Commander.'

'We'll radio Athens right away. Two things, sir. I suggest we release Andropulos and his friends for breakfast and leave them free. Sure, we've got plenty on them, but as yet no conclusive proof and the three A's – Andropulos, Aristotle and Alexander – are a close-mouthed and secretive lot and we can be certain they won't talk to us or give anything away. But they might, just might, talk among themselves. Lieutenant Denholm will lurk unobtrusively. They don't, and won't, know that he talks Greek as well as they do. Number One, would you tell McKenzie to warn the four seamen who were with us tonight that they are on no account to mention the fact that we were on the *Delos*. Keel-hauling, walking the plank, that sort of thing. One other thing. The presence of the cryptographer, when he arrives, will not go unnoticed.'

'He's not a cryptographer,' Van Gelder said. 'Peace be to Lieutenant Denholm but he's a civilian electronics specialist who's come out to fix some abstruse electronic fault that only he can fix. Also gives a splendid reason for him to use Denholm's cabin while he gets on with his decoding.'

'Well, thank you very much.' Denholm smiled and turned to Talbot. 'With the Captain's permission, I'd like to retire there right now and get some sleep before this impostor arrives.'

'An excellent idea. Vice-Admiral Hawkins, Professor Benson, Dr Wickram, I suggest you follow his example. I promise you we'll give you a shake if anything untoward occurs.'

'Another excellent idea,' Hawkins said. 'After our nightcap. *And* after you've sent your signal to Athens and I've composed a suitably stirring message to the Chairman of the Joint Chiefs of Staff in Washington.'

'Stirring?'

'Certainly. Why should I be the only one suffering from insomnia? I shall tell him that we have every reason to believe that the bomber was carrying a smuggled explosive device aboard, that its detonation was triggered by a radio wave and that we have the miscreant responsible in our hands. Reason to believe, not proof. I shall name Andropulos. I shall want to know how he knew when and from where that bomber was taking off. How did he know what it was carrying? How could this explosive device possibly have been smuggled aboard? How did he know the radio wavelength to set it off? I shall suggest that our concern should be made immediately known to the White House, Air Force Intelligence, the CIA and the FBI. I will suggest that Andropulos has been provided with top-level, ultra-secret

125

information from a very senior official. I will suggest that this should considerably narrow their field of search. I will further suggest that it seems very likely that the traitor is in his own fiefdom, the Pentagon.'

'Stirring indeed. Laying it on the line as you might say.' Talbot paused, 'It has occurred to you, Admiral Hawkins, that you might also be laying your own career on the line?'

'Only if I'm wrong.'

'Only if we're wrong.'

'In the circumstances, a bagatelle. You would do exactly the same thing.'

'Five o'clock, sir.' Talbot woke in his sea-cabin abaft the bridge to find Van Gelder bending over him. 'The *Kilcharran* is three miles out.'

'What's the latest word from sonar?'

'Still ticking away, sir. Captain Montgomery says he's going to shut down his engines in another half-mile. Sees us clearly and reckons he'll come to a stop more or less alongside. He says that if he's going to overshoot he'll use a sea anchor or drop a stern anchor and if he stops short of us he'll send a crew with a rope. From the way he talks he seems to regard either possibility as a remote contingency. Doesn't seem the shy or bashful type.'

'I gathered as much from the admiral. Has our cryptologist arrived?'

'Yes. Calls himself Theodore. Speaks perfect English but I suppose he's Greek. Installed in

Denholm's cabin. Denholm himself is up in the wardroom trying to resume his slumbers.' Van Gelder broke off to accept a sheet of paper from a seaman who had appeared in the doorway, glanced briefly at the message and handed it without a word to Talbot, who read it in turn, muttered something inaudible and swung his legs to the deck.

'He'll have to try to resume his slumbers later on. Tell him to join us in the admiral's cabin at once.'

A pyjama-clad Vice-Admiral Hawkins, propped up on the pillows of his bunk, glowered at the message in his hand and passed it across to Denholm. 'Pentagon. Unsigned. This krytron device you suggested.'

'If I were the spluttering type, which I'm not, this would be a sure fire-starter.' Denholm re-read the message. ' "Understand krytron experimental device in hand. Endeavour expedite soonest clearance." Gobbledygook, sir. Writer is ignorant or stupid or thinks he's clever. Very likely all three at once. What does he mean – "endeavour"? He can either do it or not. What does he mean – "understand"? He either knows or not. Expedite? Means to try to hurry things along. The Pentagon doesn't expedite – they demand immediate compliance. Same goes for that meaningless word "soonest". Again, should be immediate. Clearance by whom? The Pentagon can clear anything they want. What do they mean – "experimental"? Either it works or it doesn't. And doesn't the phrase "in hand" have a splendid meaningless vagueness about it. Gobbledygook, sir.'

'Jimmy's right, sir,' Talbot said, 'It's insulting. Stalling for time. What they're saying in effect is that they're not going to entrust their latest toy to their closest ally because we'd flog it to the first Russian we came across.'

'It's rich,' Denholm said, 'It's really wonderful. The Americans positively force their Stinger surface-to-air missiles on the rebels who are fighting the Marxist regime in Angola and the Contras in Nicaragua. It's no secret that those guerrilla bands contain a fair proportion of characters who are just as undesirable as the dictatorial governments they're supposed to be fighting and who would have no hesitation in disposing of those $60,000 missiles, at a fraction of their cost, to any passing terrorists who, in turn, would have no hesitation in loosing off one of those missiles at a passing Boeing 747, preferably one packed with five hundred American citizens. But that's perfectly OK for the American administration's *ad hoc* knee-jerk set of reactions that passes for their foreign policy. But it's unthinkable that they should allow the krytron into the hands of their oldest ally. It makes me sick.'

'It makes me mad,' Hawkins said. 'Let us give them a lesson on clear and unequivocal English. "Unsigned message received. Meaningless mumbo-

128

jumbo designed to stall and delay. Demand immediate repeat immediate repeat immediate dispatch of krytron or immediate repeat immediate repeat immediate explanation of why not available. Sender of message and person responsible for delay in clearance will be held directly responsible for possible deaths of thousands. Can you not imagine the world-wide reaction when it is learnt that not only is America responsible for this potential disaster but that it was almost certainly caused by treason in the highest American military echelons? A copy of this message is being sent directly to the President of the United States." That do, you think?'

'You could have pitched it a bit more strongly, sir,' Talbot said, 'but I'd have to spend the rest of the night thinking how. You spoke earlier of sleepless heads along the Potomac. I think we should now talk of heads rolling along the Potomac. If I were you, sir, I'd keep clear of Washington for some little time, by which I mean the rest of your life.' He rose. 'The *Kilcharran* will be alongside in a few minutes. I assume you are in no hurry to meet Captain Montgomery?'

'You assume right. There is no charity in me.' He looked at his watch. 'Five-thirteen. My respects to the captain and ask him to join me for breakfast at, say, eight-thirty. In my cabin here.'

Captain Montgomery, whether by luck or design – design, Talbot was certain – brought the *Kilcharran* alongside the *Ariadne* with faultless precision. Talbot stepped across the two gunwales – they were almost exactly of a height – and made his way up to the bridge. Captain Montgomery was a tall, burly character with a jutting black beard, white teeth, a slightly hooked nose and humorous eyes and, in spite of the immaculately cut uniform and four golden rings on either cuff, could easily have passed for a well-to-do and genial eighteenth-century Caribbean pirate. He extended a hand.

'You'll be Commander Talbot, of course.' The voice was deep, the Irish brogue unmistakable. 'You are welcome aboard. Has there been any further deterioration in the situation?'

'No. The only deterioration possible, Captain, is one I don't care to imagine.'

'Indeed. I shall be sadly missed in the Mountains of Mourne. We're great ones for the lamentations, the weepings and the wailings in the Mountains of Mourne. Is this atom bomb, or whatever, still ticking away?'

'It is. I suppose you might call it a deterioration when the ticking stops. You shouldn't have come here, Captain. You should have nipped into the Gulf of Corinth – you might have stood a chance there.'

'Not to be thought of for a moment. Nothing to do with heroics – heroics are for those epics they make in Hollywood – or the fact that I couldn't live with myself. I just couldn't stand the thought of what that man would say.'

'You'll be referring to Vice-Admiral Hawkins?'

'The very same. Maligning and blackening my character as usual, I dare say?'

'Hardly.' Talbot smiled. 'He did, mind you, make some casual remark about you being allergic to certain naval regulations. He also said you're the best in the business.'

'Aye. A fair man and a bloody good admiral – but don't tell him I said so. I suggest coffee in my cabin, Commander, and perhaps you'll be kind enough to tell me all you know.'

'That shouldn't take long.'

'Eleven p.m.,' the President said. 'What's the time over there?'

'Six a.m. There's a seven-hour time difference.'

'A very forthright character, this Admiral Hawkins.' The President gazed thoughtfully at the two dispatches lying on his desk. 'You know him, of course?'

'Pretty well, sir.'

'An able man, General?'

'Exceptionally so.'

'He also appears to be an exceptionally tough s.o.b.'

'That's undoubtedly true, sir. But then you have to be to command the NATO Mediterranean sea forces.'

'Do you know him, John?' This was to John Heiman, the Defence Secretary, the only other person present.

'Yes. Not as well as the General, but well enough to agree with the General's assessment.'

'Pity I never met him. Who selected him for the job, General?'

'Usual NATO committee.'

'You were on it, of course?'

'Yes. I was the chairman.'

'Ah. The man with the casting vote?'

'No casting vote. The decision was unanimous.'

'I see. He – well, he seems to have rather a low opinion of the Pentagon.'

'He doesn't exactly say that. But he does appear to have a low opinion, deep suspicions if you like, of a person or persons in the Pentagon.'

'Puts you in a rather unhappy position. I mean, there must be some stirrings in the Pentagon dovecote.'

'As you say, Mr President, a few ruffled feathers. Some are hopping mad. Others are giving the matter serious consideration. Generally, you could speak of an air of quiet consternation.'

'Are you, personally, prepared to lend any credence to this outrageous suggestion? Or what appears to be outrageous?'

'Think the unthinkable? I don't have any option, do I? Every instinct says no, this cannot be, those are all my friends and colleagues of many years standing, all honourable men. But instinct is a fallible guide, Mr President. Common sense and what little knowledge of history I have tells me that every man has his price. I have to investigate. The enquiry is already under way. I thought it prudent not to involve the intelligence arms of the four services. So, the FBI. The Pentagon does not care to be investigated by the FBI. It's an extremely difficult and delicate situation, sir.'

'Yes. One can hardly go up to an admiral of the fleet and ask him what he was doing on the night of Friday the thirteenth. I wish you luck.' The President looked at one of the papers before him. 'Your message re the krytron that provoked Hawkins's ire must have been badly handled.'

'It was. Very badly. The matter has been attended to.'

'This krytron device. Is it operational?'

'Yes.'

'Been sent?' The General shook his head, the President pressed a button and a young man entered. 'Take this message for the General here. "Krytron device en route. Would greatly appreciate up-to-date assessment of existing problems and measures being taken. Fully appreciate extreme gravity, dangers and complexities of the situation. I personally guarantee total and immediate repeat immediate repeat immediate support and cooperation in all measures undertaken." That should do it. Sign my name.'

'I hope he appreciates the three "immediates",' the General said.

*   *   *

'Eight-forty, sir,' McKenzie said. 'Admiral's apologies, but he'd like to see you. He's in his cabin with Captain Montgomery.'

Talbot thanked him, rose, washed the sleep from his face and eyes and made his way to the admiral's quarters. A shirtsleeved Hawkins beckoned him to join himself and Montgomery at the breakfast table.

'Coffee? Sorry to disturb you but these are times that are sent to try men's souls.' For a troubled soul Hawkins looked remarkably fresh, rested and relaxed and was attacking his breakfast with some gusto. 'Captain Montgomery has been reporting the state of progress and I thought you might like to hear it. Incidentally, our friend the timing device is still ticking merrily away.'

'We are making progress,' Montgomery said. 'Slow but steady – slow, because the presence of what the Admiral calls your friend the timing device does have a rather inhibitory effect and we're probably taking some quite needless precautions as far as acoustic levels are concerned. But we're dealing with a devil we don't know and we're paying the devil more than his due. Our own sonar is now locked on to this device and the sonar room has suddenly become the focal centre of interest in the *Kilcharran*.

'We have achieved two things. First, by coupling up the battery resources of our two vessels we have ample electric power to lift this wreck. Your young Lieutenant Denholm looks and talks

134

like a character out of P. G. Wodehouse, but he unquestionably knows his stuff. Your engineer officer, McCafferty, is no slouch either and neither is mine. Anyway, no problem. Secondly, we've cut away the port wing of the bomber.'

'You've what?' Talbot said.

'Well, you know how it is.' Montgomery sounded almost apologetic. 'It was three parts torn away in any case and I figured that neither you nor the US Air Force would have any further use for it. So I had it burnt off.' Despite his faint air of apology, it was quite clear that Montgomery had no regrets about what had been a wholly unilateral decision: as the only expert on the spot, he had no intention of consulting anybody. 'A difficult decision and a tricky operation. No one, as far as I know, has ever before cut away the wing of a submerged big jet. That's where the fuel tanks are located and though it seemed likely that the partial tearing away of the wing had also ruptured the fuel lines and spilled the fuel, there was no way of being sure and no one, again as far as I know, has ever come up against the problem of what happens when an oxyacetylene jet meets a fuel tank under water. But my men were very careful, there was no fuel and so no trouble. And now, at the present moment, my men are securing flotation bags and lifting slings to the plane.

'Removing this wing gives us two advantages, one minor, one major. The minor one is that with the wing and two very heavy jet engines gone we have all that less to lift although I'm certain we could have lifted the whole lot without trouble. The major one is that the wing, had it been left there, would have snagged on the underside of the *Kilcharran* as it surfaced and tilted the fuselage, maybe to so acute an angle as to make access to this damned bomb difficult or impossible.'

'Very well done, Captain,' Hawkins said. 'But surely there's still one problem. When the bomber surfaces, isn't the weight of the remaining wing and its two engines going to tilt it just as far in the other direction?'

Montgomery smiled in a kindly and tolerant fashion which any average person would have found more than wildly infuriating. Hawkins, fortunately, was not an average person.

'No problem,' Montgomery said. 'We're also securing flotation bags under that wing. When the fuselage surfaces, the wings will still be under water – you know how low wings are set on a modern jet. In the first stage of surfacing, only the top of the fuselage will be above water-level – when we cut away a rectangular section over where the bomb is located I want as much water as possible below that section to dissipate the heat of the oxyacetylene torches. After we've made that hole in the top we'll lift the fuselage high enough to drain most of the water from it.'

'How long will it take to inflate the bags and haul the plane to the surface?'

'An hour or two. I don't know.'

'An hour or two?' Hawkins made no attempt to conceal his surprise, 'I should have thought a few minutes. You don't know, you say. I would have thought those things could have been pretty closely calculated.'

'Normally, yes.' Montgomery's air of massive restraint was on a par for provocation with his kindly tolerance. 'But normally we'd use powerful diesel compressors. Out of deference to the little lady lying on the sea floor, no diesel. Electricity again but using only a fraction of the power. So, an indeterminate period. Do you think I could have some more coffee?' Montgomery clearly regarded the conversation as over.

Van Gelder knocked on the opened door and entered, a message slip in his hand. He handed it to Hawkins.

'For you, Admiral. Came in a couple of hours or so ago. Not urgent, so I didn't think it worth waking you for it.'

'A wise decision, my boy.' Hawkins read it, smiled broadly and handed it to Talbot, who glanced at it, smiled in turn and read it out aloud.

'Well, well,' Talbot said. 'Hobnobbing with presidents. Perhaps, after all, sir, you could walk down Pennsylvania Avenue without being clapped in irons or whatever they do to you over in those parts. More importantly, you have the krytron and this splendid pledge of cooperation. Your indignation – the less charitable would call it calculated gamble – has paid off. I like the "repeat

137

immediate" bit. The President would appear to have a sense of humour.'

'He would indeed. One has to be grateful to him for intervening personally. Very, very satisfactory. I note that he requires information. Would you, please.'

'Naturally. Emphasis, of course, on the gravity and the dangers?'

'Of course.'

'Another item of news, sir,' Van Gelder said to Talbot. 'I've just had a rather intriguing chat with Irene Charial.'

'I can well imagine that. Andropulos and company, of course, are now at liberty. How are they this fine morning?'

'Glowering a bit, sir. At least Andropulos and Alexander were. But the cook was in fine form and they seemed to be thawing a bit when I left them chattering away in Greek with Denholm sitting among them and not understanding a word they were saying. Irene wasn't there.'

'Oh? So, naturally, overcome by concern, you hurried up to my cabin to enquire after her health.'

'Naturally. I knew that was what you would want me to do, sir. She didn't look as if she had slept too well and admitted as much. Seemed worried, apprehensive even. At first she was rather reluctant to talk about what was bothering her. Misplaced loyalty, I should say.'

'I would say so too,' Talbot said. 'If, that is, I knew what you were talking about.'

'Sorry. Turned out she wanted to know if Uncle Adam had been sending any radio messages. It seems –'

'Uncle Adam?'

'Adamantios Andropulos. His parents have a lot to answer for. Seems that she and her pal Eugenia – both sets of parents live in Piraeus, the two girls are at the University in Athens – were in the habit of phoning home every night. She wanted their parents to know that they had had an accident, were safely aboard a Royal Navy ship and would be home soon.'

'I hope she's right,' Hawkins said.

'Me too, sir. I told her no messages had been sent and suggested that if Uncle was a businessman – I thought it better not to mention that we already knew he was a multi-millionaire businessman – he might naturally tend to be secretive and that he might also be reluctant to broadcast the fact that he had lost his yacht through what might have been his own fault. She said that was no excuse for not informing the next of kin of the three crew members of the *Delos* who had died. I asked her if she had raised the question with him and she said no. She was a bit evasive on this point. I gather she either doesn't know very much about Uncle Adam or doesn't care very much about what she does know.' Van Gelder produced a paper from his pocket, 'I told her to write a message and I would see it was sent.'

Talbot looked at the paper, 'It's in Greek. Perhaps this Uncle Adam –'

'We share the same nasty, suspicious mind, sir. I called Jimmy from the breakfast table. Quite innocent, he says.'

'I have a better idea. Take the two young ladies to the radio-room. It's a simple matter to lock into the telephone land lines through the Piraeus radio station. They can talk direct to their folks.'

'With Jimmy just happening to be there?'

'We share, as you say, the same nasty, suspicious minds. Before you do that, however, I think we'll go and see how our latest recruit is getting on.'

'Ah! Our resident cryptologist. Theodore.'

'Theodore. After we've seen him and the young ladies have finished their calls I want you to take Irene Charial aside.'

'And engage her in casual conversation?'

'What else? It would seem that she and her uncle are less than soul-mates and, of course, she will be feeling suitably grateful to you for having permitted her to speak to her folks. Find out what you can about Andropulos. Find out what she thinks of him. See what you can discover about his business or businesses. Find out who his business contacts and friends are and what she thinks of them, assuming, of course, that she's ever met any of them. And it would be very interesting to know where his travels take him – I'm not talking about his yacht cruises when she is with him – and why they take him there.'

'You are asking me, sir, in effect, to ply Irene with cunning and devious questions, to entrap her, if you will, to engage in duplicity and extract unwitting information from a sweet and innocent girl?'

'Yes.'

'A pleasure, sir.'

Theodore was a cheerful, plump man in his late forties, with a pale face and thick pebble glasses, those last a very probable consequence of having spent a lifetime poring over abstruse codes.

'You have come to check on progress, gentlemen. I am making some, I'm happy to report. Took me quite some time to find the key, the connection between the code and the *Odyssey*. Since then, it's straightforward. These sheets are in three sections and I'm now about two-thirds of the way through the first one.'

'Found anything of interest?' Talbot said.

'Interesting? Fascinating, Captain, fascinating. Statements of his accounts, bank holdings, if you like. He has his money stashed away – "stashed" is the word? – all over the world, it seems. As a matter of interest, I'm totting up the sum of his holdings as I go along. He's made it very easy for me, everything is in US dollars. So far, let me see, it's two-eighty. Yes, two-eighty. Dollars.'

'A man could retire on that,' Van Gelder said.

'Indeed. Two-eighty. Followed by six zeros.'

Talbot and Van Gelder looked at each other in silence, then bent forward over Theodore's shoulders to look at the figures he had added up. After some seconds they straightened, looked at each other again, then bent forward once more.

'Two hundred and eighty million dollars,' Talbot said. 'On that you *could* retire, Vincent.'

'If I scraped and pinched a bit, I might manage. Do you know where those bank accounts are kept, Theodore? Cities, countries, I mean?'

'Some I do, because he's given names and addresses, some I don't. For the second lot, he may have another code which I don't have or he just knows them by heart. By heart, I would guess. I have no means of knowing where at least half the accounts are. Just the amounts, that's all.'

'Could you show us some of those?' Talbot said.

'Of course.' Theodore pointed to some entries, flipped over several pages and indicated several more. 'Just amounts, as I said. As you see, there's a differing capital letter after each entry. They mean nothing to me. Maybe they do to Andropulos.'

Talbot leafed through the pages again. 'Five letters, just five, recur regularly – Z, W, V, B and G. Well, now. If you were a thrifty citizen and wanted a safe piggy-bank secure from the prying eyes of nasty parties such as police and income tax authorities, which country would you choose?'

'Switzerland.'

'I think the same far from original thought had occurred to Andropulos – for at least half his assets. Z for Zürich. W? Winterthur, perhaps. V? Off-hand, I don't know about that one.'

'Vevey?' Van Gelder said. 'On Lake Geneva?'

'I don't think so. Hardly what you might call an international banking centre. Ah! I have it. Not in Switzerland, but it might as well be. Vaduz. Liechtenstein. I don't know much about those things but I understand that once cash disappears into the vaults of Vaduz it never surfaces again. B could be Berne or Basle – Andropulos would know, of course. G has to be Geneva. How am I doing, Number One?'

'Splendidly. I'm sure you're right. I hardly like to point out, sir, that we still don't have the names and addresses of those banks.'

'True. Crest-fallen, but only slightly. We still have names and addresses of other banks. You have a list of those cities where those banks are located?'

'I don't have to,' Theodore said, 'I have it in my head. They're all over the place, west, east and in between. Places as different as Miami, Tijuana, Mexico City, Bogotá in Colombia, Bangkok, Islamabad in Pakistan, Kabul in Afghanistan. Why anyone should want to hide away money in Kabul is quite beyond me. Country is torn by war and the Russians occupy and control the capital.'

'Andropulos would appear to have friends everywhere,' Talbot said. 'Why should the poor Russians be left out in the cold? That about the lot?'

'Quite a few other places,' Theodore said. 'Mostly smaller accounts. One exception, though. The biggest deposit of the lot.'

'Where?'

'Washington, DC.'

'Well, now.' Talbot was silent for a few minutes. 'What do you make of that, Number One?'

'I think I've just about stopped making anything out of anything. My mind has kind of taken a leave of absence. But my eyes are still working, in a fashion, you might say. I think I see a faint light at the end of the tunnel.'

'I think if we think a bit more it might turn into a searchlight. How much money?'

'Eighteen million dollars.'

'Eighteen million dollars,' Van Gelder said. 'My, my. Even in Washington, DC, a man could buy a lot with eighteen million dollars.'

6

The *Angelina*, to put it at its most kindly, was a rather striking-looking craft. An eighty-tonner built of pinewood from the forests of the island of Samos, she had a dazzling white hull which contrasted strongly – some would have said violently – with her vermilion gunwale. Wide of beam and low in the water amidships, she had a pronounced flare aft and for'ard, a curved stem that projected high above the gunwale. As a sailing boat, she was well equipped with a standing-lug main and balance-lug foresail, together with two jibs. Had it been left at that, as she had originally been built, the *Angelina*, a typical example of the *Tehandiri* class, would not only have been striking but downright handsome. Unfortunately, it had not been left at that.

The owner, Professor Wotherspoon, although a self-avowed traditionalist, was also strongly attached to his creature comforts. Not content with converting the craft's very considerable hold – it was, after all, originally constructed as a cargo vessel – into cabins and bathrooms, he had constructed on the deck a bridge, saloon and galley which, while admittedly functional, detracted notably from the overall æsthetic effect.

Shortly before ten o'clock in the morning, the *Angelina*, almost slack-sailed and ghosting along under a Meltemi that hardly rated as a zephyr, tied up along the starboard side of the *Ariadne*. Talbot, accompanied by Denholm, climbed down a rope ladder to greet the owner.

The first impression that Talbot had of Wotherspoon was that he didn't look a bit like a professor or an archæologist but then, he had to admit, he had no idea what a professor or archæologist was supposed to look like. He was tall, lean, shock-haired and deeply tanned: humorous of mien and colloquial of speech, he was the last person one would expect to find wandering through the groves of Academe. He was certainly not more than forty years old. His wife, with auburn hair and laughing hazel eyes, was at least ten years younger and was also, it seemed, an archæologist.

Introductions effected by Denholm, Talbot said: 'I appreciate this very much, Professor. Very kind of you to come. Not to say very gallant. You appreciate that there is a fair chance that you might find yourself prematurely in another world? Lieutenant Denholm did explain the dangers to you?'

'In a cautious and roundabout fashion. He's become very tight-lipped since he joined the Senior Service.'

'I didn't join. I was dragooned.'

'He did mention something about vaporization. Well, one gets a bit tired of studying ancient history. Much more interesting to be a part of the making of it.'

'It might be a very short-lived interest indeed. Does Mrs Wotherspoon share your short-lived interests?'

' "Angelina", please. We had to entertain a very prim and proper Swiss lady the other day and she insisted on addressing me as Madame Professor Wotherspoon. Ghastly. No, I can't say I share all of my husband's more extravagant enthusiasms. But, alas, he does have one professorial failing. He's horribly absent-minded. Someone has to look after him.'

Talbot smiled. 'A fearful thing for so young and attractive a lady to be trapped for life. Again, thank you both very, very much. I should like it if you would join us for lunch. Meantime, I'll leave Lieutenant Denholm to explain the full horrors of the situation to you – especially the ones you'll encounter across the lunch table.'

'Gloom and despondency,' Van Gelder said, 'It ill becomes one so young and beautiful to be gloomy and despondent. What *is* the matter, Irene?'

In so far as one so young and beautiful could look morose, Irene Charial gazed out morosely over the taffrail of the *Ariadne*.

147

'I am not, Lieutenant-Commander Van Gelder, in the mood for flattery.'

'Vincent. Flattery is an insincere compliment. How can the truth be flattery? But you're right about the word "mood". You are in a mood. You're worried, upset. What's troubling you?'

'Nothing.'

'Being beautiful doesn't mean you're above telling fibs. You could hardly call that flattery, could you?'

'No.' A fleeting smile touched the green eyes. 'Not really.'

'I know this is a very unpleasant situation you find yourself in. But we're all trying to make the best of it. Or did something your parents say upset you?'

'You know perfectly well that that's not true.' Van Gelder also knew it, Denholm had reassured him on that point.

'Yes, that's so. You were hardly in a cheerful frame of mind when I first met you this morning. Something worries you. Is it so dreadful a secret that you can't tell me?'

'You've come here to pry, haven't you?'

'Yes. To pry and probe. Crafty, cunning, devious questions to extract information from you that you don't know you're giving away.' It was Van Gelder's turn to look morose, 'I don't think I'm very good at it.'

'I don't think you are, either. That man sent you, didn't he?'

'What man?'

'Now you're being dishonest. Commander Talbot. Your captain. A cold man. Distant. Humourless.'

'He's neither cold nor distant. And he's got a very considerable sense of humour.'

'Humour. I don't see any signs of it.'

'I'm beginning not to be surprised.' Van Gelder had stopped smiling. 'Maybe he thought it would be wasted on you.'

'Maybe he's right.' She appeared not to have taken offence. 'Or maybe I just don't see too much to laugh about at the moment. But I'm right about the other thing. He's remote, distant. I've met people like him before.'

'I doubt it very much. In the same way that I doubt your power of judgement. You don't seem to be very well equipped in that line.'

'Oh.' She made a *moue*. 'Flattery and charm have flown out the window, is that it?'

'I don't flatter. I've never claimed to have charm.'

'I meant no harm. Please. I see nothing wrong with being a career officer. But he lives for only two things – the Royal Navy and the *Ariadne*.'

'You poor deluded creature.' Van Gelder spoke without heat. 'But how were you to know? John Talbot lives for only two things – his daughter and his son. Fiona, aged six, and Jimmy, aged three. He dotes on them. So do I. I'm their Uncle Vincent.'

'Oh.' She was silent for some moments. 'And his wife?'

'Dead.'

'I am sorry.' She caught his arm. 'To say I didn't know is no excuse. Go ahead. Call me a clown.'

'I don't flatter, I don't charm – and I don't tell lies.'

'But you do turn a pretty compliment.' She took her hand away, leaned on the rail and looked out over the sea. After some time, she said, without looking around: 'It's my Uncle Adam, isn't it?'

'Yes. We don't know him, we don't trust him and we think he's a highly suspicious character. You will forgive me talking about your nearest and dearest in this fashion.'

'He is not my nearest and dearest.' She had turned to face him. There was neither vehemence in her voice nor marked expression in her face: at most, a slight degree of bewilderment in both. '*I* don't know him, *I* don't trust him and *I* think he's a highly suspicious character.'

'If you don't know him, what on earth are – were – you doing aboard his yacht?'

'I suppose that, too, seems suspicious. Not really. Three reasons, I would think. He's a very persuasive man. He seems to be genuinely fond of our family – my younger brother and sister and myself – for he is forever giving us presents, very expensive presents, too, and it seemed churlish to refuse his invitation. Then there was the element of fascination – I know practically nothing about him, nor what his business activities are or why he spends so much time in foreign countries. And, of course, perhaps both Eugenia and I are snobs at heart and were flattered by the invitation to go cruising on a very expensive yacht.'

'Well, good enough reasons. But still not good enough to explain why you went with him if you dislike him.'

'I didn't say I disliked him. I said I distrusted him. Not the same thing. And I didn't begin distrusting him until this trip.'

'Why start now?'

'Alexander is why.' She gave a mock shudder. 'Would you trust Alexander?'

'Candidly, no.'

'And Aristotle is almost as bad. The three of them spent hours talking together, usually in the radio-room. Whenever Eugenia or I went near them, they stopped talking. Why?'

'Obvious, isn't it? They didn't want you to hear what they were talking about. Ever been with him abroad on his business trips?'

'Good heavens, no.' She was genuinely startled at the idea.

'Not even on the *Delos*?'

'I've only been on the *Delos* once before. With my brother and sister. A short trip to Istanbul.'

He was going to have less than a sensational report to make to his captain, Van Gelder reflected. She didn't know her uncle. She didn't know what his businesses were. She never travelled with him.

And her only reason for distrusting him was that she distrusted Alexander, a feeling almost certainly shared by the majority of people who had ever met him. Van Gelder made one last try.

'Your mother's brother, of course?' She nodded. 'What does she think of him?'

'She never speaks ill of him. But she never speaks ill of anyone. She's a wonderful lady, a wonderful mother, not simple or anything like that, just a very trusting person who could never bring herself to speak ill of anyone.'

'She's obviously never met Alexander. Your father?'

'He never speaks of Uncle Adam either, but he doesn't speak in a very different way, if you follow me. My father is a very straight, very honest man, very clever, head of a big construction company, highly respected by everyone. But he doesn't speak of my uncle. I'm not as trusting as my mother. I believe my father strongly disapproves of Uncle Adam or whatever businesses he runs. Or both. I don't believe they've talked in years.' She shrugged and gave a faint smile. 'Sorry I can't be of more help. You haven't learnt anything, have you?'

'Yes, I have. I've learnt I can trust you.'

This time the smile was warm and genuine and friendly. 'You don't flatter, you don't charm and you don't tell lies. But you *are* gallant.'

'Yes,' Van Gelder said, 'I believe I am.'

* * *

'Sir John,' the President said, 'you have put me in a most damnably awkward position. I speak, you understand, more in sorrow than in anger.'

'Yes, Mr President. I am aware of that and I'm sorry for it. It is, of course, no consolation for you to know that I am in an equally awkward situation.' If Sir John Travers, the British Ambassador to the United States, did indeed find himself in such a situation, he showed no signs of it. But then Sir John was renowned throughout the diplomatic world for his *savoir-faire*, his monolithic calm and his ability to remain wholly unruffled in the most trying and difficult situations, 'I'm only the messenger boy. Grade one, of course.'

'Who the hell is this fellow Hawkins, anyway?' Richard Hollison, deputy head of the FBI, couldn't quite match Sir John's tranquil serenity but he had his obvious anger under tight control, 'I don't think I care very much for having a foreigner telling the White House, the Pentagon and the FBI how to run their business.'

'Hawkins is a Vice-Admiral in the British Navy.' The General was the fourth and only other person in the office. 'An exceptionally able man. I cannot think of any United States naval officer whom I would sooner have in his place in those near-impossible circumstances. And I don't think I need point out that I am in the most awkward situation of all. I don't want to sound overly possessive but, bloody hell, the Pentagon is *my* concern.'

'Richard Hollison,' Sir John said. 'I've known you for some years now. I know your reputation for toughness is matched only by your reputation for fairness. Be fair in this case. Admiral Hawkins, as the General has just said, is in a position of having to cope with almost impossible circumstances which, as you are in a position to know better than most, involves making almost impossible decisions. He's not telling anyone how to run their business. In order to get a message to the President, without anyone in the Government or the Pentagon seeing the message before the President, he elected to bypass the Pentagon and all the standard avenues of communication. Certainly the Pentagon knows it's already under investigation, but Hawkins didn't want anyone to know that he was pointing fingers in certain directions. If it is your intention to set a cat among the pigeons or let loose an eagle in the dovecote, you don't send a postcard in advance announcing your intentions.'

'Yes, I accept that,' Hollison said. 'With weary resignation, I accept it. But don't ask me to like it.'

'Like it or lump it,' the President said, 'I accept it, too.' He looked unenthusiastically at the paper before him on his desk. 'It would appear that this Adamantios Andropulos, who is Hawkins's temporary guest – I could well imagine that Admiral Hawkins would use the term "guest" even if this unfortunate were clapped in irons in some shipboard dungeon – has an account with a Washington bank, name and address supplied, of some eighteen million dollars, and would we kindly make enquiries to see if he has been disbursing any of this of late and, if so, in what direction. I know this lies well within your capabilities, Richard. Point is, how long will it take?'

'All depends upon how many false names, how many dud companies, how much of the usual laundering paraphernalia is involved. The villain, if there is a villain, might well have a numbered account in outer Mongolia. Unlikely, I admit, but you take my point. One hour, maybe three. We will not stand upon the order of our going. Excuse me, Mr President. Excuse me, gentlemen.' Hollison left.

'The Army and the Marines will be pleased to learn – when they do learn of it – that Admiral Hawkins does not consider them worthy of his regard,' the President went on. 'Only the Air Force and the Navy. The Air Force I can, in the circumstances, understand. But it would be interesting to know why he has deemed the Navy to be deserving of his interests. He gives no indications on that score.' The President sighed. 'Maybe he doesn't even trust me. Or maybe he knows something that we don't know.'

Sir John said placidly: 'If that is the case – that he knows something we don't – I have little doubt that he'll tell us in the fullness of time.'

The man under discussion in the White House was, at that moment, dwelling on precisely the same subject.

'Time's winged chariot, John. I forget the rest of the quotation but it's definitely on the wing.' Leaning back in a comfortable armchair, a glass of frosted lime juice in his hand, Hawkins succeeded only in giving the impression of a man with all the time in the world. 'So much to do, so little time to do it in. How stands the *Ariadne* in respect of the rest of this uncaring world?'

'I think you might say, sir, that the patient is coming along as well as could be expected. Our carpenter is aboard the *Angelina*, building a cradle for the bomb according to the specifications the Pentagon gave us. There will be two hinged clamps to secure it in even the worst weather which, as you can see for yourself, is the last thing we expect today.'

'Indeed.' The Admiral looked through the window of his cabin. 'The weather is all wrong, John. Considering the possibly apocalyptic and doom-laden task we have on hand, the least we could reasonably expect is high winds, torrential rain, thunder, lightning, tempests, tornadoes and all those other adverse weather conditions that King Lear encountered on his walkabout around the blasted heath. But what do we have? A blistering July sun, a cloudless blue sky and the wine-dark seas without even a ripple to show for themselves. Downright disappointing. Also disappointing, not to say extremely disturbing, is the likelihood that if those zero-wind conditions persist, it'll take the *Angelina* a week to get even half way towards the horizon.'

'I don't think we have to worry about that, sir. Weather conditions in the Cyclades between early July and mid-September are remarkably predictable. It's already eleven forty-five. Any minute now the Meltemi, the Etesian wind, will start up from the north-west. During the afternoon it reaches Forces 5 or 6, sometimes even 7. Usually dies away in the evening but it has been known to last all night. The Meltemi will be ideally suited for the *Angelina*. Those luggers, as Denholm said, are hopeless windward sailors but in this case it will be directly astern of them and carry them down towards the Kásos Strait to the east of the easternmost tip of Crete.'

'Sounds fine, but, well, even *if* Montgomery manages to raise this bomber, *if* he manages to cut a hole in the fuselage without blowing us all to kingdom come, *if* he manages to extract the atom bomb and *if* he manages to secure it to the *Angelina*'s cradle, what happens if the thing detonates before he reaches the Kásos Strait?'

'Then that's it for Wotherspoon and his crew. For us, the risk is low. I've been talking to Dr Wickram about this. He seems convinced of the inherent stability of the hydrogen bomb – after all, he does build the damn things. While he says it would be a hundred per cent certain to go up if an atom bomb exploded alongside it, we mustn't over-estimate the effects of a more remote explosive shock, even at a distance of a few miles. After all, those bombs did survive the effect of the explosion in the nose of the bomber and the impact of the plane hitting the water at high speed. Besides, the intervening miles of water – we hope there will be those intervening miles – should have a powerfully dampening effect.'

'There'll be no such effect for those aboard the *Angelina*. Curtains. What motivates a man like that, John? Obviously, he's incredibly brave – but, well, is he all right?'

'If you mean is he off his rocker, then we're all off our rockers. He's as sane as you or I. He's a romantic at heart, a born adventurer; a couple of hundred years ago and he'd have been somewhere on the other side of the world building up the odd empire.'

'That's as may be. But it's still a terrible thought that a man like that should die for us.'

'He won't be dying for all of us. I'm going on the *Angelina*. So is Vincent Van Gelder.'

Hawkins put down his glass and stared at him. 'Do you know what you're saying? *I* know what you're saying and I think you've taken leave of your senses. Are you mad? You and Van Gelder? Quite mad?'

'Van Gelder insists on coming along. I insist on going. That's all there is to it.'

'I absolutely forbid it.'

'With the deepest respect, Admiral, you'll forbid me nothing. Did you honestly expect me to leave a job half done? Did you honestly expect me to let him go out there and die alone? I would remind you that I am the captain of this ship and that at sea not even an admiral can take over from me or give orders which I consider to be to the detriment of this vessel.'

'Mutiny!' Hawkins waved a dismissive hand at his lime juice. 'Have we nothing stronger than this?'

'Naturally.' Talbot went to the Admiral's wine cupboard and prepared a drink while Hawkins gazed at a spot on the deck which was about a thousand miles away. 'A large scotch and water. No ice.'

'Thank you.' Hawkins drained almost half the contents. 'Mutiny, forsooth!'

'Yes, sir. Can't hang me from the yard-arm, though. It's my yard-arm. You haven't yet met Angelina – Professor Wotherspoon's wife, I mean, not the lugger. But you will. I've invited them aboard for lunch. Young, rather lovely, nice sense of humour and dotty about her husband. She has to be – dotty, I mean – to do something she clearly doesn't want to do, that is to go along from here with her husband and the bomb on the lugger.'

'I'm sure I shall be delighted to make her acquaintance.' Hawkins took another sip of his drink. 'What's she got to do with the matter in hand?'

'She's not going with the bomb and the lugger. Neither is Wotherspoon, for that matter, or his two crew members. They remain aboard the *Ariadne*. Wotherspoon, of course, will have to be forcibly restrained, but that's no problem at all. Van Gelder and I will take the *Angelina* down through the Kásos Strait. Two small medals will suffice.'

Hawkins was silent for quite some time, then said: 'How are you going to pin on a couple of posthumous VCs or whatever when you're circling the earth in a vaporized orbit?'

'One problem at a time. We can't let the girl go.'

'Good God, no. I'll never forgive myself. I never even started to think. I wonder –'

'Wonder me no wonders, sir. We don't have room for three heroes aboard the *Angelina*. Someone has to take the *Ariadne* home again, remember? Well, that's the *Angelina*. Now, the *Kilcharran*. I've just been talking to Captain Montgomery. He's just given a couple of experimental tugs on the lifting slings and he reckons the bomber, with the help of the flotation bags, of course, is nearing a state of neutral buoyancy. Twenty minutes, half an hour at the most, and he's going to start to haul away. You won't want to miss that, sir.'

'No, indeed. What did Walter de la Mare say – look your last on all things lovely every hour? This may be the last thing I'll ever see?'

'I rather hope it doesn't come to that, sir. Apart from the lugger and the recovery of the bomber, we have to wait for three other things. The reaction to the message we sent to the President via our embassy in Washington, which might take quite some time, for even the most cooperative of banks, and banks almost by definition are secretive and detest the very thought of cooperation, are going to be very reluctant to disclose any information about their important clients, because important clients don't like that sort of thing. Admittedly, Air Force Generals and Admirals are unlikely to be very important financially, but they are from the point of view of prestige and power and would, I should think, carry a disproportionate amount of clout. I do hope we haven't upset too many people over there. Then, and this I should expect very soon, there should be a reply from Greek Intelligence to our query asking for the complete list of places where Andropulos has conducted business, any kind of business, over the past few years. Then, of course, we await the arrival of this krytron device from America.'

'Which may arrive any old time. I mean, we have no idea, have we? Do the Americans have supersonic planes?'

'Sure they have. But fighters only. And their nearest refuelling point would be the Azores and I'm quite certain no fighter could fly the close on two thousand miles they'd have to travel to get there. Question of fuel capacity. Besides, it's not absolutely essential that we get this device before leaving with the bomb – always assuming, of course, that we do leave. We could always dump the bomb, drop a marker, warn all shipping to keep clear, wait for the krytron to arrive, return there and detonate the bomb.'

'Much more satisfactory if it could all be done in one fell swoop.' Hawkins thought for a moment, then smiled. 'What's the time in Washington?'

'Four a.m., I think.'

'Excellent, excellent. A short message. Ask them how it's being transported and what's the expected time of arrival. Give 'em something to do.' Talbot lifted a phone and dictated the message.

'Haven't seen your second-in-command lately,' Hawkins said. 'I understood he was prising secrets loose from Andropulos's niece?'

'Vincent normally carries out his duties with efficiency and dispatch. When the duties involve Irene Charial, it seems to take a little longer.'

'Not so many years ago it would have taken me a little longer myself. Ah!' Van Gelder had appeared in the doorway. 'Just discussing you, young man. A difficult and protracted interview, I take it?'

'One treads delicately, sir. But she told me everything she knew.' He looked reproachfully at Talbot. 'I detect a trace of scepticism in your expression, sir. Unwarranted, I assure you. I believe her, I trust her and I was not bewitched by her green eyes, owing to the fact that I was on duty at the time.'

'Less than admirable though they may be, Vincent, deviousness and low cunning have their place in the scheme of things.'

'It wasn't like that at all. I told her that you had sent me to try to trap her into making unwary and unguarded statements and unwittingly to betray herself. After that, we got along famously.'

Talbot smiled. 'Just another way of being devious. What does she know?'

'Nothing. I guarantee you'd come to the same conclusion, sir. She doesn't know her uncle, except superficially. She doesn't trust him. She thinks he's a highly suspicious character. She thinks Alexander is a highly suspicious character, although that wouldn't require any great acumen on anyone's part. She knows nothing about his businesses. She's never travelled with him. Her father, whom she obviously dotes on and has the highest respect for, thinks he's a highly suspicious character – he and Andropulos haven't spoken for years. She's convinced that her father knows a great deal about her uncle and his businesses, but Dad refuses to discuss any aspect of the matter.'

'Sounds as if we could do with Dad aboard right now,' Hawkins said, 'I have the feeling we could learn some very interesting things from him.'

'I'm sure we could, sir. One odd thing – she's convinced that her uncle is genuinely fond of her.'

Hawkins smiled, 'I think it would be rather difficult not to be fond of the young lady. However, I would point out in the passing, and apropos of nothing, that mass murderers have been known to dote on tiny tots.'

'I hardly think he's a mass murderer, sir.'

'And she's certainly not a tiny tot.' He looked speculatively at Talbot. 'A passing thought, John?'

'Yes.' Talbot looked out through the window for an unseeing moment, then back at Hawkins. 'How do we know he's not a mass murderer?'

The speculation was still in Hawkins's eyes. 'You don't normally make remarks like that. Not without good reason. You have something in mind?'

'I think I have. But it's so far back in my mind that I can't reach it. It'll come.' He turned as Denholm entered the cabin, 'I seem to recall having asked you this question before. What drags you away from the fleshpots?'

'Duty, sir.'

'You will have noticed, Admiral,' Talbot said, 'how devoted the *Ariadne*'s officers are to their duty. I thought, Jimmy, that you were supposed to be lurking and eavesdropping?'

'I have lurked, sir. And eavesdropped. I have also been plying Mr Andropulos and his friends with strong drink.'

'At this time of the morning?' Hawkins said.

'Captain's orders, sir. I hope, Captain, that the Admiralty are going to take care of my bar bill.'

'Prodigious?'

'Not as prodigious as their thirsts. They have relaxed a bit. They have apparently agreed that I'm simple-minded. They are quite certain I don't know a word of Greek but even so they're still very cautious. Much given to allusions and cryptic

164

references, all made, for good measure, in a Macedonian dialect.'

'Which you learnt at your mother's knee?'

'A bit later than that. But I'm at home in it. I don't know whether you will consider this good news or bad, sir, but Andropulos knows there are hydrogen bombs aboard that bomber. He even knows there are fifteen of them.'

There was a fairly lengthy silence while the other three men in the cabin considered the implications of Denholm's words, then Hawkins said: 'Good news and bad news. Good news for us, bad news for Andropulos. Well done, my boy. Very well done.'

'I echo that, sir,' Talbot said. 'Lieutenant Denholm is miscast as either a classicist or electronics officer. MI5 should have him. There is no way that Andropulos could have learnt aboard the *Ariadne* of the existence of those bombs. So he knew before. Proof, if that were needed, of our near-certain conviction that Andropulos has penetrated the Pentagon.'

'I would point out, sir,' Denholm said, 'that the words hydrogen bombs weren't actually used. Also, it's only my word against theirs.'

'That's irrelevant and this is no court of law. There will be no confrontation. All that matters is that we know and they don't know that we do.'

'My usefulness is over? Or do I continue to lurk?'

'Lurk, of course. The three A's must be making some contingency plans. We know now why they

165

wanted aboard the *Ariadne*. What we don't know is what they intend to do now that they are here. Resume your wassailing.'

'Wassailing?' Denholm sounded bitter, 'I have an arrangement with Jenkins whereby I consume copious quantities of tonic water, lemon and ice. Ghastly.' He turned to go but Talbot stopped him as a seaman entered and handed over a sheet of paper.

'You might as well hear what's in this.' He studied the paper briefly. 'This is in reply to a request we made of Greek Intelligence for as exhaustive a list as they could supply of all places where Andropulos is known either to do business or have contacts. No names, no addresses, just towns. Forty or fifty of them. My, my. This list wasn't compiled on the spur of the moment. Greek Intelligence must have been taking a more than passing interest in the activities of our friend Andropulos over a long period, years I would think. I wonder why. About half of those places are marked by asterisks. Again I wonder why. Was that for their own information or is it intended to suggest something to us?'

He handed the paper to Hawkins, who studied it for a moment, then said: 'I know those places marked with an asterisk. I don't see their relevance in our circumstances. I can't even remotely associate them with our problem. I'd swear that none of those places had any connection with hydrogen bombs.'

'So would I,' Talbot said. 'Maybe they handle something else. In spite of the situation we find ourselves in, maybe hydrogen bombs aren't the biggest cause for concern. If you can imagine anything worse than our present situation, that is. Could I have that back, sir?'

He sat at the desk, made some marks on the paper before him, then looked up.

'Bangkok, Islamabad, Kabul, Bogotá, Miami, Mexico City, Tijuana, San Diego, Bahamas, Ocho Rios, Ankara, Sofia – Andropulos playing both sides of the fence with those last two, the ethnic Turks are having a very bad time in Bulgaria just now, but Andropulos wouldn't let that interfere with his business interests – and Amsterdam. What does that list suggest?'

'Drugs,' Van Gelder said.

'Drugs. Heroin, cocaine, marijuana, you name. it. Now some more towns. Tehran, Baghad – Andropulos again playing both sides of the fence, Iran and Iraq had been at war for six years now – Tripoli, Damascus, Beirut, Athens, Rome, East Berlin, New York and London. That suggest something?'

'Yes.' It was Van Gelder again. 'Terrorism. I'm not quite sure why New York and London qualify.'

'I seem to remember there have been two attempts, one at John F. Kennedy, the other at Heathrow to smuggle bombs aboard planes. Both bungled, both failed. I think it's fairly safe to assume – in fact, it would be criminally negligent not to assume – that the terrorists who planned those crimes are still in residence in London and New York, waiting. Jimmy, would you please go to your cabin and bring Theodore here with whatever further results his cryptology has turned up.'

Hawkins said: 'I most sincerely hope that you are not thinking what I think you are, if you follow me.'

'It may be, sir, that I am thinking what you are, if *you* follow *me*.'

'What you are suggesting is that this Andropulos is some kind of mastermind – possible world co-ordinator – of drug-smuggling? Is that what you meant by your remark that we didn't know he wasn't a mass murderer?'

'Yes, sir. What else can that list of contacts he has in drug areas mean? Where else has he accumulated his vast wealth – and we haven't added it all up yet, not by any means.'

'There's no actual proof.'

'All depends on what you call proof. It's very powerful suggestive evidence. How far are you prepared to stretch the long arm of coincidence? To infinity?'

'And you're further suggesting he's engaged in terrorism. That he's using his vast profits from drug-smuggling to finance his terrorist activities?'

'It's possible, but I don't think so. I think the two activities are being run in tandem.'

'A drug-peddler is one thing. A terrorist quite another. Incompatibles. Poles apart. Never the twain shall meet.'

'One hesitates to contradict a senior officer. But I'm afraid you're wrong, sir. Vincent, would you enlighten the Admiral? You know what I'm talking about.'

'All too well, sir. October 1984, Admiral, our last submarine patrol. North Atlantic, about two hundred miles west of the Irish coast. I can remember it as if it were yesterday. We were asked to move into position to observe, but not to intercept, a small American ship en route from the States to Ireland and given its course and estimated time when it would pass a certain point. Neither the crew of this vessel nor its captain, a certain Captain Robert Anderson who, I believe, is still at large, knew that they had been monitored from the moment they had left port by an American spy-in-the-sky satellite. We upped periscope, identified it, then downed periscope. They never saw us. It was a New England trawler, the *Valhalla*, based on Gloucester, Massachusetts, from which it had sailed a few days earlier. It transferred its cargo to an Irish tug, the *Marita Ann*, which was duly seized by the Irish Navy.

'The cargo consisted entirely of military hardware – rifles, machine-guns, shotguns, pistols, hand grenades, rockets and, as I recall, about 70,000 rounds of ammunition, all destined for the IRA. It was to have been the IRA's biggest gun-running plot ever, but it was foiled because of what was called "Operation Leprechaun", where the CIA, our MI5 and Irish Intelligence took a healthy – or unhealthy, it all depends on your point of view – interest in the activities of Noraid, an Irish–American group that specialized – for all I know it may still be specializing – in buying American arms and shipping them to the IRA in Ireland.

'Round about the same time a Panamanian registered cargo ship by the name of the *Ramsland*, chartered by the same gang who had organized the *Valhalla*, put into Boston harbour and was promptly seized by the United States Coast Guard. The *Ramsland* had secret compartments below decks but the Coast Guard knew all about those secret compartments. They held no less than thirty tons of marijuana, another smuggling record. The proceeds from the sale of those drugs were, of course, intended to fund IRA terrorist activities.'

'We became quite interested in the drugs-terrorist connection,' Talbot said, 'and made some discreet enquiries. At least five other drug-terrorist connections had been discovered and broken up. It is believed that considerably more connections have not been discovered and so not broken up. Why should Andropulos be an exception to what appears to be a fairly well established rule?'

'A suitably chastened admiral sits before you,' Hawkins said. 'We live, we learn. You two should join Denholm and offer your services to MI5. Ah, the man himself.'

Denholm entered the cabin with Theodore, who handed over to Talbot some papers he had with him. Talbot looked at them and handed them over to Hawkins.

'Well, well, well,' Hawkins said. 'What an interesting coincidence or, in view of what I've just been learning, perhaps not all that much of a coincidence. Fifteen of the towns that Greek Intelligence asterisked – if that's the word – on their list. Only, in this case – my, my, my! – they give names and addresses. Isn't that splendid? Captain, a thought has occurred to me. There's one of those towns marked with an asterisk that you omitted to mention. Washington, DC. Does that come under D for drugs or T for terrorism?'

'Neither. B for bribery. Are you about through this list, Theodore?'

'Two-thirds, I would say.'

'And that will be the end of it?'

'No, Captain. There's still a last list.'

'It would be gratifying if it held some more revelations, but perhaps that would be too much to hope for. How long have you been up and around, Theodore?'

'Three o'clock this morning. Three-thirty. I'm not sure, I was a bit fuzzy. If I had known what would be required of me this morning I wouldn't have gone to that birthday celebration last night.'

'And it's now noon, or thereabouts. Seven hours of beating your brains out when you weren't feeling all that hot to begin with. You must be exhausted. But I would appreciate it if you could at least finish this present list off. After that, Jimmy, I suggest that Theodore has a drink, snack and snooze in that order.' The two men left. 'If you agree, Admiral, I suggest that Vincent contacts Greek Intelligence after Theodore has finished that list and furnishes them with a list of the towns together with the appropriate names and addresses. Could help.'

'And what do you imagine Greek Intelligence can do?'

'Very little, I imagine. But they can forward the list, with utmost urgency, to Interpol. Admittedly, Interpol's writ doesn't run worldwide – they would have zero clout in places, say, like Tripoli, Tehran or Beirut – and they are an information gathering and dispensing agency not an executive unit, and they know more about bad people than any other group in the world. And ask them if they suspect – suspect, not have proof – that Andropulos is engaged in drug-running.'

'Shall be done, sir. Sign it "Admiral Hawkins"?'

'Naturally.'

Hawkins shook his head. 'Admiral Hawkins here, Admiral Hawkins there, it seems he's signing his name everywhere. Or, rather somebody's signing it for him. I shall have to look to my chequebooks.'

The heavy steel derrick projected upwards and outwards from the midships side of the *Kilcharran* at an angle of about thirty degrees off the vertical. From the winch at the foot of the derrick the hawser rose upwards through the pulley at the top of the derrick and then descended vertically into the sea. The lower end of the hawser was attached to a heavy metal ring which was distanced about twenty feet above the fuselage of the sunken plane: from the ring, two shorter cables, bar-taut, were attached to the two lifting slings that had been attached fore and aft to the nose and tail of the bomber.

The winch turned with what seemed to most watchers an agonizing and frustrating slowness. There was ample electrical power available to have revolved the drum several times as quickly but Captain Montgomery was in no hurry. Standing there by the winch, he exhibited about as much anxiety and tension as a man sitting with his eyes closed in a garden deckchair on a summer's afternoon. Although it was difficult to visualize, it was possible that a sling could have loosened and slipped and Montgomery preferred not to think what might happen if the plane should slip and strike heavily against the bottom, so he just stood patiently there, personally guiding the winch's control wheel while he listened with clamped earphones to the two divers who were accompanying the plane on its ten foot a minute ascent.

After about five minutes the grotesque shape of the plane – grotesque because of the missing left wing – could be dimly discerned through the now slightly wind-ruffled surface of the sea. Another three minutes and the lifting ring came clear of the water. Montgomery centred the winch wheel, applied the brake, went to the gunwale, looked over the rail and turned to the officer by his side.

'Too close in. Fuselage is going to snag on the underside. Have to distance it a bit. More fenders fore and aft –' the side of the *Kilcharran* was already festooned with rubberized fenders '– and lay out ropes to secure the nose and tail of the plane.' He returned to the winch, eased forward on a lever and slowly lowered the derrick until it was projecting outwards from the ship's side at an angle of forty degrees above the horizontal. The plane, which could now be clearly seen only twenty feet below the surface, moved sluggishly outwards from the ship's side. Montgomery started up the winch again and soon the top of the plane's fuselage broke the surface. He stopped the winch when the top eighteen inches was clear. The starboard wing was still beneath the surface. Montgomery turned to Admiral Hawkins.

'So far, a simple and elementary exercise. With luck, the rest of it should be equally straightforward. We cut away the appropriate section on the top of the fuselage while attaching more flotation bags to the undersides of the fuselage and the wing and inflating those. Then we'll lift a bit more until the fuselage is almost clear of the water and go inside.' He lifted a ringing phone, thanked the caller and replaced the receiver. 'Well, perhaps not quite so straightforward. It would appear that the timing device has stopped ticking.'

'Has it now?' Hawkins didn't look particularly concerned and certainly not upset. 'It could have happened at a better time and a better place. But it had to happen. So our friend is armed.'

'Indeed. Still, no reason why we shouldn't go ahead as planned.'

'Especially as we have no option. Every person on both ships to be warned. No mechanical devices to be used: no banging or crashing, everyone on fairy tiptoes. They already know that, of course, but I imagine they'll now redouble their caution.'

A gangway had been lowered down the ship's side until one of its feet rested on the plane's fuselage. Carrington and Grant descended and ran a tape-measure back along the top of the fuselage from the cockpit – the internal distance from the cockpit to the exact location of the bomb had already been measured – to the corresponding area above. This they mopped dry with engine-room waste and then proceeded to paint the outline of a black rectangle to guide the two men with the oxyacetylene cutters who were already standing by.

Hawkins said: 'How long will this take?'

'I can only guess,' Montgomery said. 'An hour, maybe a bit longer. We don't know how thick the fuselage skin is or how tough it is. We don't know how thick or tough the lateral reinforcing members are. What I do know is that we're going to cut with the lowest possible flame that will do the job – even with that reduced power we're going to generate a fair amount of heat in the air-space and water below. It goes without saying that no one has ever done this sort of thing before.'

'Will your standing here, supervising operations – just looking on, rather – help things along? Resolve the unknown, I mean.'

'Not a bit of it. Ah! Lunch?'

'Whether we're here or in the wardroom of the *Ariadne*, it's not going to make all that difference if this lot goes up.'

'True, true. A millisecond here, a millisecond there. The condemned man ate a hearty breakfast. In our case, lunch.'

*   *   *

Lunch, while hardly festive, was by no means the doom-laden affair it could have been in view of the fact that most of the people at the table were well aware that they were sitting on top of a time-bomb that had now ceased to tick. Conversation flowed freely but in no way resembled the compulsive nervous chatter of those conscious of being under stress. Professor Wotherspoon spoke freely and often on any subject that arose, not through garrulity but because he was a born conversationalist who loved discussion and the free exchange of ideas. Andropulos, too, was far from silent, although he appeared to have only one idea in mind, and that was the mystery of the bomber that had just been raised from the depths. He had not been invited aboard the *Kilcharran* but had seen well enough from the *Ariadne* what had been going on. He appeared to be deeply and understandably interested in what had happened and was going to happen to the bomber but was clever enough not to ask any penetrating questions or say a word that he knew anything whatever about what was going on. Across the table Talbot caught the eye of Admiral Hawkins who nodded almost imperceptibly. It was clear that they couldn't keep him completely and totally in the dark.

'Up to now, Mr Andropulos,' Talbot said, 'we have not told you everything we know. We have not been remiss and no apology for our silence is necessary. Our sole concern, I can assure you, was not to cause unnecessary alarm and apprehension,

177

especially to your two young ladies. But a man like you must have a keen interest in international affairs, and you are, after all, a Greek and member of NATO and have a right to know.' No one could have guessed from Talbot's openness and relaxed tone that he considered Andropulos to have a keen interest in international crime, that he didn't give a damn about either Greece or NATO and had a right to know only what he, Talbot, chose to tell him.

'The plane was an American bomber and was carrying a lethal cargo, among them hydrogen and atomic bombs, almost certainly for a NATO missile base somewhere in Greece.' Andropulos's expression, at first stunned, rapidly changed to grim-faced understanding. 'We can only guess at what caused the crash. It could have been an engine explosion. On the other hand it could have been carrying a variety of weapons, and one of them – obviously of the non-nuclear variety – may have malfunctioned. We don't know, we have no means of telling and probably, almost certainly, we will never know. The crew, of course, died.'

Andropulos shook his head. The clear, innocent eyes were deeply tinged with sadness. 'Dear God, what a tragedy, what a tragedy.' He paused and considered. 'But there are terrorists in this world.' He spoke of terrorists as if they were alien beings from an alien planet. 'I know this sounds unthinkable, but could this have been a case of sabotage?'

'Impossible. This plane flew from a top secret Air Force base where security would have been absolute. Carelessness there may have been but the idea of the deliberate implantation of any explosive device passes belief. It can only be classified as an act of God.'

'I wish I shared your trust in our fellow-man.' Andropulos shook his head again. 'There are no depths which some inhuman monsters would not plumb. But if you say it was physically impossible, then I accept that, and gladly, for I would not care to be counted as a member of a human race that could proceed to such unspeakable lengths. What's past is past, I suppose, but there's also a future. What happens next, Commander?'

'Before we decide on that we'll have to wait until we get inside the plane. I understand that impacts and explosions such as those nuclear weapons have experienced can have – what shall we say? – a very disturbing effect on their delicate firing control systems.'

'You – or some member of your crew – have the expertise to pass judgement on such matters?'

'Neither I nor my crew know anything about such matters. But seated only two chairs away from you is a man who does. Dr Wickram – I will not spare his blushes – is a world-famous nuclear physicist who specializes in nuclear weaponry. We are fortunate indeed to have him aboard.'

'My word, that is convenient.' Andropulos leaned forward and half-bowed to Wickram. 'I was, of course, unaware that you were an expert on those matters. I hope you can help resolve this dreadful dilemma.'

'Hardly in the dreadful category yet, Mr Andropulos,' Talbot said. 'A problem, shall we say.' He turned as Denholm, who had not joined them for lunch, entered the wardroom. 'Lieutenant?'

'Sorry to disturb you, sir. Lieutenant McCafferty's apologies, but would you be kind enough to come to the engine-room.'

Once outside, Talbot said. 'What's the trouble in the engine-room, Jimmy?'

'Nothing. This habit of deception grows on one. A message from the Pentagon, sir, and some interesting information turned up by Theodore.'

'I thought he was resting.'

'He elected not to, sir. Just as well, as I'm sure you'll agree.' He produced a slip of paper. 'The Washington message.'

' "Krytron device en route direct New York–Athens via Concorde." My word, someone over there does carry some clout. I detect the hand of the President in this. Can't you just see the outrage of a hundred-odd Europe-bound passengers when they find themselves being dumped on the tarmac of John F. Kennedy in favour of a teeny-weeny electrical device? Not that they'll know why they have been dumped. It goes on: "Fullest cooperation British Airways, Spanish and Italian authorities." '

'Why Spain and Italy?' Denholm said. 'You don't require permission to overfly friendly countries. Just Air Control notification, that's all.'

'Except, I imagine, when you're going to upset their normal peace and quiet by a non-stop sonic boom. Message ends: "ETA your time 3 p.m." Just over an hour. We'll have to make arrangements to have a plane standing by in Athens airport. Let's see what Theodore has for us. Something of significance, I'll be bound.'

Theodore had, indeed, found something of significance, although its relevance was not immediately evident.

'I've started on the third and last list, Captain,' Theodore said, 'and this is the sixth name I've come up with. George Skepertzis. Full Washington address. Under the address, as you see, it says Ref. KK, TT. Means nothing to me.'

'Nor to me,' Talbot said. 'Anything to you, Lieutenant?'

'It might. Skepertzis is a Greek name, that's for sure. Could be a fellow-countryman of Andropulos. And if our friend has contacts in the Pentagon, you can lay odds that he wouldn't be writing to them, using their names, care of the Pentagon. You'd expect Andropulos to use a buffer-man, a go-between.'

'I'd expect anything of that character. You're probably right. So, a message to the bank asking if they have any accounts under those initials and one to the FBI to find out if there are any Air

181

Force generals or admirals with those initials. A shot in the dark, of course, but it might find a target. In the remote event of their contemplating a sound night's sleep, a personal message to the President, via the FBI, that the tick . . . tick . . . tick has stopped and that the atomic mine is armed. We'll clear it with the Admiral first. Would you ask him to join us. Have Number One and Dr Wickram come along too. I suggest the bridge. I'm sure you'll think up a suitable excuse on the way to the wardroom.'

'I don't have to think, sir. It's second nature now.'

'Fair enough.' Hawkins laid down the three radio messages that Talbot had already drafted. 'The Greek Ministry of Defence will have a plane standing by when the Concorde lands. If its estimated time of arrival is reasonably accurate we should have this krytron device in Santorini about three-thirty. Even allowing for the fact that your men will have to row to and from at least Cape Akrotiri we should have the device aboard by five p.m. There's an even chance that the messages to the FBI and the Washington bank may produce some positive results. As to the news that the mine is armed, we shall await the Presidential reaction with interest. Send these at once. You have some other matters on your mind, Captain. Urgent, I take it?'

'As you said yourself not so long ago, sir, time *is* on the wing. Questions, sir, and we'd better try to find some answers quickly. Why was Andropulos so restrained in his questioning about the bombers? Because – apart from that ticking time device – he already knew everything there was to know and saw no point in asking questions when he already held the answers.

'Why did he express no surprise at Dr Wickram here just happening to be aboard at this critical juncture? Even the most innocent of people would have thought it the most extraordinary coincidence that Dr Wickram should be here at the moment when he was most needed and would have said so.

'What's going to pass through that crafty and calculating mind when he sees us hauling that atom bomb out of the fuselage – always providing we do, of course? And what are we going to do to satisfy his curiosity?'

'I can answer your last two questions *and* explain my presence here,' Wickram said. 'I've had time to think although, to be honest, it didn't require all that much thought. You heard that the plane had hydrogen bombs aboard, you didn't know what the degree of danger was so you called in the resident expert. That's me. The resident expert informs you there is a high degree of danger. There's no way to prevent a slow but continuous degree of radioactive emanations from a hydrogen bomb, and there are fifteen of those aboard that plane. This radioactivity builds up inside the atom bomb, which is of an entirely different construction, until the critical stage is reached. Then it's goodnight, all. All a question of mass, really.'

'This really happens?'

'How the hell should I know? I've just invented it. But it sounds scientific enough and more than vaguely plausible. Your average citizen has a zero knowledge level of nuclear weaponry. Who is going to dream of questioning the word of a world-famous nuclear physicist which, in case you've forgotten Commander Talbot's words, is me.'

Talbot smiled, 'I wouldn't dream of it, Dr Wickram. Excellent. Next query. What are Andropulos's code lists doing aboard the *Ariadne*?'

'Well, to start with,' Hawkins said, 'you put them there. No need for massive restraint, Captain. You had something else in mind?'

'Wrong question. Why did he leave them behind? He forgot? Not likely. Not something as important as that. Because he thought they'd never be found? Possible, but again not likely. Because he thought that if anyone found them then it would be unlikely that that person would recognize it as a code or try to decode it? Rather more likely, but I think the real reason is that he thought it would be too dangerous to bring them aboard the *Ariadne*. The very fact that that was the only item he chose to salvage from the wreck would have been significant and suspicious in itself. So he elected to leave them behind and recover them later by diving. He may always have had this possibility in his mind and if he did he wouldn't have left them in a cardboard folder. So he chose a waterproof metal box.

'Recovery of the box from the bottom of the sea would mean the presence or availability of a diving ship. Just a hunch. I think that the *Delos* was sunk by accident and not by design. Probably Andropulos never visualized the need of a diving ship for that purpose. But a convenient diving ship would have been useful for other purposes, such as, dare I suggest, the recovery of nuclear weapons from a sunken bomber. They – whoever they are – wouldn't have brought it down anywhere in the Sea of Crete – that's the area between the Peloponnese in the west, the Dodecanese in the east, the Cyclades in the north and Crete to the south – because by far the greater part of that area is between 1,500 and 7,000 feet – much too deep for recovery by diving. Maybe it was meant to bring it down where it was brought down. Maybe this hypothetical diving ship was meant to be where we inconveniently were.'

'It's a long shot,' Hawkins said, 'but no stone unturned, is that it? What you would like to know is whether there is any diving ship based in those parts or temporarily located or cruising by. Isn't that it?' Talbot nodded. 'Finding out is no problem.'

'Heraklion in Crete?'

'Of course. The US Air Force base there is our main centre for electronic surveillance in those parts. They use AWACs and other high-flying radar planes to monitor Soviet, Libyan and other countries' military movements. The Greek Air Force use their Phantoms and Mirages for the same purpose. I know the base commander rather well. An immediate signal. They'll either find out in very short order or have the information already. A couple of hours should do it.'

'I speak in no spirit of complaint,' Captain Montgomery said to Talbot. His voice, in fact, held a marked note of complaint. 'But I think we might have been spared this.' He indicated a bank of heavy dark cloud approaching from the north-west. 'The wind's already Force 5 and we're beginning to rock a bit. Travel agents wouldn't like this at all. This is supposed to be a golden summer's day in the golden Aegean.'

'Force 5 isn't uncommon here in the afternoons, even at this time of year. Rain *is* most unusual but it looks as if we're going to have quite a lot of the unusual in the very near future. Weather forecast is poor and the barometer unhappy.' Talbot looked over the rail of the *Kilcharran*. 'And this is what makes you unhappy.'

Montgomery's ship was not, in fact, rocking at all. Headed directly north-west into the gentle three-foot swell, it was quite motionless, which couldn't be said for the plane lashed alongside. Because of its much shorter length and the fact that it was nine-tenths submerged, it was reacting quite badly to the swell, pitching rather noticeably to and fro and snubbing alternately on the ropes that secured its nose and the remnants of its tail to the *Kilcharran*. Cutting the metal and maintaining balance was becoming increasingly difficult for the oxyacetylene team on top of the fuselage as the tops of the swells periodically washed over the area on which they were working. They had already reached the stage where they were spending more time looking after their own safety than using their torches.

'Not so much unhappy as annoyed. Their rate of progress has been reduced to almost zero and God knows they were moving slowly enough even in good conditions – that fuselage and especially the transverse members are proving much tougher than expected. If things don't improve – and looking at that weather coming at us I'm sure they won't – I'm going to have to withdraw the cutters. They're in no danger, of course, but the plane might very well be. We have no way of knowing how weakened the nose or tail may be and I don't care to imagine what will happen if one of them comes off.'

'So you're going to float it astern on a single tow-rope?'

'I don't see I have any option. I'll build a cradle of ropes round the nose and wing of the plane, attach a single rope – a heavy one, to act as a spring – to it and let it drift a cable length astern. Have to inform the Admiral first.'

'No need. He never interferes with an expert. An unpleasant thought occurs, Captain. What happens if it breaks loose?'

'Send a boat out – rowing, of course – to secure it with an anchor.'

'And if that goes?'

'We puncture the flotation bags and sink it. Can't have it drifting all over the shop ready to blow the whole works whenever the first ship's engines come within auditory range.'

'And if it sinks where it is, we, of course, won't be able to move from here.'

'You can't have everything.'

'Agreed,' Hawkins said. 'Montgomery's got no option. When is he starting?'

'Any moment. Perhaps you might have a word with him. I said that there was no question but that you would agree, but I think he'd like your say-so.'

'Of course,' Hawkins said. 'What's your weather forecast?'

'Deteriorating. Any word from the Washington bank, the FBI or Heraklion?'

'Nothing. Just a lot of unsolicited rubbish from diverse heads of states, presidents, premiers and so forth commiserating with us in one breath and asking us why we aren't doing something about it in the second breath. One wonders how the news has been leaked.'

'I don't know, sir. What's more, I really don't care.'

'Nor I.' He waved to some papers on his desk. 'Want to read them? They don't know that the tick . . . tick has stopped.'

'I don't want to read them.'

'I didn't think you would. What's next for you, John?'

'I didn't have much sleep last night. It's quite possible I may lack some tonight. Now's the time. Nothing I can do.'

'An excellent idea. Same for me when I come back from the *Kilcharran*.'

When Talbot emerged from his day cabin and passed through to the bridge shortly after six o'clock in the evening it should still have been broad daylight, but so low was the level of light in the sky that it could well have been late twilight. He found Van Gelder and Denholm waiting for him.

'In this weather,' Talbot said, 'I could almost say "Well, watchmen, what of the night?" Everything running smoothly and under control while Drake was in his hammock?'

'We have not been idle,' Van Gelder said. 'Neither has Captain Montgomery. He's got the bomber strung out about a cable length to the south-east. Riding quite badly – it's either a Force 6 or 7 out there – but it seems to be holding together. He's got a searchlight – well, a six-inch signalling lamp – on it, either to check that it doesn't break away or to discourage the disaffected from snaffling it, although why there should be anyone around, or daft enough, to try that I can't imagine. I'd advise against going out on the wing to have a look, sir. You might get washed away.'

Van Gelder's advice was superfluous. The rain falling from the black and leaden skies was of the torrential or tropical downpour variety, the heavy warm drops rebounding six inches from the deck.

'I take your point.' He looked at the brown metal box lying on the deck. 'What's that?'

'*Voilà!*' Denholm seized the handle let into the top and swept off the cover with all the panache of a stage magician unveiling his latest impossible trick. 'The *pièce de résistance.*' What was presumably the control panel on the top of the box was singularly unimpressive and old-fashioned, reminiscent of a pre-war radio, with two calibrated dials, some knobs, a press-button and two orange hemispherical glass domes let into the surface.

'The krytron, I assume,' Talbot said.

'No less. Three cheers for presidents. This particular one has been as good as his word.'

'Excellent. Really excellent. Let's only hope we get the chance to use it under, let us say, optimal circumstances.'

' "Optimal" is the word,' Denholm said. 'Very simple device – as far as operating it is concerned, that is. Inside, it's probably fiendishly complicated. This particular model – there may be others – runs off a twenty-four volt battery.' He placed his forefinger on a button. 'I depress this – and hey presto!'

'If you're trying to make me nervous, Jimmy, you're succeeding. Take your finger off that damned button.'

Denholm depressed it several times. 'No battery. We supply that. No problem. And under those two orange domes are two switches that have to be rotated through 180 degrees. Specially designed, you see, for careless clowns like me. As an added precaution, you can't unscrew those domes. One sharp tap with a light metal object, the instructions say, and they disintegrate. Again, I should imagine, designed with people like me in mind, in case we remove the tops and start twiddling the switches around. Designed, if you follow me, to be a one-off operation. The only time those switches will ever be exposed is immediately before the firing button is depressed.'

'When are you going to attach the battery?'

'As an added precaution – this is *my* precaution – only immediately before use. These are positive and negative connections. We use spring-loaded crocodile clips. Two seconds to attach the clips. Three seconds to crack the domes and align the switches. One second to press the button. Nothing could be simpler. Only one other trifling requirement, sir – that we have that atom bomb, on its own and a long, long way from anywhere and us at a very prudent distance when we detonate it.'

'You ask for very little, Jimmy.' Talbot looked out at the driving rain and the dark and now white-capped seas. 'We may have to wait a little – an hour or two as an optimistic guess, all night as a pessimistic one, before we can even begin to move. Anything else?'

'I repeat, we have not been idle,' Van Gelder said. 'We've heard from the Heraklion Air Base. There is – or was – a diving vessel in the near vicinity, if you can call the western tip of Crete the near vicinity.'

'Is – or was?'

'Was. It was anchored off Souda Bay for a couple of days and apparently took off about one a.m. this morning. As you know, Souda Bay is a very hush-hush Greek naval base, and the area is very protected, very restricted. Foreign vessels, even harmless cruising yachts, are definitely not welcomed. Souda Bay naturally took an interest in this lad. It's their business to be suspicious, especially at a time when NATO are operating in the area.'

'What did they find out?'

'Precious little. It was called the *Taormina* and registered in Panama.'

'A Sicilian name? No significance. Panama – a convenience registry, some of the most successful ocean-going crooks in the world are registered there. Anyway, you don't have to be an artist to change both names in very short order – all you require is a couple of pots of paint and a set of stencils. Where had it come from?'

'They didn't know. As it had anchored off-shore it didn't have to register with either the customs or the port authorities. But they did know that it took off in a roughly north-easterly direction which, just coincidentally, is the course it would have taken if it were heading for Santorini. And as Souda Bay is just under a hundred miles from here, even a slow ship could have been in this area well before the bomber came down. So your hunch could have been right, sir. Only problem is, we've seen no sign of him.'

'Could have been a coincidence. Could have been that the *Delos* warned him off. Did Heraklion say anything about going to have a look for this ship?'

'No. Jimmy and I discussed the idea but we didn't think it important enough to disturb you when you were – ah – resting lightly. And the Admiral.'

'Probably unimportant. We should have a go. Normally, that is. Where does Heraklion lie from here? About due south?'

'Near enough.'

'A couple of planes, one carrying out a sweep to the north, the other to the east, should locate this lad, if he is in the area, in half an hour, probably less. Part of an urgent NATO exercise, you understand. But conditions aren't normal. A waste of time in near zero visibility. An option we'll keep in mind for better weather. Anything else?'

'Yes. We've heard from both the Washington bank and the FBI. Mixed results, you might say. Under the initials of KK, the bank says it has a certain Kyriakos Katzanevakis.'

'Promising. You could hardly get anything more Grecian than that.'

'Under TT, they have a Thomas Thompson. You can't have anything more Anglo-Saxon than that. The FBI say there are no high-ranking officers in the Pentagon – by which I take it they mean admirals and Air Force generals or, at the outside, vice-admirals and lieutenant-generals – with those initials.'

'On the face of it, disappointing, but it may equally well be just another step in the laundering cover-up, another step to distance themselves from their paymaster. The FBI hasn't been in touch with the bank? Of course not. We didn't even mention the bank to them. Remiss of us. No, remiss of me. The bank must have addresses for Messrs KK and TT, and although those will almost certainly turn out to be accommodation addresses they may lead to something else. And another omission, again my fault entirely. We didn't let the FBI have the name and address of this George Skepertzis. We'll do that now. There's an outside chance that the FBI may be able to link Skepertzis, KK and TT together. And what was the presidential reaction to the stopping of the tick . . . tick . . .?'

'He appears to be beyond any further reaction.'

Montgomery sipped his drink, gazed gloomily through his cabin window, winced and looked away.

194

'The weather has deteriorated in the past half-hour, Commander Talbot.'

'It couldn't possibly be any worse than it was half an hour ago.'

'I'm an expert on such matters.' Montgomery sighed. 'Makes me quite homesick for the Mountains of Mourne. We get a lot of rainfall in the Mountains of Mourne. Do you see this lot clearing up in the near future?'

'Not this side of midnight.'

'And that would be an optimistic estimate, I'm thinking. By the time we haul this damn bomber back alongside, cut away the hole in the fuselage, hoist it out of the water and extract that bomb, it'll be dawn. At least. Might possibly be well into the forenoon. You'll understand if I turn down your kind offer to join you for dinner. An early snack for me, then bed. Might have to get up any time during the night. I'll have a couple of boys on the poop all night, watching the plane and with orders to wake me as soon as they think the weather has moderated enough for us to start hauling it in.'

Dr Wickram said: 'How's that for a brief résumé of the speech I shall so reluctantly make at the table tonight? Not too much, I would have thought, and not too little?'

'Perfect. Perhaps the tone a thought more doom-laden?'

'A half octave deeper, you think? Odd, isn't it, how easily this mendacity comes to one?'

195

'Aboard the *Ariadne*, it's become positively endemic. Very catching.'

'I've just had a word with Eugenia,' Denholm said. 'I thought you ought to know.'

'That you've been neglecting your duty? Not lurking, I mean.'

'A man gets tired of lurking. I meant what she had to say.'

'You spoke to her privately, I take it?'

'Yes, sir. In her cabin. Number One's cabin, that is to say.'

'You surprise me, Jimmy.'

'If I may say so, sir, with some dignity, we had been discussing matters on a purely intellectual level. Very bright girl. Going for a double first at University. Language and literature, Greek ancient and modern.'

'Ah! Deep calling unto deep.'

'I wouldn't call it that, because I spoke only in English. I was under the impression that she was convinced that I didn't speak a word of Greek.'

'She's no longer convinced? A close observer, the young lady? Perhaps you registered a flicker of expression when something was said in Greek when you should have registered nothing. I suspect you were trapped in your innocent youth by some fiendish feminine wile.'

'How would you react, sir, if you were told that a scorpion was crawling up your shoe?'

Talbot smiled. 'She spoke in Greek, of course. You immediately carried out a hurried check to locate this loathsome monster. Anybody would have fallen for it. You have not suffered too much chagrin and mortification, I hope?'

'Not really, sir. She's too nice. And too worried. Wanted to confide in me.'

'Alas, the days when lovely young ladies wanted to confide in me appear to be over.'

'I think she's a little scared of you, sir. So is Irene. She wanted to talk about Andropulos. Girl talk, of course, and I suppose there's no one else really on the ship they can talk to. That's not quite fair, I suppose, they're clearly very close friends. Seems that Irene repeated to her, more or less verbatim, the conversation she had with Number One this morning and told her she'd told Vincent everything she knew about her Uncle Adam. It would appear that Eugenia knows something about Uncle Adam that his niece doesn't know. May I have a drink, sir? I've been awash since dawn in tonic and lemon.'

'Help yourself. Revelations, is that it?'

'I don't know how you'd classify it, sir, but I know you'll find it very interesting. Eugenia's father has quite a lot in common with Irene's father – apparently they're good friends – they're both wealthy businessmen, they both know Andropulos and both think he's a crook. Well, nothing new in that so far. We all think he's a crook. But Eugenia's father, unlike Irene's, is willing to talk freely and at length about Andropulos and Eugenia hasn't talked about it to Irene, because she doesn't wish to hurt her feelings.' Denholm sampled his drink and sighed in satisfaction. 'It would seem that Adamantios Spyros Andropulos has a pathological hatred of Americans. Who would suspect such a charming, courteous, urbane and civilized gentleman to have a pathological hatred of anyone?'

'I would. Well, we all know he's intelligent so he had to have a reason.'

'He had. Two. His son and only nephew. Apparently, he doted on them. Eugenia quite believes this, because she says that Andropulos is unquestionably fond of Irene and herself, a feeling, I'm glad to say, that they don't reciprocate.'

'What about his son and nephew?'

'Disappeared in most mysterious circumstances. Never to be seen again. Andropulos is convinced that they were done in by the American CIA.'

'The CIA has a reputation, justified or not, for eliminating people they regard as undesirables. But they usually have a reason, again whether that is justifiable or not. Does Eugenia's old man know the reason?'

'Yes. He says – and he's convinced of this – that the two young men were heroin peddlers.'

'Well, well. Ties in all too well with what we have been increasingly suspecting. There are times, Jimmy, when I regard the CIA as being a much maligned lot.'

* * *

The atmosphere at the dinner table that night was noticeably, but not markedly, less relaxed than it had been at lunch-time. Conversation flowed rather less freely than it had then, and three men in particular, Hawkins, Talbot and Van Gelder, seemed more given than usual to brief and introspective silences, occasionally gazing at some object or objects that lay beyond a distant horizon. There was nothing that one could put a finger on and the insensitive would quite have failed to recognize that there was anything amiss. Andropulos proved that he was not one of those.

'I do not wish to pry, gentlemen, and I may be quite wrong, I frequently am, but do I not detect a certain aura of uneasiness, even of tension at the table tonight?' His smile was as open and ingenuous as his words had been frank and candid. 'Or is it my imagination? You are surprised, perhaps, Commander Talbot?'

'No, not really.' The only thing that surprised Talbot was that Andropulos had taken so long in getting around to it. 'You are very perceptive, Mr Andropulos. I'm rather disappointed, I must say. I thought – or hoped – that our concern was better concealed than that.'

'Concern, Captain?'

'To a slight degree only. No real anxiety yet. No reason in the world why you shouldn't know as much as we do.' As Dr Wickram had said, Talbot reflected, mendacity required little practice to become second nature: there was every reason in the world why Andropulos should not know as much as he did. 'You know, of course, that the bad weather has forced us to suspend operations on the bomber?'

'I have seen that it is riding several hundred metres astern of us. Operations? What operations, Captain. You are trying to recover those wicked weapons?'

'Just one of them. An atom bomb.'

'Why only one?'

'Dr Wickram? Would you kindly explain?'

'Certainly. Well, as far as I can. What we have here is a situation of considerable complexity and doubt, because we are dealing largely with the unknown. You will be aware that a nuclear explosion occurs when a critical mass of uranium or plutonium is reached. Now, there's no way to prevent a slow but continuous degree of radioactive emanations from a hydrogen bomb, and there are fifteen of them aboard that plane. This radioactivity builds up inside the atom bomb, which is of an entirely different construction, until the critical mass of the atom bomb is reached. Then the atom bomb goes poof! Unfortunately, because of something we call sympathetic detonation, the hydrogen bombs also go poof! I will not dwell on what will happen to us.

'Normally, because of this well-known danger, hydrogen bombs and atom bombs are never stored together, not, at least, for any period of time. Twenty-four hours is regarded as a safe period and a plane, as in this instance, can easily make a long-distance flight with them together, at the end of which, of course, they would immediately be stored separately. What happens after twenty-four hours, we simply don't know although some of us – I am one – believe that the situation deteriorates very rapidly thereafter.

'Incidentally, that's why I have asked the Captain to stop all engines and generators. It is an established fact that acoustical vibrations hasten the onset of the critical period.'

Wickram's deep, solemn and authoritative voice carried absolute conviction. Had he not known, Talbot thought, that Dr Wickram was talking scientific malarkey he, for one, would have believed every word he said.

'So you will readily appreciate that it is of the utmost urgency that we remove that atom bomb from the plane as soon as possible and then take it away – by sail, of course, that's why the *Angelina* is alongside, the critical mass will decay only very slowly – to some distant spot. Some very distant spot. There we will deposit it gently on the ocean floor.'

'How will you do that?' Andropulos said. 'Deposit it gently, I mean. The ocean could be thousands of feet deep at the spot. Wouldn't the bomb accelerate all the way down?'

Wickram smiled tolerantly. 'I have discussed the matter with Captain Montgomery of the *Kilcharran*.' He had not, in fact, discussed the matter with anybody. 'We attach a flotation bag to the bomb, inflate it until it achieves a very slight negative buoyancy and then it will float down like a feather to the ocean floor.'

'And then?'

'And then nothing.' If Wickram were having visions of a passenger cruise liner passing over an armed atomic mine, he kept his visions to himself. 'It will decay and corrode slowly over the years, perhaps even over the centuries. May give rise to a few digestive upsets for some passing fish. I don't know. What I do know is that if we don't get rid of that damned beast with all dispatch we're going to suffer more than a few digestive problems. Better that some of us – those concerned with the recovery of the bomb – have a sleepless night than that we all sleep forever.'

8

Talbot stirred, half sat up in his bunk and blinked at the overhead light that had suddenly come on in his day cabin. Van Gelder was standing in the doorway.

'Two-thirty. An unChristian hour, Vincent. Something is afoot. Weather moderated and Captain Montgomery hauling in the plane?'

'Yes, sir. But there's something more immediately urgent. Jenkins is missing.'

Talbot swung his feet to the deck. 'Jenkins? I won't say, "Missing?" or "How can he be missing?" If you say he is, he is. You've had a search carried out, of course?'

'Of course. Forty volunteers. You know how popular Jenkins is.' Talbot knew. Jenkins, their Mess steward and a Marine of fifteen years' standing, a man whose calmness, efficiency and resource were matched only by his sense of humour, was highly regarded by everyone who knew him.

'Can Brown cast any light on this?' Marine Sergeant Brown, a man as rock-like and solid as Chief McKenzie, was Jenkins's closest friend on the ship. Both men were in the habit of having a tipple in the pantry when the day's work was done, an illicit practice which Talbot tacitly and readily condoned. Their tipple invariably stopped at that, just one: even in the élite Royal Marines it would have been difficult to find two men like them.

'Nothing, sir. They went down to their Mess together. Brown turned in while Jenkins started on a letter to his wife. That was the last Brown saw of him.'

'Who discovered his absence?'

'Carter. The Master-at-arms. You know how he likes to prowl around at odd hours of the day and night looking for non-existent crime. He went up to the wardroom and pantry, found nothing, returned to the Marine Mess-deck and woke Brown. They carried out a brief search. Again nothing. Then they came to me.'

'It would be pointless to ask you if you have any ideas?'

'Pointless. Brown seems convinced he's no longer aboard the ship. He says that Jenkins never sleep-walked, drank only sparingly and was devoted to his wife and two daughters. He had no problems – Brown is certain of that – and no enemies aboard the ship. Well, among the crew, that is. Brown is further convinced that Jenkins stumbled across something he shouldn't have or saw something he shouldn't have seen, although how he could do anything like that while sitting in the mess writing to his wife is difficult to imagine. His suspicions immediately centred on Andropulos and company – I gather he and Jenkins have talked quite a lot about them – and he was all for going down to Andropulos's cabin and beating the living daylights out of him. I had some difficulty in restraining him, although privately, I must say, I found it rather an appealing prospect.'

'An understandable reaction on his part.' Talbot paused, 'I can't see how Andropulos or his friends could have any possible connection with this or have any conceivable reason for knocking him off. Do you think there's a remote chance that he might have gone aboard the *Kilcharran*?'

'No earthly reason why he should have but the thought did occur. I asked Danforth – he's the *Kilcharran*'s chief officer – if he'd have a look around, so he collected some of his crew and carried out a search. There aren't many places you can hide – or be hidden – on a diving ship. Took them less than ten minutes to be sure he wasn't anywhere aboard.'

'Nothing we can do at the moment. I have the uncomfortable feeling that there's nothing we're going to be able to do either. Let's go and see how Captain Montgomery is getting on.'

The wind had dropped to Force 3, the sea was no more than choppy and the rain had eased, but only slightly, from torrential to heavy. Mont-gomery, clad in streaming oilskins, was at the winch: the plane, still bobbing rather uncomfort-ably, was slowly but steadily nearing the stern of the diving ship. The oxyacetylene crew, also in oil-skins, were standing by the guard-rail, torches at the ready.

Talbot said: 'Your men are going to be able to maintain their footing?'

'It won't be easy. The plane should steady up a bit when we secure it fore and aft and we'll have ropes on the men, of course. And this confounded rain doesn't help. I think we should be able to make some progress but it'll be slow. Point is, this may be as good weather as we're going to get. No point in your remaining, Commander, you'd be better off in your bunk. I'll let you know when we've cut away the section and are ready to lift.' He wiped rain away from his eyes. 'I hear you've lost your chief steward. Bloody odd, isn't it? Do you suspect foul play?'

'I'm at the stage where I'm about ready to sus-pect anything or anybody. Van Gelder and I are agreed that it couldn't have happened accidentally so it must have happened on purpose and not, of course, his purpose. Yes, foul play. As to what kind of foul play and the identity of the person or per-sons responsible, we don't have a clue.'

It should have been dawn, but wasn't, when Van Gelder roused Talbot shortly after six-thirty in the morning. The sky was still heavy and dark, and neither the wind nor the steadily drumming rain had improved in the past four hours.

'So much for your breathless Aegean dawns,' Talbot said, 'I take it that Captain Montgomery has cut away that section of the plane's fuselage?'

'Forty minutes ago. He's got the fuselage more than half way out of the water already.'

'How are the winch and the derrick taking the strain?'

'Very little strain, I believe. He's secured four more flotation bags under the fuselage and wing and is letting compressed air do most of the work. He asks if you'd like to come along. Oh, and we've had a communication from Greek Intelligence about Andropulos.'

'You don't seem very excited about it.'

'I'm not. Interesting, but doesn't really help us. It just confirms that our suspicions about Uncle Adam are far from groundless. They've passed on our messages to Interpol. It seems – the message, I must say, is couched in very guarded language – that both Greek Intelligence and Interpol have been taking a considerable interest in Andropulos for several years. Both are certain that our friend is engaged in highly illegal activities but if this was a trial in a Scottish court of law the verdict would be "not proven". They have no hard evidence. Andropulos acts through intermediaries who operate though other intermediaries and so on until either the trail runs cold or, occasionally, ends up in shell companies in Panama and the Bahamas, where much of his money is stashed away. The banks there consistently refuse to acknowledge letters and cables, in fact they won't even acknowledge his existence. No cooperation from the Swiss banks, either. They'll only open up their books if the depositor has been convicted of what is also regarded as a crime in Switzerland. He hasn't been convicted of anything.'

'Illegal activities? What illegal activities?'

'Drugs. Message ends with a request – sounds more like a demand the way they put it – that this information be treated in total secrecy, utter and absolute confidentiality. Words to that effect.'

'What information? They haven't given us any information that we didn't already suspect or have. No mention of the one item of information we'd like to know. Who, either in the government, the civil service or the top echelons in the armed forces, is Andropulos's powerful protector and friend? Possibly they don't know, more probably they don't want us to know. Nothing from Washington?'

'Not a word. Maybe the FBI don't work at night.'

'More likely that other people don't work at night. It's eleven-thirty p.m., their time, the banks are shut and all the staffs to hell and gone until tomorrow morning. We may have to wait hours before we hear anything.'

* * *

208

'We're nearly there,' Captain Montgomery said. 'We'll stop hoisting – in this case more lifting from below than hoisting – when the water-level drops below the floor of the cabin. That way we won't get our feet wet when we go inside.'

Talbot looked over the side to where a man, torch in his hand pointing downwards, sat with his legs dangling through the rectangular hole that had been cut in the fuselage.

'We're going to get a lot more than our feet wet before we get there. We've got to pass first through the compartment under the flight deck and that will still have a great deal of water in it.'

'I don't understand,' Montgomery said. 'I mean we don't have to. We just drop down through the hole we've made in the fuselage.'

'That's fine, if all we want to do is to confine ourselves to the cargo hold. But you can't get into the flight deck from there. There's a heavy steel door in the bulkhead and the clamps are secured on the for'ard side. So if we want to get at those clamps you have to do it from the flight-deck side, and to do that you must pass through the flooded compartment first.'

'Why should we want to open that door at all?'

'Because the clamps holding the atom bomb in place have padlocks. Where is one of the first places you'd look if you were searching for a key to the padlocks?'

'Ah! Of course. The pockets of the dead men.'

'Enough, Captain,' the man on the fuselage called out. 'Deck's clear.'

Montgomery centred the winch and applied the brake, then checked the fore and aft securing ropes. When he had them adjusted to his satisfaction he said: 'Won't be long, gentlemen. Just going to have a first-hand look.'

'Van Gelder and I are coming with you. We've brought our suits.' Talbot checked the level of the top of the jagged hole in the nose cone relative to the surface of the sea. 'I don't think we'll be needing our helmets.'

They did not, as it proved, require their helmets, the compartment under the flight-deck was no more than two-thirds full. They moved along to the opened hatch and hauled themselves up into the space behind the pilots' seats. Montgomery looked at the two dead men and screwed his eyes momentarily shut.

'What a bloody awful mess. And to think that the fiend responsible is still walking around free as air.'

'I don't think he will be for much longer.'

'But you've said yourself you don't have the evidence to convict him.'

'Andropulos will never come to trial. Vincent, would you bang open that door and show Captain Montgomery where our friend is.'

'No banging. Maybe our friend doesn't like banging.' Van Gelder produced a large stilson wrench. 'Persuasion. Aren't you coming, sir?'

'In a moment.' They left and Talbot addressed himself to the highly distasteful task of searching through the dead men's pockets. He found nothing. He searched through every shelf, locker and compartment in the cockpit. Again, nothing. He moved aft and joined Montgomery and Van Gelder.

'Nothing, sir?'

'Nothing. And nothing I can find anywhere in the flight-deck.'

Montgomery grimaced. 'You were, of course, looking through the pockets of the dead men. Sooner you than me. This is a very big plane, the key – if there ever was a key – could have been tucked away anywhere. I don't give much for our chances of recovering it. So, other methods. Your Number One suggests a corrosive to cut through those clamps. Wouldn't it be easier just to use an old-fashioned hacksaw?'

'I wouldn't recommend it, sir,' Van Gelder said. 'If you were to try I'd rather be a couple of hundred miles away at the time. I don't know how intelligent this armed listening device is, but I would question whether it's clever enough to tell the difference between the rhythmic rasping of a hacksaw and the pulse of an engine.'

'I agree with Vincent,' Talbot said. 'Even if it were only a one in ten thousand chance – and for all we know it might be a one in one chance – the risk still isn't worth taking. Lady Luck has been riding with us so far but she might take a poor view of our pushing her too far.'

211

'So corrosives, you think? I have my doubts.' Montgomery stopped to examine the clamps more closely. 'I should have carried out some preliminary test aboard, I suppose, but I never thought those clamps would be so thick nor made, as I suspect they are, of hardened steel. The only corrosive I have aboard is sulphuric acid. Neat sulphuric, H_2SO_4 at specific gravity 1800 – vitriol, if you like – is a highly corrosive agent when applied to most substances, which is why it is usually carried in glass carboys which are immune to the corrosive action of acids. But I think it would find this a very tough meal to digest. Patience and diligence, of course, and I'm sure it would do the trick, but it might take hours.'

Talbot said: 'What do you think, Vincent?'

'I'm no expert. I should imagine Captain Montgomery is quite correct. So, no corrosives, no hacksaws, no oxyacetylene torches.' Van Gelder hoisted the big stilson in his hand. 'This.'

Talbot looked at the clamps and their mountings, then nodded. 'Of course. That. We're not very bright, are we? At least I'm not.' He looked at the way the clamps were secured to the side of the fuselage and the floor: each of the bases of the four retaining arms of the clamps was fitted over two bolts and were held in place by heavy inch-and-a-half nuts. 'We leave the clamps *in situ* and free the bases instead. See how stiff those nuts are, will you?'

Van Gelder applied the stilson to one of the nuts, adjusted the grip and heaved. The nut was big and

212

tightly jammed in position but a stilson wrench affords great leverage: the nut turned easily.

'Simple,' Van Gelder said.

'Indeed.' Talbot looked at the length of the retaining arms, which projected at ninety degrees from each other, then gauged the width of the hole that had been cut overhead. 'What's not so simple is getting the bomb up through the hole. With those arms in position there's just not enough clearance for it to go through. We'll have to widen the hole. You can do that, Captain?'

'No bother. Just means that we'll have to lower the fuselage down to its previous position. I'm coming around to Van Gelder's view about taking zero chances. I want as much water as possible in this compartment to dissipate the heat of the torches. It'll take a couple of hours, maybe longer, to do the job, but better two or three hours late down here than twenty years early you-know-where.'

Van Gelder said: 'Do I undo those nuts now?'

'No. We're stable enough at the moment. But if the fuselage returns to its previous position of being almost submerged and then the weather blows up – well, I don't think it would be a very clever idea to have an armed atomic mine rolling about all over the shop.'

'I don't think so, either.'

Talbot and Van Gelder were back aboard the *Ariadne* and having coffee in the deserted wardroom when a seaman from the radio-room entered and handed Talbot a message. Talbot read it and handed it to Van Gelder, who read it twice, then looked at his captain with a certain thoughtful surprise.

'Looks as if I have been casting unjust aspersions on the FBI, sir. It further looks as if they do work at night.'

'Even better, it seems as if they have no compunction about waking others, such as bank managers, in the middle of the night and making them work also. One gathers from the message that Andropulos's mysterious friend George Skepertzis, does know the even more mysterious Kyriakos Katzanevakis and Thomas Thompson.'

'If GS deposits one million dollars each in the accounts of KK and TT and has given them smaller sums on previous occasions one gathers that they are more than passing acquaintances. Unfortunately, it seems that the one person who could identify them, the bank clerk who handled the accounts of all three men, had been transferred elsewhere. They say that they are pursuing enquiries, whatever that means.'

'It means, I'm certain, that the FBI are going to drag this unfortunate bank clerk from his bed and have him conduct an identity parade.'

'I find it hard, somehow, to visualize generals and admirals voluntarily consenting to line up for inspection.'

'They won't have to. The FBI or the Pentagon itself is bound to have pictures of them.' Talbot looked out of the window. 'Dawn is definitely in the sky and the rain has eased off to no more than a drizzle – I suggest we contact Heraklion Air Base and ask them if they'll kindly go and have a look for the diving ship *Taormina*.'

Together with the Admiral and the two scientists, Talbot and Van Gelder were just finishing breakfast when a messenger arrived from the *Kilcharran*. Captain Montgomery, he informed them, had just finished enlarging the opening on the top of the bomber's fuselage, was now about to raise the plane again. Would they care to come across? He had made especial mention of Lieutenant-Commander Van Gelder.

'It's not me he wants,' Van Gelder said. 'It's my trusty stilson wrench. As if he doesn't have a dozen aboard.'

'I wouldn't miss this,' Hawkins said. He looked at Benson and Wickram. 'I'm sure you gentlemen wouldn't want to miss this either. It will, after all, be a historic moment when, for the first time in history, they drop a live atomic mine on the deck of a ship.'

'You have a problem, Captain Montgomery?' the Admiral asked. Montgomery, winch stopped, was leaning over the guard-rail and looking down at the fuselage which had been raised to its previous position with its cargo deck just above the level of the sea. 'You look a mite despondent.'

215

'I am not looking despondent, Admiral. I am looking thoughtful. The next step is to hoist the bomb from the plane. After that, we have to load it aboard the *Angelina*. And then the *Angelina* sails away. Correct?' Hawkins nodded and Montgomery wet his forefinger and held it up. 'To sail away you require wind. Unfortunately and most inconveniently, the Meltemi has died completely.'

'It has, hasn't it?' Hawkins said. 'Most inconsiderate, I must say. Well, if we manage to get the bomb aboard the *Angelina* without blowing ourselves to smithereens we'll just tow it away.'

'How will we do that, sir?' Van Gelder said.

'The *Ariadne*'s whaler. Not the engine, of course. We row.'

'How do we know that the cunning little brain of this explosive device can differentiate between the repeated creaking of oars and the pulse of an engine? After all, sir, it is primarily an acoustic device.'

'Then we'll go back to the naval days of yore. Muffled oars.'

'But the *Angelina* displaces between eighty and a hundred tons, sir. Even with the best will and the strongest backs in the world it wouldn't be possible to make as much as one nautical mile in an hour. And that's with men continuously pulling with all their strength. Even the strongest, fittest and most highly trained racing crews – Oxford, Cambridge, Thames Tideway – approach complete exhaustion after twenty minutes. Not being Oxbridge Blues, our limit would probably be nearer ten minutes. Half a nautical mile, if we're lucky. And then, of course, the periods between successive onsets of exhaustion would become progressively shorter. Cumulative effects, if you follow me, sir. A quarter of a mile an hour. It's close on a hundred miles to the Kásos Strait. Even assuming they can row night and day, which they can't, and discounting the possibility of heart attacks, it's going to take them at least a fortnight to get to the Kásos Strait.'

'When it comes to comfort and encouragement,' Hawkins said, 'I couldn't ask for a better man to have around. Bubbling over with optimism. Professor Wotherspoon, you live and sail in these parts. What's your opinion?'

'It's been an unusual night, but this is a perfectly normal morning. Zero wind. The Etesian wind – the Meltemi as they call it in these parts – starts up around about noon. Comes from the north or north-west.'

'What if the wind comes from the south or south-west instead?' Van Gelder said. 'It would be impossible for the rowers to make any headway against it. The reverse, rather. Can't you just picture it, the *Angelina* being driven on to the rocks of Santorini?'

'Job's comforter,' Hawkins said. 'Would it be too much to ask you kindly to cease and desist?'

'Not Job, sir, nor his comforter. I see myself more in the role of Cassandra.'

217

'Why Cassandra?'

'Beautiful daughter of Priam, King of Troy,' Denholm said. 'The prophecies of the princess, though always correct, were decreed by Apollo never to be believed.'

'I'm not much of a one for Greek mythology,' Montgomery said. 'Had it been a leprechaun or a brownie, now, I might have listened. As it is, we have work to do. Mr Danforth —' this to his chief officer '— detail half-a-dozen men, a dozen, to haul the *Angelina* round to our port quarter. Once the bomb has been removed we can pull the fuselage for'ard and the *Angelina* can then move for'ard in her turn to take its place.'

Under Montgomery's instructions, the derrick hook was detached from the lifting ring and the derrick itself angled slightly aft until the hook dangled squarely over the centre of the rectangular opening that had been cut in the fuselage. Montgomery, Van Gelder and Carrington descended the companionway to the top of the fuselage, Van Gelder with his stilson, Carrington with two adjustable rope grommets to which were attached two slender lengths of line, one eight feet in length, the other perhaps four times as long. Van Gelder and Carrington lowered themselves into the cargo bay and slipped and secured the grommets over the tapered ends of the mine while Montgomery remained above guiding the winch driver until the lifting fork was located precisely over the centre of the mine. The hook was lowered until it was four feet above the mine.

None of the eight securing clamp nuts offered more than a token resistance to Van Gelder's stilson and as each clamp came free Carrington tightened or loosened the pressure on the two shorter ropes which had been attached to the hook. Within three minutes the atomic mine was free of all restraints that had attached it to the bulkhead and floor of the cargo bay and in less than half that time it had been winched upwards, slowly and with painstaking care, until it was clear of the plane's fuselage. The two longer ropes attached to the grommets were thrown up on to the deck of the *Kilcharran*, where they were firmly held to ensure that the mine was kept in a position precisely parallel to the hull of the ship.

Montgomery climbed aboard and took over the winch. The mine was hoisted until it was almost level with the ship's deck and then, by elevating the angle of the derrick, carefully brought alongside until it was resting against the rubber-cushioned sides of the *Kilcharran*, a manœuvre that was necessary to ensure that the mine did not snag against the port stays of the foremast of the *Angelina* when that vessel was brought alongside.

It took what seemed like an unconscionably long time – in fact, it took just over half an hour – to bring the *Angelina* alongside. Hauling the plane's fuselage forward to leave space for the lugger had been a quick and simple task, but then, because of the supporting air bags the fuselage was in a state of neutral buoyancy and one man could have accomplished the task with ease. But the Angelina displaced upwards of eighty tons and even the dozen men assigned to the task of towing it found it a laborious task just to get it under way, a difficulty that amply confirmed Van Gelder's assertion that towing it any distance at all by a whaler propelled only by oars was a virtual impossibility. But eventually, brought alongside it was, the mine gently lowered into its prepared cradle and clamped into position.

'Routine,' Montgomery said to Hawkins. If he was experiencing any feelings of relief and satisfaction, and he would have been less than human not to have done, he showed no signs of them. 'Nothing should have gone wrong and nothing did go wrong. All we need now is a tiny puff of wind, the lugger's on her way and all our troubles are over.'

'Maybe all our troubles are just beginning,' Van Gelder said.

Hawkins looked at him suspiciously. 'And what, may we ask, are we expected to gather from that cryptic remark?'

'There is a tiny puff of wind, sir.' Van Gelder wetted a forefinger and held it upwards. 'Unfortunately, it's not from the north-west, it's from the south-east. The beginning, I'm afraid, of what is called the Euros.' Van Gelder had assumed a conversational tone. 'Reading about it last night.

Rare in the summer months but not unknown. I'm sure Professor Wotherspoon will confirm this.' Wotherspoon's unsmiling nod did indeed confirm it. 'Can turn very nasty, very stormy. Gusting up to Force 7 or 8. I can only assume that the radio operators on the *Kilcharran* and the *Ariadne* have – what shall I say? – relaxed their vigilance a bit. Understandable, after what they've been through. Must have been something about it in the weather forecasts. And if this wind increases, and according to the book there is no doubt it will, any attempt to sail or row the *Angelina* anywhere will end up in her banging not against the rocks of Santorini, as I suggested, but against those of Síphinos or Folégandros, which I believe are rather sparsely populated. But if the Euros backs more to the east, which I understand it occasionally does, then it would bang into Mílos. Five thousand people on Mílos. So it says in the book.'

'I speak with restraint, Van Gelder,' Hawkins said. 'I don't exactly see myself in the role of an ancient Roman Emperor but you do know what happened to messengers who brought bad news to them?'

'They got their head chopped off. "Twas ever thus, sir. A prophet hath no honour in his own country."'

Bearers of bad news were having a hard time of it on both sides of the Atlantic that morning.

*　　*　　*

221

The President of the United States was no longer a young man and at half past five on that morning in the Oval Office he was showing every year of his age. The lines of care and concern were deeply entrenched in his face and the skin, beneath the permanent tan, had a greyish tinge to it. But he was alert enough and his eyes were as clear as could be expected of an elderly man who had had no sleep whatsoever that night.

'I am beginning, gentlemen, to feel almost as sorry for myself and ourselves as I am for those unfortunates in Santorini.' The 'gentlemen' he was addressing were the Chairman of the Joint Chiefs of Staff, Richard Hollison of the FBI, John Heiman, the Defense Secretary, and Sir John Travers, the British Ambassador. 'I suppose I should, in all decency, apologize for bringing you all together at this unearthly hour of the morning, but, frankly, I have no decency left in me. I'm right at the undisputed top of my self-pity list.' He rifled some papers on his desk. 'Admiral Hawkins and his men are sitting on top of a ticking time-bomb and it seems that nature and circumstances are conspiring to thwart their every attempt to rid themselves of this canker in their midst. With his latest report I had thought that I had reached the ultimate nadir. Inevitably, I was wrong.' He looked sorrowfully at the deputy head of the FBI. 'You had no right to do this to me, Richard.'

'I am sorry about that, Mr President.' Hollison may well have meant what he said but the sorrow was completely masked by the expression and tone of bitter anger. 'It's not just bad news or damnably bad news, it's shattering news. Shattering for you, shattering for me, most of all shattering for the General. I still can hardly bring myself to believe it.'

'I might be prepared to believe it,' Sir John Travers said, 'and might well be prepared to be shattered along with the rest of you. If, that is, I had the slightest idea what you are talking about.'

'And *I* am sorry about that,' the President said. 'We have not really been remiss, there just hasn't been time yet. Richard, the Ambassador has not yet read the relevant documents. Could you put him in the picture, please?'

'That shouldn't take too long. It's a most damnably ugly picture, Sir John, because it reflects badly – just how badly it's only now beginning to dawn on me – on both Americans in general and the Pentagon in particular.

'The central figure in the scenario, of whom you have of course heard, is a certain Adamantios Spyros Andropulos who is rapidly emerging as an international criminal of staggering proportions. As you know, he is at present being held aboard the frigate *Ariadne*. He is an exceptionally wealthy man – I'm talking merely of hundreds of millions of dollars, it could be billions for all I so far know – and he has money, laundered money under false names, hidden away in various deposit accounts all over the world. Marcos of the Philippines and Duvalier of Haiti are, or were, rather good at this sort of thing, but they're being found out, they should have employed a real expert like Andropulos.'

'He can't be all that expert, Richard,' Sir John said. 'You've found out about him.'

'A chance in a million, a break that comes to a law agency once in a lifetime. In any but the most exceptional and extraordinary circumstances he would have taken the secret to the grave with him. And I didn't find out about him – there is no possible way I ever could have done – and no credit whatsoever attaches to us. That he was found out is due entirely to two things – an extraordinary stroke of luck and an extraordinary degree of astuteness by those aboard the *Ariadne*. I have, incidentally, have had cause to revise my earlier – and I must admit prejudiced and biased opinion of Admiral Hawkins. He insists that none of the credit belongs to him but to the captain and two of his officers aboard the *Ariadne*. It takes quite a man to insist on that sort of thing.

'Among his apparently countless worldwide deposits Andropulos had tucked away eighteen million dollars in a Washington bank through an intermediary or nominee by the name of George Skepertzis. This nominee had transferred over a million dollars apiece to the accounts of two men registered in the bank as Thomas Thompson and Kyriakos Katzanevakis. The names, inevitably, are fictitious – no such people exist. The only bank clerk who could identify all three men, inasmuch as he was the person who had handled all three accounts, had left the bank. We tracked him down – he was understandably a bit upset about being dragged out of his bed at midnight – and showed him a group of photographs. Two of them he recognized immediately but none of the photographs remotely resembled the man going by the name of George Skepertzis.

'But he was able to give us some additional – and very valuable – information about Skepertzis, who seemed to have taken him into some limited degree of confidence. No reason why he shouldn't, of course – Skepertzis has – had – every reason to believe that his tracks were completely covered. This was approximately two months ago. He wanted to know about the banking facilities in certain specified towns in the United States and Mexico. The bank clerk – his name is Bradshaw – gave him what information he could. It took Bradshaw about a week to find out the details Skepertzis wanted. I should imagine that he was well rewarded for his labours although, of course, Bradshaw didn't say so. There were no criminal charges that we could have laid against him for that – not that we would, even if we could have.

'Bradshaw provided our agent with the names and addresses of the banks concerned. We checked those against two lists regarding Andropulos's banking activities that we had just received from the *Ariadne* and Greek Intelligence – a third, if you count Interpol. Skepertzis had made enquiries about banks in five cities and, lo and behold and to nobody's surprise, all five also appeared on the lists concerning Andropulos.

'We instituted immediate enquiries. Bankers – especially senior banking officials – have profound objections to being woken in the middle of the night but among our eight thousand FBI agents in those United States we have some very tough and persistent individuals who are also very good at putting the fear of God into even the most law-abiding citizens. And we have some very good friends in Mexico. It turns out that friend Skepertzis has bank accounts in all five cities. All under his own name.'

'You're ahead of me here,' the President said. 'This is news to me. When did you find this out?'

'Just over half an hour ago. I'm sorry, Mr President, but there just hasn't been the time to confirm everything and tell you until now. In two of those banks – in Mexico City and San Diego – we struck gold. In each of those banks close on three-quarters of a million dollars have been transferred to the accounts of a certain Thomas Thompson and a certain Kyriakos Katzanevakis. It's a measure of those two gentlemen's belief in their immunity to investigation that they hadn't even bothered to change their names. Not that that would have mattered in the long run – not after we had got around to circulating photographs. One final point of interest. Two weeks ago the bank in Mexico City received a draft of two million dollars in favour of George Skepertzis from a reputable or supposedly reputable, bank in Damascus, Syria. A week later exactly the same amount was transferred to a certain Philip Trypanis in Greece. We have the name of the Athens bank and have asked Greek Intelligence to find out who or what Trypanis is or for whom he is fronting. A cent gets a hundred dollars that it is a pal of Andropulos.'

A silence ensued, a silence that was long and profound and more than a little gloomy. It was the President himself who finally broke it.

'A stirring tale, is it not, Sir John?'

'Stirring, indeed. Richard had the right term for it – shattering.'

'But – well, have you no questions?'

'No.'

The President looked at him in near disbelief. 'Not even one little question?'

'Not even one, Mr President.'

'But surely you must want to know the identities of Thompson and Katzanevakis?'

'I don't want to know. If we must refer to them at all I'd rather just refer to them as the general and the admiral.' He looked at Hollison. 'That would be about right, Richard?'

'I'm afraid so. A general and an admiral. Your Admiral Hawkins, Sir John, is smarter than your average bear.'

'I would agree. But you have to be fair to yourselves. He had access to information that you hadn't had until now. I, too, have an advantage that you people lack. You're deep in the middle of the wood. I'm on the outside looking in.

'Two things, gentlemen. As a representative of Her Majesty's Government I am bound to report any developments of significance to the Foreign Office and Cabinet. But if I specifically lack certain information, such as specific names, then I can't very well report them, can I? We ambassadors have the power to exercise a very wide range of discretion. In this particular instance, I choose to exercise that discretion.

'The second point is that you all seem convinced – there appears to be a certain doom-laden certainty about this – that this affair, this top-level treason, if you will, is bound to become public knowledge. I have one simple question. Why?'

'Why? Why?' The President shook his head as if bemused or stunned by the naïveté of the question. 'God damn it, Sir John, it's bound to come out. It's inevitable. How else are we going to explain things away? If we are at fault, if we are the guilty party, we must in all honesty openly confess to that guilt. We must stand up and be counted.'

'We have been friends for some years now, Mr President. Friends are allowed to speak openly?'

'Of course, of course.'

'Your sentiments, Mr President, do you the greatest possible credit but hardly reflect what, fortunately or unfortunately, goes on in the more rarefied strata of international diplomacy. I am not speaking of deception and deviousness, I *am* referring to what is practical and politic. It's bound to come out, you say. Certainly it will – but only if the President of the United States decides that it must. How, you ask, are we going to explain things away? Simple. We don't. You give me one valid reason why we should move this matter into the realm of the public domain or, as you appear to suggest, make a clean breast of things, and I'll give you half a dozen reasons – reasons equally valid if not more so – why we shouldn't.' Sir John paused as if to marshal his facts but was, in fact, merely waiting for one of the four intent listeners to voice an objection: he had already marshalled his facts.

'I think, Mr President, that it might do us no harm to hear what Sir John as to say.' Hollison smiled. 'Who knows, we might even learn something. As the senior ambassador of a vastly experienced Foreign Office, it seems likely that Sir John must have gained some little expertise along the way.'

'Thank you, Richard. Bluntly and undiplomatically, Mr President, you have a duty not to speak out. There is nothing whatsoever to be gained, and a very great deal to be lost. At best you will be hanging out a great deal of dirty washing in public and all to no avail, to no purpose: at worst, you will be providing invaluable ammunition for your enemies. Such open and, if I may say so, ill-advised confession will achieve at best an absolute zero and at worst a big black minus for you, the Pentagon and the citizens of America. The Pentagon, I am sure, is composed of honourable men. Sure, it may have its quota of the misguided, the incompetent, even the downright stupid: name me any large and powerful bureaucratic élite that has never had such a quota. All that matters, finally and basically, is that they *are* honourable men and I see no earthly justification for dragging the reputations of honourable men through the dust because we have discovered two rotten apples at the bottom of the barrel.

'You yourself, Mr President, are in an even worse position. You have devoted a considerable deal of your presidential time to combating terrorism in every shape and form. How will it look to the world if it comes out that two senior members of your armed forces have been actively engaged in promoting terrorism for material gain? You may hardly know the two gentlemen concerned but they will, of course, be elevated to the status of highly trusted aides, and that's just looking on the bright side. On the dark side, you will not only be accused of harbouring men who are engaged in terrorism but of aiding, abetting and inciting them to new levels of terrorism. Can't you just see the headlines smeared across the front pages of the tabloids and yellow press throughout the world? By the time they have finished with you, you will be remembered in history for one thing and one thing only, the ultimate byword for hypocrisy, the allegedly noble and high-principled president who had spent his life in encouraging and promoting the one evil he had sworn to destroy. Throughout the countries of the world that dislike or fear America because of its power, authority and wealth – and that, like it or not, means most countries – your reputation would lie in tatters. Because of your exceptionally high level of popularity in your own country you will survive but I hardly think that that consideration would affect you: what would and should affect you is that your campaign against terrorism would be irrevocably destroyed. No phoenix would arise from those particular ashes. As a world force for justice and decency you would be a spent man. To put it in the most undiplomatic terms, sir, to go ahead as you propose to do you'd have to be more than slightly off your rocker.'

The President stared into the middle distance for quite some time, then said in a voice that was almost plaintive: 'Does anyone else think I'm off my rocker?'

'Nobody thinks you're off your rocker, Mr President,' the General said. 'Least of all, I would say, Sir John here. He is merely saying what our unfortunately absent Secretary of State would advocate if he were here. Both gentlemen are high on pragmatism and cold logic and low on unconsidered and precipitate action. Maybe I'm not the ideal person to be passing judgement on this issue. I would obviously be delighted if whatever reputation the Pentagon has survives intact, but I do feel most strongly that, before jumping off the top of the Empire State or whatever one should give some thought to the fatal and irrevocable consequences.'

'I can only nod emphatic agreement,' John Heiman, the Defense Secretary said. 'If I may mix up two metaphors – if I am mixing them – we have only two options. We can let sleeping dogs lie or let slip the dogs of war. Sleeping dogs never harmed anyone but the dogs of war are an unpredictable bunch. Instead of biting the enemy they may well turn, in this case almost certainly would turn, and savage us.'

The President looked at Hollison. 'Richard?'

'You're in the card-game of your life, Mr President. You've got only one trump and it's marked "Silence".'

'So it's four to one, is it?'

'No, Mr President,' Heiman said, 'it's not and you know it. It's five to zero.'

'I suppose, I suppose.' The President ran a weary hand across his face. 'And how do we propose to mount this massive display of silence, Sir John?'

'Sorry, Mr President, but not me. If I am asked for my opinions I am not, as you have seen, slow to give them. But I know the rules and one of them is that I cannot be a party to formulating the policy of a sovereign state. Decisions are for you and for what is, in effect, your war cabinet here.'

A messenger entered and handed a slip of paper to the president. 'Dispatch from the *Ariadne*, Mr President.'

'I don't have to brace myself for this,' the President said. 'As far as dispatches from the *Ariadne* are concerned, I am permanently braced. Some day I'll get some good news from that ship.' He read the message. 'But not, of course, this time. "Atomic mine removed from cargo bay of bomber and safely transferred to sailing vessel *Angelina*." Excellent news as far as it goes, but then: "Unexpected 180 degree change in wind course makes sailing departure impossible. Anticipated delay three to six hours. Hydrogen weapons from plane's cargo bay being transferred to diving ship *Kilcharran*. Expect to complete transfer by nightfall." End of message. Well, where does that leave us?'

Sir John Travers said: 'It leaves you, Mr President, with a few hours' breathing space.'

'Meaning?'

'Masterly inactivity. Nothing that can be profitably done at the moment. I am merely thinking out loud.' He looked at the Chairman of the Joint Chiefs of Staff. 'Tell me, General, do those two gentlemen in the Pentagon know they are under suspicion? Correction. Do they know that you have proof of their treason?'

'No. And I agree with what you are about to say. No point will be served by acquainting them with that fact at the present moment.'

'None. With the President's permission, I would like to retire and ponder the problems of state and international diplomacy. With the aid of a pillow.'

The President smiled one of his increasingly rare smiles.

'What a splendid suggestion. I also shall do exactly that. It's close on six now, gentlemen. May I suggest that we foregather again at ten-thirty a.m.?'

At 2.30 that afternoon Van Gelder, message sheet in hand, joined Talbot on the bridge of the *Ariadne*.

'Radio from Heraklion, sir. Seems that a Phantom of the Greek Air Force located the diving ship *Taormina* less than ten minutes after taking off from base. It was just east of Avgó Island, which the chart tells me is about forty miles north-east of Heraklion. Very conveniently positioned to break through the Kásos Strait.'

'What direction was it headed?'

'No direction. Having no wish to raise any suspicion the Greek pilot didn't hang around but he reports that the *Taormina* was stopped in the water.'

'Lurking. Lurking, one wonders, for what. Speaking of lurking, what's Jimmy doing at the moment?'

'Last seen, he was lurking with two young ladies in the wardroom. No dereliction of duty, I assure you. The three A's have retired, to their cabins, presumably for the afternoon. The girls report a far from subtle change in their behaviour. They have stopped discussing the predicament they find themselves in, in fact they have stopped discussing anything. They appear unusually calm, relaxed and not very concerned about anything, which may mean that they have philosophically resigned themselves to whatever fate may hold in store or they may have made up their minds about some plan of action, although what that could be I couldn't even begin to imagine.'

'What would your guess be, Vincent?'

'A plan of action. I know it's only the slenderest of clues but it's just possible that they may be resting up this afternoon because they don't expect to be doing much resting during the coming night.'

'I have the oddest feeling that we won't be doing much resting ourselves tonight.'

'Aha! The second sight, sir? Your non-existent Scottish blood clamouring for recognition.'

'When it clamours a bit more, I'll let you know. I just keep wondering about Jenkins's disappearance.' A phone rang and Talbot picked it up. 'A message for the Admiral from the Pentagon? Bring it here.' Talbot hung up and gazed out through the for'ard screens of the bridge. The *Angelina*, to protect it from the buffeting of the four-foot-high waves generated by the now very brisk Euros wind from the south-east, had been moved to a position where it lay snugly in the still waters between the bows of the *Ariadne* and the stern of the *Kilcharran*.

'Speaking of the Pentagon, it's only an hour since we told them that we expected the unloading of the hydrogen missiles to be completed by nightfall. And what do we have? A Force 6 and the plane's fuselage streamed out a cable length to the north-west. Lord only knows when the unloading will be finished now. Do you think we should so inform them?'

'I should think not, sir. The President of the United States is a much older man than we are and the kind of cheery communications he has been receiving from the *Ariadne* of late can't be doing his heart any good.'

'I suppose you're right. Ah, thank you, Myers.'

'Bloody funny signal if you ask me, sir. Can't make head nor tail of it.'

'These things are sent to try us.' Talbot waited till Myers had left, then read out the signal.

' "Identity of cuckoos in the nest established. Irrefutable proof that they are linked to your generous benefactor friend. Sincerest congratulations to Admiral Hawkins and the officers of the *Ariadne*." '

'Recognition at last,' Van Gelder said.

'You are the last to arrive, Sir John,' the President said. 'I have to advise you that we have already made up our minds what to do.'

236

'A very difficult decision, I assume, Mr President. Probably the most difficult you have ever been called upon to make.'

'It has been. Now that the decision is made and is irrevocable, you can no longer be accused of meddling with the affairs of a sovereign state. What would you have done, Sir John?'

'Perfectly straightforward. Exactly what you have done. No one is to be informed except two people and those two people are to be informed that the President has suspended them indefinitely from duty, pending the investigation of allegations and statements that have been laid against them.'

'Well, damn your eyes, Sir John.' The President spoke without heat. 'Instead of sleeping all the time I spent a couple of hours wrestling with my conscience to arrive at the same conclusion.'

'It was inevitable, sir. You had no option. And I would point out that it's easy enough for us to arrive at decisions. You, and only you, can give the executive order.'

'I will not insult your intelligence by asking if you are aware what this executive order means.'

'I am perfectly aware of what it means. Now that my opinion is no longer called for I have no hesitation in saying that I would have done exactly the same thing. It is a death sentence and it can be no consolation at all that you will not be called upon to carry out, or to order to be carried out, the execution of that death sentence.'

'Manhattan Project?' Admiral Hawkins said. 'What on earth does she mean by "Manhattan Project"?'

'I don't know, sir,' Denholm said. 'Eugenia doesn't know either. She just caught the words as she walked into the wardroom. Only Andropulos, Alexander and Aristotle were there. The phrase was repeated twice and she thought it odd enough – I think it's very odd, too – to pass it on to me. When they became aware of her presence the subject was switched. She said that whatever the nature of the subject was they seemed to find it rather amusing.'

Talbot said: 'Even Alexander was amused?'

'Humour, sir, is not Alexander's forte. Nobody's seen him smile since he came aboard the *Ariadne*, I would doubt if anyone has ever seen him smile. Besides, it was Alexander who was discussing the subject. Maybe he doesn't laugh at his own jokes.'

'I know you know something about those things, Denholm,' Hawkins said. 'Doesn't it suggest anything to you?'

'Zero, sir. The immediate and obvious – far too obvious – connection is the atom bomb. The Manhattan Project, of course, was that immensely long, immensely complicated and immensely expensive project that led to the invention of the atom bomb. "Manhattan" was only a code word. The actual research was carried out in New Mexico and Nevada or thereabouts. I'm sorry, sir, but the significance, the relevance of the phrase in our present situation, quite escapes me.'

'At least I've got company,' Hawkins said. He picked up two slips of paper from his table in the admiral's cabin. 'Those two messages have come in since last we saw you. In this case, I don't think their significance will escape you.'

'Ah! This one from the White House itself. "Two of your philanthropist's beneficiaries are no longer with us. Beneficiary A has been involved in a fatal automobile accident." ' Denholm looked up from the paper. 'Has he now? For Beneficiary A I take it we can read either Admiral X or General Y. Did he fall, did he jump or was he pushed?' He looked at the paper again. 'And I see that Beneficiary B has just disappeared. Again I assume that Beneficiary B was either X or Y. How very inconvenient for them, how very convenient for us.' Denholm looked from Hawkins to

Talbot. 'From the very restrained wording I take it that this news is not to be broadcast from the house-tops.'

'I shouldn't have thought so,' Hawkins said. 'We have already arranged for the coded original to be destroyed.'

'I take it then, sir, that speculation about their abrupt departure is pointless.'

'Indeed. Not only pointless but needless. They have fallen upon their swords. One does not wish to sound cynical nor stand in condemnation but it's probably the only faintly honourable thing they have done for a long time. The second signal, Denholm?'

'The one from Heraklion. Interesting, sir. It seems that the *Taormina*'s last port of call was Tobruk. Furthermore, although it's registered in Panama, it appears to be permanently based in Tobruk. It's more than interesting, it's intriguing, especially considering that that well-known philanthropist sitting in our wardroom seems to have considerable business interests in Tripoli. It's most damnably frustrating, sir.'

'What is?'

'That we haven't a single shred of evidence to adduce against him, far less proof.'

'I have this feeling,' Talbot said, 'that neither evidence nor proof will ever be required. Andropulos will never come to trial.'

Hawkins looked at him for a few thoughtful moments. 'That's the second time you've said that, Captain. You have access to some information that we lack?'

'Not at all, sir. Maybe I've just got blind faith in this blindfolded goddess of justice. You know, the lady who holds the scales in her hands.' Talbot smiled. 'Or maybe, as Van Gelder keeps on hinting, I have some traces of Highland blood in me. Says I'm fey, the second sight or some nonsense like that. Ah, the man himself.'

'A radio message from Greek Intelligence,' Van Gelder said. He proffered the paper he held in hand.

'Just tell me,' Hawkins said. 'Gently. I'm becoming allergic to bad news.'

'Not all that bad, sir. Not for us, at any rate. Says that someone attached to the department for Middle East and North African affairs – they carefully don't give his name, I suppose he's a minister of some sort, I suppose we could find out easily enough but it seems unimportant – took off by government plane on a routine visit to Canea, the town close by the Souda Bay air base. Never got there. But at exactly the time he should have got there a patrolling Greek Mirage spotted a plane very like the one he was flying in – too much of a coincidence for it not to have been the same plane – passing directly over Heraklion.'

'So, of course,' Talbot said, 'you consulted the chart and arrived at the conclusion that he was heading for some place. What place?'

'Tobruk.'

'And you also arrived at the conclusion that he wouldn't be coming back from there?'

'Allowing for the vagaries of human nature, sir, I would not have thought so. Greek Intelligence have also established the fact that the vanishing minister, if minister he was, held an account at the same Athens bank that Philip Trypanis honours with his custom. It would appear, to coin a phrase, that they are now hot on the trail of Mr Trypanis. Whether they nab Mr Trypanis or not hardly seems a matter of concern for us.'

'I would think,' Hawkins said, 'if our philanthropist friend in the wardroom knew of the fate of his pal in government here and those of A and B – or X and Y – in Washington his humour might be in marked abeyance by now. And if he knew that we knew of the *Taormina* and that its home base was Tobruk, he would be downright thoughtful. Was that all, Van Gelder?'

'On that subject, sir, yes. Captain Montgomery, Professor Wotherspoon and I have been discussing the weather.'

'You have?' Hawkins looked at him suspiciously. 'Don't tell me that Cassandra has you in her clutches again?'

'Certainly not, sir. The Euros has died away. Completely. We suspect it will only be a matter of time before the weather returns to normal. A very short time. Latest met. reports confirm that. The *Angelina*, at the present moment, is lying between our ship and the *Kilcharran*, facing north-west. If the Meltemi starts up – also from the north-west, of course – we won't be able to sail her out of her present position. It might be wise to tow her alongside us now.'

'Of course,' Talbot said. 'See to it now, would you, Number One. After that, let us foregather for the last supper.'

Van Gelder looked through the opened doorway. 'It's already getting dark, sir. You don't feel like waiting for the dawn before we take off?'

'Nothing I'd like better than to wait for the dawn. But we have this duty to our fellow man.'

'We have to be brave, noble and self-sacrificing?'

'The sooner we take off, the easier will lie the heads along the Potomac. Not to mention, of course, those on the *Kilcharran* and *Ariadne*.'

Denholm looked from Talbot to Van Gelder. His face registered an expression of near incredulity.

'Am I to understand, Captain, that you and Lieutenant-Commander Van Gelder are sailing on the *Angelina*?'

Talbot shook his head. 'I suppose it had to come to this, Number One. Junior officers questioning our nautical expertise.'

'I don't understand, sir. Why on earth are you and Number One going along on the *Angelina*? I mean –'

'We are not going along on the *Angelina*. We are taking the *Angelina*. Professor Wotherspoon and his wife are the people who are not going. They

243

don't know that yet, of course. The good Professor is going to be very wroth but it's difficult to please everybody.'

'I see, sir. Yes, I see. I should have guessed. I'd like to come along, sir.'

'Yes and no. You shall come along, but not on the *Angelina*. You will take the launch. You won't start up the engine until we're at least three miles clear. We don't want, you understand, to precipitate any premature big bangs.'

'And then we follow you at that distance?'

'Not so much follow us as circle us at, of course, the same prudent distance of three miles. Your purpose, again, of course, is to ward off and warn off any unsuspecting vessels that come too close.'

'And then help tow you back here?'

'When we've dumped the mine and sailed on a sufficiently safe distance, we'll start the engine and head back. A tow would help. Or perhaps the Admiral will fetch us in the *Ariadne*. We haven't decided yet and at the moment it's not important. But what I'm about to say *is* important.

'You will take along with you Chief Petty Officer McKenzie, Marine Sergeant Brown and Petty Officer Myers to operate the radio. Most importantly, you will also take with you, suitably wrapped in plastic, the krytron detonating device and conceal it well. I suggest under the floor-boards of the wheelhouse. You will instruct Petty Officer Myers to take along the smallest portable transceiver he can lay hands on and conceal it in the same place. Make sure the floorboards are securely nailed down afterwards.'

'May I ask the reason for this excessive secrecy, sir?'

'You may not for the excellent reason that I have no reason to give you. The best I can do is to wave a vague hand and say that I am preparing for unforeseen eventualities. The trouble with the unforeseen is that it is unforeseeable. You understand?'

'I think so, sir.'

'I suggest you go now and alert your crew. And for God's sake don't let anyone see you wandering around with the krytron under your arm.'

Lieutenant Denholm left. Hawkins said: 'There are times, Captain, when I feel I have to say, with regret of course, that the truth is not always with you. I mean the truth, the whole truth and nothing but the truth.'

'I agree, sir,' Van Gelder said. 'Sets a very bad example for junior officers.'

Talbot smiled. 'Be ye as pure as snow ye shall not escape calumny. Something like that. We captains become inured to such injustices. I have the odd feeling – all right, all right, Vincent, let's settle for just a few microscopic traces of Highland blood – that Andropulos is going to be asking the odd casual question at table tonight. I suggest we have Dr Wickram up here.'

*   *   *

Andropulos did indeed have the odd casual question to ask at table that night but he was in no hurry to introduce them. It was not until after they had finished the main course that he said: 'We do not wish to pry, Captain, nor ask questions about purely naval matters which should be none of our concern. But whatever *is* happening surely does concern us, whether directly or indirectly, and we are but human and very, very curious. We can all see that the *Angelina* is alongside with that highly suspect atomic mine lashed down in its cradle on the deck. I thought the intention was to sail it away with all possible speed?'

'We shall be doing just that, Mr Andropulos. In the fullness of time, by which I mean after we've finished dinner. You will not be happy until it is gone?'

'I confess I will feel a considerable degree of relief when I see the *Angelina* disappearing over the horizon, and with a clear sky and an almost full moon we should be able to see just that. Selfish? Cowardly? Maybe, maybe not.' Andropulos sighed. 'I do not see myself in the role of hero.'

'I don't see myself as such. No sensible person does.'

'But, surely – well, that atomic mine is still highly unstable, is it not?'

'I don't think it's quite so highly dangerous as it was. But why ask me? You're sitting next to the expert.'

'Of course. Dr Wickram. How do you see things now, sir?'

'The Captain is right, or I hope he is. The radioactive emanations of the hydrogen missiles, from which of course the atomic mine is now separated, have an extremely limited range. They are no longer affecting the mine which should be now slowly beginning to stabilize itself. But I have to emphasize that it's a slow process.'

'How long will it be before it has fully stabilized itself? By which I mean when will it reach a condition when a passing vessel's engines will have no effect on it?'

'Ah. Well, now.' Wickram's tone was the verbal equivalent of a shrug. 'As I've said, we're in the realms of the unknown, the untested, but I have been making some calculations. Difficult calculations involving some rather advanced mathematics so I won't bother you with those, but my estimate is that the mine should be quite safe in twelve hours at the most. Possibly even in six hours. At a lesser time than that – well, the risk would be unacceptably high.'

'Damn you to hell, Talbot,' Wotherspoon said. His voice was low and controlled but the ivory-knuckled fists showed the depths of his anger. 'It's *my* boat you're talking about. It's not the property of your damned Navy!'

'I am aware of that, Professor, and I'm most damnably sorry about it.' Talbot was with Hawkins,

Wotherspoon and his wife in the admiral's cabin. 'But you are not coming along. Did you honestly imagine that the Royal Navy would idly stand by and let you, civilians, risk your lives for us?' Talbot smiled. 'It's not only our duty but we're getting paid for it.'

'It's not only bloody high-handed, it's piracy! Hijack. That sort of illegal behaviour you're sworn to destroy. You are, of course, prepared to resort to force in order to restrain me.'

'If we have to, yes.' Talbot nodded to the opened, darkened doorway. Wotherspoon turned, caught sight of three large figures half-hidden in the gloom. When he turned back, he was literally speechless with fury. 'It's the last thing we want to do,' Talbot said, 'and it's totally unnecessary.' He let an element of coldness creep into his voice. 'Quite frankly, Wotherspoon, my primary concern is not your welfare. I think you're being most extraordinarily selfish and totally inconsiderate. How long have you been married, Mrs Wotherspoon?'

'How long have –' She tried to smile but her heart wasn't in it. 'Almost six months.'

'Less than six months.' Talbot looked at Wotherspoon without enthusiasm. 'And yet you're willing to expose her to danger and – the chance is very real – to send her to her death because your stiff-necked pride has been wounded. You must be proud of yourself. Do you really want to go, Mrs Wotherspoon?'

'Angelina.' The correction was automatic and this time she did smile almost certainly because of the incongruity of it in the circumstances. 'You put me in an impossible situation.' She paused, then went on quickly: 'No. No, you don't. I *don't* want to go. I don't want James to go either. Delving around in antiquities is our business, not violence and death. Heaven knows I'm no latter-day Amazon and if there are any dragons waiting around to be killed I don't want my husband to be St George. *Please*, James.'

Hawkins spoke for the first time. 'I make no appeal to your emotions, Professor. All I ask you is to put yourself in Commander Talbot's position. I think you would agree it is a pretty impossible one.'

'Yes.' Wotherspoon had unclenched his fists. 'I see that.'

'I think three signals are in order, John,' Hawkins said. The Wotherspoons had left. 'One to the White House, one to General Carson in Rome and one to Rear-Admiral Blyth. The same signal, coded of course, to each. How about "Settled weather with favourable north-west wind. *Angelina* about to sail with armed mine. Transfer of hydrogen missiles from plane to *Kilcharran* continuing smoothly." That should fit the bill?'

'Admirably. It should come as quite a shock to them all.'

'We haven't of late, I must admit, been sending them much in the way of good news.'

A small knot of interested spectators were gathered round the head of the gangway, the foot of which offered easy access to both the stern of the *Angelina*, whose sails were already hoisted, and the bows of the *Ariadne*'s launch. Among the more interested of the spectators was Andropulos.

He turned to Talbot and said: 'How much longer now, Captain?'

'Ten minutes. Thereabouts.'

Andropulos shook his head as if in disbelief. 'And then all our troubles will be over?'

'It's beginning to look that way, isn't it?'

'It is indeed. Tell me, why is the launch there?'

'Simple. It's coming with us.'

'Going with you? I don't understand. Won't the sound of its engines –'

'Maybe trigger off the mine? The launch won't start up until we're at least three miles clear. It will then proceed to circle us, again at a distance of three miles, to warn off any vessels – powered vessels, that is – that threaten to come too close to us. We haven't come this far, Mr Andropulos, to take any chances.'

'The thought, the precaution, never occurred to me. Alas, I fear I will never make a man of action.'

Talbot gave him what Andropulos misinterpreted as a kindly smile. 'One cannot be all things to all men, sir.'

'You are ready to go, Captain?' Hawkins said. He had just joined them.

'A few minutes, sir. Sails are filling rather nicely, aren't they?'

'*You* are going, Captain?' Andropulos seemed a trifle disconcerted.

'Certainly. I've always rather fancied myself as the skipper of an Aegean lugger. You seem rather surprised, Mr Andropulos?'

'I am. Rather, I was. But not now.' He looked down to the deck of the *Angelina* where Van Gelder was adjusting a halyard on the foresail. 'And of course, inevitably, Lieutenant-Commander Van Gelder. Hand-picked men, eh, Captain? Hand-picked by yourself, of course. I congratulate you. I also salute you. I suspect that this is a much more dangerous mission than you have led us to understand, a mission so perilous that you have chosen not to delegate some members of your crew to carry it out.'

'Nonsense, Mr Andropulos. You exaggerate. Well, Admiral, we're off. Taking a median estimate on Dr Wickram's time limits we should be disposing of this mine in nine hours' time – six a.m. tomorrow. If the wind holds – there's no guarantee that it will, of course – we'll be well on our way to the Kásos Strait by then.'

Hawkins nodded. 'And with luck – although I don't see why the factor luck should enter into it – we should be picking you up in the early afternoon tomorrow. We shall remain with Captain

251

Montgomery until he has finished loading the hydrogen missiles and until the destroyer I've radioed for comes to pick him up and escort him to Thessalonika. That should be between nine and ten in the morning. Then we'll come looking for you.' He turned his head. 'You're off, Mr Andropulos? I should have thought you would have remained to witness this rather historic moment.'

'I intend to do just that. I also intended to record this historic moment. I go to fetch my trusty Leica. Well, Lieutenant Denholm's trusty Leica. He lent it to me less than an hour ago.'

Talbot chatted briefly with Hawkins, said his goodbye, climbed down the gangway, had a brief word with Denholm on the launch and then boarded the *Angelina*. Van Gelder had already pulled in and coiled the bow rope. Talbot stooped over the cleat on the poop-deck to do the same with the stern rope when he became aware of a certain commotion and exclamations about his head. He straightened and looked up.

Andropulos had made his reappearance not with his trusty Leica but with what was probably an equally trusty and much more unpleasant Navy Colt .44, the muzzle of which was pressed against the temple of a plainly terrified Angelina Wotherspoon. Behind him loomed Alexander and Aristotle, both men similarly armed and both with the muzzles of their pistols similarly pointed at temples, those of Irene Charial and her friend Eugenia, neither of whom looked any happier

252

than Angelina, which was to say that they looked very unhappy indeed. Having a pistol grinding into one's temple is an unpleasant sensation for even the most hardened: for three young ladies whose nearest previous approach to violence must have been the printed page or some of the less-regarded TV psycho-dramas the effect must have been traumatic.

'Don't cast off quite yet, Captain,' Andropulos said. 'We're coming with you.'

'What in God's name is the meaning of this devilry?' Hawkins's expression reflected an equal degree of shock and anger. 'Have you taken leave of your senses?'

'We have not taken leave of our senses. We are just taking leave of you.'

'I don't understand,' Hawkins said, 'I just don't understand. This is the way you repay us for having saved your lives and offered you every hospitality?'

'We thank you both for your care and your kindness. However, we have no wish to overstay our welcome or impose upon you further.' He jabbed Angelina's temple with a force that made her gasp with pain. 'After you, Mrs Wotherspoon.'

The six of them descended the gangway in succession and boarded the *Angelina*. Andropulos transferred the attention of his Colt from Angelina to Talbot and Van Gelder.

'Nothing rash or heroic or gallant, if you please,' Andropulos said. 'Especially gallant. It could only have the most distressing consequences, both for you and the three young ladies.'

'Is this a joke?' Talbot said.

'Ah! Do I detect a certain loss of composure, a crack in the monolithic calm? If I were you, Captain, I would not take me for a joker.'

'I don't.' Talbot made no attempt to conceal his bitterness. 'I took you for a wealthy businessman and a man of honour. I took you at your face value. I suppose we all learn from our mistakes.'

'You are too late to learn from this mistake. You are correct in one respect – I freely confess to being a wealthy businessman. A very wealthy one. As to the second charge?' He shrugged his indifference. 'Honour is in the eye of the beholder. Let us not waste time. Instruct this young man –' Denholm standing in the bows of the launch was less than six feet away '– to follow his orders precisely. The orders, I understand, that you have given him, Captain. That is, not to start his engines until we have put three miles away from him and then to circle us, at that same distance, to fend off unwanted intruders.'

'Lieutenant Denholm understands his orders perfectly clearly.'

'In which case, cast off.'

The wind was fresh, but not strong, and it took the *Angelina* quite some time to overcome its initial inertia and reach a speed of three or four knots. Slowly the *Ariadne* dropped astern and after fifteen minutes it was at least a mile distant.

'Excellent,' Andropulos said. 'Rather gratifying, is it not, when things go exactly according to plan.' There was no hint of undue satisfaction in his voice. 'Tell me, Commander Talbot, would you believe me when I say that I am genuinely fond, very fond, of my niece and her friend Eugenia and might even come to regard Mrs Wotherspoon in the same light?'

'I don't know why I should believe you and I don't see why it should concern me. It could be.'

'And would you believe me when I say I wouldn't harm a hair of their heads.'

'I'm afraid I do.'

'Afraid?'

'Others wouldn't believe it, or wouldn't know whether to believe it or not. Which makes them perfect hostages.'

'Exactly. I don't need to say that they will come to no harm in my hands.' He looked thoughtfully at Talbot. 'You are singularly incurious as to the reasons for my conduct.'

'I am very curious. But one does not become a wealthy businessman by engaging in idle tittle-tattle. If I were to ask you, you would tell me exactly what you wanted to tell me. No more, no less.'

'How very true. Now, a different point entirely. The three young ladies pose absolutely no threat to me. You and Van Gelder are a very different kettle of fish. My two friends and I regard you as highly dangerous individuals. We think you are capable of concocting devious and cunning plans and using a great deal of violence in putting those plans to the test – if, that is, you thought there was the slightest chance of success. You will understand, therefore, that we will have to immobilize you. I will remain by the wheel here. You two gentlemen, accompanied by the three ladies, will proceed to the saloon where Aristotle who, as you will readily understand, is very good at knots, will tie you hand and foot, while Alexander, who is every bit as proficient with a gun as Aristotle is with ropes, will ensure that proceedings are conducted in a peaceful fashion.'

Hawkins was bent over Professor Wotherspoon who was lying half propped-up on a sofa in the wardroom. Wotherspoon, dazed and making odd choking noises that were part way between moans and curses, was struggling to open his eyes. Finally, with the aid of his fingers, he managed to do just that.

'What the hell has happened?' The watchers had to strain to catch his words, which were no more than an asthmatic croak. 'Where am I?'

'Take this.' Hawkins put an arm around his shoulders and a glass of brandy to his lips. Wotherspoon sipped, gagged, then drained the contents.

'What *has* happened?'

'You've been banged over the back of the head,' Grierson said, 'and not lightly, either. "Sapped", I believe, is the current term. By the butt of the revolver, I should guess.'

Wotherspoon struggled to a sitting position. 'Who?'

'Andropulos,' Hawkins said. 'Or one of his criminal friends. Some more brandy is in order, Doctor?'

'Normally, no,' Grierson said. 'In this case, yes. I know the back of your head must hurt badly, Professor, but don't touch it. Bruised, bleeding, puffy but no fracture.'

'Andropulos has hijacked your vessel,' Hawkins said. 'Along, of course, with the atomic mine. He has also taken hostages.'

Wotherspoon nodded and winced at the pain it caused him. 'My wife, of course, is one of them.'

'I am sorry. Along with Irene Charial and her friend Eugenia. There was no way we could stop them.'

'Did you try?'

'Would you have tried if you saw the barrel of a Colt screwing into your wife's temple? And two other guns screwed into the temples of the two other ladies?'

'I hardly think so.' Wotherspoon shook his head. 'I'm trying to come to terms with the situation. With a head like an over-ripe pumpkin about to burst, it's not easy. Talbot and Van Gelder. What's happened to them?'

'We don't know, of course. Clapped in irons, handcuffed or some such, I should imagine.'

'Or permanently disposed of. What in God's name is behind all this, Admiral? Do you think this fellow Andropulos has gone off his rocker?'

'By his own standards, he's probably under the impression that he's perfectly sane. We have every reason to believe that he is a long-term and highly professional criminal operating on a hitherto unprecedented international scale. Terrorism and drugs would appear to be his forte. There is no time to go into that at the moment. The immediate point is that Lieutenant Denholm is very shortly leaving in the launch to follow them. Do you feel up to accompanying him?'

'Follow them? Board and capture them? I should say.'

'As you as much as said yourself, Professor, your mind isn't yet firing on all cylinders. If the launch were to go within a couple of miles of the *Angelina* its engine beat would probably detonate the atomic mine.'

'As you say, I'm not at my best. But if you have any spare rifles or pistols there would be no harm in taking them along. Just in case.'

'There will be no firearms. If there were to be any exchange of fire you know where the first bullet would lodge, don't you?'

'Yes. You do put things so nicely. Less than an hour ago you were prepared to restrain me at all costs. You seem to have changed your mind, Admiral.'

'It's not my mind that has changed. It's the circumstances.'

'A rapid change in circumstances,' the President said, 'does give one a rather more balanced view of life. I wouldn't go so far as to say that I enjoyed that lunch, but then, a couple of hours ago I didn't expect or wish to have any today. Although the memory of the treachery will be with us for a long time one has to admit that the discreet if tragic settlement of the Pentagon question removes a major burden of worry. But that was only a local and, let us confess it, a basically selfish concern.' He waved the paper he held in his hand. 'This, of course, is what matters. The good ship *Angelina*, with this damned bomb aboard, is heading steadily south-east and with every second that passes it is putting another yard – or is it two? – between itself and all the horrors of Santorini. It is not too much to say, gentlemen, that a holocaust of unimaginable proportions has been averted.' He raised his glass. 'I give you a toast, Sir John. The Royal Navy.'

The President had barely returned his glass to the table when a messenger entered. The President glanced at him briefly, looked away, then looked at him again. All traces of satisfaction drained from his face.

'Bad news, Johnson?'

'I'm afraid so, Mr President.'

'The worst? The very worst?'

'Not the very worst. But bad enough.'

The President took the message, read it in silence, then looked up and said: 'I'm afraid our celebrations have been rather premature. The *Angelina* has been hijacked.'

Nobody repeated the word 'hijacked'. Nobody said anything. There didn't seem to be anything to say.

'Message reads: "*Angelina* and armed mine hijacked by Andropulos and two criminal associates. Five hostages taken – Commander Talbot, Lieutenant-Commander Van Gelder and three ladies, one of whom is Andropulos's niece. Physically impossible for *Angelina* to return to area so major danger no longer exists. Will keep you posted hourly. Our major and only concern now recovery of hostages." '

'Dear me, dear me,' Sir John said. 'This *is* distressing. Both ominous and confusing. Here we have this madman – or genius, who knows how much truth there is in the old maxim that they are the two sides of the same coin – loose in the Levant with an armed atomic mine aboard. Does he know that it's armed? One rather suspects he doesn't. Where have the three ladies suddenly appeared from and what were they doing aboard one of Her Majesty's frigates in the first place? Why, of all improbabilities, should this villain elect to kidnap his own niece? And why, not to mention how, did this same villain kidnap the captain of the frigate and one of his senior officers? And where, in the name of all that's holy, does he hope to sail his ship, cargo and prisoners, when he must know that every ship and plane in NATO will be searching for him? But he does so hope. That is obvious. His long and spectacularly successful criminal career, undetected until now, proves that he is a devious, cunning and brilliant operator. He has another scheme in mind. Not a man, as we have now learnt to our cost and should have known from his record, to be underestimated. A villain, indeed, but a very resourceful villain.'

'Indeed,' the President said. 'One can only hope that Commander Talbot proves to be even more resourceful.'

'I have the uncomfortable feeling,' Sir John said, 'that at the present moment Talbot is in no position to prove anything.'

10

On the hour of midnight, Eastern Mediterranean time, Commander Talbot was in no position to prove anything and, judging from his uncomfortable position on a sofa in the *Angelina*'s saloon, with his ankles lashed together and his hands bound behind his back, it didn't seem that he would be in a position to prove anything for quite some time to come. Van Gelder, equally uncomfortable at the other end of the sofa, was in no better case. Aristotle, with a wholly unnecessary pistol held loosely across his knee, was seated very comfortably indeed in a large armchair facing the sofa. The three ladies were in smaller armchairs towards the after end of the saloon and didn't look at all comfortable. They hadn't exchanged a word for upwards of two hours. There didn't seem to be much to talk about and all three, understandably enough, were preoccupied with their own thoughts.

Talbot said: 'Tell Andropulos I want to speak to him.'

'Do you now?' Aristotle lowered the glass from which he had been sipping. 'You are not in a position, Captain, to give orders to anyone.'

'Would you kindly present my compliments to the captain and say I would like to talk to him.'

'That is better.' Aristotle rose, crossed to the short flight of steps leading up to the wheelhouse and said something in Greek. Andropulos appeared almost at once. He, too, was needlessly armed. There was a relaxed and confident, even cheerful, air about him.

'When you were aboard my ship,' Talbot said, 'we catered for your every desire. Whatever you wanted, you had but to ask. I wish I could say the same for Greek hospitality. Well, your version of it.'

'I think I take your point. It can't be easy for you to lie there and watch Aristotle steadily lowering the level in a bottle of retsina. You are thirsty?'

'Yes.'

'That's easily remedied.'

In very short order, Aristotle had their bonds quickly and skilfully re-arranged, with Talbot's left wrist and Van Gelder's right loosely but securely attached to each other. Their free hands now held a glass apiece.

'I am becoming suspicious, Captain,' Andropulos said. He neither looked nor sounded suspicious. 'You seem totally unconcerned as to the immediate past and the immediate future. I find it very curious indeed.'

'There's nothing curious about it. It's your behaviour that I find extraordinarily curious although I have to admit that that is based entirely on my complete ignorance of what is going on. I fail to understand why you, a very wealthy and, I assume, highly respected businessman, should suddenly decide to put yourself outside the bounds of law. I don't have to tell you that, by hijacking the *Angelina*, you have done just that. I can't even begin to understand why you should jeopardize your career, perhaps even risk a prison sentence, although I have no doubt that with the kind of money you must possess you wouldn't have too much trouble in bending the law in your direction. Most of all, I don't understand how you can possibly hope to get away with it. By six o'clock, possibly seven, tomorrow morning every ship and plane in NATO will be looking for you and you must know that it will take very little time to locate you.'

'You have this famous Royal Navy signal, locate, engage and destroy. Locate, yes. Destroy, no.' Andropulos was quite undisturbed. 'Not with the kind of cargo and very select group of hostages I have on board. As for jeopardizing my career, well, I think the time comes in many people's lives when they should abandon the old ways and strike out in a fresh direction. Don't you, Captain?'

'Not where I'm concerned. And perhaps, where you are concerned, it's not a choice but a necessity.

You appear to have taken a fresh step along the road to crime. It's just possible – it's difficult to imagine but it is possible – that many of your past steps have led along that same road and that your past is catching up with you. But that's just empty speculation. I really don't know and, to be honest, I no longer care. Could I have some more wine?'

'What are you going to do with us?' Irene Charial was trying to keep her voice steady but the undercurrent of strain was there. 'What is going to happen to us?'

'Don't be ridiculous, my dear. Nothing is going to happen to you. You heard me saying that to Commander Talbot when we came aboard. Unthinkable that you should come to any harm at my hands.'

'Where are you taking us?'

'I'm not taking you anywhere. Oh dear, that does sound ominous. To what will probably be my lifelong regret, I shall be parting company with you. Dear, dear, that doesn't sound much better. Within a very short time I shall be transferring you aboard the *Ariadne*'s launch and bidding you farewell.'

'And the two officers here? Do you shoot them or just tie their hands up again and throw them overboard?'

'I must protest, Irene,' Van Gelder said. 'Don't go around putting ideas into the man's head.'

'I had looked for more intelligence from my niece,' Andropulos said. 'If it had been my intention

265

to dispose of them, I should have done so immediately we came aboard.'

'What's to stop them from coming after you? You know they can call for help.'

'The Lord help us,' Van Gelder said. 'One shudders to think of the minimal levels of university entrance these days.'

'I'm afraid I have to agree with both Van Gelder and your uncle,' Talbot said. 'You are naïve.' He cocked his fingers, pistol fashion. 'Poof! Exit engine. Poof! Exit radio.'

Andropulos smiled. 'As you say, a double poof should do it nicely.'

Denholm looked out at the light flickering from the north. 'What does the *Angelina* say, Myers?'

' "Stop two miles south-east of us and cut engines." How shall I answer, sir?'

'We don't have any option. "Wilco." ' He waited until Myers had triggered the reply, then said: 'What's the latest news about the *Taormina*?' The *Ariadne* had been monitoring the radio traffic between the *Angelina* and the *Taormina* for almost three hours and had the position of the *Taormina* – and themselves – pinpointed to within a few hundred yards.

'Just ten miles north of Avgó Island and moving, pretty slowly, north.'

'Proceeding, in what one might say in happier circumstances, with admirable caution.' The *Ariadne* had picked up Andropulos's warning to the *Taormina* of the danger of their coming together too soon. 'How long before they make contact?'

'Three hours, give or take. A bit longer, I should think, if the *Angelina* stops off alongside for a bit.'

'Do you think,' Wotherspoon said, 'that they might have in mind to sink us, Lieutenant?'

'I would be grateful, Professor, if you didn't even think of such things.'

Under the watchful eyes of three men with three guns McKenzie and Brown took and secured the ropes of the *Angelina* as it came alongside. First aboard was Andropulos himself, followed by Angelina Wotherspoon, who immediately seemed bent on strangling the Professor, then the two girls, Talbot and Van Gelder with their hands still bound behind their backs and finally Alexander and Aristotle, the last carrying a bag.

'We will not stay long,' Andropulos said. 'One or two small things to attend to first, then we shall be on our way.'

'May one ask what is in that bag?' Wotherspoon said. 'A delayed action bomb?'

'Mankind has so little trust in one another these days,' Andropulos said. He shook the bag gently and a slight tinkling noise resulted. 'To while away the time while you await rescue. Commander Talbot's idea, really. After all, it's your liquor, Wotherspoon. This, I take it, is the radio.'

'Do me a last favour,' Talbot said. 'A favour to all of us. Don't blow it apart with a bullet. Just tap it gently with the butt of your revolver. Similarly with the engine. It requires very little effort to destroy the distributor and the plugs.' He nodded towards the armed mine lying in its cradle. 'I'm not at all sure how our friend here would react to the explosive crack of a pistol shot.'

'A well taken point,' Andropulos said. 'We just don't know how temperamental that mine is.' He reversed his grip on the pistol, levered open the face-plate of the radio and swept the butt across the transistors. It took him scarcely more time to attend to the engine. He next turned his attention to the signalling lamp, smashed it thoroughly and turned to Myers. 'Is there a spare?'

Myers swore at him softly, and Andropulos raised his gun. Talbot said: 'Don't be a fool, Myers. Give it to him.'

Myers, tight-lipped, handed over a small hand-signalling lamp. Andropulos broke the face and threw it into the water. He then turned his attention to a small metal box attached to the deck just outside the wheelhouse and jerked his gun in McKenzie's direction. 'The distress flares there. Over the side with them, if you please.' He was silent for a moment, as if considering. 'Engine, radio, signalling lamps, distress flares. No, I don't think there's any other way you can communicate with anyone. Not that there's anyone around to communicate with. I trust you do not have too long and uncomfortable a wait before you are picked up.' He turned to Irene Charial. 'Well, then, my dear, I will say goodbye.'

She did not answer him, did not even look at him. Andropulos shrugged, stepped across the gunwales and disappeared inside the *Angelina's* wheelhouse. Alexander and Aristotle followed him aboard, retrieved the lines that had secured them to the launch and pushed off with boat-hooks. The *Angelina* got slowly under way and headed off once more towards the south-east.

McKenzie used his seaman's knife to slice through the ropes that bound the wrists of Talbot and Van Gelder. 'Someone,' he said, 'certainly used a lot of enthusiasm to tie those knots.'

'That they did.' Talbot flexed painful and swollen wrists and hands and looked at the bag Aristotle had brought aboard. 'However, using two hands, I might just be able to hold something in them.'

Irene Charial looked at him. 'Is that all you have to say?'

'Make it a generous measure.'

She stared some more at him, looked away and reached for the bag. Wotherspoon said: 'Are you sure you're all right, Captain? How can you be so abnormally calm? You've lost out, haven't you? Lost out all along the line.'

'That's one way of putting it.' The wind was fresh, the sky cloudless and the full moon, abnormally large and bright, laid a golden bar across the

269

Sea of Crete. Even at the distance of half a mile every detail of the *Angelina* was startlingly clear. 'The world, of course, will say that Andropulos has lost out. Andropulos and his two murderous friends.' Irene was still staring at him, her expression blank and uncomprehending. 'Things never quite work out the way you want them to.'

'I'm sure you know what you're talking about.' Wotherspoon's tone of voice left no doubt that he was quite sure that Talbot didn't know what he was talking about. 'And you took a hell of a chance there, if I may say so, Captain. He could have killed you and Van Gelder.'

'He could have tried. Then he would have died himself. Himself, Alexander and Aristotle.'

'You had your hands tied behind your back. And Van Gelder.' Wotherspoon was openly incredulous. 'How could you –'

'Chief Petty Officer McKenzie and Marine Sergeant Brown are highly trained and highly qualified marksmen. The only two on the *Ariadne*. With hand-guns, they are quite deadly. That is why they are along. Andropulos and his friends would have died without knowing what had hit them. Show the Professor, Chief.'

McKenzie reached under the small chart table, brought out two Navy Colts and handed them without a word to Wotherspoon. Quite some seconds passed in silence, then he looked up from the guns and said in a quiet voice: 'You *knew* those guns were there.'

'I put them there.'

'You put them there.' He shook his head as if in disbelief. 'You could have *used* those guns.'

'Killed them, you mean?'

'Well, no. That wouldn't have been necessary. Wounded them, perhaps. Or just taken them prisoner.'

'What were your orders, Chief?'

'Shoot to kill.'

'Shoot to kill.' It was a night for silences. 'But you didn't, did you?'

'I elected not to.'

Irene Charial clutched her arms and shivered, as if a sudden chill had fallen on the evening air. Nor was she alone in sensing the sudden and almost tangible drop in temperature. Both Eugenia and Angela Wotherspoon were staring at him, their eyes wide with uncertainty, then with fear and then with a sudden sick foreknowledge. Talbot's words still hung in the air, the fading echo of a sentence of execution.

Talbot said to Myers: 'The radio, if you would, Chief.'

'Two minutes, sir.' Myers moved aft, returned with a hammer and chisel and began to attack the floorboards of the wheelhouse. He pulled up a creaking plank, reached under and brought out a small compact radio with speaker attached. 'You talk in here, sir. Reply comes from the box. After, that is, you've cranked the handle.' Talbot nodded and spun the handle.

271

'HMS *Ariadne* here.' The voice was very distinct, very clear and unquestionably the voice of Admiral Hawkins.

'Talbot, sir. The three ladies, Van Gelder and I have been returned to the launch. Well and unharmed. Andropulos and his two friends are on their way again, moving south-east.'

'Well, thank God for that, anyway. Damn your eyes, Talbot, you've guessed right again. You've made up your mind what to do?'

'I have, sir.'

'For the record, do you want a direct order?'

'Off or on the record, no order will be necessary. But thank you. Do you have an estimate of their meeting time, sir.'

'Yes, I do. At their current speeds – the *Taormina* is still drifting along – and on their converging courses, about two hours. Three-thirty.'

'Thank you, sir. I'll call again in one hour.'

'The *Taormina*?' Wotherspoon said. 'Who or what the hell is the *Taormina*?'

'A diving ship, in which Andropulos has an interest. By interest, I mean that he probably owns the damn thing.'

'Commander Talbot?' Irene Charial's voice was very low.

'Yes?'

'Admiral Hawkins said "you've guessed right again". What did he mean by that?'

'Just what he meant, I suppose.'

'Please.' She essayed a smile but gave up. 'You all seem to think that I'm not very bright, but I don't deserve that.'

'I'm sorry.'

'I'm beginning to think that you're not much given to guessing.' She looked at the two guns. 'You didn't guess that those were here. I don't think you guessed, I think you knew, that my uncle and the other two were armed.'

'I knew.'

'How?'

'Jenkins, our wardroom steward, had been writing a letter to his family. For some reason, maybe he'd forgotten something, he went back up to the wardroom. He came across your uncle, or his associates, opening up a box in the passageway outside the wardroom. That box – it's a standard fitting on most naval ships – contained Colt .44s. So they killed Jenkins and threw him over the side. I *am* sorry, Irene, really and truly sorry. I know how terrible all this must be for you.'

This time she did manage a smile although it was a pretty wan attempt.

'Terrible, yes, but not as terrible as I thought it might be. Did you guess that my uncle would try to hijack the *Angelina*?'

'Yes.'

'And take the two of you hostages?'

'Yes.'

'Did you guess he would take three young ladies as hostages?'

273

'No. I make guesses and I take chances, but I would never have taken a chance like that. If I'd even dreamed of the possibility, I'd have killed them there and then. On the *Ariadne*.'

'I made a mistake about you, Captain. You talk a lot about killing but I think you're a very kind man.'

'I wouldn't go as far as to say that.' Talbot smiled. 'You made a mistake?'

'Irene is a pretty fair judge of character, sir,' Van Gelder said. 'She had you down as a cruel and inhuman monster.'

'I said nothing of the kind! When you talked to my uncle on the *Angelina* you said you knew nothing about what was going on. That wasn't true, was it? You knew all along.'

'Well, it's as you say. I'm a pretty fair old guesser. I have to admit that I had a lot of help from Lieutenant-Commander Van Gelder and Lieutenant Denholm is no slouch at the guessing game either. I'm afraid you'll have to know about your uncle some time, and you may as well know now. It sounds an exaggeration, but it is not, to say that he's a criminal in the world class, if not in a class of his own, and a totally ruthless killer. He specializes in, organizes and dominates international drug-smuggling and international terrorism. God only knows how many hundreds, more likely thousands, lie dead at his hands. We know, and know beyond any doubt, that he is as guilty as any man can be, but it might take months, even years, to amass the necessary proof. By that time, he would have disappeared. That's what he's doing now – disappearing. Even in the past couple of days he's been doing not too badly. He murdered the engineer, cook and steward on the *Delos*. They found out too much. What, we shall probably never know.'

'How on earth can you know this?' All the colour had left her face and her face registered pure shock. Not grief or horror, just shock. 'How on earth can you *guess* that, far less prove it?'

'Because Van Gelder and I went down to examine the hull on the bottom. He also blew up his own yacht in order to get aboard the *Ariadne*. You weren't to know this, of course. Neither, unfortunately for your uncle, did he. For good measure, he's also been responsible for the suicides of a very senior general and a very senior admiral, both Americans, in the past few hours. He doesn't know that, but if he did I'm sure it might cost him anything up to a minute's sleep.' He looked at McKenzie. 'Chief, this retsina is dreadful. Can you do no better than this for your long-suffering captain?'

'It is pretty awful, sir. I've tried it. All respects to Professor Wotherspoon, but I'm afraid Greek plonk is very much an acquired taste. There seems to be a bottle of scotch and one of gin in a locker in the wheelhouse. Don't know how it got there. Sergeant Brown appears to think that it's marked up in your Mess bill.'

'I'll court-martial you both later. Meantime, don't just hang around.'

'He's going to die, isn't he, sir?' Brown said, 'I'm sorry, miss, but if half of what the Captain says is true, then he's an inhuman man who doesn't belong in a human world. And I believe *everything* the Captain has said is true.'

'I know Jenkins was your best friend, Sergeant, and I cannot say how sorry I am. He will die and by his own hand. He is his own executioner.' Talbot turned to Eugenia. 'You heard him mention the words "Manhattan Project"?'

'Yes, I did. I didn't know what he meant.'

'Neither did we, at first. But we worked it out. Andropulos wasn't interested in the hydrogen bombs. There's no way you can use a hydrogen bomb as a terrorist weapon. It's too final, it would achieve nothing and no terrorist would dare admit the responsibility of using it. It would have been impossible for any terrorist to transport anyway. But he *was* interested in atomic mines and he knew there were three of those aboard this plane. His original plan, we think, was to dump those in the sea approaches to some of the world's greatest seaports, like San Francisco, New York, London or Rotterdam and let the respective countries know of it. He would inform those countries that he had the means to detonate those mines by means of a long-range, pre-set radio signal and that any attempt to locate, remove or neutralize them might or might not activate the mine and, of course, destroy the investigating vessel.

'It would have effectively paralysed all seaborne trade and passenger traffic in and out of those ports. It would also have had the additional holier-than-thou advantage that if any such atomic explosion did occur the fault would lie squarely at the door of the country responsible for the explosion and not at the door of the terrorists. The Manhattan Project mine would have been laid somewhere in the Ambrose Channel on the approaches to the Lower New York Bay. It was a brilliant scheme, typical of a brilliant but twisted mind. It had one drawback. It wouldn't have worked. Andropulos had no means of knowing that. But we did.'

'How in the world could you know that?' Wotherspoon said.

'I'll come to that. So, Andropulos gets his bomb. Perfect for his purposes, or so he thinks. But there was something else he didn't know. When the plane crashed it activated a timing mechanism inside the mine. When that mechanism ran out the mine was armed and ready to explode at the first sound of a ship's engines. Any kind of engine, in fact. That mine aboard the *Angelina* is armed. But Andropulos fell for that gobbledygook that Wickram fed him about its being temporarily unstable because of the radioactive emanations from the hydrogen bombs. It's permanently unstable and just waiting to go. Chief, you are being strangely remiss.'

'Sorry, sir.' McKenzie handed over a glass of scotch. 'You can hardly blame me, sir. A man doesn't often get a chance to listen to a story like this.'

Talbot sampled his drink, 'It is to be hoped that you will never hear another like it again.'

'So what's going to happen?' Wotherspoon asked.

'One of two things *could* happen. He could try to transfer the mine to the *Taormina*, the sound of whose engines would blow them all to a better world. Well, in the case of Andropulos and his friends, we would hope a much worse world. The crew of the *Taormina* may be a relatively innocent bunch. Or he could elect to sail it to Tobruk, his final destination. Don't forget, he would think it perfectly safe to do so because, as far as he knows, the world would still think that he has five hostages aboard. At the sound of the first ship's or industrial engine in Tobruk, the mine is activated. How many guiltless people dead? Ten thousand? A minimum estimate. Lieutenant Denholm, I grow tired of my own voice. You are alleged to be the *Ariadne*'s electronics officer. Would you show them this device and explain its purpose.'

'It's called the krytron,' Denholm said. 'Looks like a small and rather old-fashioned portable radio, doesn't it? This is what the Captain meant when he said that if Andropulos knew of the existence of this instrument he wouldn't have gone to all the vast trouble of obtaining an atomic mine. By carrying out a very few simple actions – it is in fact an extraordinarily complex mechanism and I know practically nothing about it – you can send an electronic impulse on a selected wave-length and detonate an atomic bomb. If Andropulos were to have laid this mine in the Ambrose Channel it could have been destroyed from almost any given distance without a ship or a plane going anywhere near it.'

Wotherspoon said: 'Is one allowed to ask how you so conveniently came by this lethal instrument?'

'We sent to America for it. It arrived yesterday.'

'That implies two things. You had prior knowledge of the existence of this device and you've known for quite some time about exactly what Andropulos was up to. Did anyone else know?'

'The Captain disapproves of his officers gossiping.'

Wotherspoon turned to Talbot. 'You're going to blow up the *Angelina*? *My Angelina*!'

'Well, yes. I dare say there will be some form of compensation.'

'What compensation?'

'How should I know? I'm not sufficiently senior to make any offers. I'll have to ask the Admiral.'

'Does it have to be done this way?' Irene said. 'You do have a radio. Couldn't you just tell him to drop the bomb over the side and then have him picked up later?'

'Apart from the fact that he wouldn't believe me, I wouldn't do it anyway. I have told you that obtaining proof against him might take months, even years. I suggest that you and Eugenia ask your respective fathers about him. You will find that they will totally agree with what I am about to do, and that is not to let a mad dog run loose in the world.'

Van Gelder said: 'This is what you meant by saying, not once but many times, that Andropulos would never come to trial?'

'He has been tried.'

At 2.30 a.m. Talbot called up the *Ariadne* and was through to the Admiral immediately.

'It's two-thirty, sir. Has the *Kilcharran* brought all the hydrogen missiles aboard?'

'It has.'

'So we go. Two small points, sir. Professor Wotherspoon seems somewhat peeved by the imminent – ah – demise of the *Angelina*.'

'Tell him it's all in a good cause.'

'Yes, sir. Do you think the Ministry of Defence could run to a replacement?'

'Guaranteed.'

'He also mentioned something about gold-plated taps in his bathroom.'

'Good God! The other small point? A mercifully small point, one trusts.'

'A bagatelle, sir. How do you view the suggestion that, after all their harrowing experiences, the crew of the *Ariadne* deserves some leave?'

'Precisely the same thought had occurred to me. A week, I think. Where do you suggest?'

'Piræus, sir. I thought it would be rather a nice gesture to take the two girls back home. It would also be an excellent centre for Professor Wotherspoon and his lady to start looking round for gold-plated taps. We will call again in five minutes.'

Talbot replaced the telephone and said to McKenzie and Brown: 'A couple of sweeps out, if you please, and have the bows lined up to the south-east. Well, Professor, what do you think of the Admiral's generous offer?'

'I'm staggered.'

'So you might well be, as the Admiralty was under no obligation whatsoever to replace it. You must be well aware that Andropulos intended to sink it anyway. Lieutenant Denholm, pass me the krytron.'

'It's my job, sir. You can't have forgotten that I'm your electronics officer.'

'It's also your job to call to mind the rules and regulations about seniority,' Van Gelder said. 'Pass it to me.'

Talbot reached out and took the krytron, already connected to a battery, from Denholm. 'Neither of you. When we get to Piraeus, I think that those two young ladies will feel under a moral obligation to show you around the University precincts and indulge in other such-like cultural activities. I don't think, somehow, that they would feel entirely comfortable in the presence of whoever pressed this button.'

Talbot cracked both orange domes with the hammer, rotated the switches through 180° and pressed the button.

' "Commander Talbot has elected to destroy and has destroyed the *Angelina* by detonating the atomic mine. He had my one hundred per cent encouragement and support. Andropulos and his two friends were aboard the *Angelina*." '

The President shook his head in disbelief and laid the message down. 'This Commander Talbot. A totally ruthless and highly resourceful man.'

'Not ruthless, sir,' Sir John said. 'A kind and thoughtful man. If he were ruthless, he could have permitted the destruction of a ship or a city. But resourceful? Yes, I rather think he is.'

ALISTAIR MACLEAN

Alistair MacLean, the son of a Scots minister, was brought up in the Scottish Highlands. In 1941, at the age of eighteen, he joined the Royal Navy. After the war he read English at Glasgow University and became a school-master. The two and a half years he spent aboard a wartime cruiser were to give him the background for *HMS Ulysses*, his remarkably successful first novel, published in 1955. He is now recognized as one of the outstanding popular writers of the 20th century, the author of twenty-nine worldwide bestsellers, many of which have been filmed, including *The Guns of Navarone*, *Where Eagles Dare*, *Fear is the Key* and *Ice Station Zebra*. In 1983, he was awarded a D.Litt. from Glasgow University. Alistair MacLean died in 1987.

By Alistair MacLean

FICTION

HMS Ulysses
The Guns of Navarone
South by Java Head
The Last Frontier
Night Without End
Fear is the Key
The Dark Crusader
The Golden Rendezvous
The Satan Bug
Ice Station Zebra
When Eight Bells Toll
Where Eagles Dare
Force 10 from Navarone
Puppet on a Chain
Caravan to Vaccarès
Bear Island
The Way to Dusty Death
Breakheart Pass
Circus
The Golden Gate
Seawitch
Goodbye California
Athabasca
River of Death
Partisans
Floodgate
San Andreas
The Lonely Sea (stories)
Santorini

NON-FICTION

Captain Cook

ALISTAIR MACLEAN

San Andreas

HarperCollins*Publishers*

HarperCollins*Publishers*
1 London Bridge Street,
London SE1 9GF

www.harpercollins.co.uk

HarperCollins*Publishers*
1st Floor, Watemarque Building, Ringsend Road
Dublin 4, Ireland

This paperback edition 2021
1

Previously published in paperback by HarperCollins 2009
and by Fontana 1985

First published in Great Britain by
William Collins Sons & Co. Ltd. 1984

Copyright © HarperCollins*Publishers* 1984

Alistair MacLean asserts the moral right to
be identified as the author of this work

ISBN: 978-0-00-833669-1

Typeset in Meridien by Palimpsest Book Production Limited,
Falkirk, Stirlingshire

Printed and bound in Great Britain by
CPI Group (UK) Ltd, Croydon CR0 4YY

MIX
Paper from
responsible sources

FSC
www.fsc.org **FSC™ C007454**

To David and Judy

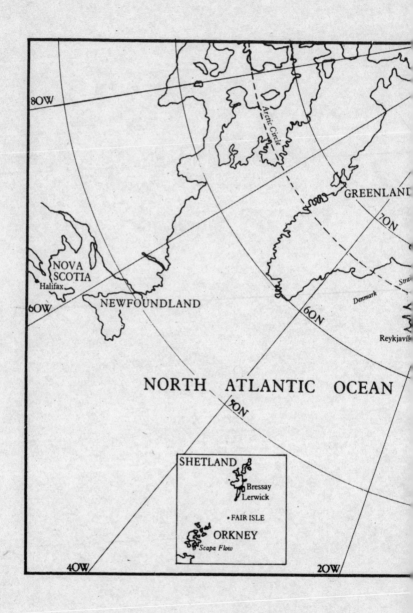

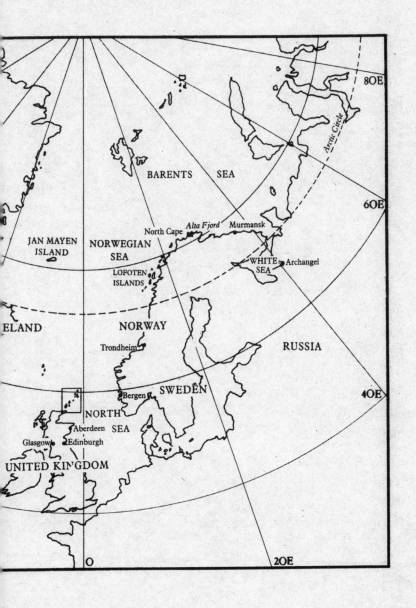

PROLOGUE

There are three distinct but inevitably interlinked elements in this story: the Merchant Navy (officially the Mercantile Marine) and the men who served in it: Liberty Ships: and the units of the German forces, underseas, on the seas and in the air, whose sole mission was to seek out and destroy the vessels and crews of the Merchant Navy.

1   At the outbreak of war in September 1939 the British Merchant Navy was in a parlous state indeed – 'pitiable' would probably be a more accurate term. Most of the ships were old, a considerable number unseaworthy and some no more than rusting hulks plagued by interminable mechanical breakdowns. Even so, those vessels were in comparatively good shape compared to the appalling living conditions of those whose misfortune it was to serve aboard those ships.

The reason for the savage neglect of both ships and men could be summed up in one word – greed.

The fleet owners of yesteryear – and there are more than a few around today – were grasping, avaricious and wholly dedicated to their high priestess – profits at all costs, provided that the cost did not fall on them. Centralization was the watchword of the day, the gathering in of over-lapping monopolies into a few rapacious hands. While crews' wages were cut and living conditions reduced to barely subsistence levels, the owners grew fat, as did some of the less desirable directors of those companies and a considerable number of carefully hand-picked and favoured shareholders.

The dictatorial powers of the owners, discreetly exercised, of course, were little short of absolute. Their fleets were their satrap, their feudal fiefdom, and the crews were their serfs. If a serf chose to revolt against the established order, that was his misfortune. His only recourse was to leave his ship, to exchange it for virtual oblivion, for, apart from the fact that he was automatically black-balled, unemployment was high in the Merchant Navy and the few vacancies available were for willing serfs only. Ashore, unemployment was even higher and even if it had not been so, seamen find it notoriously difficult to adapt to a landlubber's way of life. The rebel serf had no place left to go. Rebel serfs were very few and far between. The vast majority knew their station in life and kept to it. Official histories tend to gloss over this state of affairs or, more commonly, ignore it altogether, an understandable myopia.

The treatment of the merchant seamen between the wars and, indeed, during the Second World War, does not form one of the more glorious chapters in British naval annals.

Successive governments between the wars were perfectly aware of the conditions of life in the Merchant Navy – they would have had to be more than ordinarily stupid not to be so aware – so successive governments, in largely hypocritical face-saving exercises, passed a series of regulations laying down minimum specifications regarding accommodation, food, hygiene and safety. Both governments and owners were perfectly aware – in the case of the ship-owners no doubt cheerfully aware – that regulations are not laws and that a regulation is not legally enforceable. The recommendations – for they amounted to no more than that – were almost wholly ignored. A conscientious captain who tried to enforce them was liable to find himself without a command.

Recorded eyewitness reports of the living conditions aboard Merchant Navy ships in the years immediately prior to the Second World War – there is no reason to question those reports, especially as they are all so depressingly unanimous in tone – describe the crews' living quarters as being so primitive and atrocious as to beggar description. Medical inspectors stated that in some instances the crews' living quarters were unfit for animal, far less human, habitation. The quarters were invariably cramped and bereft of any form of

3

comfort. The decks were wet, the men's clothes were wet and the mattresses and blankets, where such luxuries were available, were usually sodden. Hygiene and toilet facilities ranged from the primitive to the non-existent. Cold was pervasive and heating of any form – except for smoking and evil-smelling coal stoves – was rare, as, indeed was any form of ventilation. And the food, which as one writer said would not have been tolerated in a home for the utterly destitute, was even worse than the living quarters.

The foregoing may strain the bounds of credulity or, at least, seem far-fetched, but respectively, they should not and are not. Charges of imprecision and exaggeration have never been laid at the doors of the London School of Hygiene and Tropical Medicine or the Registrar General. The former, in a pre-war report, categorically stated that the mortality rate below the age of fifty-five was twice as high for seamen as it was for the rest of the male population, and statistics issued by the latter showed that the death rate for seamen of all ages was 47% in excess of the national average. The killers were tuberculosis, cerebral hæmorrhage and gastric or duodenal ulcers. The incidence of the first and last of those is all too understandable and there can be little doubt that the combination of those contributed heavily to the abnormal occurrence of strokes.

The prime agent of death was unquestionably tuberculosis. When one looks around Western

Europe today, where TB sanatoria are a happily and rapidly vanishing species, it is difficult to imagine just how terrible a scourge tuberculosis was just over a generation ago. It is not that tuberculosis, worldwide, has been eliminated: in many underdeveloped countries it still remains that same terrible scourge and the chief cause of death, and as recently as the early years of this century TB was still the number one killer in Western Europe and North America. Such is no longer the case since scientists came up with the agents to tame and destroy the tubercle bacillus. But in 1939 it was still very much the case: the discovery of the chemotherapeutic agents, rifampin, para-aminosalicylic acid, isoniazid and especially streptomycin, still lay far beyond a distant horizon.

It was upon those tuberculosis-ridden seamen, ill-housed and abominably fed, that Britain depended to bring food, oil, arms and ammunition to its shores and those of its allies. It was the *sine qua non* conduit, the artery, the lifeline upon which Britain was absolutely dependent: without those ships and men Britain would assuredly have gone under. It is worth noting that those men's contracts ended when the torpedo, mine or bomb struck. In wartime as in peacetime the owners protected their profits to the bitter end: the seaman's wages were abruptly terminated when his ship was sunk, no matter where, how, or in what unimaginable circumstances. When an owner's ship went down he shed no salt tears, for his ships were insured, as often as not grossly over-insured: when a seaman's ship went down he was fired.

The Government, Admiralty and ship-owners of that time should have been deeply ashamed of themselves: if they were, they manfully concealed their distress: compared to prestige, glory and profits, the conditions of life and the horrors of death of the men of the Merchant Navy were a very secondary consideration indeed.

The people of Britain cannot be condemned. With the exception of the families and friends of the Merchant Navy and the splendid volunteer charitable organizations that were set up to help survivors – such humanitarian trifles were of no concern to owners or Whitehall – very few knew or even suspected what was going on.

2   As a lifeline, a conduit and an artery, the Liberty Ships were on a par with the British Merchant Navy: without them, Britain would have assuredly gone down in defeat. All the food, oil, arms and ammunition which overseas countries – especially the United States – were eager and willing to supply were useless without the ships in which to transport them. After less than two years of war it was bleakly apparent that because of the deadly attrition of the British Merchant fleets there must soon, and inevitably, be no ships left to carry anything and that Britain would, inexorably and not slowly, be starved into surrender. In 1940, even the indomitable Winston

Churchill despaired of survival, far less ultimate victory. Typically, the period of despair was brief but heaven only knew that he had cause for it.

In nine hundred years, Britain, of all the countries in the world, had never been invaded, but in the darkest days of the war such invasion seemed not only perilously close but inevitable. Looking back today over a span of forty and more years it seems inconceivable and impossible that the country survived: had the facts been made public, which they weren't, it almost certainly would not.

British shipping losses were appalling beyond belief and beggar even the most active imagination. In the first eleven months of the war Britain lost 1,500,000 tons of shipping. In some of the early months of 1941, losses averaged close on 500,000 tons. In 1942, the darkest period of the war at sea, 6,250,000 tons of shipping went to the bottom. Even working at full stretch British shipyards could replace only a small fraction of those enormous losses. That, together with the fact that the number of operational U-boats in that same grim year rose from 91 to 212 made it certain that, by the law of diminishing returns, the British Merchant Navy would eventually cease to exist unless a miracle occurred.

The name of the miracle was Liberty Ships. To anyone who can recall those days the term Liberty Ships was automatically and immediately linked with Henry Kaiser. Kaiser – in the circumstances it was ironic that he should bear the same name as the title of the late German Emperor – was an American engineer of unquestioned genius. His career until then had been a remarkably impressive one: he had been a key figure in the construction of the Hoover and Coulee dams and the San Francisco bridge. It is questionable whether Henry Kaiser could have designed a rowing-boat but that was of no matter. He almost certainly had a better understanding of prefabrication based on a standard and repeatable design than any other person in the world at the time and did not hesitate to send out contracts for part-construction to factories in the United States that lay hundreds of miles from the sea. Those sections were transmitted to shipyards for assembly, originally to Richmond, California, where Kaiser directed the Permanente Cement Co., and eventually to other shipyards under Kaiser's control. Kaiser's turnover and speed of production stopped just short of the incredible: he did for the production of merchant vessels what Henry Ford's assembly lines had done for the Model T Ford. Until then, as far as ocean-going vessels were concerned, mass production had been an alien concept.

Mistakenly, but understandably, there existed a widely-held belief that the Liberty Ships originated in the design offices of the Kaiser shipyards. The design and prototypes were, in fact, English and were conceived by the design staff of the shipbuilders J.L. Thompson of North Sands, Sunderland. The first of what was to become a very long line indeed, the *Embassage*, was completed in 1935 – the prefix 'Liberty' did not come into existence for another seven years, and only for some of the Kaiser-built vessels. The *Embassage*, 9,300 tons, with a raked stem and rounded stern and three triple-expansion coal-burning engines, was a non-starter in the æsthetic stakes, but then J.L. Thompson were not interested in æsthetics: what they had aimed at was a modern, practical and economical cargo vessel and in this they succeeded admirably. Twenty-four more similar vessels were built before the outbreak of war.

Those ships were built in Britain, the United States and Canada, the great preponderance in the Kaiser yards. Hull designs remained identical but the Americans, and only the Americans, introduced two changes which they regarded as refinements. One of those changes, using oil instead of coal as fuel, may well have been: the other, which concerned the accommodation of officers and crew, was not. While the Canadians and British retained the original concept of having the living quarters both fore and aft the Americans elected to have all the crew, officers and men – and the navigating bridge – in a superstructure surrounding the funnel. In retrospect – hindsight and bitter experience make for a splendid conductor to belated wisdom – it was a blunder. The Americans had all their eggs in one basket.

Those vessels were armed – after a fashion. They had four-inch low-angle and twelve-pounder anti-aircraft guns, neither of which was particularly effective, together with Bofors and rapid-firing Oerlikons: the Oerlikons were deadly in trained hands – but there were few trained hands around. They also had weird devices such as rocket-fired parachutes and cables carrying coils of wire and grenades: these were as dangerous to those using them as the aircraft they were supposed to bring down. Some few of these ships had catapult-launched Hurricane fighters – the nearest equivalent to the suicidal Japanese kamikaze planes that Britain ever had. The pilots could not, of course, return to their ships: they had the uncomfortable option of either baling out or ditching. In the Arctic, in winter, their survival rate was not high.

3 From the air, on the sea and under the sea the Germans, often with brilliance, always with tenacity and ruthlessness, used every means in their power to destroy the Merchant Navy convoys.

Basically, they used five main types of aircraft. Their standard or conventional bomber was the Dornier which flew at pre-determined heights and released their bombs in pre-determined patterns: they were useful planes and had their successes but were not particularly effective.

Much more feared, in ascending order, were the Heinkel, the Heinkel III and the Stuka. The Heinkel was a torpedo-bomber, which attacked at wave-top level, its pilot releasing the torpedo at the last possible moment, then using the lightened weight of his aircraft to lift over the ship it was attacking. Those planes had an unusual degree of immunity from destruction: when the anti-aircraft gunners on the merchant ships peered over the sights of their Oerlikons, Bofors or pom-poms – two-pounders – the thought that 'He gets me or I get him' didn't make for the degree of cool detachment which would have been helpful in the circumstances. In the Arctic winter, those torpedo-bombers were not infrequently at a disadvantage, especially for the gallant but unfortunate pilots who flew them: ice could freeze up their torpedo release mechanisms and their burdened aircraft were unable to lift off over their targets. This made little difference to the equally unfortunate crews of the merchant vessels: whether the torpedo was running free or still attached to the aircraft when it crashed into the ship, the results were equally devastating.

The Heinkel III used glider bombers. These were highly effective, exposed their pilots to a much lesser degree of risk and the bombs, once released, were virtually impossible to shoot down: fortunately for the Merchant Navy, the Germans did not have too many of these highly specialized planes.

The Stuka, the dihedral – gull-winged Junker 87 dive-bomber – was the most feared of all. It was their customary practice to fly at high altitude

11

in level formation, then peel off successively in near-vertical dives. Forty years later, the seamen and soldiers – the Germans used the Junker 87 in every theatre of war – who survived those attacks and are still alive will never forget the sound of the banshee shrieking as the Stuka pilots switched on their sirens in their plummeting dive. The sound, to say the least, was unnerving and considerably reduced the effectiveness of anti-aircraft gunners. The Royal Navy used searchlights, customarily of the 44-inch variety, in an attempt to blind the Stuka pilots, until it was pointed out to them that the pilots, who were well aware of this tactic, used dark glasses to reduce the blinding glare to mere pinpoints of light which enabled them to home in even more accurately on their targets. From the German point of view the Stukas had only one drawback: they were essentially short-range planes and could operate effectively only against convoys moving to the north of Norway en route to Murmansk and Archangel.

But, oddly enough, the most effective air weapon the Germans had was the essentially non-combative Focke-Wulf Condor 200. True, it could and did carry 250-kilo bombs and had a fairly formidable array of machine-guns, but with bombs removed and extra fuel tanks fitted in their place, it became an invaluable reconnaissance plane. For that comparatively early flying era, in the early Forties, its flying range was quite remarkable. Condors flew almost daily from Trondheim, in

German-occupied Norway, round the western coast of the British Isles to German-occupied France: more importantly, they were capable of patrolling the Barents Sea, the Greenland Sea and, most damagingly of all, the justly dreaded Denmark Strait, between Iceland and Greenland, for it was through that strait that the Russian-bound convoys from Canada and the United States passed. For such a convoy, the sight of a Condor was the guarantee of inevitable disaster.

Flying high and safely out of reach of anti-aircraft fire, the Condor would literally circle the convoy, its crew noting down the number of ships, the convoy's speed, course and precise latitude and longitude. This information was radioed to Alta Fjord or Trondheim and then transmitted to Lorient, the French HQ of Admiral Karl Doenitz, almost certainly the best submarine C-in-C of his time or any time. From there the information was re-transmitted to the growing submarine wolfpack or packs, instructing them when and where exactly to position themselves to intercept the convoy.

As far as surface warships were concerned, the Germans were more than adequately prepared at the outbreak of war. By the Anglo-German agreement of 1937 Germany could build 100% of the British equivalent of submarines but only 35% of surface ships. In fact they built twice as many submarines and completely ignored the other 35% restriction. The *Deutschland*, *Admiral Graf Spee* and

Admiral Scheer were nominally 10,000 ton cruisers: they were, in fact, fast and powerful commerce raiders, in effect pocket battleships of a far greater tonnage than purported. The *Scharnhorst* and *Gneisenau*, 26,000 ton battle-cruisers, were completed in 1938 and it was in that year that the *Bismarck* and *Tirpitz* were laid down in the Blohm and Voess shipyards in Hamburg. Those were the best and most powerful battleships ever built, a statement that remains true to this day. By treaty limitations they were restricted to 35,000 tons: they were, in fact, 53,000 tons.

The *Bismarck* had a brief but spectacular career, the *Tirpitz* no career at all. It spent its war holed up in northern Norway, where it none the less performed the invaluable function of tying up major units of the British Home Fleet which feared that the giant battleship might slip its moorings in Alta Fjord and break out into the Atlantic. It was at those moorings that the *Tirpitz* was ultimately destroyed by ten-ton bombs from RAF Lancasters.

Although the British had a very considerable advantage in battleships, they were, individually, no match for those of the Germans, as was tragically proved when the *Bismarck* sank the battle-cruiser *Hood*, pride and darling of the Royal Navy, with a single salvo.

Underwater, the Germans used mines and submarines. Less than three months after the outbreak of war the Germans had come up with a rather unpleasant device – the magnetic mine.

Unlike the standard type, which had to come into physical contact with a vessel before being activated, the magnetic mine was set off by the electrical current generated by the ship's hull. Those mines could be laid by either ships or aircraft and in the first four days after their introduction no fewer than fifteen ships were sent to the bottom – the fact that they were nearly all neutrals seemed of no great concern to the Germans: magnetic mines are very clever devices but not clever enough to discriminate between a neutral and an enemy. The British managed to retrieve one intact, took it to pieces – not without considerable danger to those engaged in the dismantling – and came up with electronic counter-measures which enabled minesweepers to detonate the magnetic mine at a respectful distance.

Submarines, of course, were the most deadly enemies the Merchant Navy had to face. The toll taken in the first three and a half years of war was savage beyond belief. It wasn't until the early summer of 1943 that the menace was brought under some form of control, but it wasn't until the end of 1944 – during the two years 1943–4 480 German submarines were destroyed – that those stealthy pursuers and silent killers ceased to be a factor of consequence.

It was inevitable that the U-boats should be selected as *the* target for hatred and their crews depicted, both during the war and subsequently, as cunning, treacherous and ice-cold murderers, fanatical Nazis to a man, who hunted down unsuspecting innocents, closed in unheard and unseen, destroyed their victims without mercy or compunction, then moved on again, still unheard and unseen. To a limited extent, this view was valid. The pattern for this belief was set on the very first day of the war when the liner *Athenia* was torpedoed. In no way could the *Athenia* have been mistaken for anything other than what it was: a peaceful passenger vessel crammed with civilians – men, women and children. This must have been known to the far from gallant Oberleutnant Fritz-Julius Lemp, commander of the German U-boat that sent the *Athenia* to the bottom. There is no record that Lemp was ever reprimanded for his action.

The same charge of ruthlessness, of course, could have been levelled against Allied submariners – to a lesser extent, admittedly, it is true, but that was only because they had a much more limited choice of targets.

The overall U-boat picture is false. Ruthless Nazis there may have been among the crews but they were a tiny minority: the men were motivated principally by an intense pride in the traditions of the Imperial German Navy. Certainly there were acts of brutality by individual U-boat commanders but there were also acts of humanity, gallantry and compassion. What was undeniable was the immense personal courage and spirit of self-sacrifice of those men. It has to be remembered that, out of a total of 40,000 U-boat submariners, 30,000 died, the most shocking casualty rate in the history of naval warfare. While the actions of those men are not to be condoned, the men themselves are not to be condemned. Ruthless they were – the nature of their job demanded it – but they were brave beyond belief.

Such then were the conditions in which the men of the Merchant Navy had to live and die: such, too, were their enemies, who sought, implacably, to destroy them. The odds against the health and lives of the merchantmen surviving, respectively, their living conditions and the attentions of the enemy were high indeed: theirs was a classic no-win situation. In the circumstances it was an astonishing and commonplace fact that men who had survived two or three torpedoings and sinkings would immediately, on their return to Britain, seek out another ship to take them to sea again. By definition, those men were noncombatants but their endurance, tenacity and determination – they would have laughed at words like gallantry and courage – matched those of the men who hunted them down.

ONE

Silently, undramatically, without any forewarning, as in any abrupt and unexpected power cut in a city, the lights aboard the *San Andreas* died in the hour before the dawn. Such blackouts were rare but not unknown and gave rise to no particular alarm as far as the handling and navigation of the vessel were concerned. On the bridge, the binnacle light that illuminated the compass, the chart light and the essential telephone line to the engine-room remained unaffected because, operating as they did on a lower voltage, they had their own separate generator. The overhead lights were on the main generator but this was of no consequence as those lights were switched off: the bridge, any bridge, was always darkened at night. The only item on the bridge that did fail was the Kent screen, an inset circular plate of glass directly ahead of the helmsman which spun at high speed and offered a clear view in all conditions. Third Officer Batesman, the officer of the watch, was unworried: to the best of his belief there were neither land nor ships within a hundred miles of him with the exception of the frigate HMS *Andover*. He had no idea where the frigate was and it didn't matter: the frigate always knew where he was, for it was equipped with highly sophisticated radar.

In the operating theatre and recovery room it was a case of business as usual. Although the surrounding sea and sky were still dark as midnight, the hour was not early: in those high latitudes and at that time of year daylight, or what passed for daylight, arrived about 10.00 a.m. In those two rooms, the most important in a hospital ship, for that was what the *San Andreas* was, battery-powered lights came on automatically when the main power failed. Throughout the rest of the ship emergency lighting was provided by hand-hung nickel-cadmium lamps: a twist of the base of such a lamp provided at least a bare minimum of illumination.

What did give rise to concern was the complete failure of the upper deck lights. The hull of the *San Andreas* was painted white – more correctly, it had been white but time and the sleet, hail, snow and ice spicules of Arctic storms had eroded the original to something between a dingy off-white and an equally dingy light grey. A green band ran all the way around the hull. Very big red crosses had been painted on both her sides, as well as on the fore and after-decks. During night-time those red crosses were illuminated by powerful floodlights:

at that time darkness accounted for twenty hours out of the twenty-four.

Opinion as to the value of those lights was fairly evenly divided. According to the Geneva Convention, those red crosses guaranteed immunity against enemy attacks, and as the *San Andreas* had so far been reassuringly immune those aboard her who had never been subjected to an enemy attack of any kind tended to believe in the validity of the Geneva Convention. But the crew members who had served aboard before her conversion from a Liberty cargo carrier to her present status regarded the Convention with a very leery eye. To sail at night lit up like a Christmas tree went against all the instincts of men who for years had been conditioned to believe, rightly, that to light a cigarette on the upper deck was to attract the attention of a wandering U-boat. They didn't trust the lights. They didn't trust the red crosses. Above all, they didn't trust the U-boats. There was justification for their cynicism: other hospital boats, they knew, had been less fortunate than they had been but whether those attacks had been deliberate or accidental had never been established. There are no courts of law on the high seas and no independent witnesses. Either from reasons of delicacy or because they thought it pointless the crew never discussed the matter with those who lived in what they regarded as a fool's paradise – the doctors, the sisters, the nurses and the ward orderlies.

The starboard screen door on the bridge opened and a figure, torch in hand, entered. Batesman said: 'Captain?'

'Indeed. One of these days I'll get to finish my breakfast in peace. Some lamps, will you, Third?'

Captain Bowen was of medium height, running to fat – 'well-built' was his preferred term – with a cheerful white-bearded face and periwinkle-blue eyes. He was also well past retirement age but had never asked to retire and never been asked to: in both ships and men the Merchant Navy had suffered crippling losses and a new ship could be made in a tiny fraction of the time it took to make a new captain: there weren't too many Captain Bowens left around.

The three emergency lamps didn't give much more light than a similar number of candles would have done but it was enough to see just how quickly the Captain's coat had been covered in snow in the brief seconds it had taken him to cover the distance from the saloon. He removed the coat, shook it out through the doorway and hurriedly closed the door.

'Bloody generator having one of its fits again,' Bowen said. He didn't seem particularly upset about it, but then, no one had ever seen the Captain upset about anything. 'Kent screen on the blink, of course. No odds. Useless anyway. Heavy snow, thirty knot wind and visibility zero.' There was a certain satisfaction in Bowen's voice and neither Batesman nor Hudson, the helmsman, had to ask why. All three belonged to the group of thought that had minimal belief in the Geneva Convention: no plane, ship or submarine could hope to locate them in those conditions. 'Been through to the engine-room?'

'I have not.' Batesman spoke with some feeling and Bowen smiled. Chief Engineer Patterson, a north-easterner from the Newcastle area, had a high pride in his undoubted skill, a temper with a notoriously short fuse and a rooted aversion to being questioned about his activities by anyone as lowly as a third officer. 'I'll get the Chief, sir.'

He got the Chief. Bowen took the phone and said: 'Ah, John. Not having much luck this trip, are we? Overload coil? Brushes? Fuse? Ah! The standby, then – I do hope we're not out of fuel again.' Captain Bowen spoke in tones of grave concern and Batesman smiled: every member of the crew, down even to the pantry-boy, knew that Chief Patterson was totally devoid of any sense of humour. Bowen's reference to fuel referred to the occasion when, with Chief Patterson off duty, the main generator had failed and the young engineer in charge had forgotten to turn the cock on the fuel line to the auxiliary. Patterson's comments were predictable. With a pained expression on his face, Bowen held the phone a foot from his ear until the crackling in the earpiece had ceased, spoke briefly again, then hung up and said diplomatically: 'I think Chief Patterson is having rather more trouble than usual in locating electrical faults. Ten minutes, he says.'

Only two minutes later the phone rang.

'Bad news, for a fiver.' Bowen lifted the phone, listened briefly, then said: 'You want a word with me, John? But you *are* having a word with me . . . Ah. I see. Very well.' He hung up. 'The Chief wants to show me something.'

Bowen did not, as Batesman might have assumed, go to the engine-room. He went, instead, to his cabin where he was joined within a minute by the Chief Engineer. A tall, lean man, with an unremarkable face and a permanent five o'clock shadow, he was, like a number of men who are humourless and unaware of it, given to smiling at frequent intervals and usually at inappropriate moments. He was not, however, smiling at that particular moment. He produced three pieces of what appeared to be black carbon and arranged them on the Captain's table until they formed an oblong shape.

'What do you make of that, then?'

'You know me, John, just a simple seaman. An armature brush for a dynamo or generator or whatever?'

'Exactly.' Patterson was much better at being grim than he was at smiling.

'Hence the power failure?'

'Nothing to do with the power failure. Overload coil thrown. Short somewhere. Jamieson's taken a

23

bridge-megger and gone off to locate it. Shouldn't take him long to locate it.'

This Bowen was prepared to believe. Jamieson, the Second Engineer, was a very bright young man with the unusual distinction of being an A.M.I.E.E. – an Associate Member of the Institute of Electrical Engineers. He said: 'So this brush comes from the auxiliary generator; it's broken, you seem unhappy about it, so I take it this is unusual.'

'Unusual? It's unknown. At least, I've never known of it. The brush is under constant spring-loaded pressure against the face of the armature. There is no way it could have broken in this particular fashion.'

'Well, it did happen. First time for everything.' Bowen touched the broken pieces with his finger. 'A one-off job? Flaw in manufacture?'

Patterson didn't answer. He dug into an overall pocket, brought out a small metal box, removed the lid and placed the box on the table beside the broken brush. The two brushes inside were identical in shape and size to the one that Patterson had reassembled. Bowen looked at them, pursed his lips, then looked at Patterson.

'Spares?' Patterson nodded. Bowen picked one up but only one half came away in his hand: the other half remained in the bottom of the box.

'Our only two spares,' Patterson said.

'No point in examining the other?'

'None. Both generators were examined and in good shape when we were in Halifax – and we've used the auxiliary twice since leaving there.'

'One broken brush could be an extraordinary fluke. Three broken ones don't even make for a ludicrous coincidence. Doesn't even call for thoughtful chin-rubbing, John. We have an ill-intentioned crank in our midst.'

'Crank! Saboteur, you mean.'

'Well, yes, I suppose. At least, someone who is ill-disposed to us. Or towards the *San Andreas*. But saboteur? I wonder. Saboteurs go in for varied forms of wholesale destruction. Breaking three generator brushes can hardly be classified as wholesale destruction. And unless the character responsible is deranged he's not going to send the *San Andreas* to the bottom – not with him inside it. Why, John, why?'

They were still sitting there, darkly pondering why, when a knock came at the door and Jamieson entered. Young, red-headed and with an ebullient and carefree attitude to life, he was being anything but ebullient and carefree at that moment: he had about him an air of gravity and anxiety, both quite alien to his nature.

'Engine-room told me I'd find you here. I thought I should come at once.'

'As the bearer of bad news,' Captain Bowen said. 'You have discovered two things: the location of the short and evidence of, shall we say, sabotage?'

'How the hell – I'm sorry, sir, but how could you possibly –'

'Tell him, John,' Bowen said.

'I don't have to. Those broken brushes are enough. What did you find, Peter?'

'For'ard. Carpenter's shop. Lead cable passing through a bulkhead. Clips on either side seemed to have worked loose where it passed through the hole in the bulkhead.'

Bowen said: 'Normal ship's vibration, weather movement – doesn't take much to chafe through soft lead.'

'Lead's tougher than you think, sir. In this case a pair of hands helped the normal chafing along. Not that that matters. Inside the lead sheathing the rubber round the power cable has been scorched away.'

'Which one would expect in a short?'

'Yes, sir. Only, I know the smell of electrically burnt rubber and it doesn't smell like sulphur. Some bright lad had used an igniting match-head or heads to do the trick. I've left Ellis on the repair job. It's simple and he should be about through now.'

'Well, well. So it's as easy as that to knock out a ship's electrical power.'

'Almost, sir. He'd one other little job to do. There's a fuse-box just outside the carpenter's shop and he removed the appropriate fuse before starting work. Then he returned to the fuse-box and shorted out the line – insulated pliers, ditto screwdriver, almost anything would do – then replaced the fuse. If he'd replaced the fuse before shorting out the line it would have blown, leaving the rest of the electrical system intact. Theoretically, that is – on very rare occasions the fuse is not so obliging and doesn't go.' Jamieson smiled faintly. 'Fact of the matter is, if I'd had a cold in the nose he might have got away with it.'

The phone rang. Captain Bowen lifted it and handed it over to Patterson who listened, said: 'Sure. Now,' and handed the phone back. 'Engine-room. Power coming on.'

Perhaps half a minute passed, then Captain Bowen said mildly: 'You know, I don't think the power *is* coming on.'

Jamieson rose and Bowen said: 'Where are you going?'

'I don't know, sir. Well, first of all to the engine-room to pick up Ellis and the bridge-megger and then I don't know. It would seem that old Flannelfoot has more than one string to his bow.'

The phone rang again and Bowen, without answering, handed it over to Patterson, who listened briefly, said: 'Thank you. Mr Jamieson is coming down,' and handed the phone back. 'Same again. I wonder how many places our friend *has* jinxed and is just waiting for the opportunity to activate them.'

Jamieson hesitated at the door. 'Do we keep this to ourselves?'

27

'We do not.' Bowen was positive. 'We broadcast it far and wide. Granted, Flannelfoot, as you call him, will be forewarned and forearmed, but the knowledge that a saboteur is at large will make everyone look at his neighbour and wonder what a saboteur looks like. If nothing else, it will make this lad a great deal more circumspect and, with any luck, may restrict his activities quite a bit.' Jamieson nodded and left.

Bowen said: 'I think, John, you might double the watch in the engine-room or at least bring two or three extra men – not, you understand, for engine-room duties.'

'I understand. You think, perhaps –'

'If you wanted to sabotage, incapacitate a ship, where would you go?'

Patterson rose, went to the door and, as Jamieson had done, stopped there and turned. 'Why?' he said. 'Why, why, why?'

'I don't know why. But I have an unpleasant feeling about the where and the when. Here or hereabouts and sooner than we think, quicker than we want. Somebody,' Captain Bowen said as if by way of explanation, 'has just walked over my grave.' Patterson gave him a long look and closed the door quietly behind him.

Bowen picked up the phone, dialled a single number and said: 'Archie, my cabin.' He had no sooner replaced the receiver when it rang again. It was the bridge. Batesman didn't sound too happy.

'Snowstorm's blowing itself out, sir. *Andover* can see us now. Wants to know why we're not showing any lights. I told them we had a power failure, then another message just now, why the hell are we taking so long to fix it?'

'Sabotage.'

'I beg your pardon, sir.'

'Sabotage. S for Sally, A for Arthur, B for Bobby, O for –'

'Good God! Whatever – I mean, why –'

'I do not know why.' Captain Bowen spoke with a certain restraint. 'Tell them that. I'll tell you what I know – which is practically nothing – when I come up to the bridge. Five minutes. Maybe ten.'

Archie McKinnon, the Bo'sun, came in. Captain Bowen regarded the Bo'sun – as indeed many other captains regarded their bo'suns – as the most important crew member aboard. He was a Shetlander, about six feet two in height and built accordingly, perhaps forty years of age, with a brick-coloured complexion, blue-grey eyes and flaxen hair – the last two almost certainly inheritances from Viking ancestors who had passed by – or through – his native island a millennium previously.

'Sit down, sit down,' Bowen said. He sighed. 'Archie, we have a saboteur aboard.'

'Have we now.' He raised eyebrows, no startled oaths from the Bo'sun, not ever. 'And what has he been up to, Captain?'

Bowen told him what he had been up to and said: 'Can you make any more of it than I can, which is zero?'

'If you can't, Captain, I can't.' The regard in which the Captain held the Bo'sun was wholly reciprocated. 'He doesn't want to sink the ship, not with him aboard and the water temperature below freezing. He doesn't want to stop the ship – there's half a dozen ways a clever man could do that. I'm thinking myself that all he wanted to do is to douse the lights which – at night-time, anyway – identify us as a hospital ship.'

'And why would he want to do that, Archie?' It was part of their unspoken understanding that the Captain always called him 'Bo'sun' except when they were alone.

'Well.' The Bo'sun pondered. 'You know I'm not a Highlander or a Western Islander so I can't claim to be fey or have the second sight.' There was just the faintest suggestion of an amalgam of disapproval and superiority in the Bo'sun's voice but the Captain refrained from smiling: essentially, he knew, Shetlanders did not regard themselves as Scots and restricted their primary allegiance to the Shetlands. 'But like yourself, Captain, I have a nose for trouble and I can't say I'm very much liking what I can smell. Half an hour – well, maybe forty minutes – anybody will be able to see that we are a hospital ship.' He paused and looked at the Captain with what might possibly have been a hint of surprise which

was the nearest the Bo'sun ever came to register-
ing emotion. 'I can't imagine why but I have the
feeling that someone is going to have a go at us
before dawn. At dawn, most likely.'

'I can't imagine why either, Archie, but I have
the same feeling myself. Alert the crew, will
you? Ready for emergency stations. Spread the
word that there's an illegal electrician in our
midst.'

The Bo'sun smiled. 'So that they can keep an
eye on each other. I don't think, Captain, that
we'll find the man among the crew. They've been
with us for a long time now.'

'I hope not and I think not. That's to say, I'd like
to think not. But it was someone who knew his
way around. Their wages are not exactly on a
princely scale. You'd be surprised what a bag of
gold can do to a man's loyalty.'

'After twenty-five years at sea, there isn't a
great deal that can surprise me. Those survivors we
took off that tanker last night – well, I wouldn't
care to call any of them my blood-brother.'

'Come, come, Bo'sun, a little of the spirit of
Christian charity, if you please. It was a Greek
tanker – Greece is supposed to be an ally, if you
remember – and the crew would be Greek. Well,
Greek, Cypriot, Lebanese, Hottentot if you like.
Can't expect them all to look like Shetlanders. I
didn't see any of them carrying a pot of gold.'

'No. But some of them – the uninjured ones, I
mean – were carrying suitcases.'

'And some of them were carrying overcoats and at least three of them were wearing ties. And why not? The *Argos* spent six hours there wallowing around after being mined: time and enough for anyone to pack his worldly possessions or such few possessions as Greek seamen appear to have. It would be a bit much I think, Archie, to expect a crippled Greek tanker in the Barents Sea to have aboard a crewman with a bag of gold who just happened to be a trained saboteur.'

'Aye, it's not a combination that one would expect to find every day. Do we alert the hospital?'

'Yes. What's the latest down there?' The Bo'sun invariably knew the state of everything aboard the *San Andreas* whether it concerned his department or not.

'Dr Singh and Dr Sinclair have just finished operating. One man with a broken pelvis, the other with extensive burns. They're in the recovery room now and should be okay. Nurse Magnusson is with them.'

'My word, Archie, you do appear to be singularly well-informed.'

'Nurse Magnusson is a Shetlander,' the Bo'sun said, as if that explained everything. 'Seven patients in Ward A, not fit to be moved. Worst is the Chief Officer of the *Argos*, but not in danger, Janet says.'

'Janet?'

'Nurse Magnusson.' The Bo'sun was a difficult man to put off his stride. 'Ten in recuperating

Ward B. The *Argos* survivors are in the bunks on the port side.'

'I'll go down there now. Go and alert the crew. When you've finished, come along to the sick-bay – and bring a couple of your men with you.'

'Sick-bay?' The Bo'sun regarded the deckhead. 'You'd better not let Sister Morrison hear you call it that.'

Bowen smiled. 'Ah, the formidable Sister Morrison. All right, hospital. Twenty sick men down there. Not to mention sisters, nurses and ward orderlies who –'

'And doctors.'

'And doctors who have never heard a shot fired in their lives. A close eye, Archie.'

'You are expecting the worst, Captain?'

'I am not,' Bowen said heavily, 'expecting the best.'

The hospital area of the *San Andreas* was remarkably airy and roomy, remarkably but not surprisingly, for the *San Andreas* was primarily a hospital and not a ship and well over half of the lower deck space had been given over to its medical facilities. The breaching of watertight bulkheads – a hospital ship, theoretically, did not require watertight bulkheads – increased both the sense and the actuality of the spaciousness. The area was taken up by two wards, an operating theatre, recovery room, medical store, dispensary, galley – quite separate from and independent of the crew's galley – cabins for the medical staff, two messes – one for the staff, the other for recuperating patients – and a small lounge. It was towards the last of these that Captain Bowen now made his way.

He found three people there, having tea: Dr Singh, Dr Sinclair and Sister Morrison. Dr Singh was an amiable man of 'Pakistan' descent, middle-aged and wearing a pince-nez – he was one of the few people who looked perfectly at home with such glasses. He was a qualified and competent surgeon who disliked being called 'Mister'. Dr Sinclair, sandy-haired and every bit as amiable as his colleague, was twenty-six years old and had quit in his second year as an intern in a big teaching hospital to volunteer for service in the Merchant Navy. Nobody could ever have accused Sister Morrison of being amiable: about the same age as Sinclair, she had auburn hair, big brown eyes and a generous mouth, all three of which accorded ill with her habitually prim expression, the steel-rimmed glasses which she occasionally affected and a faint but unmistakable aura of aristocratic hauteur. Captain Bowen wondered what she looked like when she smiled: he wondered if she ever smiled.

He explained, briefly, why he had come. Their reactions were predictable. Sister Morrison pursed her lips, Dr Sinclair raised his eyebrows and Dr Singh, half-smiling, said: 'Dear me, dear me. Saboteur or saboteurs, spy or spies aboard a British vessel. Quite unthinkable.' He meditated briefly. 'But then, not everybody aboard is strictly British. I'm not, for one.'

'Your passport says you are.' Bowen smiled. 'As you were operating in the theatre at the time that our saboteur was operating elsewhere that automatically removes you from the list of potential suspects. Unfortunately, we don't have a list of suspects, potential or otherwise. We do indeed, Dr Singh, have a fair number of people who were not born in Britain. We have two Indians – lascars – two Goanese, two Singhalese, two Poles, a Puerto Rican, a Southern Irishman and, for some odd reason, an Italian who, as an official enemy, ought to be a prisoner-of-war or in an internment camp somewhere. And, of course, the survivors of the *Argos* are non-British to a man.'

'And don't forget me,' Sister Morrison said coldly. 'I'm half German.'

'You are? With a name like Margaret Morrison?'

She pursed her lips, an exercise which seemed to come naturally to her. 'How do you know that my name is Margaret?'

'A captain holds the crew lists. Like it or not, you are a member of the crew. Not that any of this matters. Spies, saboteurs, can be of any nationality and the more unlikely they are – in this case being British – the more efficiently they can operate. As I say, that's at the moment irrelevant. What is relevant is that the Bo'sun and two of his men will be here very shortly. Should an emergency arise he will assume complete charge except, of course, for the handling of the very ill. I assume you all know the Bo'sun?'

'An admirable man,' Dr Singh said. 'Very reassuring, very competent, couldn't imagine anyone I'd rather have around in times of need.'

'We all know him.' Sister Morrison was as good with her cold tones as she was with her pursed lips. 'Heaven knows he's here often enough.'

'Visiting the sick?'

'Visiting the sick! I don't like the idea of an ordinary seaman pestering one of my nurses.'

'Mr McKinnon is not an ordinary seaman. He's an extraordinary seaman and he's never pestered anyone in his life. Let's have Janet along here to see if she bears out your preposterous allegations.'

'You – you know her name.'

'Of course I know her name.' Bowen sounded weary. It was not the moment, he thought, to mention the fact that until five minutes ago he had never heard of anyone called Janet. 'They come from the same island and have much to talk about. It would help, Miss Morrison, if you took as much interest in your staff as I do in mine.'

It was a good exit line, Bowen thought, but he wasn't particularly proud of himself. In spite of the way she spoke he rather liked the girl because

36

he suspected that the image she projected was not the real one and that there might be some very good reason for this: but she was not Archie McKinnon.

The Chief Officer, one Geraint Kennet, an unusual name but one that he maintained came from an ancient aristocratic lineage, was awaiting Bowen's arrival on the bridge. Kennet was a Welshman, lean of figure and of countenance, very dark and very irreverent.

'You are lost, Mr Kennet?' Bowen said. Bowen had long ago abandoned the old habit of addressing a Chief Officer as 'Mister'.

'When the hour strikes, sir, Kennet is there. I hear of alarms and excursions from young Jamie here.' 'Young Jamie' was Third Officer Batesman. 'Something sinister afoot, I gather.'

'You gather rightly. Just how sinister I don't know.' He described what little had happened. 'So, two electrical breakdowns, if you could call them that, and a third in the process of being investigated.'

'And it would be naïve to think that the third is not connected with the other two?'

'Very naïve.'

'This presages something ominous.'

'Don't they teach you English in those Welsh schools.'

'No, sir. I mean, yes, sir. You have reached a conclusion, not, perhaps, a very nice one?'

The phone rang. Batesman took it and handed the phone to Bowen who listened briefly, thanked the caller and hung up.

'Jamieson. In the cold room, this time. How could anyone get into the cold room? Cook's got the only key.'

'Easily,' Kennet said. 'If a man was a saboteur, trained in his art – if that's the word I want – one would expect him to be an expert picklock or at least to carry a set of skeleton keys around with him. With respect, sir, I hardly think that's the point. When will this villain strike again?'

'When indeed. Flannelfoot – that's Jamieson's term for him – seems to be a villain of some resource and foresight. It is more than likely that he has some further surprises. Jamieson is of the same mind. If there's another power failure when they switch on again he says he's going to go over every inch of wiring with his bridge-megger, whatever that is.'

'Some sort of instrument for detecting voltage leaks – you know, breaks in a circuit. It's occurred to me –'

Chief Radio Officer Spenser appeared at the hatchway of his wireless office, paper in hand. 'Message from the *Andover*, sir.'

Bowen read out: 'Continued absence of lights very serious. Essential expedite matters. Has saboteur been apprehended?'

Kennet said: 'Cue, I think for angry spluttering.'

'Man's a fool,' Bowen said. 'Commander Warrington, I mean, captain of the frigate. Spenser, send: "If you have any members of the Special Branch or CID with you they are welcome aboard. If not, kindly refrain from sending pointless signals. What the hell do you think we're trying to do?"'

Kennet said: 'In the circumstances, sir, a very restrained signal. As I was about to say —'

The phone rang again. Batesman took the call, listened, acknowledged, hung up and turned to the Captain.

'Engine-room, sir. Another malfunction. Both Jamieson and Third Engineer Ralson are on their way up with meggers.'

Bowen brought out his pipe and said nothing. He gave the impression of a man temporarily bereft of words. Kennet wasn't, but then, Kennet never was.

'Man never gets to finish a sentence on this bridge. Have you arrived at any conclusion, sir, however unpleasant?'

'Conclusion, no. Hunch, suspicion, yes. Unpleasant, yes. I would take odds that by or at dawn someone is going to have a go at us.'

'Fortunately,' Kennet said, 'I am not a betting man. In any event I wouldn't bet against my own convictions. Which are the same as yours, sir.'

'We're a hospital ship, sir,' Batesman said. He didn't even sound hopeful.

Bowen favoured him with a morose glance. 'If you are immune to the sufferings of the sick and

39

dying and care to exercise a certain cold-blooded and twisted logic, then we are a man-of-war even though we are completely defenceless. For what do we do? We take our sick and wounded home, fix them up and send them off again to the front or to the sea to fight the Germans once more. If you were to stretch your conscience far enough you could make a good case out of maintaining that to allow a hospital ship to reach its homeland is tantamount to aiding and abetting the enemy. Oberleutnant Lemp would have torpedoed us without a second thought.'

'Oberleutnant who?'

'Lemp. Chap who sent the *Athenia* to the bottom – and Lemp knew that the *Athenia* carried only civilians as passengers, men, women and children who – he knew this well – would never be used to fight against the Germans. The *Athenia* was a case much more deserving of compassion than we are, don't you think, Third?'

'I wish you wouldn't talk like that, sir.' Batesman was now not only as morose as the Captain had been, but positively mournful. 'How do we know that this fellow Lemp is not lurking out there, just over the horizon?'

'Fear not,' Kennet said. 'Oberleutnant Lemp has long since been gathered to his ancestors, for whom one can feel only a certain degree of sympathy. However, he may have a twin brother or some kindred souls out there. As the Captain so rightly infers, we live in troubled and uncertain times.'

Batesman looked at Bowen. 'Is it permitted, Captain, to ask the Chief Officer to shut up?'

Kennet smiled broadly, then stopped smiling as the phone rang again. Batesman reached for the phone but Bowen forestalled him. 'Master's privilege, Third. The news may be too heavy for a young man like you to bear.' He listened, cursed by way of acknowledgment and hung up. When he turned round he looked – and sounded – disgusted.

'Bloody officers' toilet!'

Kennet said, 'Flannelfoot?'

'Who do you think it was? Santa Claus?'

'A sound choice,' Kennet said judiciously. 'Very sound. Where else could a man work in such peace, privacy and for an undetermined period of time, blissfully immune, one might say, from any fear of interruption? Might even have time to read a chapter of his favourite thriller, as is the habit of one young officer aboard this ship, who shall remain nameless.'

'The Third Officer has the right of it,' Bowen said. 'Will you kindly shut up?'

'Yes, sir. Was that Jamieson?'

'Yes.'

'We should be hearing from Ralson any time now.'

'Jamieson has already heard from him. Seamen's toilet this time, port side.'

For once, Kennet had no observation to make and for almost a minute there was silence on the bridge for the sufficient reason that there didn't seem to be any comment worth making. When the silence was broken it was, inevitably, by Kennet.

'A few more minutes and our worthy engineers might as well cease and desist. Or am I the only person who has noticed that the dawn is in the sky?'

The dawn, indeed, was in the sky. Already, to the south-east, off the port beam, the sky had changed from black, or as black as it ever becomes in northern waters, to a dark grey and was steadily lightening. The snow had completely stopped now, the wind had dropped to twenty knots and the *San Andreas* was pitching, not heavily, in the head seas coming up from the north-west.

Kennet said, 'Shall I post a couple of extra look-outs, sir? One on either wing?'

'And what can those look-outs do? Make faces at the enemy?'

'They can't do a great deal more, and that's a fact. But if anyone is going to have a go at us, it's going to be now. A high-flying Condor, for instance, you can almost see the bombs leaving the bay and there's an even chance in evasive action.' Kennet didn't sound particularly enthusiastic or convinced.

'And if it's a submarine, dive-bomber, glider-bomber or torpedo-bomber?'

'They can still give us warning and time for a prayer. Mind you, probably a very short prayer, but still a prayer.'

'As you wish, Mr Kennet.'

Kennet made a call and within three minutes his look-outs arrived on the bridge, duffel-coated and scarfed to the eyebrows as Kennet had instructed. McGuigan and Jones, a Southern Irishman and a Welshman, they were boys only, neither of them a day over eighteen. Kennet issued them with binoculars and posted them on the bridge wings, Jones to port, McGuigan to starboard. Seconds only after closing the port door, Jones opened it again.

'Ship, sir! Port quarter.' His voice was excited, urgent. 'Warship, I think.'

'Relax,' Kennet said. 'I doubt whether it's the *Tirpitz*.' Less than half a dozen people aboard knew that the *Andover* had accompanied them during the night. He stepped out on to the wing and returned almost immediately. 'The good shepherd,' he said. 'Three miles.'

'It's almost half-light now,' Captain Bowen said. 'We could be wrong, Mr Kennet.'

The radio room hatchway panel banged open and Spenser's face appeared.

'*Andover*, sir. Bandit, bandit, one bandit . . . 045 . . . ten miles . . . five thousand.'

'There now,' Kennet said. 'I knew we weren't wrong. Full power, sir?' Bowen nodded and Kennet gave the necessary instructions to the engine-room.

'Evasive action?' Bowen was half-smiling; knowledge, however unwelcome that knowledge, always comes as a relief after uncertainty. 'A Condor, you would guess?'

'No guess, sir. In those waters, only the Condor flies alone.' Kennet slid back the port wing door and gazed skywards. 'Cloud cover's pretty thin now. We should be able to see our friend coming up – he should be practically dead astern. Shall we go out on the wing, sir?'

'In a minute, Mr Kennet. Two minutes. Gather flowers while we may – or, at least, keep warm as long as possible. If fate has abandoned us we shall be freezing to death all too soon. Tell me, Mr Kennet, has any profound thought occurred to you?'

'A lot of thoughts have occurred to me but I wouldn't say any of them are profound.'

'How on earth do you think that Condor located us?'

'Submarine? It could have surfaced and radioed Alta Fjord.'

'No submarine. The *Andover*'s sonar would have picked him up. No plane, no surface ships, that's a certainty.'

Kennet frowned for a few seconds, then smiled. 'Flannel-foot,' he said with certainty. 'A radio.'

'Not necessarily even that. A small electrical device, probably powered by our own mains system, that transmits a continuous homing signal.'

'So if we survive this lot it's out with the fine-tooth comb?'

'Indeed. It's out with –'

'*Andover*, sir.' It was Spenser again. 'Four bandits, repeat four bandits . . . 310 . . . eight miles . . . three thousand.'

'I wonder what we've done to deserve this?' Kennet sounded almost mournful. 'We were even more right than we thought, sir. Torpedo-bombers or glider-bombers, that's for sure, attacking out of the darkness to the north-west and us silhouetted against the dawn.'

The two men moved out on the port wing. The *Andover* was still on the port quarter but had closed in until it was less than two miles distant. A low bank of cloud, at about the same distance, obscured the view aft.

'Hear anything, Mr Kennet? See anything?'

'Nothing, nothing. Damn that cloud. Yes, I do. I hear it. It's a Condor.'

'It's a Condor.' Once heard, the desynchronized clamour of a Focke-Wulf 200's engine is not readily forgotten. 'And I'm afraid, Mr Kennet, that you'll have to postpone your evasive action practice for another time. This lad sounds as if he is coming in very low.'

'Yes, he's coming in low. And I know why.' Most unusually for Kennet, he sounded very bitter. 'He intends to do some pinpoint precision bombing. He's under orders to stop us or cripple us but not sink us. I'll bet that bastard Flannelfoot feels as safe as houses.'

'You have it to rights, Mr Kennet. He could stop us by bombing the engine-room, but doing that is a practical guarantee that we go to the bottom. There he comes, now.' The Focke-Wulf Condor had broken through the cloud and was heading directly for the stern of the *San Andreas*. Every gun on the *Andover* that could be brought to bear had opened up as soon as the Focke-Wulf had cleared the cloud-bank and within seconds the starboard side of the *Andover* was wreathed in smoke. For a frigate, its anti-aircraft fire-power was formidable: low-angle main armament, pom-poms, Oerlikons and the equally deadly Boulton-Paul Defiant turrets which loosed off a devastating 960 rounds a minute. The Focke-Wulf must have been hit many times but the big Condor's capacity to absorb punishment was legendary. Still it came on, now no more than two hundred feet above the waves. The sound of the engines had risen from the clamorous to the thunderous.

'This is no place for a couple of honest seamen to be, Mr Kennet.' Captain Bowen had to shout to make himself heard. 'But I think it's too late now.'

'I rather think it is, sir.'

Two bombs, just two, arced lazily down from the now smoking Condor.

TWO

Had the Americans retained the original British design concept for accommodation aboard the Liberty Ships, the tragedy, while still remaining such, would at least have been minimized. The original Sunderland plans had the accommodation both fore and aft: Henry Kaiser's designers, in their wisdom – blind folly as it turned out – had *all* their accommodation, for both officers and men, including also the navigating bridge, grouped in a single superstructure surrounding the funnel.

The Bo'sun, Dr Sinclair by his side, had reached the upper deck before the Condor reached the *San Andreas;* they were almost immediately joined by Patterson for whom the *Andover'*s barrage had sounded like a series of heavy metallic blows on the side of his engine-room.

'Down!' the Bo'sun shouted. Two powerful arms around their shoulders bore them to the deck, for the Focke-Wulf had reached the *San Andreas* before the bombs did and the Bo'sun was well aware that the Focke-Wulf carried a fairly lethal array of machine guns which it did not hesitate to use when the occasion demanded. On this occasion, however, the guns remained silent, possibly because the gunners were under instructions not to fire, more probably because the gunners were already dead, for it was plain that the Condor, trailing a huge plume of black smoke, whether from fuselage or engines it was impossible to say, and veering sharply to starboard, was itself about to die.

The two bombs, contact and not armour-piercing, struck fore and aft of the funnel, exploded simultaneously and just immediately after passing through the unprotected deck-heads of the living quarters, blowing the shattered bulkheads outwards and filling the air with screaming shards of metal and broken glass, none of which reached the three prone men. The Bo'sun cautiously lifted his head and stared in disbelief as the funnel, seemingly intact but sheared off at its base toppled slowly over the port side and into the sea. Any sound of a splash that there may have been was drowned out by the swelling roar of more aero engines.

'Stay down, stay down!' Flat on the deck, the Bo'sun twisted his head to the right. There were four of them in line abreast formation, Heinkel torpedo-bombers, half a mile away, no more than twenty feet above the water and headed directly for the starboard side of the *San Andreas*. Ten seconds, he thought, twelve at the most and the dead men in the charnel house of that shattered superstructure would have company and to spare. Why had the guns of the *Andover* fallen silent? He twisted his head to the left to look at the frigate and immediately realized why. It was impossible that the gunners on the *Andover* could not hear the sound of the approaching Heinkels but it was equally impossible that they could see them. The *San Andreas* was directly in line between the frigate and the approaching bombers which were flying below the height of their upper deck.

He twisted his head to the right again and to his momentary astonishment saw that this was no longer the case. The Heinkels were lifting clear of the water with the intention of flying over the *San Andreas*, which they did seconds later, not much more than ten feet above the deck, two on each side of the twisted superstructure. The *San Andreas* had not been the target, only the shield for the Heinkels: the frigate was the target and the bombers were half way between the *San Andreas* and the frigate before the bemused defenders aboard the *Andover* understood what was happening.

When they did understand their reaction was sharp and violent. The main armament was virtually useless. It takes time to train and elevate a gun of any size and against a close-in and fast-moving target there just isn't time. The anti-aircraft guns, the two-pounders, the Oerlikons and the Defiants

49

did indeed mount a heavy barrage but torpedo-bombers were notoriously difficult targets, not least because the gunners were acutely aware that death was only seconds away, a realization that made for less than a controlled degree of accuracy.

The bombers were less than three hundred yards away when the plane on the left-hand side of the formation pulled up and banked to its left to clear the stern of the *Andover*: almost certainly neither the plane nor the pilot had been damaged: as was not unknown, the torpedo release mechanism had iced up, freezing the torpedo in place. At about the same instant the plane on the right descended in a shallow dive until it touched the water – almost certainly the pilot had been shot. A victory but a Pyrrhic one. The other two Heinkels released their torpedoes and lifted clear of the *Andover*.

Three torpedoes hit the *Andover* almost simultaneously, the two that had been cleanly released and the one that was still attached to the plane that had crashed into the water. All three torpedoes detonated but there was little enough in the way of thunderclaps of sound or shock waves: water always has this same muffling effect on an underwater explosion. What they did produce, however, was a great sheet of water and spray which rose to two hundred feet into the sky and then slowly subsided. When it finally disappeared the *Andover* was on its beam ends and deep in the water. Within twenty seconds, with only a faint hissing as the water flooded the engine-room and with curiously little in the way of bubbles, the *Andover* slid beneath the surface of the sea.

'My God, my God, my God!' Dr Sinclair, swaying slightly, was on his feet. As a doctor, he was acquainted with death, but not in this shocking form: he was still dazed, not quite aware of what was going on around him. 'Good God, that big plane is coming back again!'

The big plane, the Condor, was indeed coming back again, but it offered no threat to them. Dense smoke pouring from all four engines, it completed a half circle and was approaching the *San Andreas*. Less than half a mile away it touched the surface of the sea, momentarily dipped beneath it, then came into sight again. There was no more smoke.

'God rest them,' Patterson said. He was almost abnormally calm. 'Damage control party first, see if we're making water, although I shouldn't have thought so.'

'Yes, sir.' The Bo'sun looked at what was left of the superstructure. 'Perhaps a fire-control party. Lots of blankets, mattresses, clothes, papers in there – God only knows what's smouldering away already.'

'Do you think there will be any survivors in there?'

'I wouldn't even guess, sir. If there are, thank heavens we're a hospital ship.'

Patterson turned to Dr Sinclair and shook him gently. 'Doctor, we need your help.' He nodded towards the superstructure. 'You and Dr Singh – and the ward orderlies. I'll send some men with sledges and crowbars.'

'An oxy-acetylene torch?' said the Bo'sun.

'Of course.'

'We've got enough medical equipment and stores aboard to equip a small town hospital,' Sinclair said. 'If there are any survivors all we'll require is a few hypodermic syringes.' He seemed back on balance again. 'We don't take in the nurses?'

'Good God, no.' Patterson shook his head vehemently. 'I tell you, *I* wouldn't like to go in there. If there are any survivors they'll have their share of horrors later.'

McKinnon said: 'Permission to take away the lifeboat, sir?'

'Whatever for?'

'There could be survivors from the *Andover*.'

'Survivors! She went down in thirty seconds.'

'The *Hood* blew apart in one second. There were three survivors.'

'Of course, of course. I'm not a seaman, Bo'sun. You don't need permission from me.'

'Yes, I do, sir.' The Bo'sun gestured towards the superstructure. 'All the deck officers are there. You're in command.'

'Good God!' The thought, the realization had never struck Patterson. 'What a way to assume command!'

'And speaking of command, sir, the *San Andreas* is no longer under command. She's slewing rapidly to port. Steering mechanism on the bridge must have been wrecked.'

'Steering can wait. I'll stop the engines.'

Three minutes later the Bo'sun eased the throttle and edged the lifeboat towards an inflatable life raft which was roller-coasting heavily near the spot where the now vanished Condor had been. There were only two men in the raft – the rest of the air-crew, the Bo'sun assumed, had gone to the bottom with the Focke-Wulf. They had probably been dead anyway. One of the men, no more than a young-ster, very seasick and looking highly apprehensive – he had every right, the Bo'sun thought, to be apprehensive – was sitting upright and clinging to a lifeline. The other lay on his back in the bottom of the raft: in the regions of his left upper chest, left upper arm and right thigh his flying overalls were saturated with blood. His eyes were closed.

'Jesus' sake!' Able Seaman Ferguson, who had a powerful Liverpool accent and whose scarred face spoke eloquently of battles lost and won, mainly in bar-rooms, looked at the Bo'sun with a mixture of disbelief and outrage. 'Jesus, Bo'sun, you're not going to pick those bastards up? They just tried to send us to the bottom. Us! A hospital ship!'

'Wouldn't you like to know *why* they bombed a hospital ship?'

'There's that, there's that.' Ferguson reached out with a boathook and brought the raft along-side.

'Either of you speak English?'

The wounded man opened his eyes: they, too, seemed to be filled with blood. 'I do.'

'You look badly hurt. I want to know where before we try to bring you aboard.'

'Left arm, left shoulder, I think, right thigh. And I believe there's something wrong with my right foot.' His English was completely fluent and if there was any accent at all it was a hint of southern standard English, not German.

'You're the Condor Captain, of course.'

'Yes. Still want to bring me aboard?'

The Bo'sun nodded to Ferguson and the two other seamen he had along with him. The three men brought the injured pilot aboard as carefully as they could but with both lifeboat and raft rolling heavily in the beam seas it was impossible to be too careful. They laid him in the thwarts close to where the Bo'sun was sitting by the controls. The other survivor huddled miserably amidships. The Bo'sun opened the throttle and headed for the position where he estimated the *Andover* had gone down.

Ferguson looked down at the injured man who was lying motionless on his back, arms spread-eagled. The red stains were spreading. It could have been that he was still bleeding quite heavily: but it could have been the effect of sea-water.

'Reckon he's a goner, Bo'sun?'

McKinnon reached down and touched the side of the pilot's neck and after a few seconds he located the pulse, fast, faint and erratic, but still a pulse.

'Unconscious. Fainted. Couldn't have been an easy passage for him.'

Ferguson regarded the pilot with a certain grudging respect. 'He may be a bloody murderer, but he's a bloody tough bloody murderer. Must have been in agony, but never a squawk. Shouldn't we take him back to the ship first? Give him a chance, like?'

'I thought of it. No. There just may be survivors from the *Andover* and if there are they won't last long. Sea temperature is about freezing or just below it. A man's usually dead inside a minute. If there's anyone at all, a minute's delay may be a minute too late. We owe them that chance. Besides it's going to be a very quick trip back to the ship.'

The *San Andreas*, slewing to port, had come around in a full half-circle and, under reverse thrust, was slowing to a stop. Patterson had almost certainly done this so as to manoeuvre the temporarily rudderless ship as near as possible to the spot where the *Andover* had been torpedoed.

Only a pathetic scattering of flotsam and jetsam showed where the frigate had gone down, baulks of timber, a few drums, carley floats, lifebuoys and life jackets, all empty – and four men. Three of the men were together. One of them, a man with what appeared to be a grey stocking hat, was keeping the head of another man, either unconscious or dead, out of the water: with his other hand he waved at the approaching lifeboat. All three men were wearing life jackets and, much more importantly, all three were wearing wet suits, which was the only reason they were still alive after fifteen minutes in the ice-cold waters of an Arctic winter.

All three were hauled inboard. The young, bareheaded man who had been supported by the man with the grey stocking hat was unconscious, not dead. He had every reason, the Bo'sun thought, to be unconscious: there was a great swelling bruise still oozing blood just above the right temple. The third man – it seemed most incongruous in the circumstances – wore the peaked braided cap of a naval commander. The cap was completely saturated. The Bo'sun made to remove it, then changed his mind when he saw the blood at the back of the cap: the cap was probably stuck to his head. The commander was quite conscious, he had courteously thanked the Bo'sun for being pulled out of the sea: but his eyes were vacant, glazed and sightless. McKinnon passed a hand before his eyes, but there was no reaction: for the moment, at any rate, the commander was quite blind.

Although he knew he was wasting his time, the Bo'sun headed towards the fourth man in the water but he backed off when he was still five yards away. Although his face was deep in the water he hadn't died from drowning but from freezing: he wasn't wearing a wet suit. The Bo'sun turned the lifeboat back to the *San Andreas* and touched the commander gently on the shoulder.

'How do you feel, Commander Warrington?'

'What? How do I feel? How do you know I'm Commander Warrington?'

'You're still wearing your cap, sir.' The Commander made as if to touch the peak of his cap but the Bo'sun restrained him. 'Leave it, sir. You've cut your head and your hat's sticking to it. We'll have you in hospital inside fifteen minutes. Plenty of doctors and nurses there for that sort of thing, sir.'

'Hospital.' Warrington shook his head as if trying to clear it. 'Ah, of course. The *San Andreas*. You must be from her.'

'Yes, sir. I'm the Bo'sun.'

'What happened, Bo'sun? The *Andover*, I mean.' Warrington touched the side of his head. 'I'm a bit foggy up here.'

'No bloody wonder. Three torpedoes, sir, almost simultaneously. You must have been blown off the bridge, or fell off it, or most likely been washed off it when your ship went down. She was on her beam ends then, sir, and it took only just over twenty seconds.'

'How many of us – well, how many have you found?'

'Just three, sir. I'm sorry.'

'God above. Just three. Are you sure, Bo'sun?'

'I'm afraid I'm quite sure, sir.'

'My yeoman of signals –'

57

'I'm here, sir.'

'Ah. Hedges. Thank heavens for that. Who's the third?'

'Navigating officer, sir. He's taken a pretty nasty clout on the head.'

'And the First Lieutenant?' Hedges didn't answer, he had his head buried in his hands and was shaking it from side to side.

'I'm afraid Hedges is a bit upset, Commander. Was the First Lieutenant wearing a red kapok jacket?' Warrington nodded. 'Then we found him, sir. I'm afraid he just froze to death.'

'He would, wouldn't he? Freeze to death, I mean.' Warrington smiled faintly. 'Always used to laugh at us and our wet suits. Carried a rabbit's foot around with him and used to say that was all the wet suit he'd ever need.'

Dr Singh was the first man to meet the Bo'sun when he stepped out of the lifeboat. Patterson was with him, as were two orderlies and two stokers. The Bo'sun looked at the stokers and wondered briefly what they were doing on deck, but only very briefly: they were almost certainly doing a seaman's job because there were very few seamen left to do it. Ferguson and his two fellow seamen had been in the for'ard fire-control party and might well be the only three left: all the other seamen had been in the superstructure at the time of the attack.

'Five,' Dr Singh said. 'Just five. From the frigate and the plane, just five.'

'Yes, Doctor. And even they had the devil's own luck. Three of them are pretty wobbly. Commander looks all right but I think he's in the worst condition. He seems to have gone blind and the back of his head has been damaged. There's a connection, isn't there, Doctor?'

'Oh dear. Yes, there's a connection. We'll do what we can.'

Patterson said: 'A moment, Bo'sun, if you will.' He walked to one side and McKinnon followed him. They were half way towards the twisted superstructure when Patterson stopped.

'As bad as that is it, sir?' the Bo'sun said. 'No eavesdroppers. I mean, we have to trust someone.'

'I suppose.' Patterson looked and sounded tired. 'But damned few. Not after what I've seen inside that superstructure. Not after one or two things I've found out. First things first. The hull is still structurally sound. No leaks. I didn't think there would be. We're fixing up a temporary rudder control in the engine-room: we'll probably be able to reconnect to the bridge which is the least damaged part of the superstructure. There was a small fire in the crew's mess, but we got that under control.' He nodded to the sadly twisted mass of metal ahead of them. 'Let's pray for calm weather to come. Jamieson says the structural supports are so weakened that the whole lot is liable to go over the side if we hit heavy seas. Would you like to go inside?'

'Like? Not like. But I have to.' The Bo'sun hesitated, reluctant to hear the answer to the question he had to ask. 'What's the score so far, sir?'

'Up to now we've come across thirteen dead.' He grimaced. 'And bits and pieces. I've decided to leave them where they were meantime. There may be more people left alive.'

'More? You have found some?'

'Five. They're in a pretty bad way, some of them. They're in the hospital.' He led the way inside the twisted entrance at the after end of the superstructure. 'There are two oxy-acetylene teams in there. It's slow work. No fallen beams, no wreckage as such, just twisted and buckled doors. Some of them, of course – the doors, I mean – were just blown off. Like this one here.'

'The cold room. Well, at least there would have been nobody in there. But there were three weeks' supply of beef, all kinds of meat, fish and other perishables in there: in a couple of days' time we'll have to start heaving them over the side.' They moved slowly along the passageway. 'Cool room intact, sir, although I don't suppose a steady diet of fruit and veg. will have much appeal. Oh God!'

The Bo'sun stared into the galley which lay across the passage from the cool room. The surfaces of the cooking stoves were at a peculiar angle, but all the cupboards and the two work tables were intact. But what had caught the Bo'sun's horrified attention was not the furniture but the two men

60

who lay spreadeagled on the floor. They seemed unharmed except for a little trickle of blood from the ears and noses.

'Netley and Spicer,' the Bo'sun whispered. 'They don't seem – they're dead?'

'Concussion. Instantaneous,' Patterson said.

The Bo'sun shook his head and moved on.

'Tinned food store,' he said. 'Intact. It would be. And the liquor store here, not a can dented or a bottle broken.' He paused. 'With your permission, sir, I think this is a very good time to breach the liquor store. A hefty tot of rum all round – or at least for the men working in here. Pretty grim work and it's the custom in the Royal Navy when there's grim work to be done.'

Patterson smiled slightly, a smile that did not touch the eyes. 'I didn't know you were in the Royal Navy, Bo'sun.'

'Twelve years. For my sins.'

'An excellent idea,' Patterson said. 'I'll be your first customer.' They made their way up a twisted but still serviceable companionway to the next deck, the Bo'sun with a bottle of rum and half a dozen mugs strung on a wire in the other. This was the crew accommodation deck and it was not a pretty sight. The passageway had a distinct S-bend to it, the deck was warped so that it formed a series of undulations. At the for'ard end of the passageway, two oxy-acetylene teams were at work, each attacking a buckled door. In the short space between the head of the companionway

61

and where the men were working were eight doors, four of them hanging drunkenly on their hinges, four that had been cut open by torches: seven of those had been occupied, and the occupants were still there, twelve of them in all. In the eighth cabin they found Dr Sinclair, stooping over and administering a morphine injection to a prone but fully conscious patient, a consciousness that was testified to by the fact that he was addressing nobody in particular in an unprintable monologue.

The Bo'sun said: 'How do you feel, Chips?' Chips was Rafferty, the ship's carpenter.

'I'm dying.' He caught sight of the rum bottle in the Bo'sun's hand and his stricken expression vanished. 'But I could make a rapid recovery –'

'This man is not dying,' Dr Sinclair said. 'He has a simple fracture of the tibia, that's all. No rum – morphine and alcohol make for bad bedfellows. Later.' He straightened and tried to smile. 'But I could do with a tot, if you would, Bo'sun – a generous one. I feel in need of it.' With his strained face and pale complexion he unquestionably looked in need of it: nothing in Dr Sinclair's brief medical experience had even remotely begun to prepare him for the experience he was undergoing. The Bo'sun poured him the requisite generous measure, did the same for Patterson and himself, then passed the bottle and mugs to the men with the torches and the two ward orderlies who were standing unhappily by, strapped stretcher at the ready: they looked in no better case than Dr Sinclair but cheered up noticeably at the sight of the rum.

The deck above held the officers' accommodation. It too, had been heavily damaged, but not so devastatingly so as the deck below. Patterson stopped at the first cabin they came to: its door had been blown inwards and the contents of the cabin looked as if a maniac had been let loose there with a sledgehammer. The Bo'sun knew it was Chief Patterson's cabin.

The Bo'sun said, 'I don't much care for being in an engine-room, sir, but there are times when it has its advantages.' He looked at the empty and almost as badly damaged Second Engineer's cabin opposite. 'At least Ralson is not here. Where is he, sir?'

'He's dead.'

'He's dead,' the Bo'sun repeated slowly.

'When the bombs struck he was still in the seamen's toilet fixing that short-circuit.'

'I'm most damnably sorry, sir.' He knew that Ralson had been Patterson's only close friend aboard the ship.

'Yes,' Patterson said vaguely. 'He had a young wife and two kids – babies, really.'

The Bo'sun shook his head and looked into the next cabin, that belonging to the Second Officer. 'At least Mr Rawlings is not here.'

'No. He's not here. He's up on the bridge.' The Bo'sun looked at him, then turned away and went into the Captain's cabin which was directly opposite and which, oddly enough, seemed almost undamaged. The Bo'sun went directly to a small wooden cupboard on the bulkhead, produced his knife, opened up the marlinspike and inserted its point just below the cupboard lock.

'Breaking and entering, Bo'sun?' The Chief Engineer's voice held puzzlement but no reproof: he knew McKinnon well enough to know that the Bo'sun never did anything without a sound reason.

'Breaking and entering is for locked doors and windows, sir. Just call this vandalism.' The door sprang open and the Bo'sun reached inside, bringing out two guns. 'Navy Colt 45s. You know about guns, sir?'

'I've never held a gun in my hand in my life. *You* know about guns – as well as rum?'

'I know about guns. This little switch here – you press it so. Then the safety-catch is off. That's really all you require to know about guns.' He looked at the broken cupboard and then the guns and shook his head again. 'I don't think Captain Bowen would have minded.'

'Won't. Not wouldn't. Won't.'

The Bo'sun carefully laid the guns on the Captain's table. 'You're telling me that the Captain is not dead?'

'He's not dead. Neither is the Chief Officer.'

The Bo'sun smiled for the first time that morning, then looked accusingly at the Chief Engineer. 'You might have told me this, sir.'

'I suppose. I might have told you a dozen things. You would agree, Bo'sun, that we both have a great deal on our minds. They're both in the sick bay, both pretty savagely burnt about the face but not in any danger, not, at least, according to Dr Singh. It was being far out on the port wing of the bridge that saved them – they were away from the direct effects of the blast.'

'How come they got so badly burnt, sir?'

'I don't know. They can hardly speak, their faces are completely wrapped in bandages, they look more like Egyptian mummies than anything else. I asked the Captain and he kept mumbling something like Essex, or Wessex or something like that.'

The Bo'sun nodded. 'Wessex, sir. Rockets. Distress flares. Two lots kept on the bridge. The shock must have triggered some firing mechanism and it went off prematurely. Damnable ill luck.'

'Damnably lucky, if you ask me, Bo'sun. Compared to practically everybody else in the superstructure.'

'Does he – does he know yet?'

'It hardly seemed the time to tell him. Another thing he kept repeating, as if it was urgent. "Home signal, home signal," something like that. Over and over again. Maybe his mind was wandering, maybe I couldn't make him out. Their mouths are the only part of their faces that aren't covered with bandages but even their lips are pretty badly burnt. And, of course, they're loaded with morphine. "Home signal." Mean anything to you?'

'At the moment, no.'

A young and rather diminutive stoker appeared in the doorway. McCrimmon, in his middle twenties, was a less than lovable person, his primary and permanent characteristics being the interminable mastication of chewing gum, truculence, a fixed scowl and a filthy tongue: at that moment, the first three were in abeyance.

'Bloody awful, so it is, down there. Just like a bloody cemetery.'

'Morgue, McCrimmon, morgue,' Patterson said. 'What do you want?'

'Me. Nothing, sir. Jamieson sent me. He said something about the phones no' working and you would be wanting a runner, maybe.'

'Second Engineer to you, McCrimmon.' Patterson looked at the Bo'sun. 'Very thoughtful of the Second Engineer. Nothing we require in the engine-room – except to get that jury rudder fixed. Deck-side, Bo'sun?'

'Two look-outs, although God knows what they'll be looking out for. Two of your men, sir, the two ward orderlies below, Able Seaman Ferguson and Curran. Curran is – used to be – a sailmaker. Don't envy him his job but I'll give him a hand. Curran will know what to bring. I suggest, sir, we have the crew's mess-deck cleared.'

'Our mortuary?'

'Yes, sir.'

'You heard, McCrimmon? How many men?'

'Eight, sir.'

'Eight. Two look-outs. The two seamen to bring up the canvas and whatever required. The other four to clear the crew's mess. Don't you try to tell them, they'd probably throw you overboard. Tell the Second Engineer and he'll tell them. When they've finished have them report to me, here or on the bridge. You too. Off you go.' McCrimmon left.

The Bo'sun indicated the two Colts lying on the table. 'I wonder what McCrimmon thought of those.'

'Probably old hat to him. Jamieson picked the right man – McCrimmon's tough and hasn't much in the way of finer feelings. Irish-Scots from some Glasgow slum. Been in prison. In fact, if it wasn't for the war that's probably where he'd be now.'

The Bo'sun nodded and opened another small wall locker – this one had a key to it. It was a small liquor cupboard and from a padded velvet retainer McKinnon removed a rum bottle and laid it on the Captain's bunk.

'I don't suppose the Captain will mind that either,' Patterson said. 'For the stretcher-bearers?'

'Yes, sir.' The Bo'sun started opening drawers in the Captain's table and found what he was looking for in the third drawer, two leather-bound folders which he handed to Patterson. 'Prayer book and burial service, sir. But I should think the burial service would be enough. Somebody's got to read it.'

'Good God. I'm not a preacher, Bo'sun.'

'No, sir. But you're the officer commanding.'

'Good God,' Patterson repeated. He placed the folders reverently on the Captain's table. 'I'll look at those later.'

' "Home signal",' the Bo'sun said slowly. 'That's what the Captain said, wasn't it? "Home signal".'

'Yes.'

' "Homing signal" is what he was trying to say. "Homing signal". Should have thought of it before – but I suppose that's why Captain Bowen is a captain and I'm not. How do you think the Condor managed to locate us in the darkness? All right, it was half dawn when he attacked but he *must* have been on the course when it was still night. How did he know where we were?'

'U-boat?'

'No U-boat. The *Andover*'s sonar would have picked him up.' The Bo'sun was repeating the words that Captain Bowen had used.

'Ah.' Patterson nodded. 'Homing signal. Our saboteur friend.'

'Flannelfoot, as Mr Jamieson calls him. Not only was he busy fiddling around with our electrical circuits, he was transmitting a continuous signal. A directional signal. The Condor knew where we were to the inch. I don't know whether the Condor was equipped to receive such signals, I know nothing about planes, but it wouldn't have mattered, some place like Alta Fjord could have picked up the signal and transmitted our bearing to the Condor.'

'You have it, of course, Bo'sun, you have it to rights.' Patterson looked at the two guns. 'One for me and one for you.'

'If you say so, sir.'

'Don't be daft, who else would have it?' Patterson picked up a gun. 'I've never even held one of these things in my hand, far less fired one. But you know, Bo'sun, I don't really think I would mind firing a shot once. Just one.'

'Neither would I, sir.'

Second Officer Rawlings was lying beside the wheel and there was no mystery as to how he had died: what must have been a flying shard of metal had all but decapitated him.

'Where's the helmsman?' the Bo'sun asked. 'Was he a survivor, then?'

'I don't know. I don't know who was on. Maybe Rawlings had sent him to get something. But there were two survivors up here, apart from the Captain and Chief Officer – McGuigan and Jones.'

'McGuigan and Jones? What were they doing up here?'

'It seems Mr Kennet had called them up and posted them as look-outs, one on either wing. I suppose that's why they survived, just as Captain Bowen and Mr Kennet survived. They're in the hospital, too.'

'Badly hurt?'

'Unharmed, I believe. Shock, that's all.'

The Bo'sun moved out to the port wing and Patterson followed. The wing was wholly undamaged, no signs of metal buckling anywhere. The Bo'sun indicated a once grey but now badly scorched metal box which was attached just below the wind-breaker: its top and one side had been blown off.

'That's where they kept the Wessex rockets,' the Bo'sun said.

They went back inside and the Bo'sun moved towards the wireless office hatchway: the sliding wooden door was no longer there.

'I wouldn't look, if I were you,' Patterson said.

'The men have got to, haven't they?'

Chief Radio Officer Spenser was lying on the deck but he was no longer recognizable as such. He was just an amorphous mass of bone and flesh and torn, blood-saturated clothing: had it not been for the clothing it could have been the shattered remnants of any animal lying there. When McKinnon looked away Patterson could see that some colour had drained from the deeply-tanned face.

'The first bomb must have gone off directly beneath him,' the Bo'sun said. 'God, I've never seen anything like it. I'll attend to him myself. Third Officer Batesman. I know he was the officer of the watch. Any idea where he is, sir?'

'In the chart room. I don't advise you to go there either.'

Batesman was recognizable but only just. He was still on his chair, half-leaning, half-lying on

70

the table, what was left of his head pillowed on a blood-stained chart. McKinnon returned to the bridge.

'I don't suppose it will be any comfort to their relatives to know that they died without knowing. I'll fix him up myself, too. I couldn't ask the men.' He looked ahead through the totally shattered windscreens. At least, he thought, they wouldn't be needing a Kent clear-view screen any more. 'Wind's backing to the east,' he said absently. 'Bound to bring more snow. At least it might help to hide us from the wolves – if there are any wolves around.'

'You think, perhaps, they might come back to finish us off?' The Chief was shivering violently but that was only because he was accustomed to the warmth of the engine-room: the temperature on the bridge was about 6°F – twenty-six degrees of frost – and the wind held steady at twenty knots.

'Who can be sure, sir? But I really don't think so. Even one of those Heinkel torpedo-bombers could have finished us off if they had had a mind to. Come to that, the Condor could have done the same thing.'

'It did pretty well as it was, if you ask me.'

'Not nearly as well as it could have done. I know that a Condor normally carries 250-kilo bombs – that's about 550 lbs. A stick of those bombs – say three or four – would have sent us to the bottom. Even two might have been enough – they'd have

71

certainly blown the superstructure out of existence, not just crippled it.'

'The Royal Navy again, is that it, Bo'sun?'

'I know explosives, sir. Those bombs couldn't have been any more than fifty kilos each. Don't you think, sir, that we might have some interesting questions to ask that Condor captain when he regains consciousness?'

'In the hope of getting some interesting answers, is that it? Including the answer to the question why he bombed a hospital ship in the first place.'

'Well, yes, perhaps.'

'What do you mean – perhaps?'

'There's just a chance – a faint one, I admit – that he didn't know he was bombing a hospital ship.'

'Don't be ridiculous, Bo'sun. Of course he knew he was attacking a hospital ship. How big does a red cross have to be before you see it?'

'I'm not trying to make any excuses for him, sir.' There was a touch of asperity in McKinnon's voice and Patterson frowned, not at the Bo'sun but because it was most unlike the Bo'sun to adopt such a tone without reason. 'It was still only half-dawn, sir. Looking down, things look much darker than they do at sea level. You've only got to go up to a crow's nest to appreciate that.' As Patterson had never been in a crow's nest in his life he probably fell ill-equipped to comment on the Bo'sun's observation. 'As he was approaching from dead astern he couldn't possibly have seen the markings on the ship's sides and as he was flying very low he couldn't have seen the red cross on the foredeck – the superstructure would have blocked off his view.'

'That still leaves the red cross on the afterdeck. Even though it might have been only half light, he *must* have seen that.'

'Not with the amount of smoke you were putting up under full power.'

'There's that. There is a possibility.' He was unconvinced and watched with some impatience as the Bo'sun spun the now useless wheel and examined the binnacle compass and the standby compass, now smashed beyond any hope of repair.

'Do we have to remain up here?' Patterson said. 'There's nothing we can do here at the moment and I'm freezing to death. I suggest the Captain's cabin.'

'I was about to suggest the same, sir.'

The temperature in the cabin was no more than freezing point, but that was considerably warmer than it had been on the bridge and, more importantly, there was no wind there. Patterson went straight to the liquor cabinet and extracted a bottle of Scotch.

'If you can do it I can do it. We'll explain to the Captain later. I don't really like rum and I need it.'

'A specific against pneumonia?'

'Something like that. You will join me?'

'Yes, sir. The cold doesn't worry me but I think I'm going to need it in the next hour or so. Do you think the steering can be fixed, sir?'

'It's possible. Have to be a jury job. I'll get Jamieson on to it.'

'It's not terribly important. I know all the phones are out but it shouldn't take too long to reconnect them and you're fixing up a temporary rudder control in the engine-room. Same with the electrics – it won't take long to run a few rubber cables here and there. But we can't start on any of those things until we get this area – well, cleared.'

Patterson lowered the contents of his glass by half. 'You can't run the *San Andreas* from the bridge. Two minutes up there was enough for me. Fifteen minutes and anyone would be frozen to death.'

'You can't run it from any other place. Cold is the problem, I agree. So we'll board it up. Plenty of plywood in the carpenter's shop.'

'You can't see through plywood.'

'Could always pop our heads through the wing doors from time to time, but that won't be necessary. We'll let some windows into the plywood.'

'Fine, fine,' Patterson said. The Scotch had apparently restored his circulation. 'All we need is a glazier and some windows and we haven't got either.'

'A glazier we don't need. We don't need to have cut glass or fitted windows. You must have rolls

74

and rolls of insulating tape in your electrical department.'

'I've got a hundred miles of it and I still don't have any windows.'

'Windows we won't need. Glass, that's all. I know where the best glass is – and plate glass at that. The tops of all those lovely trolleys and trays in the hospital.'

'Ah! I do believe you have it, Bo'sun.'

'Yes, sir. I suppose Sister Morrison will let you have them.'

Patterson smiled one of his rare smiles. 'I believe I'm the officer commanding, however temporary.'

'Indeed, sir. Just don't let me be around when you put her into irons. Those are all small things. There are three matters that give a bit more concern. First, the radio is just a heap of scrap metal. We can't contact anyone and no one can contact us. Secondly, the compasses are useless. I know you had a gyro installed, but it never worked, did it? But worst of all is the problem of navigation.'

'Navigation? Navigation! How can that be a problem?'

'If you want to get from A to B, it's the biggest problem of all. We have – we had – four navigating officers aboard this ship. Two of those are dead and the other two are swathed in bandages – in your own words, like Egyptian mummies. Commander Warrington could have navigated, I know, but he's blind and from the look in Dr Singh's eyes I should think the blindness is permanent.' The Bo'sun paused for a moment, then shook his head. 'And just to make our cup overflowing, sir, we have the *Andover*'s navigating officer aboard and he's either concussed or in some sort of coma, we'll have to ask Dr Singh. If a poker-player got dealt this kind of hand of cards, he'd shoot himself. Four navigating officers who can't see and if you can't see you can't navigate. That's why the loss of the radio is so damned unfortunate. There must be a British warship within a hundred or two miles which could have lent us a navigating officer. Can you navigate, sir?'

'Me? Navigate?' Patterson seemed positively affronted. 'I'm an engineer officer. But you, McKinnon: you're a seaman – *and* twelve years in the Royal Navy.'

'It doesn't matter if I had been a hundred years in the Royal Navy, sir. I still can't navigate. I was a Torpedo Petty Officer. If you want to fire a torpedo, drop a depth charge, blow up a mine or do some elementary electrics, I'm your man. But I'd barely recognize a sextant if I saw one. Such things as sunsights, moonsights – if there is such a thing – and starsights are just words to me. I've also heard of words like deviation and variation and declination and I know more about Greek than I do about those.

'We do have a little hand-held compass aboard the motor lifeboat, the one I took out today, but that's useless. It's a magnetic compass, of course, and that's useless because I do know the magnetic north pole is nowhere near the geographical north pole: I believe it's about a thousand miles away from it. Canada, Baffin Island or some such place. Anyway, in the latitudes we're in now the magnetic pole is more west than north.' The Bo'sun sipped some Scotch and looked at Patterson over the rim of his glass. 'Chief Patterson, we're lost.'

'Job's comforter.' Patterson stared moodily at his glass, then said without much hope: 'Wouldn't it be possible to get the sun at noon? That way we'd know where the south was.'

'The way the weather is shaping up we won't be able to *see* the sun at noon. Anyway, what's noon, sun-time – it's certainly not twelve o'clock on our watches? Supposing we were in the middle of the Atlantic, where we might as well be, and knew where south was, would that help us find Aberdeen, which is where I believe we are going? The chronometer, incidentally, is kaput, which doesn't matter at all – I still wouldn't be able to relate the chronometer to longitude. And even if we did get a bearing on due south, it's dark up here twenty hours out of the twenty-four and the auto-pilot is as wrecked as everything else on the bridge. We wouldn't, of course, be going around in circles, the hand compass would stop us from doing that, but we still wouldn't know in what direction we were heading.'

'If I want to find some optimism, Bo'sun, I'll know where not to look. Would it help at all if we knew approximately where we were?'

'It would help, but all we know, approximately, is that we're somewhere north or north-west of Norway. Anywhere, say, in twenty thousand square miles of sea. There are only two possibilities, sir. The Captain and Chief Officer must have known where we were. If they're able to tell us, I'm sure they will.'

'Good God, of course! Not very bright, are we? At least, I'm not. What do you mean – "if"? Captain Bowen was able to talk about twenty minutes ago.'

'That was twenty minutes ago. You know how painful burns can be. Dr Singh is sure to have given them painkillers and sometimes the only way they can work is by knocking you out.'

'And the other possibility?'

'The chart house. Mr Batesman was working on a chart – he still had a pencil in his hand. I'll go.'

Patterson grimaced. 'Sooner you than me.'

'Don't forget Flannelfoot, sir.' Patterson touched his overalls where he had concealed his gun. 'Or the burial service.'

Patterson looked at the leather-covered folder in distaste. 'And where am I supposed to leave that? On the operating table?'

'There are four empty cabins in the hospital, sir. For recuperating VIPs. We don't have any at the moment.'

'Ah. Ten minutes, then.'

*   *   *

78

The Bo'sun was back in five minutes, the Chief Engineer in fifteen. An air of almost palpable gloom hung over Patterson.

'No luck, sir?'

'No, dammit. You guessed right. They're under heavy sedation, may be hours before they come to. And if they do start coming to, Dr Singh says, he's going to sedate them again. Apparently, they were trying to tear the bandages off their faces. He's got their hands swathed in bandages – even an unconscious man, the doctor says, will try to scratch away at whatever irritates him. Anyway, their hands *were* burnt – not badly, but enough to justify the bandages.'

'They've got straps for tying wrists to the bed-frames.'

'Dr Singh did mention that. He said he didn't think Captain Bowen would take too kindly to waking up and finding himself virtually in irons on his own ship. By the way, the missing helmsman was Hudson. Broken ribs and one pierced his lung. Doctor says he's very ill. What luck did *you* have?'

'Same as you, sir. Zero. There was a pair of parallel rules lying beside Mr Batesman so I assume he must have been pencilling out a course.'

'You couldn't gather anything from the chart?'

'It wasn't a chart any more. It was just a blood-stained rag.'

THREE

It was snowing heavily and a bitter wind blew from the east as they buried their dead in the near-Stygian darkness of the early afternoon. A form of illumination they did have, for the saboteur, probably more than satisfied with the results of his morning's activities, was now resting on his laurels and the deck floodlights were working again, but in that swirling blizzard the light given off was weak, fitful and almost ineffectual, serving only to intensify the ghoulish effect of the burial party hastening about their macabre task and the ghostlike appearance of the bare dozen of snow-covered mourners. Flashlight in hand, Chief Engineer Patterson read out the burial service, but he might as well have been quoting the latest prices on the stock exchange for not a word could be heard: one by one the dead, in their weighted canvas shrouds, slipped down the tilted plank, out from under the Union flag and vanished, silently, into the freezing water of the Barents Sea. No bugle calls, no Last Post for the Merchant Navy, not ever: the only requiem was the lost and lonely keening of the wind through the frozen rigging and the jagged gaps that had been torn in the superstructure.

Shivering violently and mottled blue and white with the cold, the burial party and mourners returned to the only reasonably warm congregating space left on the *San Andreas* – the dining and recreational area in the hospital between the wards and the cabins.

'We owe you a very great debt, Mr McKinnon,' Dr Singh said. He had been one of the mourners and his teeth were still chattering. 'Very swift, very efficient. It must have been a gruesome task.'

'I had six willing pairs of hands,' the Bo'sun said. 'It was worse for them than it was for me.' The Bo'sun did not have to explain what he meant: everybody knew that anything would always be worse for anybody than for that virtually indestructible Shetlander. He looked at Patterson. 'I have a suggestion, sir.'

'A Royal Naval one?'

'No, sir. Deep-sea fisherman's. Anyway, it's close enough, these are the waters of the Arctic trawlers. A toast to the departed.'

'I endorse that, and not for traditional or sentimental reasons.' Dr Singh's teeth still sounded like castanets. 'Medicinal. I don't know about the rest of you but my red corpuscles are in need of some assistance.'

The Bo'sun looked at Patterson, who nodded his approval. McKinnon turned and looked at an undersized, freckle-faced youth who was hovering at a respectful distance. 'Wayland.'

Wayland came hurrying forward. 'Yes, Mr McKinnon, sir?'

'Go with Mario to the liquor store. Bring back some refreshments.'

'Yes, Mr McKinnon, sir. Right away, Mr McKinnon, sir.' The Bo'sun had long given up trying to get Wayland Day to address him in any other fashion.

Dr Singh said: 'That won't be necessary, Mr McKinnon. We have supplies here.'

'Medicinal, of course?'

'Of course.' Dr Singh watched as Wayland went into the galley. 'How old is that boy?'

'He claims to be seventeen or eighteen, says he's not sure which. In either case, he's fibbing. I don't believe he's ever seen a razor.'

'He's supposed to be working for you, isn't he? Pantry boy, I understand. He spends nearly all his day here.'

'I don't mind, Doctor, if you don't.'

'No, not at all. He's an eager lad, willing and helpful.'

'He's all yours. Besides, we haven't a pantry left. He's making eyes at one of the nurses?'

'You underestimate the boy. Sister Morrison, no less. At a worshipful distance, of course.'

'Good God!' the Bo'sun said.

Mario entered, bearing, one-handed and a few inches above his head, a rather splendid silver salver laden with bottles and glasses, which, in the circumstances, was no mean feat, as the *San Andreas* was rolling quite noticeably. With a deft, twirling movement, Mario had the tray on the table without so much as the clink of glass against glass. Where the salver had come from was unexplained and Mario's business. As became the popular conception of an Italian, Mario was darkly and magnificently mustachioed, but whether he possessed the traditional flashing eyes was impossible to say as he invariably wore dark glasses. There were those who purported to see in those glasses a connection with the Sicilian Mafia, an assertion that was always good-humouredly made, as he was well-liked. Mario was overweight, of indeterminate age and claimed to have served in the Savoy Grill, which may have been true. What was beyond dispute was that there lay behind Mario, a man whose rightful home Captain Bowen considered to be either a prisoner-of-war or internment camp, a more than usually chequered career.

After no more than two fingers of Scotch, but evidently considering that his red corpuscles were back on the job, Dr Singh said: 'And now, Mr Patterson?'

'Lunch, Doctor. A very belated lunch but starving ourselves isn't going to help anyone. I'm afraid it will have to be cooked in your galley and served here.'

'Already under way. And then?'

'And then *we* get under way.' He looked at the Bo'sun. 'We could, temporarily, have the lifeboat's compass in the engine-room. We already have rudder control there.'

'It wouldn't work, sir. There's so much metal in your engine-room that any magnetic compass would have fits.' He pushed back his chair and rose. 'I think I'll pass up lunch. I think you will agree, Mr Patterson, that a telephone line from the bridge to the engine-room and electric power on the bridge – so that we can see what we are doing – are the two first priorities.'

Jamieson said: 'That's already being attended to, Bo'sun.'

'Thank you, sir. But the lunch can still wait.' He was speaking now to Patterson. 'Board up the bridge and let some light in. After that, sir, we might try to clear up some of the cabins in the superstructure, find out which of them is habitable and try to get power and heating back on. A little heating on the bridge wouldn't come amiss, either.'

'Leave all that other stuff to the engine-room staff – after we've had a bite, that is. You'll be requiring some assistance?'

'Ferguson and Curran will be enough.'

'Well, that leaves only one thing.' Patterson regarded the deckhead. 'The plate glass for your bridge windows.'

'Indeed, sir. I thought you –'

'A trifle.' Patterson waved a hand to indicate how much of a trifle it was. 'You have only to ask, Bo'sun.'

'But I thought you – perhaps I was mistaken.'

'We have a problem?' Dr Singh said.

'I wanted some plate glass from the trolleys or trays in the wards. Perhaps, Dr Singh, you would care –'

'Oh no.' Dr Singh's reply was as quick as it was decisive. 'Dr Sinclair and I run the operating theatre and look after our surgical patients, but the running of the wards has nothing to do with us. Isn't that so, Doctor?'

'Indeed it is, sir.' Dr Sinclair also knew how to sound decisive.

The Bo'sun surveyed the two doctors and Patterson with an impassive face that was much more expressive than any expression could have been and passed through the doorway into Ward B. There were ten patients in this ward and two nurses, one very much a brunette, the other very much a blonde. The brunette, Nurse Irene, was barely in her twenties, hailed from Northern Ireland, was pretty, dark-eyed and of such a warm and happy disposition that no one would have dreamed of calling her by her surname, which no one seemed to know anyway. She looked up as the Bo'sun entered and for the first time since she'd joined she failed to give him a welcoming smile. He patted her shoulder gently and walked to the other end of the ward where

Nurse Magnusson was rebandaging a seaman's arm.

Janet Magnusson was a few years older than Irene and taller, but not much. She had a more than faintly windswept, Viking look about her and was unquestionably good-looking: she shared the Bo'sun's flaxen hair and blue-grey eyes but not, fortunately, his burnt-brick complexion. Like the younger nurse, she was much given to smiling: like her, the smile was in temporary abeyance. She straightened as the Bo'sun approached, reached out and touched his arm.

'It was terrible, wasn't it, Archie?'

'Not a thing I would care to do again. I'm glad you weren't there, Janet.'

'I didn't mean that – the burial, I mean. It was you who sewed up the worst of them – they say that the Radio Officer was, well, all bits and pieces.'

'An exaggeration. Who told you that?'

'Johnny Holbrook. You know, the young orderly. The one that's scared of you.'

'There's nobody scared of me,' the Bo'sun said absently. He looked around the ward. 'Been quite some changes here.'

'We had to turf some of the so-called recuperating patients out. You'd have thought they were being sent to their deaths. Siberia, at least. Nothing the matter with them. Not malingerers, really, they just liked soft beds and being spoiled.'

'And who was spoiling them, if not you and Irene? They just couldn't bear to be parted from you. Where's the lioness?'

Janet gave him a disapproving look. 'Are you referring to Sister Morrison?'

'That's the lioness I mean. I have to beard her in her den.'

'You don't know her, Archie. She's very nice really. Maggie's my friend. Truly.'

'Maggie?'

'When we're off duty, always. She's in the next ward.'

'Maggie! Good lord! I thought she disapproved of you because she disapproves of me because she disapproves of me talking to you.'

'Fiddlesticks. And Archie?'

'Yes?'

'A lioness doesn't have a beard.'

The Bo'sun didn't deign to answer. He moved into the adjacent ward. Sister Morrison wasn't there. Of the eight patients, only two, McGuigan and Jones, were visibly conscious. The Bo'sun approached their adjacent beds and said: 'How's it going, boys?'

'Ach, we're fine, Bo'sun,' McGuigan said. 'We shouldn't be here at all.'

'You'll stay here until you're told to leave.' Eighteen years old. He was wondering how long it would take them to recover from the sight of the almost decapitated Rawlings lying by the wheel when Sister Morrison entered by the far door.

'Good afternoon, Sister Morrison.'

'Good afternoon, Mr McKinnon. Making your medical rounds, I see.'

The Bo'sun felt the stirrings of anger but contented himself with looking thoughtful: he was probably unaware that his thoughtful expression, in certain circumstances, could have a disquieting effect on people.

'I just came to have a word with you, Sister.' He looked around the ward. 'Not a very lively bunch, are they?'

'I hardly think this is the time or place for levity, Mr McKinnon.' The lips were not as compressed as they might have been but there was an appreciable lack of warmth behind the steel-rimmed spectacles.

The Bo'sun looked at her for long seconds, during which time she began to show distinct signs of uneasiness. Like most people – with the exception of the timorous Johnny Holbrook – she regarded the Bo'sun as being cheerful and easy-going, with the rider, in her case, that he was probably a bit simple: it required only one glance at that cold, hard, bleak face to realize how totally wrong she had been. It was an unsettling experience.

The Bo'sun spoke in a slow voice. 'I am not in the mood for levity, Sister. I've just buried fifteen men. Before I buried them I had to sew them up in their sheets of canvas. Before I did that I had to gather up their bits and pieces and stick their guts back inside. Then I sewed them up. Then I buried them. I didn't see you among the mourners, Sister.'

The Bo'sun was more than aware that he shouldn't have spoken to her like that and he was also aware that what he had gone through had affected him more than he had thought. Under normal circumstances it was impossible that he should have been so easily provoked: but the circumstances were abnormal and the provocation too great.

'I've come for some plate glass, such as you have on the tops of your trolleys and trays. I need them urgently and I don't need them for any light-hearted purposes. Or do you require an explanation?'

She didn't say whether she required an explanation or not. She didn't do anything dramatic like sinking into a chair, reaching out for the nearest support or even putting a hand to her mouth. Only her colour changed. Sister Morrison had the kind of complexion that, like her eyes and lips, was in marked contrast to her habitually severe expression and steel-rimmed glasses, the kind of complexion that would have had the cosmetic tycoons sending their scientists back to the bench: at that moment, however, the peaches had faded from the traditional if rarely seen peaches and cream of the traditional if equally rarely seen English rose.

The Bo'sun removed the glass top from a table by Jones's bedside, looked around for trays, saw none, nodded to Sister Morrison and went back to Ward B. Janet Magnusson looked at him in surprise.

'Is that what you went for?' The Bo'sun nodded. 'Maggie – Sister Morrison – had no objection?'

'Nary an objection. Have you any glass-topped trays?'

Chief Patterson and the others had already begun lunch when the Bo'sun returned, five sheets of plate glass under his arm. Patterson looked faintly surprised.

'No trouble then, Bo'sun?'

'One only has to ask. I'll need some tools for the bridge.'

'Fixed,' Jamieson said. 'I've just been to the engine-room. There's a box gone up to the bridge – all the tools you'll require, nuts, bolts, screws, insulating tape, a power drill and a power saw.'

'Ah. Thank you. But I'll need power.'

'Power you have. Only a temporary cable, mind you, but the power is there. And lights, of course. The phone will take some time.'

'That's fine. Thank you, Mr Jamieson.' He looked at Patterson. 'One other thing, sir. We have a fair number of nationalities in our crew. The captain of the Greek tanker – Andropolous, isn't it? – might have a mixed crew too. I should think there's a fair chance, sir, that one of our men and one of the Greek crew might have a common language. Perhaps you could make enquiries, sir.'

'And how would that help, Bo'sun?'

'Captain Andropolous can navigate.'

'Of course, of course. Always the navigation, isn't it, Bo'sun?'

'There's nothing without it, sir. Do you think you could get hold of Naseby and Trent – they're the two men who were with me here when we were attacked? Weather's worsening, sir, and we have ice forming on the deck. Would you have them rig up lifelines between here and the superstructure?'

'Worsening?' Dr Singh said. 'How much worse, Mr McKinnon?'

'Quite a bit, I'm afraid. Bridge barometer is smashed but I think the one in the Captain's cabin is intact. I'll check.' He brought out the hand compass which he'd removed from the lifeboat. 'This thing's virtually useless but at least it does show changes in direction. We're wallowing in the troughs port side to, so that means the wind and the sea are coming at us on the port beam. Wind direction is changing rapidly, we've backed at least five degrees since we came down here. Wind's roughly north-east. If experience is any guide that means heavy snow, heavy seas and a steadily dropping temperature.'

'No slightest light in the gloom, is that it, Mr McKinnon?' Dr Singh said. 'Where every prospect pleases and only man is vile. Except this is the other way round.'

'A tiny speck of light, Doctor. If the temperature keeps falling like this, the cold room is going to stay cold and the frozen meat and fish should stay that way. And we do have a vile man – or men – aboard or we shouldn't be in the state we are. You're worried about your patients, aren't you, Doctor – especially the ones in Ward A?'

'Telepathy, Mr McKinnon. If conditions deteriorate much more they're going to start falling out of their beds – and the last thing I want to do is to start strapping wounded men to their beds.'

'And the last thing I want is for the superstructure to topple over the side.'

Jamieson had pushed back his chair and was on his feet. 'I have my priorities right, no, Bo'sun?'

'Indeed, Mr Jamieson. Thank you very much.'

Dr Singh half-smiled. 'Not more telepathy?'

The Bo'sun smiled back. Dr Singh appeared to be very much the right man in the right place. 'I think he's gone to have a word with the men rigging up the telephone line from the bridge to the engine-room.'

'And then I press the button,' Patterson said.

'Yes, sir. And then south-west. I don't have to tell you why.'

'You might tell a landlubber why,' Dr Singh said.

'Of course. Two things. Heading south-west will mean that the wind and the seas from the north-east are dead astern. That should eliminate all rolling so that you don't have to put your patients in straitjackets or whatever. There'll be some pitching, of course, but not much and even then Mr Patterson can smooth that out by adjusting the ship's speed to the wave speed. The other big advantage is that by heading south-west there's no land we can bump into for hundreds of miles to come. If you will excuse me, gentlemen.' The Bo'sun left, together with his sheets of plate glass and hand compass.

'Doesn't miss much, does he?' Dr Singh said. 'Competent, you would say, Mr Patterson?'

'Competent? He's more than that. Certainly the best bo'sun I've ever sailed with – and I've never known a bad bo'sun yet. If we ever get to Aberdeen – and with McKinnon around I rate our chances better than even – I won't be the man you'll have to thank.'

The Bo'sun arrived on the bridge, a bridge now over-illuminated with two garish arc lamps, to find Ferguson and Curran already there, with enough plywood of various shapes and sizes to build a modest hut. Neither of the two men could be said to be able to walk, not in the proper sense of the term. Muffled to the ears and with balaclavas and hoods pulled low over their foreheads, they were so swaddled in layers of jerseys, trousers and coats that they were barely able to waddle: given a couple of white fur coats they would have resembled nothing so much as a pair of polar bears that had given up on their diet years ago. As it was, they were practically white already: the snow, driving almost horizontally, swept, without let or hindrance, through the yawning gaps where the port for'ard screens and the upper wing door screen had once been. Conditions weren't improved by the fact that, at a height of some forty feet above the hospital, the effects of the rolling were markedly worse than they had been down below, so bad, in fact, that it was very difficult to keep one's footing, and that only by hanging on to something. The Bo'sun carefully laid the plate glass in a corner and wedged it so that it wouldn't slide all over the deck. The rolling didn't bother him, but the creaking and groaning of the superstructure supports and the occasional juddering vibration that shook the bridge bothered him a very great deal.

'Curran! Quickly! Chief Engineer Patterson. You'll find him in the hospital. Tell him to start up and turn the ship either into the wind or away from the wind. Away is better – that means hard a-starboard. Tell him the superstructure is going to fall over the side any minute.'

For a man usually slow to obey any order and handicapped though he was by his constricted lower limbs, Curran made off with remarkable alacrity. It could have been that he was a good man in an emergency, but more likely he didn't fancy being on the bridge when it vanished into the Barents Sea.

Ferguson eased two layers of scarf from his mouth. 'Difficult working conditions, Bo'sun.

Impossible, a man might say. And have you seen the temperature?'

The Bo'sun glanced at the bulkhead thermometer which was about the only thing still working on the bridge. 'Two above,' he said.

'Ah! Two above. But two above what? Fahrenheit, that's what it's above. That means thirty degrees of frost.' He looked at the Bo'sun in what he probably regarded as a meaningful fashion. 'Have you ever heard of the chill factor, eh?'

The Bo'sun spoke with commendable restraint. 'Yes, Ferguson, I have heard of the chill factor.'

'For every knot of wind the temperature, as far as the skin is concerned, falls by one degree.' Ferguson had something on his mind and as far as he was concerned the Bo'sun had never heard of the chill factor. 'Wind's at least thirty knots. That means it's *sixty* below on this bridge. Sixty!' At that moment, at the end of an especially alarming roll, the superstructure gave a very loud creak indeed, more of a screech than a creak, and it didn't require any kind of imagination to visualize metal tearing under lateral stress.

'If you want to leave the bridge,' the Bo'sun said, 'I'm not ordering you to stay.'

'Trying to shame me into staying, eh? Trying to appeal to my better nature? Well, I got news for you. I ain't got no better feelings, mate.'

The Bo'sun said, mildly: 'Nobody aboard this ship calls me "mate".'

'Bo'sun.' Ferguson made no move to carry out his implied threat and he wasn't even showing any signs of irresolution. 'Do I get danger money for this? Overtime, perhaps?'

'A couple of tots of Captain Bowen's special malt Scotch. Let's spend our last moments usefully, Ferguson. We'll start with some measuring.'

'Already done.' Ferguson showed the spring-loaded steel measuring tape in his hand and tried hard not to smile in smug self-satisfaction. 'Me and Curran have already measured the front and side screens. Written down on that bit of plywood there.'

'Fine, fine.' The Bo'sun tested both the electric drill and electric saw. Both worked. 'No problem. We'll cut the plywood three inches wider and higher than your measurements to get the overlap we need. Then we'll drill holes top, bottom and sides, three-quarters of an inch in, face the plywood up to the screen bearers, mark the metal and drill the holes through the steel.'

'That steel is three-eighths of an inch. Take to next week to drill all those holes.'

The Bo'sun looked through the tool box and came up with three packets of drills. The first he discarded. The drills in the second, all with blue tips, he showed to Ferguson.

'Tungsten. Goes through steel like butter. Mr Jamieson doesn't miss much.' He paused and cocked his head as if listening, though it was a purely automatic reaction, any sound from the after end of the ship was carried away by the wind: but there was no mistaking the throbbing that pulsed through the superstructure. He looked at Ferguson, whose face cracked into what might almost have been a smile.

The Bo'sun moved to the starboard wing door – the sheltered side of the ship – and peered through the gap where the screen had been in the upper half of the door. The snow was so heavy that the seas moving away from the *San Andreas* were as much imagined as seen. The ship was still rolling in the troughs. A vessel of any size that has been lying dead in the water can take an unconscionable time – depending, of course, on the circumstances – to gather enough momentum to have steerage way on, but after about another minute the Bo'sun became aware that the ship was sluggishly answering to the helm. He couldn't see this but he could feel it: a definite quartering motion had entered into the rolling to which they had been accustomed for some hours.

McKinnon moved away from the wing door. 'We're turning to starboard. Mr Patterson has decided to go with the wind. We'll soon have both sea and snow behind us. Fine, fine.'

'Fine, fine,' Ferguson said. This was about twenty seconds later and the tone of his voice indicated that everything was all but fine. He was, indeed, acutely uneasy and with reason. The *San Andreas* was heading almost due south, the heavy seas bearing down on her port quarter were making her corkscrew violently and the markedly increased creaking and groaning of the superstructure was doing little enough for his morale. 'God's sake, why couldn't we have stayed where we were?'

'A minute's time and you'll see why.' And in a minute's time he did see why. The corkscrewing and rolling gradually eased and ceased altogether, so did the creaking in the superstructure and the *San Andreas*, on an approximately south-west course, was almost rock-steady in the water. There was a slight pitching, but, compared to what they had just experienced, it was so negligible as not to be worth the mentioning. Ferguson, with a stable deck beneath his feet, the fear of imminent drowning removed and the snowstorm so squarely behind them that not a flake reached the bridge, had about him an air of profound relief.

Shortly after the Bo'sun and Ferguson had started sawing out the rectangles of plywood, four men arrived on the bridge – Jamieson, Curran, McCrimmon and another stoker called Stephen. Stephen was a Pole and was called always by his first name: nobody had ever been heard to attempt the surname of Przynyszewski. Jamieson carried a telephone, Curran two black heaters, McCrimmon two radiant heaters and Stephen two spools of rubber-insulated cable, one thick, one thin, both of which he unreeled as he went.

'Well, this is more like it, Bo'sun,' Jamieson said. 'A millpond, one might almost call it. Done a power of good for the morale down below. Some people have even rediscovered their appetites. Speaking of appetites, how's yours? You must be the only person aboard who hasn't had lunch today.'

'It'll keep.' The Bo'sun looked to where McCrimmon and Stephen were already attaching wires from the heaters to the heavy cable. 'Thanks for those. They'll come in handy in an hour or two when we've managed to keep all this fresh air out.'

'More than handy, I should have thought.' Jamieson shivered. 'My word, it is fresh up here. What's the temperature?'

The Bo'sun looked at the thermometer. 'Zero. That's two degrees it's dropped in a few minutes. I'm afraid, Mr Jamieson, that we're going to be very cold tonight.'

'Not in the engine-room,' Jamieson said. He unscrewed the back of the telephone and started connecting it to the slender cable. 'Mr Patterson thinks this is an unnecessary luxury and that you just want it so that you can talk to someone when you feel lonely. Says that keeping the stern on to wind and seas is child's play and that he could do it for hours without deviating more than two or three degrees off course.'

'I've no doubt he could. That way we'll never see Aberdeen. You can tell Mr Patterson that the wind is backing and that if it backs far enough and he still keeps stern on to the wind and sea we'll end up by making a small hole in the north of Norway and a large hole in ourselves.'

Jamieson smiled. 'I'll explain that to the Chief. I don't think the possibility has occurred to him – it certainly didn't to me.'

'And when you go below, sir, would you send up Naseby? He's an experienced helmsman.'

'I'll do that. Need any more help up here?'

'No, sir. The three of us are enough.'

'As you say.' Jamieson screwed the back of the telephone in place, pressed the call-up button, spoke briefly and hung up. 'Satisfaction guaranteed. Are you through, McCrimmon? Stephen?' Both men nodded, and Jamieson called the engine-room again, asked for power to be switched on and told McCrimmon and Stephen to switch on one heater apiece, one black, one radiant. 'Still require McCrimmon as a runner, Bo'sun?'

The Bo'sun nodded towards the telephone. 'Thanks to you, I've got my runner.'

One of McCrimmon's radiant heaters had started to glow a dim red. Stephen removed a hand from the black heater and nodded.

'Fine. Switch off. It would seem, Bo'sun, that Flannelfoot has knocked off for the day. We'll go below now, see what cabins we can make habitable. I'm afraid there won't be many. The only way we can make a cabin habitable – the clearing up won't take long, I've already got a couple of our boys working on that – is to replace defective heating systems. That's all that matters. Unfortunately, most of the doors have been blasted off their hinges or cut away by the oxy-acetylene torches and there's no point in replacing heating if we can't replace the doors. We'll do what we can.' He spun the useless wheel. 'When we've finished below and you've finished here – and when the temperature is appropriate for myself and other hothouse plants from the engine-room – we'll come and have a go at this steering.'

'Big job, sir?'

'Depends upon what damage in the decks, below. Don't hold me to it, Bo'sun, but there's a fair chance that we'll have it operational, in what you'll no doubt regard as our customary crude fashion, some time this evening. To give me some leeway, I won't specify what time.'

The temperature on the bridge continued to drop steadily and because numbing cold slows up a man both physically and mentally it took McKinnon and his two men well over two hours to complete their task: had the temperature been anything like normal they could probably have done it in less than half the time. About three-quarters of the way through the repairs they had switched on all four heaters and the temperature had begun to rise, albeit very slowly.

McKinnon was well enough satisfied with their end product. Five sheets of hardboard had been bolted into position, each panel fitted with an inlet oblong of plate glass, one large, the other four, identical in shape, about half the size. The large one was fitted in the centre, directly ahead of where the helmsman normally stood: two of the others were fitted on either side of this and the remaining two on the upper sections of the wing doors. The inevitable gaps between the glass and the plywood and between the plywood and the metal to which they had been bonded had been sealed off with Hartley's compound, a yellow plastic material normally used for waterproofing external electrical fittings. The bridge was as draughtproof as it was possible to make it.

Ferguson put away the last of the tools and coughed. 'There was some mention of a couple of tots of Captain Bowen's special malt.'

McKinnon looked at him and at Curran. Their faces were mottled blue and white with cold and both men were shivering violently: chronic complainers, neither had complained once.

'You've earned it.' He turned to Naseby. 'How's she bearing?'

Naseby looked at his hand-held compass in distaste. 'If you can trust this thing, two-twenty. Give or take. So the wind's backed five degrees in the past couple of hours. We don't bother the engine-room for five degrees?'

George Naseby, a solid, taciturn, dark-haired and swarthy Yorkshireman – he hailed from Whitby, Captain Cook's home town – was McKinnon's alter ego and closest friend. A bo'sun himself on his two previous ships, he had elected to sail on the *San Andreas* simply because of the mutual regard that he and McKinnon shared. Although he held no official ranking, he was regarded by everyone, from the Captain down, as the number two on the deckside.

'We don't bother them. Another five, perhaps, ten degrees off, then we bother them. Let's go below – ship can look after itself for a few minutes. Then I'll have Trent relieve you.'

The level of Scotch in the Captain's bottle of malt had fallen quite rapidly – Ferguson and Curran had their own ideas as to what constituted a reasonably sized tot. McKinnon, in between rather more frugal sips, examined the Captain's sextant, thermometer and barometer. The sextant, as far as the Bo'sun could tell, was undamaged – the felt lining of its wooden box would have cushioned it from the effects of the blast. The thermometer, too, appeared to be working: the mercury registered I7°F., which was about what McKinnon reckoned the cabin temperature to be. The Captain's cabin was one of the few with its door still intact and Jamieson had already had a black heater installed.

He gave the thermometer to Naseby, asking that it be placed on one of the bridge wings, then turned his attention to the barometer. This was functioning normally, for when he tapped the glass the black needle fell sharply to the left.

'Twenty-nine point five,' the Bo'sun said. 'Nine nine nine millibars – and falling.'

'Not good, eh?' Ferguson said.

'No. Not that we need a barometer to tell us that.'

McKinnon left and went down from deck to the officers' quarters. He found Jamieson at the end of the passageway.

'How's it coming, sir?'

'We're about through. Should be five cabins fit for human habitation – depending, of course, upon what your definition of human is.'

The Bo'sun tapped the bulkhead beside him. 'How stable do you reckon this structure is, sir?'

'Highly unstable. Safe enough in those conditions, but I gather you think those conditions are about to change.'

'If the wind keeps backing and we keep holding to this course then we're going to have the seas on the starboard quarter and a lot of nasty corkscrewing. I was thinking perhaps –'

'I know what you were thinking. I'm a ship's engineer, Bo'sun, not a constructive engineer. I'll have a look. Maybe we can bolt or weld a few strengthening steel plates at the weakest points. I don't know. There's no guarantee. First of all, we'll go have a look at the steering on the bridge. How are things up top?'

'Draught-free. Four heaters. Ideal working conditions.'

'Temperature?'

'Fifteen.'

'Above freezing, or below?'

'Below.'

'Ideal. Thank you very much.'

McKinnon found four people in the staff dining area – Chief Engineer Patterson, Dr Singh, and Nurses Janet Magnusson and Irene. The nurses were off-duty – the *San Andreas*, as did all hospital ships, carried an alternate nursing staff. The Bo'sun went to the galley, asked for coffee and sandwiches, sat at the table and made his report to the Chief Engineer. When he was finished he said: 'And how did you get on, sir? Finding a translator, I mean?'

Patterson scowled. 'With our luck?'

'Well, I didn't really have any hope, sir. Not, as you say, with our luck.' He looked at Janet Magnusson. 'Where's Sister Morrison?'

'In the lounge.' Neither her voice nor her eyes held much in the way of warmth. 'She's upset. You upset her.'

'She upset me.' He made an impatient, dismissive gesture with his hand. 'Tantrums. This is neither the time nor the place. If ever there is a time and a place.'

'Oh, come now.' Dr Singh was smiling. 'I don't think either of you is being quite fair. Sister Morrison is not, as you suggest, Mr McKinnon, sulking in her tent and, Nurse, if she's feeling rather unhappy, it's not primarily the Bo'sun's fault. She and Mr Ulbricht are not quite seeing eye to eye.'

'Ulbricht?' the Bo'sun said.

'Flight-Lieutenant Karl Ulbricht, I understand. The captain of the Condor.'

'He's conscious?'

'Very much so. Not only conscious but wanting out of bed. Quite remarkable powers of recuperation. Three bullet wounds, all flesh, all superficial. Bled a great deal, mind you, but he's had a transfusion: one hopes that the best British blood goes well with his own native Aryan stock. Anyway, Sister Morrison was with me when he came to. She called him a filthy Nazi murderer. Hardly makes for the ideal nurse-patient relationship.'

'Not very tactful, I agree,' Patterson said. 'A wounded man recovering consciousness might expect to be entitled to a little more sympathy. How did he react?'

'Very calmly. Mild, you might say. Said he wasn't a Nazi and had never murdered anyone in his life. She just stood and glared at him – if you can imagine Sister Morrison glaring at anybody – and –'

'I can imagine it very easily,' the Bo'sun said with some feeling. 'She glares at me. Frequently.'

'Perhaps,' Nurse Magnusson said, 'you and Lieutenant Ulbricht have a lot in common.'

'Please.' Dr Singh held up a hand. 'Lieutenant Ulbricht expressed deep regrets, said something about the fortunes of war, but didn't exactly call for sackcloth and ashes. I stopped it there – it didn't look like being a very profitable discussion.

Don't be too hard on the Sister, Bo'sun. She's no battleaxe, far less a termagant. She feels deeply and has her own way of expressing her feelings.'

McKinnon made to reply, caught Janet's still far from friendly eye and changed his mind. 'How are your other patients, Doctor?'

'The other aircrew member – a gunner, it seems, by the name of Helmut Winterman – is okay, just a scared kid who expects to be shot at dawn. Commander Warrington, as you guessed, Mr McKinnon, is badly hurt. How badly, I don't know. His occiput is fractured but only surgery can tell us how serious it is. I'm a surgeon but not a brain surgeon. We'll have to wait until we get to a mainland hospital to ease the pressure on the sight centre and find out when, if ever, he'll see again.'

'The *Andover*'s navigator?'

'Lieutenant Cunningham?' Dr Singh shook his head. 'I'm sorry – in more ways than one, I'm afraid this may be your last hope gone – that the young man won't be doing any more navigating for some time to come. He's in a coma. X-ray shows a fracture of the skull and not a hairline fracture either. Pulse, respiration, temperature show no sign of organic damage. He'll live.'

'Any idea when he might come to, Doctor?'

Dr Singh sighed. 'If I were a first-year intern, I'd hazard a fairly confident guess. Alas, it's twenty-five years since I was a first-year intern. Two days, two weeks, two months – I simply don't know. As for the others, the Captain and Chief Officer are still under sedation and when they wake up I'm going to put them to sleep again. Hudson, the one with the punctured lung, seems to have stabilized – at least, the internal bleeding has stopped. Rafferty's fractured tibia is no problem. The two injured crewmen from the *Argos*, one with a broken pelvis, the other with multiple burns, are still in the recovery room, not because they're in any danger but because Ward A was full and it was the best place to keep them. And I've discharged two young seamen, I don't know their names.'

'Jones and McGuigan.'

'That's the two. Shock, nothing more. I understand they're lucky to be alive.'

'We're all lucky to be alive.' McKinnon nodded his thanks as Mario put coffee and sandwiches before him, then looked at Patterson. 'Do you think it might help, sir, if we had a word with Lieutenant Ulbricht?'

'If you're halfway right on your way of thinking, Bo'sun, it might be of some help. At least, it can be of no harm.'

'I'm afraid you'll have to wait a bit,' Dr Singh said. 'The Lieutenant was getting a little bit too active – or beginning to feel too active – for his own good. It'll be an hour, perhaps two. A matter of urgency, Mr McKinnon?'

'It could be. Or a matter of some importance, at least. He might be able to tell us *why* we're all so lucky as to be still alive. And if we knew, then we

108

might have some idea, or a guess at least, as to what lies in store for us.'

'You think the enemy is not yet finished with us?'

'I should be surprised if they are, Doctor.'

McKinnon, alone now in the dining area, had just finished his third cup of coffee when Jamieson and three of his men entered, to the accompaniment of much arm-flapping and teeth-chattering. Jamieson went to the galley, ordered coffee for himself and his men and sat beside McKinnon.

'Ideal working conditions, you said, Bo'sun. Snug as a bug in a rug, one might say. Temperature's soaring – it's almost ten degrees up there. Minus.'

'Sorry about that, sir. How's the steering?'

'Fixed. For the moment, at least. Not too big a job. Quite a bit of play on the wheel, but Trent says it's manageable.'

'Fine. Thank you. We have bridge control?'

'Yes. I told the engine-room to cease and desist. Chief Patterson seemed quite disappointed – seems to think that he can do a better job than the bridge. What's next on the agenda?'

'Nothing. Not for me, that is.'

'Ah! I take your point. Our idle hands, is that it? We'll have a look at the chances of bracing the superstructure in a moment – a moment depending on how long it takes us to get defrosted.'

'Of course, sir.' The Bo'sun looked over his shoulder. 'I have noticed that Dr Singh doesn't bother to keep the hospital's private liquor cabinet locked.'

'Well, now. A little something in our coffee, perhaps?'

'I would recommend it, sir. Might help to speed up the defrosting process.'

Jamieson gave him an old-fashioned look, rose and crossed towards the cabinet.

Jamieson drained his second cup of reinforced coffee and looked at McKinnon. 'Something bothering you, Bo'sun?'

'Yes.' McKinnon had both hands on the table, as if preparing to rise. 'Motion's changed. A few minutes back the ship started quartering a little, not too much, as if Trent was making a slight course adjustment, but now she's quartering too damn much. It could be that the steering has failed again.'

McKinnon left at speed, Jamieson close behind him. Reaching the now smoothly ice-coated deck, McKinnon grabbed a lifeline and stopped.

'Corkscrewing,' he shouted. He had to shout to make himself heard above the near gale-force wind. 'Twenty degrees off course, maybe thirty. Something far wrong up there.'

And indeed, when they arrived on the bridge, there was something far wrong. Both men paused momentarily, and McKinnon said: 'My apologies, Mr Jamieson. It wasn't the steering after all.'

Trent was lying, face up, just behind the wheel, which was mindlessly jerking from side to side in response to the erratic seas striking against the rudder. Trent was breathing, no doubt about that, his chest rising and falling in a slow, rhythmic fashion. McKinnon bent over to examine his face, looked more closely, sniffed, wrinkled his nose in distaste and straightened.

'Chloroform.' He reached out for the wheel and began to bring the *San Andreas* back on course again.

'And this.' Jamieson stooped, picked up the fallen compass and showed it to McKinnon. The glass was smashed, the needle irremediably twisted out of position. 'Flannelfoot strikes again.'

'So it would appear, sir.'

'Ah. You don't seem particularly surprised, Bo'sun?'

'I saw it lying there. I didn't have to look. There are quite a few other helmsmen aboard. That was our only compass.'

FOUR

'Whoever was responsible for this must have had access to the dispensary,' Patterson said. He was with Jamieson and McKinnon in the hospital's small lounge.

'That won't help, sir,' McKinnon said. 'Since ten o'clock this morning everybody aboard this ship – except, of course, the wounded, the unconscious and those under sedation – have had access to the dispensary. There's not a single person who hasn't been in the hospital area, either to eat, sleep or just rest.'

'Maybe we're not looking at it in the right way,' Jamieson said. '*Why* should anyone want to smash the compass? It can't just be to stop us from following whatever course we were following or that we might outrun someone. The chances are high that Flannelfoot is still transmitting his homing signal and that the Germans know exactly where we are.'

'Maybe he's hoping to panic us,' McKinnon said. 'Maybe he's hoping we'll slow down, rather than travel around in circles, which could easily happen if the weather deteriorates, the sea becomes confused, and if we have no compass. Perhaps there's a German submarine in the vicinity and he doesn't want us to get too far away. There's an even worse possibility. We've been assuming that Flannelfoot has only a transmitter: maybe he has a transceiver, what if he's in radio contact with Alta Fjord or a U-boat or even a reconnaissance Condor? There could be a British warship in the vicinity and the last thing they would want is that we make contact with it. Well, we couldn't contact it: but its radar could pick us up ten, fifteen miles away.'

'Too many "ifs", "maybes" and "perhaps this" and "perhaps that".' Patterson's voice was decisive, that of a man who has made up his mind. 'How many men do you trust aboard this ship, Bo'sun?'

'How many – ' McKinnon broke off in speculation. 'The three of us here and Naseby. And the medical staff. Not that I have any particular reason to trust them – nor do I have any particular reason to distrust them – but we *know* that they were here, all present and accounted for, when Trent was attacked, so that rules them out.'

'Two doctors, six nursing staff, three orderlies and the four of us. That makes fifteen,' Jamieson said. He smiled. 'Apart from that, everyone is a suspect?'

The Bo'sun permitted himself a slight smile in return. 'It's difficult to see kids like Jones, McGuigan and Wayland Day as master spies.

Those apart, I wouldn't put my hand in the fire for any of them, that's to say I've no reason to trust them in a matter of life and death.'

Patterson said: 'The crew of the *Argos*? Survivors? Guests by happenstance?'

'Ridiculous, I know, sir. But who's to say the nigger is not in the most unlikely woodpile? I just don't trust anyone.' The Bo'sun paused. 'Am I wrong in thinking that it is your intention to search through the quarters and possessions of everyone aboard?'

'You are not wrong, Bo'sun.'

'With respect sir, we'll be wasting our time. Anyone as smart as Flannelfoot is too smart to leave anything lying around, or at least to leave it in any place where it might be remotely associated with him. There are hundreds of places aboard where you can hide things and we are not trained rummagers. On the other hand, it's better than doing nothing. But I'm afraid that's what we'll find, Mr Patterson. Nothing.'

They found nothing. They searched every living quarter, every wardrobe and cupboard, every case and duffel bag, every nook and cranny, and they found nothing. A rather awkward moment had arisen when Captain Andropolous, a burly, dark-bearded and seemingly intemperate character who had been given one of the empty cabins normally reserved for recuperating patients, objected violently and physically to having his quarters searched: McKinnon, who had no Greek, resolved

114

this impasse by pointing his Colt at the Captain's temple, after which, probably realizing that McKinnon wasn't acting for his own amusement, the Captain had been cooperation itself, even to going to the extent of accompanying the Bo'sun and ordering his crew to open up their possessions for scrutiny.

The two Singhalese cooks in the hospital galleys were more than competent and Dr Singh, who appeared to be something of a connoisseur in such matters, produced some Bordeaux that would not have been found wanting in a Michelin restaurant, but poor justice was done to the food and, more surprisingly, the wine at dinner that evening. The atmosphere was sombre. There was an uneasiness about, even a faint air of furtiveness. It is one thing to be told that there is a saboteur at large: it is quite another to have your luggage and possessions searched on the basis of the possibility that you might be the saboteur in question. Even, or perhaps especially, the hospital staff seemed unduly uncomfortable: their possessions had not been searched so they were not, officially, in the clear. An irrational reaction it may have been but, in the circumstances, understandable.

Patterson pushed back his unfinished plate and said to Dr Singh: 'This Lieutenant Ulbricht. Is he awake?'

'He's more than awake.' Dr Singh sounded almost testy. 'Remarkable recuperative powers.

Wanted to join us for dinner. Forbade it, of course. Why?'

'The Bo'sun and I would like to have a word with him.'

'No reason why not.' He pondered briefly. 'Two possible minor complications. Sister Morrison is there – she's just relieved Sister Maria for dinner.' He nodded towards the end of the table where a fair-haired, high-cheekboned girl in a sister's uniform was having dinner. Apart from Stephen Przybyszewski she was the only Polish national aboard and as people found her surname of Szarzynski, like Stephen's, rather difficult, she was invariably and affectionately referred to as Sister Maria.

'We'll survive,' Patterson said. 'The other complication?'

'Captain Bowen. Like Lieutenant Ulbricht, he has a high tolerance to sedatives. Keeps surfacing – longer and longer spells of consciousness and when he is awake he's in a very bad humour. Who has ever seen Captain Bowen in ill humour?'

Patterson rose. 'If I were the Captain I wouldn't be very much in the mood for singing and dancing. Come on, Bo'sun.'

They found the Captain awake, very much so, and, indeed, in a more than irritable frame of mind. Sister Morrison was seated on a stool by his bedside. She made to rise but Patterson waved to her to remain where she was. Lieutenant Ulbricht was half-sitting, half-lying in the next bed, his right hand behind his neck: Lieutenant Ulbricht was very wide awake.

'How do you feel, Captain?'

'How do I feel, Chief?' Briefly and forcefully Bowen told him how he felt. He would no doubt have expressed himself even more forcefully had he not been aware that Sister Morrison was sitting by his side. He raised a bandaged hand to cover a cough. 'All's gone to hell and breakfast, isn't it, Chief?'

'Well, yes, things could be better.'

'Things couldn't be worse.' Captain Bowen's words were blurred and indistinct: speaking through those blistered lips had to be agonizing. 'Sister has told me. Even the boat compass smashed. Flannelfoot.'

'Flannelfoot?'

'He's still around. Flannelfoot.'

'Flannelfeet,' McKinnon said.

'Archie!' It said much for the Captain's state of mind that, for the first time ever, he had, in company, addressed the Bo'sun by his first name. 'You're here.'

'Bad pennies, sir.'

'Who's on watch, Bo'sun?'

'Naseby, sir.'

'That's all right. Flannelfeet?'

'There's more than one, sir. There has to be. I know. I don't know how I know, but I know.'

'You never mentioned this to me,' Patterson said.

'That's because I didn't think about it until now. And there's another thing I didn't think about until now. Captain Andropolous.'

'The Greek master,' Bowen said. 'What about him?'

'Well, sir, you know we're having a little trouble with the navigation?'

'A *little*? That's not how Sister Morrison tells it.'

'Well, then, a lot. We thought Captain Andropolous might give us a hand if we could communicate with him. But we can't. Maybe we don't have to. Maybe if we just show him your sextant, Captain, and give him a chart, that might be enough. Trouble is, the chart's ruined. Blood.'

'No problem,' Bowen said. 'We always carry duplicates. It'll be under the table or in the drawers at the after end of the chart room.'

'I should be back in fifteen minutes,' the Bo'sun said.

It took him considerably longer and, when he did return, his set face and the fact that he was carrying with him the sextant in its box and a chart bespoke a man who had come to report the failure of a mission.

Patterson said: 'No cooperation? Or Flannelfoot?'

'Flannelfoot. Captain Andropolous was lying on his bunk, snoring his head off. I tried to shake him but I might as well have shaken a sack of potatoes. My first thought was that the same person who had been to attend to Trent had also been to see the captain, but there was no smell of chloroform. I fetched Dr Singh, who said he had been heavily drugged.'

'Drugged!' Bowen tried to express astonishment but his voice came out as a croak. 'God's sake, is there no end to it? Drugged! How in heaven's name could he have been drugged?'

'Quite easily, it would seem, sir. Dr Singh didn't know what drug it was but he said he must have taken it with something he'd eaten or drunk. We asked Achmed, the head cook, if the captain had had anything different to eat from the rest of us and he said he hadn't but also said that he had had coffee afterwards. Captain Andropolous had his own idea as to how coffee should be made – half coffee, half brandy. Dr Singh said that that amount of brandy would have disguised the taste of any drug he knows of. There was a cup and saucer by the captain's bunkside table. It was empty.'

'Ah.' Patterson looked thoughtful. 'There must have been dregs. I know nothing about those things, of course, but couldn't Dr Singh have analysed those dregs?'

'There were none. The captain could have done it himself – washed the cup, I mean. More likely, I think it was Flannelfoot covering his tracks. There was no point in making enquiries about who might or might not have been seen going into or leaving the captain's cabin.'

'No communication, is that it?' Patterson said.

'That's it. Only his own crew were around at the time.'

Patterson said: 'Assuming that our saboteur has been at work again – and I don't think we can assume anything else – where the hell would he have got hold of powerful drugs like this?'

'Where did he get hold of the chloroform? I would think that Flannelfoot is well-stocked with what he considers essentials. Maybe he's not only a bit of a chemist, too. Maybe he knows what to look for in the dispensary.'

'No,' Bowen said. 'I asked Dr Singh. The dispensary is kept locked.'

'Yes, sir,' McKinnon said. 'But if this person is a professional, a trained saboteur, then among what he rates essentials I would think that a set of skeleton keys comes pretty high on his list.'

'My cup overfloweth,' Bowen mumbled. 'As I said, all gone to hell and breakfast. If the weather breaks down much more, and I understand it's doing just that, we can end up any place. Coast of Norway, most like.'

'May I speak, Captain?' It was Lieutenant Ulbricht.

Bowen twisted his head to one side, an ill-advised move that made him grunt in pain. 'Is that Lieutenant Ulbricht?' There was little encouragement in his voice and, had his eyes not been bandaged, it was quite certain that there would have been none there either.

'Yes, sir. I can navigate.'

'You are very kind, Lieutenant.' Bowen tried to sound icy but his blistered mouth wasn't up to it.

'You're the last person in the world I would ever turn to for help. You have committed a crime against humanity.' He paused for some seconds but it was no pause for reflection, a combination of anger and pain was making speech very difficult. 'If we get back to Britain you will be shot. You? God!'

McKinnon said: 'I can understand how you feel, sir. Because of his bombs, fifteen men are dead. Because of his bombs, you are the way you are. So are the Chief Officer, Hudson and Rafferty. But I still think you should listen to him.'

The Captain was silent for what seemed an unconscionably long time. It said much for the regard in which he held the Bo'sun that probably no other man could have given him pause for so long. When he spoke his voice was thick with bitterness. 'Beggars can't be choosers. That's it, isn't it?' McKinnon made no reply. 'Anyway, navigating a plane is quite different from navigating a ship.'

'I can navigate a ship,' Ulbricht said. 'In peacetime I was at a *Marine Schule* – a marine school. I have a marine navigation certificate.' He smiled briefly. 'Not on me, of course, but I have one. Besides, I have many times taken starsights from a plane. That is much more difficult than taking sight from the bridge of a ship. I repeat, I can navigate.'

'Him! That monster!' Sister Morrison sounded even more bitter than the Captain but maybe that was because her lips weren't blistered. 'I'm quite sure he can navigate, Captain Bowen. I'm also sure that he would navigate us straight to Alta

Fjord or Trondheim or Bergen – some place in Norway, anyway.'

Ulbricht said: 'That's a very silly statement, Sister. Mr McKinnon may not be a navigator but he must be a very experienced seaman and it would require only one glimpse of the sun or the Pole Star to let him know whether we were steering roughly south-east instead of roughly south-west.'

'I still don't trust him an inch,' Sister Morrison said. 'If what he says is true, then I trust him even less.' Her eyes were coldly appraising, her lips firmly compressed, one could see that she had missed out on her profession, she was well on the way to being the headmistress of Roedean with Ulbricht cast in the unlikely role of a trembling and errant pig-tailed third-former. 'Look what happened to Trent. Look what happened to that Greek captain. Why shouldn't the same thing happen to Mr McKinnon?'

'With respect, Sister,' McKinnon said in a voice notably lacking in respect, 'I have to repeat what Lieutenant Ulbricht said – that's a very silly statement indeed. It's silly for two reasons. The first is Naseby is also a bo'sun and a very fine one, too. Not that I would expect you to know that.' The Bo'sun put an unnecessary emphasis on the word 'you'. 'Trent, Ferguson and Curran can also tell the difference between north and south. So, I'm sure, can Chief Patterson and Mr Jamieson. There could be half-a-dozen others among the crew. Are you suggesting that by some mysterious means that passes my comprehension – but not, it would seem, yours – Lieutenant Ulbricht is going to have us *all* immobilized?'

Sister Morrison parted lips that had been tightly, even whitely, compressed. 'And the second reason?'

'If you think that Lieutenant Ulbricht is in cahoots with the persons who were responsible for the destruction of his plane and, near as a whisker, the loss of his own life – well, if you believe that, you'll believe anything.'

If it is possible to clear a throat in a soothing fashion, Patterson did just that. 'I think, Captain, that the Lieutenant here might not be quite as black a villain as you and Sister think.'

'Not a villain! The black-hearted – ' Bowen broke off and when he spoke again his voice was quiet and almost thoughtful. 'You would not say that without a reason, Chief. What makes you think so?'

'It was the Bo'sun who first came up with the suggestion. I think I agree with him. Bo'sun, tell the Captain what you told me.'

'I've had time to think about this,' McKinnon said apologetically. 'You haven't. From what Dr Singh tells me about the pain you must be suffering, it must be a damn hard job to think at all. It's my belief, sir, that the Lieutenant's Luftwaffe have sold him down the river.'

'Sold him down – what the devil is that meant to mean?'

'I don't think he knew he was attacking a hospital ship. Sure, he knows now. But he didn't when he dropped the bombs.'

'He didn't know! Bomber pilots, I would remind you, Bo'sun, are supposed to have excellent eyesight. All those red crosses –'

'I don't think he saw them, sir. The lights were off. It was half dark. As he was approaching from dead astern, he certainly couldn't have seen the crosses on the sides and he was so low the superstructure would have blocked off any view of the for'ard cross. As for the cross aft, we were making so much smoke at the time that it might have been obscured. And I can't imagine for a moment that Lieutenant Ulbricht would have made so suicidal an approach, so suicidal an attack on the *San Andreas*, if he had known there was a British frigate only a couple of miles away. I wouldn't have put his chances of survival very high.'

'Neither did I.' Lieutenant Ulbricht spoke with feeling.

'And the clincher, sir. Those four Heinkel torpedo-bombers. I know you didn't see them, sir, even hear them, you were unconscious at the time. But Chief Patterson and I saw them. They deliberately avoided us – lifted over us – and headed straight for the *Andover*. So what do you make of it, sir? A Condor attacks us – I'm sure it must have been with low-power bombs – and the Heinkels, who could have sent us to the bottom, didn't. The Heinkel pilots *knew* the *Andover* was there: Lieutenant Ulbricht did not. The Luftwaffe, Captain, would seem to have two hands, with the left hand not telling the right hand what it was doing. I'm more than ever convinced that the Lieutenant was sold down the river, sold by his own high command and the saboteur who blacked out our Red Cross lights.

'Besides, he doesn't *look* like a man who would bomb a hospital ship.'

'How the hell can I tell what he looks like?' Bowen spoke with, understandably, some irritation. 'A babyface with a harp can be no less of a murderer, no matter what he looks like. But yes, I agree, Bo'sun, it does raise some very odd questions. Questions that seem to call for some very odd answers. Don't you agree, Sister?'

'Well, yes, perhaps.' Her tone was doubtful, grudging. 'Mr McKinnon could be right.'

'He *is* right.' The voice was Kennet's and it was very firm.

'Mr Kennet.' Bowen turned to the bed on the other side of him and cursed, not too *sotto voce*, as his neck and head reminded him that sudden movements were not advisable. 'I thought you were asleep.'

'Never more awake, sir. Just that I don't feel too much like talking. Of course the Bo'sun's right. Has to be.'

'Ah. Well.' More carefully, this time, Bowen turned back to face Ulbricht. 'No apologies for what you have done but maybe you're not the black-hearted murderer we thought you were. Bo'sun, Chief tells me that you've been smashing furniture in my cabin.'

'No more than I had to, sir. Couldn't find the keys.'

'The keys are in the back left-hand corner of the left drawer in my desk. Look in the right-hand locker under my bunk. There's a chronometer there. See if it's working.'

'A *spare* chronometer, sir?'

'Many captains carry one. I always have done. If the sextant has survived the blast, maybe the chronometer has too. The sextant is functioning, isn't it?'

'As far as I can tell.'

'May I see it?' Lieutenant Ulbricht said. He examined it briefly. 'It works.'

McKinnon left, taking the sextant and chart with him.

When he returned, he was smiling. 'Chronometer is intact, sir. I've put Trent back on the wheel and Naseby in your cabin. There he can see anybody who tries to go up the bridge ladder and, more important, clobber any unauthorized person who tries to come into your cabin. I've told him the only authorized people are Mr Patterson, Mr Jamieson and myself.'

'Excellent,' Bowen said. 'Lieutenant Ulbricht, we may yet call upon your services.' He paused. 'You are aware, of course, that you will be navigating yourself into captivity?'

'Not a firing squad?'

'That would be a poor return for your – ah – professional services. No.'

'Better a live prisoner-of-war than floating around and frozen to death in a rubber raft, which I would have been but for Mr McKinnon here.' Ulbricht propped himself up in his bed. 'Well, no time like the present.'

McKinnon placed a restraining hand on his shoulder. 'Sorry, Lieutenant, it'll have to wait.'

'You mean – Dr Singh?'

'He wouldn't be too happy but it's not that. Blizzard. Zero visibility. No stars, and there'll be none tonight.'

'Ah.' Ulbricht lay back in bed. 'I wasn't feeling all that energetic, anyway.'

It was then that, for the third time that day, the lights failed. McKinnon switched on his torch, located and switched on four nickel-cadmium emergency lights and looked thoughtfully at Patterson. Bowen said: 'Something up?'

'Sorry, sir,' Patterson said. He had momentarily forgotten that the Captain couldn't see. 'Another blasted power-cut.'

'Another. Jesus!' The Captain sounded less concerned and angry than just disgusted. 'No sooner do we think we have cleared up one problem than we have another. Flannelfoot, I'll be bound.'

'Maybe, sir,' McKinnon said. 'Maybe not. I don't imagine the lights have failed because someone has been drugged or chloroformed. I don't imagine they've failed because someone wanted to douse our topside Red Cross lights, because visibility is zero and it would serve no point. If it's sabotage, it's sabotage for some other reason.'

'I'll go see if they can tell me anything in the engine-room,' Patterson said. 'Looks like another job for Mr Jamieson.'

'He's working in the superstructure,' McKinnon said. 'I was going there anyway. I'll get him for you. Meet you back here, sir?' Patterson nodded and hurried from the ward.

On the now relatively stable upper deck the lifelines were no longer needed as such but were invaluable as guidelines, for, with the absence of deck-lights and the driving snow, McKinnon literally could not see an inch before his face. He brought up short as he bumped into someone.

'Who's that.' His voice was sharp.

'McKinnon? Jamieson. Not Flannelfoot. He's been at it again.'

'Looks like it, sir. Mr Patterson would like to see you in the engine-room.'

On the deck level of the superstructure the Bo'sun found three of the engine-room crew welding a cross-plate to two beams, the harsh glare of the oxy-acetylene flame contrasting eerily with the utter blackness around. Two decks up he came across Naseby in the Captain's cabin, a marlin-spike, butt end cloth-wrapped, in his hand and a purposeful expression on his face.

'No visitors, George?'

'Nary a visitor, Archie, but it looks as if some-one has been visiting somewhere.'

The Bo'sun nodded and went up to the bridge, checked with Trent and descended the ladder again. He stopped outside the Captain's cabin and looked at Naseby. 'Notice anything?'

'Yes, I notice something. I notice that the engine revs have dropped, we're slowing. This time, perhaps, a bomb in the engine-room?'

'No. We'd have heard it in the hospital.'

'A gas grenade would have done just as well.'

'You're getting as bad as I am,' McKinnon said.

He found Patterson and Jamieson in the hospital dining area. They were accompanied, to McKinnon's momentary surprise, by Ferguson. But the surprise was only momentary.

'Engine-room's okay, then?' McKinnon said.

Patterson said: 'Yes. Reduced speed as a precaution. How did you know?'

'Ferguson here is holed up with Curran in the carpenter's shop, which is as far for'ard as you can get in this ship. So the trouble is up near the bows – nothing short of an earthquake would normally get Ferguson out of his bunk – or what-ever he's using for a bunk up there.'

Ferguson looked and sounded aggrieved. 'Just dropping off, I was, when Curran and me heard this explosion. Felt it, too. Directly beneath us. Not so much an explosion as a bang or a clang. Something metallic, anyway. Curran shouted that we'd been mined or torpedoed but I told him not to be daft, if a mine or torpedo had gone off beneath us we wouldn't have been alive to talk about it. So I came running aft – well, as fast as you can run on that deck – it's like a skating rink.'

McKinnon said to Patterson: 'So you think the ship's hull is open to the sea?'

'I don't know what to think, but if it is then the slower we go the less chance of increasing the damage to the hull. Not too slow, of course, if we lose steerage way then we'll start rolling or corkscrewing or whatever and that would only increase the strain on the hull. I suppose Captain Bowen has the structural plans in his cabin?'

'I don't know. I suppose he has but it doesn't matter. I know the lay-out. I'm sure Mr Jamieson does as well.'

'Oh dear. That means I don't?'

'Didn't say that, sir. Let me put it this way. Next time I see a chief engineer crawling around the bilges will be the first time. Besides, you have to stay up top, sir. If an urgent decision has to be taken the bilges are no place for the commanding officer to be.'

Patterson sighed. 'I often wonder, Bo'sun, where one draws a line between commonsense and diplomacy.'

'This is it, you think, Bo'sun?'

'It has to be, sir.' Jamieson and the Bo'sun, together with Ferguson and McCrimmon, were in the paint store, a lowermost deck compartment on the port side for'ard. Facing them was an

130

eight-clamped door set in a watertight bulkhead. McKinnon placed the palm of his hand against the top of the door and then against the bottom. 'Normal temperatures above – well, almost normal – and cold, almost freezing, below. Sea-water on the other side, sir – not more than eight-een inches, I would think.'

'Figures,' Jamieson said. 'We're not more than a few feet below the waterline here and that's as much as the compressed air will let in. That's one of the ballast rooms, of course.'

'That's *the* ballast room, sir.'

'And this is *the* paint store.' Jamieson gestured at the irregularly welded patch of metal on the ship's side. 'Chief Engineer never did have any faith in what he called those Russkie shipwrights.'

'That's as maybe, sir. But I don't see any Russian shipwrights leaving a time-bomb in the ballast room.'

Russian shipwrights had indeed been aboard the *San Andreas*, which had sailed from Halifax, Nova Scotia, as the freighter *Ocean Belle, Ocean* being a common prefix for American-built Liberty Ships. At the time of sailing, the *Ocean Belle* was neither fish nor fowl but was, in fact, a three-parts com-pleted hospital ship. Its armament, at that stage, had been removed, its magazines emptied, all but the essential watertight bulkheads breached or par-tially cut away, the operating theatre completed, as were the cabins for the medical staff and the dispensary, already fully stocked: the medical store was almost finished, the galley partially so, whereas work had not yet begun on the wards, the recovery room and messes. The medical staff, which had come from Britain, were already on board.

Orders were received from the Admiralty that the *Ocean Belle* was to join the next fast convoy to Northern Russia, which had already assembled at Halifax. Captain Bowen had not refused – refusal of an Admiralty order was not permitted – but he had objected in a fashion so strongly as to be tantamount to refusal. He was damned, he said, if he was going to sail to Russia with a shipload of civilians aboard. He was referring to the medical staff aboard and, as they constituted only a round dozen, they could hardly have been called a shipload: he was also conveniently overlooking the fact that every member of the crew, from himself downwards, was also, technically, a civilian.

The medical staff, Bowen had maintained, were a different kind of civilian. Dr Singh had pointed out to him that ninety per cent of the medical staff of the armed forces were civilians, only they wore different kinds of uniforms: the staff on board the *San Andreas* wore different kinds of uniforms too, which happened to be white. Captain Bowen had then fallen back on his last defence: he was not, he said, going to take women through a war zone – he was referring to the six nursing staff aboard. A by now thoroughly irritated escort commander forcefully made three points that had forcefully been made to him by the Admiralty: thousands of women and children had been in war zones while being transported as refugees to the United States and Canada: in the current year, as compared to the previous two years, U-boat losses had quadrupled while Mercantile Marine losses had been cut by eighty per cent: and the Russians had requested, or rather insisted, that as many wounded Allied personnel as possible be removed from their over-crowded Archangel hospitals. Captain Bowen, as he should have done at the beginning, had capitulated and the *Ocean Belle*, still painted in its wartime grey but carrying adequate supplies of white, red and green paint, had sailed with the convoy.

As convoys to Northern Russia went, it had been an exceptionally uneventful one. Not one merchant ship and not one escort vessel had been lost. Only two incidents had occurred and both had involved the *Ocean Belle*. Some way south of Jan Mayen Island they had come across a venerable V and W class destroyer, stopped in the water with an engine breakdown. This destroyer had been a unit of the destroyer screen escorting a previous convoy and had stopped to pick up survivors from a sinking cargo vessel, which had been heavily on fire. The time had been about 2.30 p.m., well after sunset, and the rescue operation had been inter-rupted by a brief air attack. The attacker had not been seen but had obviously no difficulty in seeing the destroyer, silhouetted as it was against the blazing cargo ship. It had been assumed that the attacker was a reconnaissance Condor, for it had dropped no bombs and contented itself with raking the bridge with machine gun fire, which had effectively destroyed the radio office. Thus, when the engines had broken down some hours later – the breakdown had nothing to do with the Condor, the V and Ws were superannuated, overworked and much plagued by mechanical troubles – they had been unable to contact the vanished convoy.*

The wounded survivors were taken aboard the *Ocean Belle*. The destroyer itself, together with its crew and unwounded survivors, was taken in tow by an S-class destroyer. It was later learnt that both vessels had reached Scapa Flow intact.

---

* Throughout the wartime convoy sailings to Murmansk and Archangel the use of rescue ships remained a bone of contention between the Royal Navy at sea and the Royal Navy on land – the latter being the London-based Admiralty which acquitted itself with something less than distinction during the long years of the Russian convoys. In the earlier days, the use of rescue ships was the rule, not the exception. After the loss of the *Zafaaran* and the *Stockport*, which was lost with all hands including the many survivors that had been picked up from other sunken vessels, the Admiralty forbade the further use of rescue ships.

This was a rule that was observed in the breach. In certain convoys a self-selected member of the escort group, usually a destroyer or smaller, would assign to itself the role of rescue ship, an assignment in which the force commander would acquiesce or to which he turned a blind eye. The task of the rescue ships was a hazardous one indeed. There was never any question of a convoy stopping or of their escorts leaving the convoy, so that, almost invariably the rescue ship was left alone and unprotected. The sight of a Royal Naval vessel stopped in the water alongside a sinking vessel was an irresistible target for many U-boat commanders.

Three days afterwards, somewhere off North Cape, they had come across an equally ancient 'Kingfisher' corvette, which had no business whatever in those distant waters. It, too, was stopped, and so deep in the water astern that its poop was already awash. It, too, had survivors aboard – the survivors of the crew of a Russian submarine that had been picked up from a burning oil-covered sea.* The Russians, for the most part badly burned, had been transferred, inevitably, to the *Ocean Belle*, the crew being transferred to an escort destroyer. The corvette was sunk by gunfire. It was during this transfer that the *Ocean Belle* had been holed twice, just below the water line, on the port side, in the paint store and ballast room. The reason for the damage had never been established.

The convoy had gone to Archangel but the *Ocean Belle* had put in to Murmansk – neither Captain Bowen nor the escort commander had thought it wise that the *Ocean Belle* should proceed any further than necessary in its then present condition – slightly down by the head and with a list to port. There were no dry dock facilities available but the Russians were masters of improvisation – the rigours of war had forced them to be. They topped up the after tanks,

---

* It was neither appreciated nor reported that the Russians had a few submarines operational in the area at that time. One of them almost certainly damaged the *Tirpitz* sufficiently to make it return to its moorings in Alta Fjord.

drained the for'ard tanks and removed the for'ard slabs of concrete ballast until the holes in the paint store and ballast room were just clear of the water, after which it had taken them only a few hours to weld plates in position over the holes. The equalization of the tanks and the replacement of ballast had then brought the *Ocean Belle* back to an even keel.

While those repairs were being effected a small army of Russian carpenters had worked, three shifts in every twenty-four hours, in the hospital section of the ship, fitting out the wards, recovery room, messes, galley and medical store. Captain Bowen was astonished beyond measure. On his previous visits to the two Russian ports he had encountered from his allies, blood brothers who should have been in tears of gratitude for the dearly-bought and vital supplies being ferried to their stricken country, nothing but sullenness, indifference, a marked lack of cooperation and, not occasionally, downright hostility. The baffling sea-change he could only attribute to the fact that the Russians were only showing their heartfelt appreciation for the *Ocean Belle* having brought their wounded submariners back home.

When they sailed it was as a hospital ship – Bowen's crew, paintbrushes in hands, had worked with a will during their brief stay in Murmansk. They did not, as everyone had expected, proceed through the White Sea to pick up the wounded servicemen in Archangel. The Admiralty's orders had been explicit: they were to proceed, and at all speed, to the port of Aberdeen in Scotland.

Jamieson replaced the cover of the small electrical junction box, having effectively isolated the ballast room from the main power system. He tapped the watertight door. 'Short in there – could have been caused by the blast or sea-water, it doesn't matter – should have blown a fuse somewhere. It didn't. Somewhere or other there's a fuse, that's been tampered with – fuse-wire replaced by a nail or some such. That doesn't matter either. I'm not going to look for it. McCrimmon, go ask the engine-room to try the generator.'

McKinnon tapped the same door. 'And what do we do here?'

'What, indeed?' Jamieson sat on a paint drum and thought. 'Three choices, I would say. We can get an air compressor down here, drill a hole through the bulkhead at about shoulder level and force the water out which would be fine if we knew where the level of the hole in the hull is. We don't. Besides, the chances are that the compressed air in the ballast room would escape before we could get the nozzle of the compressed air hose into the hole we drilled which could only mean that more water would pour into the ballast room. Or we could reinforce the bulkhead. The third choice is to do nothing. I'm for the third choice. It's a pretty solid bulkhead. We'd have to reduce speed, of course. No bulkhead is going to stand up to the pressure at full speed if there's a hole the size of a barn door in the hull.'

'A barn door would not be convenient,' McKinnon said, 'I think I'll go and have a look.'

It was a very cold and rather bruised McKinnon who half-climbed and was half-pulled up to the foredeck of the *San Andreas*, which, engines stopped, was wallowing heavily in quartering seas. In the pale half-light given by the again functioning deck arc lamps they presented a strange quartet, Jamieson, Ferguson and McCrimmon, wraithlike figures completely shrouded in snow, McKinnon a weirdly-gleaming creature, the sea water on his rubber suit, aqualung and waterproof torch already, in that 35° below temperature, beginning to harden into ice. At a gesture from Jamieson, McCrimmon left for the engine-room while Ferguson pulled in the rope-ladder: Jamieson took McKinnon's arm and led him, the newly-formed ice on the rubber suit crackling as he stumbled along, towards the shelter of the superstructure where McKinnon pulled off his aqualung. His teeth were chattering uncontrollably.

'Pretty bad down there, Bo'sun?'

'Not that, sir. This damned rubber suit.' He fingered a waist-high gash in the material. 'Tore it on a jagged piece of metal. From here down the suit is filled with water.'

'Good God! You'll freeze to death, man. Hurry, hurrry!' In what was left of his cabin McKinnon

138

began to strip off his rubber suit. 'You located the damage?'

'No problem – and no barn door. Just a ragged hole about the size of my fist.'

Jamieson smiled. 'Worth risking pneumonia to find that out. I'm going to the bridge. See you in the Captain's cabin.'

When McKinnon, in dry clothing but still shivering violently, joined Jamieson and Naseby in the Captain's cabin, the *San Andreas* was back on course and steadily picking up speed. Jamieson pushed a glass of Scotch across to him.

'I'm afraid the Captain's supplies are taking a fearful beating, Bo'sun. This shouldn't increase the risk of pneumonia – I've left the water out. I've been speaking to Mr Patterson and the Captain – we've got a line through to the hospital now. When I told him you'd been over the side in this weather, he didn't say thank-you or anything like that, just said to tell you that you're mad.'

'Captain Bowen is not often wrong and that's a fact.' McKinnon's hands were shaking so badly that he spilt liquid from his admittedly brimming glass. 'Any instructions from the Captain or Mr Patterson?'

'None. Both say they're quite happy to leave the topside to you.'

'That's kind of them. What they really mean is that they have no option – there's only George and myself.'

'George?'

139

'Sorry, sir. Naseby, here. He's a bo'sun, too. We've been shipmates on and off, friends for twenty years.'

'I didn't know.' Jamieson looked thoughtfully at Naseby. 'I can see it now. You've made arrangements for up here, Bo'sun?'

'About to, sir. George and I will take turns here, looking after the family jewels, so to speak. I'll have Trent, Ferguson and Curran spell one another on the wheel. I'll tell them to give me a shake – if I'm asleep – when or if the weather clears.'

'Cue for Lieutenant Ulbricht?'

'Indeed. I would like to make a suggestion, sir, if I may. I would like to have some people keeping watch at the fore and aft exits of the hospital, just to make absolutely certain that nobody's going to start sleepwalking during the night.'

'Who's going to watch the watchers?'

'A point, sir. The watchers I would suggest are Jones, McGuigan, McCrimmon and Stephen. Unless they're wonderful actors, the first two are too young and innocent to be criminals. McCrimmon may, indeed, have a criminal bent, but I think he's an honest criminal. And Stephen strikes me as being a fairly trustworthy lad. More important, he's not likely to forget that it was a naval minesweeper that picked him up out of the North Sea.'

'I didn't know that, either. You seem to be better informed about my own department than I am. I'll arrange for Stephen and McCrimmon, you

140

look after the others. Our resident saboteur is not about to give up all that easily?'

'I would be surprised if he did. Wouldn't you?'

'Very much. I wonder what form of sabotage his next attempt to nobble us will take?'

'I just have no idea. But another thought occurs, sir. The person you have keeping an eye on the aft exit from the hospital might also keep an eye on the entrance to A Ward.'

'A Ward? That bunch of crooks? Whatever for?'

'The person or persons who are trying to slow us and are doing their best to get us lost might think it a rather good idea to nobble Lieutenant Ulbricht.'

'Indeed they might. I'll stay in the ward myself tonight. There's a spare bed. If I do drop off, the duty nurse can always give me a shake if anyone comes in who shouldn't be coming in.' Jamieson was silent for a few moments. 'What's behind it all, Bo'sun?'

'I think you know as well as I do, sir. Somebody, somewhere, wants to take over the *San Andreas*, although *why* anyone should want to take over a hospital ship I can't even begin to imagine.'

'No more can I. A U-boat, you think?'

'It would have to be, wouldn't it? I mean, you can't capture a ship from the air and they're hardly likely to send the *Tirpitz* after us.' McKinnon shook his head. 'A U-boat? Any fishing boat, with a few armed and determined men, could take us over whenever they felt like it.'

FIVE

McKinnon, deep in sleep though he was, was instantly awake at Naseby's shake and swung his legs over the edge of Captain Bowen's bunk.

'What's the time, George?'

'Six a.m. Curran's just been down from the bridge. Says the blizzard has blown itself out.'

'Stars?'

'He didn't say.'

The Bo'sun pulled on an extra jersey, duffel coat and sea-boots, made his way up to the bridge, spoke briefly to Curran and went out on the starboard wing. Within only a second or two, bent double and with his back to the gale-force wind, coughing and gasping as the ice-chilled air reached down into his lungs, he was beginning to wish himself anywhere except where he was. He switched on his torch and picked up the thermometer. It showed −8°, 40° of frost on the Fahrenheit scale. Combined with the strong wind the temperature, expressed in terms of the chill factor on exposed skin, was in the region of −80°F.

He straightened slowly and looked out towards the bows. In the light of the Red Cross arc lamps on the foredeck it was at once clear, as Curran had said, that the blizzard had blown itself out. Against the deep indigo of the sky, the stars were preternaturally bright and clear. Breathing through a mittened hand that covered both mouth and nose, McKinnon turned into the wind and looked aft.

At first he could see nothing, for the bitter wind brought instantaneous tears to his eyes. He ducked below the shelter of the canvas wind-breaker, fumbled a pair of goggles from his coat pocket, strapped them under his duffel hood, straightened again, and, by dint of wiping the back of his free mitten against the glasses, was able to see, intermittently, what was going on astern.

The waves – the weather had not yet worsened to the extent that the seas had become broken and confused – were between twelve and fifteen feet in height, their lee sides whitely streaked with spume and half-hidden in flying spray as the wind tore their tops away. The stars were as brilliant as they had been in the other direction and McKinnon soon located the Pole Star, off the star-board quarter. The wind was no longer backing to the north and the *San Andreas*, as far as he could judge, was still heading roughly between south-west and south-south-west.

McKinnon moved back into the bridge, thankfully closed the door and pondered briefly. Their present course, it was safe to assume, offered no danger: on the other hand it was not safe to assume that they would or could maintain their present course. The weather, in this grey and undefined area between the Barents and Norwegian Seas, was notoriously fickle. He had not, for instance, expected – and had said as much – that the skies would clear that night: there was equally no guarantee that they would remain clear and that the wind would not back further to the north. He descended two decks, selected an armful of warm clothing from the now mostly abandoned crew's quarters and made for the hospital area. Crossing the dangerously slippery upper deck and guided only by the lifeline, he became acutely and painfully aware that a change was already under way, a factor that he had not experienced on the starboard wing only a few minutes ago. Needle-pointed ice spicules were beginning to lance into the unprotected areas of his skin. It augured ill.

In the hospital mess-deck he came across both Jones and McGuigan, both of whom assured him that no one was or had been abroad. He passed into B ward, at the far end of which Janet Magnusson was seated at her desk, her elbows propped on it, her chin propped on her hands, and her eyes closed.

'Aha!' McKinnon said. 'Asleep on the job, Nurse Magnusson.'

She looked up, startled, blinked and tried to sound indignant. 'Asleep? Of course not.' She peered at his armful of clothing. 'What on earth is that for? Have you moved into the old rags trade, Archie? No, don't tell me. It's for that poor man in there. Maggie's in there too – she won't be pleased.'

'As far as your precious Maggie is concerned, I would have thought that a little suffering for Lieutenant Ulbricht would be preferable to none. No salt tears for either Sister Morrison or the Lieutenant.'

'Archie!' She was on her feet. 'Your face. Blood!'

'As far as the Lieutenant and myself are both concerned that should please your friend.' He wiped the blood off his face. 'It's not nice up top.'

'Archie.' She looked at him uncertainly, concern in the tired eyes.

'It's all right, Janet.' He touched her shoulder and passed into A ward. Sister Morrison and Lieutenant Ulbricht were both awake and drinking tea, the sister at her desk, Ulbricht sitting up in bed: clear-eyed and rested, the German pilot, as Dr Singh had said, unquestionably had quite remarkable recuperative powers. Jamieson, fully clothed and stretched out on the top of a bed, opened an eye as McKinnon passed by.

''Morning, Bo'sun. It *is* morning, isn't it?'

'Six-twenty, sir.'

'Good lord. Selfishness, that's what it is – I've been asleep for seven hours. How are things?'

'A quiet night up top. Here, too?'

'Must have been – no one gave me a shake.' He looked at the bundle of clothing that McKinnon was carrying, then at Ulbricht. 'Stars?'

'Yes, sir. At the moment, that is. I don't think they'll be there for long.'

'Mr McKinnon!' Sister Morrison's voice was cold, with a touch of asperity, as it usually was when addressing the Bo'sun. 'Do you intend to drag that poor man out of bed on a night like this? He's been shot several times.'

'I know he's been shot several times – or have you forgotten who picked him out of the water?' The Bo'sun was an innately courteous man but never at his best when dealing with Sister Morrison. 'So he's a poor man, now – well, it's better than being a filthy Nazi murderer. What do you mean – on a night like this?'

'I mean the weather, of course.' Her fists were actually clenched. Jamieson surveyed the ward deckhead.

'What do you know about the weather? You haven't been out of here all night. If you had been, I would have known.' He turned a dismissive back on her and looked at Ulbricht. 'How do you feel, Lieutenant?'

'I have an option?' Ulbricht smiled. 'I feel well enough. Even if I didn't I'm still coming. Don't be too hard on the ward sister, Bo'sun – even your lady with a lamp in the Crimea had a pretty short way with difficult patients – but she's overlooking my natural selfishness. I'm on this ship too.' He climbed stiffly out of bed and, with the assistance of McKinnon and Jamieson, started to pull clothing on over his pyjamas while Sister Morrison looked on in frigid disapproval. The disapproval finally culminated in the drumming of fingertips on the table.

'I think,' she said, 'that we should have Dr Singh in here.'

McKinnon turned slowly and looked at her and when he spoke his voice was as expressionless as his face. 'I don't think it matters very much what you think, Sister. I suggest you just give a shake to Captain Bowen there and find out just how much your thinking matters.'

'The Captain is under heavy sedation. When he regains consciousness, I shall report you for insolence.'

'Insolence?' McKinnon looked at her with indifference. 'I think he would prefer that to stupidity – the stupidity of a person who is trying to endanger the San Andreas and all those aboard her. It's a pity we don't have any irons on this ship.'

She glared at him, made to speak, then turned as Dr Sinclair came into the ward. Sleepy-eyed and tousle-haired, he looked in mild astonishment at the spectacle before him.

'Dr Sinclair! Thank heavens you're here!' Rapidly and urgently she began to explain the situation to him. 'Those – those men want starsights or navigation or something and in spite of all my

147

protests they insist on dragging a seriously ill man up to the bridge or wherever and –'

'I can see what's happening,' Sinclair said mildly. 'But if the Lieutenant is being dragged he's not putting up much in the way of resistance, is he? And by no stretch of the imagination can you describe him as being seriously ill. But I do take your point, Sister. He should be under constant medical supervision.'

'Ah! Thank you, Doctor.' Sister Morrison came very close to permitting herself a smile. 'So it's back to bed for him.'

'Well, no, not quite. A duffel coat, a pair of sea boots, my bag of tricks and I'll go up with them. That way the Lieutenant will be under constant medical supervision.'

Even with three men lending what assistance they could, it took twice as long as expected to help Lieutenant Ulbricht as far as the Captain's cabin. Once there, he sank heavily into the chair behind the table.

'Thank you very much, gentlemen.' He was very pale, his breathing shallow and abnormally rapid. 'Sorry about that. It would seem that I am not as fit as I thought I was.'

'Nonsense.' Dr Sinclair was brisk. 'You did splendidly. It's that inferior English blood that we had to give you this morning, that's all.' He made free with Captain Bowen's supplies. 'Superior Scotch blood. Effects guaranteed.'

Ulbricht smiled faintly. 'Isn't there something about opening pores?'

'You won't be out in the open long enough to give your pores a chance to protest.'

Up on the bridge McKinnon adjusted Ulbricht's goggles, then scarfed him so heavily above and below the goggles that not a square millimetre of skin was left exposed. When he was finished, Lieutenant Ulbricht was as immune to the weather as it was possible for anyone to be: two balaclavas and a tightly strung duffel hood made sure of that.

McKinnon went out on the starboard wing, hung a trailing lamp from the canvas wind-breaker, went back inside, picked up the sextant, took Ulbricht by his right arm – the undamaged one – and led him outside. Even although he was so cocooned against the elements, even though the Bo'sun had warned him and even though he had already had an ominous foretaste of what lay in store in their brief journey across the upper deck, he was totally unprepared for the power and savagery of the wind that caught him as soon as he stepped out on the wing. His weakened limbs were similarly unprepared. He took two short sharp steps forward, and though he managed to clutch the top of the wind-breaker, would probably have fallen but for McKinnon's sustaining hand. Had he been carrying the sextant he would almost certainly have dropped it.

With McKinnon's arm around him Ulbricht took three starsights, to the south, west and north, clumsily noting down the results as he did so. The first two sights were comparatively quick and simple: the third, to the north, took much longer and was far more difficult, for Ulbricht had to keep clearing away the ice spicules from his goggles and the sextant. When he had finished he handed the sextant back to McKinnon, leant his elbows on the after edge of the wing and stared out towards the stern, occasionally and mechanically wiping his goggles with the back of his hand. After almost twenty seconds of this McKinnon took his good arm and almost literally dragged him back into the shelter of the bridge, banging the door to behind him. Handing the sextant to Jamieson, he quickly removed Ulbricht's duffel hood, balaclavas and goggles.

'Sorry about that, Lieutenant, but there's a time and a place for everything and daydreaming or sightseeing out on that wing is not one of them.'

'The funnel.' Ulbricht looked slightly dazed. 'What's happened to your funnel?'

'It fell off.'

'I see. It fell off. You mean – I –'

'What's done is done,' Jamieson said philosophically. He handed a glass to the Lieutenant. 'To help you with your calculations.'

'Thank you. Yes.' Ulbricht shook his head as if to clear it. 'Yes. My calculations.'

Weak though he was and shivering constantly – this despite the fact that the bridge temperature was already over 55°F. – Ulbricht left no doubt that, as a navigator, he knew precisely what he was about. Working from starsights, he had no need to worry about the vagaries of deviation and variation. With a chart, dividers, parallel rules, pencils and chronometer, he completed his calculations in remarkably short order and made a tiny cross on the chart after having consulted navigational tables.

'We're here. Well, near enough. 68.05 north, 7.20 east – more or less due west of the Lofotens. Our course is 218. Is one permitted to ask our destination?'

Jamieson smiled. 'Quite frankly, Lieutenant Ulbricht, you wouldn't be much use to us if you didn't. Aberdeen.'

'Ah! Aberdeen. They have a rather famous prison there, do they not? Peterhead, isn't it? I wonder what the cells are like.'

'It's a prison for civilians. Of the more intractable kind. I should hardly think you'd end up there. Or in any prison.' Jamieson looked at him with some curiosity. 'How do you know about Peterhead, Lieutenant?'

'I know Scotland well. I know England even better.' Ulbricht did not seek to elaborate. 'So, Aberdeen. We'll stay on this course until we get to the latitude of Trondheim, then south until we get to the latitude of Bergen – or, if you like Mr McKinnon, the latitude of your home islands.'

'How did you know I'm a Shetlander?'

'Some members of the nursing staff don't seem to mind talking to me. Then on a more westerly course. That's speaking roughly, we'll work out the details as we go along. It's a very simple exercise and there's no problem.'

'Of course it's no problem,' Jamieson said, 'neither is playing Rachmaninoff, not as long as you are a concert pianist.'

Ulbricht smiled. 'You overrate my simple skills. The only problem that will arise is when we make our landfall, which of course will have to be in daylight. At this time of year North Sea fogs are as common as not and there's no way I can navigate in a fog without a radio and compass.'

'With any luck, there shouldn't be all that much of a problem,' McKinnon said. 'War or no war, there's still pretty heavy traffic on the east coast and there's more than an even chance that we can pick up a ship and be guided into harbour.'

'Agreed,' Ulbricht said. 'A Red Cross ship is not easily overlooked – especially one with its funnel missing.' He sipped his drink, pondered briefly, then said: 'Is it your intention to return me to the hospital?'

'Naturally,' Sinclair said. 'That's where you belong. Why do you ask?'

Ulbricht looked at Jamieson. 'I would, of course, be expected to do some more navigating?'

'Expecting, Lieutenant? "Depending" is the word you're after.'

'And at frequent intervals if cloud or snow conditions permit. We never know when the set of the sea and the wind may change without our being aware of it. Point is, I don't much fancy dragging myself back down to the hospital, then coming back up here again every time I have to take starsights. Couldn't I just lie down in the Captain's cabin?'

'No objections,' Jamieson said. 'Dr Sinclair?'

'Makes sense. Lieutenant Ulbricht is hardly on the critical list and it could only help his recuperation. I'll pop up every two or three hours to see how he's getting on.'

'Bo'sun?'

'Fine by me. Fine by Sister Morrison too, I should imagine.'

'I shall have company, of course?'

'Company?' Sinclair said. 'You mean a nurse, Lieutenant?'

'I don't mean a nurse. With all respect to your charming young ladies, Dr Sinclair, I don't think any of them would be much use if this fellow you call Flannelfoot came up to remove or destroy the sextant and chronometer and the way I'm feeling I couldn't fight off a determined fly. Also, of course, he'd have to dispose of witnesses and I don't much fancy that.'

'No problem, Lieutenant,' the Bo'sun said. 'He'll have to try to dispose of either Naseby or myself and I don't much think he would fancy that. We would, though.'

Sinclair shook his head sadly. 'Sister Morrison isn't going to like this one little bit. Further usurpment of her authority. After all, the Lieutenant is her patient, not mine.'

'Again no problem,' McKinnon said. 'Just tell her the Lieutenant fell over the side.'

'And how are your patients this morning, sir?' McKinnon was having breakfast with Dr Singh.

'No dramatic changes, Bo'sun. The two *Argos* crewmen in the recovery room are much of a muchness – as well as can be expected when one has a fractured pelvis and the other massive burns. The condition of Commander Warrington and his navigating officer is unchanged – Cunningham is still in deep coma and is being fed intravenously. Hudson is stabilized – the lung bleeding has stopped. Chief Officer Kennet is definitely on the mend although heaven knows how long it will be before we can take those bandages off his face. The only one that gives some cause for worry is the Captain. It's nothing critical, not even serious, just worrisome. You saw how he was when you last saw him – breathing hellfire and brimstone in all directions. He's gone strangely quiet now, almost lethargic. Or maybe he's just more calm and relaxed now that he knows the ship's position and course. That was a fine job you did there, Bo'sun.'

'No credit to me, sir. It was Lieutenant Ulbricht who did the fine job.'

'Be that as it may, Captain Bowen appears to be in at least a more philosophical mood. I suggest you come along and see him.'

When a man's face is completely obscured by bandages it is difficult to say what kind of mood he is in. He had the stem of a rather evil-smelling briar stuck between his burnt lips and again it was impossible to say whether he was enjoying it or not. When he heard McKinnon's voice he removed the pipe.

'We are still afloat, Bo'sun?' The enunciation was clearer than it had been and was costing him less effort.

'Well, sir, let's say we're no longer all gone to hell and breakfast. No more alarms and excursions either. As far as I can tell, Lieutenant Ulbricht is very much of an expert – I don't think you'd hesitate to have him as your navigating officer. He's lying down on the bunk in your cabin, sir – but you will have been told that and the reasons why.'

'Broaching my rapidly dwindling supplies, I have no doubt.'

'He did have a couple of tots, sir. He needed it. He's still a pretty sick man and very weak and the cold out there on the wing bridge was vicious, I don't think I've ever known it worse in the Arctic. Anyway, he wasn't doing any broaching when I left him. He was sound asleep.'

'As long as he keeps on acting in this fashion he can do as much broaching as he likes. Give him my sincere thanks.'

'I'll do that. Have you any instructions, sir?'

'Instructions, Bo'sun? Instructions? How can I give any instructions?'

'I wouldn't know, sir. I've never been a captain.'

'You bloody well are now. I'm in no position to give anyone instructions. Just do what you think best – and from what I've heard to date your best seems to be very good indeed. Not,' Bowen added deprecatingly, 'that I would have expected anything else of Archie McKinnon.'

'Thank you, sir. I'll try.' McKinnon turned to leave the ward but was stopped by Sister Morrison. For once, she was looking at him as if he might even belong to the human race.

'How is he, Mr McKinnon?'

'The Lieutenant? Resting. He's a lot weaker than he says he is but he'd never admit it. A very brave man. And a fine navigator. And a gentleman. When he says he didn't know the *San Andreas* was a hospital ship I believe him absolutely. I don't believe many people absolutely.'

'I'm quite sure you don't.' The return to the old asperity proved to be momentary. 'I don't think I believe he knew it either. In fact, I don't believe it.'

'That's nice.' McKinnon smiled at her, the first time, he reflected with some astonishment, that he'd ever smiled at her. 'Janet – Nurse Magnusson – tells me you come from the east coast. Would it be impertinent to ask where exactly?'

'Of course not.' She smiled and McKinnon realized with an even greater sense of shock that this was the first time she'd ever smiled at him. 'Aberdeen. Why?'

'Odd. Lieutenant Ulbricht seems to know Aberdeen rather well. He certainly seems to know about Peterhead prison and isn't all that keen on ending up there.'

A brief flicker of what could have been concern registered on her face. 'Will he?'

'Not a chance. If he brings this ship back to Aberdeen they'll probably give him a medal. Both your parents from Aberdeen, Sister?'

'My father is. My mother's from Kiel.'

'Kiel?'

'Yes. Germany. Didn't you know?'

'Of course not. How should I have known? Now that I do know, is that supposed to make a difference?'

'I'm half German.' She smiled again. 'Aren't you surprised, Mr McKinnon? Shocked, perhaps?'

'No, I'm not shocked.' McKinnon looked gloomy. 'I have troubles of my own in that direction. My sister Jean is married to an Italian. I have a niece and a nephew, two bambinos who can't – or couldn't before the war – speak a word of English to their old uncle.'

'It must make – must have made – communication a bit difficult.'

'Luckily, no. I speak Italian.'

She removed her glasses as if to examine them more closely. 'You speak Italian, Mr McKinnon?'

157

'Yes. And Spanish. And German. You must be able to speak German – you can try me any time. Surprised, Sister? Shocked?'

'No.' She shook her head slowly and smiled a third time. It was borne in upon McKinnon that a smiling Margaret Morrison, with her warm, friendly brown eyes was a totally different creature from the Sister Morrison he thought he had come to know. 'No, I'm not. Really.'

'You come from seafaring people, Sister?'

'Yes.' This time she was surprised. 'How did you know?'

'I didn't. But it was a fair guess. It's the Kiel connection. Many British sailors know Kiel well – I do myself – and it has, or did have, the finest regatta in Europe. Your father's from Aberdeen. A fisherman? A seaman of some sort?'

'A seaman of some sort.'

'What sort?'

'Well . . . .' She hesitated.

'Well what?'

'He's a captain in the Royal Navy.'

'Good Lord!' McKinnon looked at her in mild astonishment, then rubbed an unshaven chin. 'I shall have to treat you with more respect in future, Sister Morrison.'

'I hardly think that will be necessary, Mr McKinnon.' The voice was formal but the smile that followed was not. 'Not now.'

'You sound almost as if you were ashamed of being the daughter of a Royal Navy captain.'

'I am not. I'm very proud of my father. But it can be difficult. Do you understand?'

'Yes. I think I do.'

'Well, now, Mr McKinnon.' The glasses were back in position and Sister Morrison was back in business. 'You'll be seeing Lieutenant Ulbricht up top?' McKinnon nodded. 'Tell him I'll be up to see him in an hour, maybe two.'

McKinnon blinked, which was about as far as he ever permitted himself to go in the way of emotional expression. 'You?'

'Yes. Me.' If bridling hadn't gone out of fashion she would have bridled.

'But Dr Sinclair said he would come –'

'Dr Sinclair is a doctor, not a nurse.' Sister Morrison made it sound as if there was something faintly discreditable in being a doctor. 'I'm the Lieutenant's sister-in-charge. He'll probably require to have his bandages changed.'

'When exactly will you be coming?'

'Does it matter? I can find my own way.'

'No, Sister, you won't. You don't know what it's like up top. There's a full gale blowing, it's forty below, black as the Earl of Hell's waistcoat and the deck's like a skating rink. No one goes up top without my permission and most certainly not nurses. You will phone and I will come for you.'

'Yes, Mr McKinnon,' she said primly. She gave a slight smile. 'The way you put it, it doesn't leave much room for argument.'

'I'm sorry. No offence. Before you come up, put on as much warm clothing as you think you will need. Then double the amount.'

Janet Magnusson was in B ward when he passed through it. She took one quick look at his face and said: 'What's the matter with you?'

'Prepare thyself, Nurse Magnusson. The end is nigh.'

'What on earth do you mean, Archie?'

'The dragon next door.' He jerked a thumb towards A ward. 'She has just –'

'Dragon? Maggie? Yesterday she was a lioness.'

'Dragon. She's stopped breathing fire. She *smiled* at me. First time since leaving Halifax. Smiled. Four times. Unsettles a man.'

'Well!' She shook his shoulders. 'I *am* pleased. So you admit you misjudged her.'

'I admit it. Mind you, I think she may have misjudged me a bit, too.'

'I told you she was nice, Archie. Remember?'

'Indeed I remember. And indeed she is.'

'Very nice. Very.'

McKinnon regarded her with suspicion. 'What's that meant to mean?'

'She smiled at you.'

The Bo'sun gave her a cold look and left.

Lieutenant Ulbricht was awake when McKinnon returned to the Captain's cabin.

'Duty calls, Mr McKinnon? Another fix?'

'Rest easy, Lieutenant. No stars. Overcast. More snow, I'm thinking. How do you feel?'

'Well enough. At least when I'm lying down. That's physically, I mean.' He tapped his head. 'Up here, not so well. I've been doing a lot of wondering and thinking.'

'Wondering and thinking why you're lying here?'

'Exactly.'

'Haven't we all? At least, I've been doing nothing else but wondering about it. Haven't got very far, though. In fact, I haven't got anywhere.'

'I'm not saying it would help any, just call it curiosity if you like, but would you mind very much telling me what's been happening to the *San Andreas* since you left Halifax? Not, of course, if it means telling me naval secrets.'

McKinnon smiled. 'I don't have any. Besides, even if I did have and told you, what would you do with them?'

'You have a point. What indeed?'

McKinnon gave a brief résumé of what had happened to the ship since leaving Nova Scotia and when he had finished Ulbricht said: 'Well, now let me see if I can count.

'As far as I can make out there were seven different parties involved in the movements of the *San Andreas* – actually aboard it, that is. To begin with, there was your own crew. Then there were the wounded survivors picked up from this crippled destroyer. After that came the Russian submarine

161

survivors you took from this corvette you had to sink. Then you picked up some wounded servicemen in Murmansk. Since leaving there you've picked up survivors from the *Argos*, the *Andover* and Helmut and myself. That makes seven?'

'That makes seven.'

'We can eliminate the survivors from the broken-down destroyer and the sinking frigate. Their presence aboard your ship could only have been due to sheer happenstance, nothing else. We can equally forget Commander Warrington and his two men and Helmut Winterman and myself. That leaves just your crew, the survivors from the *Argos* and the sick men you picked up in Murmansk.'

'I couldn't imagine a more unlikely trio of suspects.'

'Neither could I, Bo'sun. But it's not imagination we're concerned with here, it's logic. It has to be one of those three. Take the sick men you picked up in Murmansk. One of them could have been suborned. I know it sounds preposterous but war itself is preposterous, the most unbelievable things happen in preposterous circumstances, and if there is one thing that is for certain it is that we are not going to find the answer to this enigma in the realms of the obvious. How many sick men are you repatriating from Russia?'

'Seventeen.'

'Do you happen to know the nature of their injuries?'

McKinnon regarded the Lieutenant speculatively. 'I have a fair idea.'

'All seriously wounded?'

'There are no seriously wounded, far less critically injured patients aboard. If they were, they wouldn't be here. Poorly, you might call them, I suppose.'

'But bedridden? Immobile?'

'The wounded are.'

'They are not all wounded?'

'Only eight.'

'Good God! Eight! You mean to tell me that there are nine who are *not* injured?'

'It all depends upon what you mean by injured. Three are suffering from advanced cases of exposure – frostbite, if you like. Then there are three with tuberculosis and the remaining three have suffered mental breakdowns. Those Russian convoys take a pretty vicious toll, Lieutenant, in more ways than one.'

'You have no cause to love our U-boats, our Luftwaffe, Mr McKinnon.'

The Bo'sun shrugged. 'We do send the occasional thousand bombers over Hamburg.'

Ulbricht sighed. 'I suppose this is no time for philosophizing about how two wrongs can never make a right. So we have nine unwounded. All of them mobile?'

'The three exposure cases are virtually immobile. You've never seen so many bandages. The other six – well, they can get around as well as you and I. Well, that's not quite accurate – as well as I can and a damned sight better than you can.'

'So. Six mobiles. I know little enough of medicine but I do know just how difficult it is to gauge how severe a case of TB is. I also know that a man in a pretty advanced stage can get around well enough. As for mental breakdowns, those are easy enough to simulate. One of those three may be as rational as we are – or think we are. Come to that, all three of them may be. I don't have to tell you, Mr McKinnon, that there are those who are so sick of the mindlessness, the hellishness, of war that they will resort to any means to escape from it. Malingerers, as they are commonly and quite often unfairly called. Many of them have quite simply had enough and can take no more. During the First World War quite a number of British soldiers were affected by an incurable disease that was a sure-fire guarantee for a one-way ticket to Blighty. DAH it was called – Disorder Affecting the Heart. The more unfeeling of the British doctors commonly referred to it as Desperate Affection for Home.'

'I've heard of it. Lieutenant, I'm not by nature an inquisitive person, but may I ask you a personal question?'

'Of course.'

'Your English. So much better than mine. Thing is, you don't sound like a foreigner talking English. You sound like an Englishman talking English, an Englishman who's been at an English public school. Funny.'

'Not really. You don't miss much, Mr McKinnon, and that's a fact. I was educated in an English public school. My mother is English. My father was for many years an attaché in the German Embassy in London.'

'Well, well.' McKinnon shook his head and smiled. 'It's too much. It's really too much. Two shocks like this inside twenty minutes.'

'If you were to tell me what you are talking about –'

'Sister Morrison. You and she should get together. I've just learnt that she's half-German.'

'Good God! Goodness gracious me.' Ulbricht could hardly be said to be dumbfounded but he was taken aback. 'German mother, of course. How extraordinary! I tell you, Bo'sun, this could be a serious matter. Her being my nurse, I mean. Wartime. International complications, you know.'

'I don't know and I don't see it. You're both just doing your job. Anyway, she's coming up to see you shortly.'

'Coming to see me? That ruthless Nazi killer?'

'Maybe she's had a change of heart.'

'Under duress, of course.'

'It's her idea and she insists on it.'

'It'll be a hypodermic syringe. Lethal dose of morphine or some such. To get back to our six walking unwounded. Widens the field a bit, doesn't it? A suborned malingerer or ditto TB patient. How do you like it?'

'I don't like it at all. How many suborned men, spies, saboteurs, do you think we've picked up among the survivors from the *Argos*? Another daft thought, I know, but as you've more or less said yourself, we're looking for daft answers to daft questions. And speaking of daft questions, here's another one. How do we know the *Argos* really was mined? We know that tankers are extremely tough, heavily compartmented and that this one was returning with empty tanks. Tankers don't die easily and even laden tankers have been torpedoed and survived. We don't even *know* the *Argos* was mined. How do we know it wasn't sabotaged so as to provide the opportunity to introduce a saboteur or saboteurs aboard the *San Andreas*? How do you like that?'

'Like yourself, I don't like it at all. But you're not seriously suggesting that Captain Andropolous would deliberately –'

'I'm not suggesting anything about Captain Andropolous. For all I know, he may be as double-dyed a villain as is sailing the seas these days. Although I'm willing to consider almost any crazy solution to our questions, I can't go along with the idea that any captain would sacrifice his ship for any imaginable purpose. But a person or persons to whom the *Argos* meant nothing might quite happily do just that. It would be interesting to know whether Andropolous had taken on any extra crew members in Murmansk, such as fellow nationals who had survived a previous sinking.

Unfortunately, Andropolous and his crew speak nothing but Greek and nobody else aboard speaks Greek.'

'I speak a little Greek, very little, schoolboy stuff – English public schools are high on Greek – and I've forgotten most of that. Not that I can see that it would do much good anyway even if we were to find out that a person or x number of persons joined the *Argos* at Murmansk. They would only assume expressions of injured innocence, say they don't know what we are talking about and what could we do then?' Ulbricht was silent for almost a minute, then suddenly said: 'The Russian shipwrights.'

'What Russian shipwrights?'

'The ones that fixed the damage to the hull of your ship and finished off your sick-bay. But especially the hull repairers.'

'What about them?'

'Moment.' Ulbricht thought some more. 'I don't know just how many niggers in the woodpile there may be aboard the *San Andreas*, but I'm all at once certain that the original one was a member of your own crew.'

'How on earth do you figure that out? Not, mind you, that anything would surprise me.'

'You sustained this hull damage to the *San Andreas* while you were alongside the sinking corvette, before you sunk her by gunfire. That is correct?'

'Correct.'

'How did it happen?'

'I told you. We don't know. No torpedoes, no mines, nothing of that nature. A destroyer was along one side of the corvette, taking off her crew, while we were on the other taking off the survivors of the sunken Russian submarine. There was a series of explosions inside the corvette before we could get clear. One was a boiler going off, the others could have been gun-cotton, two-pounders, anything – there was some sort of fire inside. It was at that time that the damage must have happened.'

'I suggest it didn't happen that way at all. I suggest, instead, that it was then that a trusty member of your crew detonated a charge in the port ballast room. I suggest that it was someone who knew precisely how much explosive to use to ensure that it didn't sink the ship but enough to inflict sufficiently serious damage for it to have to make for the nearest port where repair facilities were available, which, in this case, was Murmansk.'

'It makes sense. It could have happened that way. But I'm not convinced.'

'In Murmansk, did anyone see the size or type of hole that had been blown in the hull?'

'No.'

'Did anyone try to see?'

'Yes. Mr Kennet and I.'

'But surprise, surprise, you didn't. You didn't because you weren't allowed to see it.'

'That's how it was. How did you know?'

'They had tarpaulins rigged all around and above the area under repair?'

'They had.' McKinnon was beginning to look rather thoughtful.

'Did they give any reasons?'

'To keep out the wind and snow.'

'Was there much in the way of those?'

'Very little.'

'Did you ask to get behind the tarpaulins, see behind them?'

'We did. They wouldn't let us. Said it was too dangerous and would only hold up the work of the shipwrights. We didn't argue because we didn't think it was all that important. There was no reason why we should have thought so. If you know the Russians at all you must know how mulish they can be about the most ridiculous things. Besides, they were doing us a favour and there was no reason why we should have been suspicious. All right, all right, Lieutenant, there's no reason to beat me over the head with a two-by-four. You don't have to be an engineer or a metallurgist to recognize a hole that has been blown from the inside out.'

'And does it now strike you as strange that the second damage to the hull should have occurred in precisely the same ballast compartment?'

'Not now it doesn't. Our gallant – ours, not yours – our gallant allies almost certainly left the charge in the ballast room with a suitable length of fuse conveniently attached. You have the right of it, Lieutenant.'

'So all we have to do now is to find some member of your crew with a working knowledge of explosives. You know of any such, Mr McKinnon?'

'Yes.'

'What!' Ulbricht propped himself up on an elbow. 'Who?'

McKinnon raised his eyes to the deckhead. 'Me.'

'That's a help.' Ulbricht lowered himself to his bunk again. 'That's a great help.'

SIX

It was shortly after ten o'clock in the morning that
the snow came again. McKinnon had spent
another fifteen minutes in the Captain's cabin,
leaving only when he saw the Lieutenant was
having difficulty in keeping his eyes open, then
had spoken in turn with Naseby, Patterson
and Jamieson, who was again supervising the
strengthening of the superstructure. All three had
agreed that Ulbricht was almost certainly correct
in the assessment he had made: and all three
agreed with the Bo'sun that this fresh knowledge,
if knowledge it were, served no useful purpose whatsoever. McKinnon had returned to the
bridge when the snow came.

He opened a wing door in a duly circumspect
fashion but, for all his caution, had it torn from his
grasp to crash against the leading edge of the
bridge, such was the power of the wind. The snow,
light as yet, was driving along as nearly horizontally as made no difference. It was quite impossible

to look into it, but with his back to it and looking out over the bows, he could see that the wave pattern had changed: the dawn was in the sky now and in its light he could see that the last semblance of serried ranks had vanished and that the white-veined, white-spumed seas were now broken walls of water, tending this way and that in unpredictable formless confusion. Even without the evidence of his eyes he would have known that this was so: the deck beneath his feet was beginning to shake and shudder in a rather disconcerting manner. The cold was intense. Even with his very considerable weight and strength, McKinnon found it no easy task to heave the wing door shut behind him as he stepped back into the bridge.

He was in desultory conversation with Trent, who had the helm, when the phone rang. It was Sister Morrison. She said she was ready to come up to the Captain's cabin.

'I wouldn't recommend it, Sister. Things are pretty unpleasant up top.'

'I would remind you that you gave me your promise.' She was speaking in her best sister's voice.

'I know. It's just that conditions have worsened quite a bit.'

'Really, Mr McKinnon —'

'I'm coming. On your own head.'

In Ward B, Janet Magnusson looked at him with disapproval. 'A hospital is no place for a snowman.'

'Just passing through. On a mission of mercy. At least, your mule-headed friend imagines she is.'

She kept her expression in place. 'Lieutenant Ulbricht?'

'Who else? I've just seen him. Looks fair enough to me. I think she's daft.'

'The trouble with you, Archie McKinnon, is that you have no finer feelings. Not as far as caring for the sick is concerned. In other ways too, like as not. And if she's daft, it's only because she's been saying nice things about you.'

'About me? She doesn't know me.'

'True, Archie, true.' She smiled sweetly. 'But Captain Bowen does.'

McKinnon sought briefly for a suitable comment about captains who gossiped to ward sisters, found none and moved into Ward A. Sister Morrison, suitably bundled up, was waiting. There was a small medical case on a table by her side. McKinnon nodded at her.

'Would you take those glasses off, Sister?'

'Why?'

'It's the Lothario in him,' Kennet said. He sounded almost his old cheerful self again. 'He probably thinks you look nicer without them.'

'It's no morning for a polar bear, Mr Kennet, far less a Lothario. If the lady doesn't remove her glasses the wind will do the job for her.'

'What's the wind like, Bo'sun?' It was Captain Bowen.

'Force eleven, sir. Blizzard. Eight below. Nine-ninety millibars.'

'And the seas breaking up?' Even in the hospital the shuddering of the vessel was unmistakable.

'They are a bit, sir.'

'Any problems?'

'Apart from Sister here seeming bent on suicide, none.' Not, he thought, as long as the superstructure stayed in place.

Sister Morrison gasped in shock as they emerged on to the upper deck. However much she had mentally prepared herself, she could not have anticipated the savage power of that near hurricane force wind and the driving blizzard that accompanied it, could not even have imagined the lung-searing effect of the abrupt 80°F drop in temperature. McKinnon wasted no time. He grabbed Sister Morrison with one hand, the lifeline with the other, and allowed the two of them to be literally blown across the treacherous ice-sheathed deck into the shelter of the superstructure. Once under cover, she removed her duffel hood and stood there panting, tenderly massaging her ribs.

'Next time, Mr McKinnon – if there is a next time – I'll listen to you. My word! I never dreamt – well, I just never dreamt. And my ribs!' She felt carefully as if to check they were still there. 'I've got ordinary ribs, just like anyone else. I think you've broken them.'

'I'm sorry about that,' McKinnon said gravely. 'But I don't think you'd have much fancied going over the side. And there will be a next time, I'm afraid. We've got to go back again and against the wind, and that will be a great deal worse.'

'At the moment, I'm in no hurry to go back, thank you very much.'

McKinnon led her up the companionway to the crew's quarters. She stopped and looked at the twisted passageway, the buckled bulkheads, the shattered doors.

'So this is where they died.' Her voice was husky. 'When you see it, it's all too easy to understand how they died. But you have to see it first to understand. Ghastly – well, ghastly couldn't have been the word for it. Thank God I never saw it. And you had to clear it all up.'

'I had help.'

'I know you did all the horrible bits. Mr Spenser, Mr Rawlings, Mr Batesman, those were the really shocking cases, weren't they? I know you wouldn't let anyone else touch them. Johnny Holbrook told Janet and she told me.' She shuddered. 'I don't like this place. Where's the Lieutenant?'

McKinnon led her up to the Captain's cabin, where Naseby was keeping an eye on the recumbent Lieutenant.

'Good morning again, Lieutenant. I've just had a taste of the kind of weather Mr McKinnon has been exposing you to. It was awful. How do you feel?'

'Low, Sister. Very low. I think I'm in need of care and attention.'

She removed oilskins and duffel coat. 'You don't look very ill to me.'

'Appearances, appearances. I feel very weak. Far be it from me to prescribe for myself, but what I need is a tonic, a restorative.' He stretched out a languid hand. 'Do you know what's in that wall cupboard there?'

'No.' Her tone was severe. 'I don't know. I can guess, though.'

'Well, I thought, perhaps – in the circumstances, you understand –'

'Those are Captain Bowen's private supplies.'

'May I repeat what the Captain told me?' McKinnon said. 'As long as Lieutenant Ulbricht keeps navigating, he can keep on broaching my supplies. Words to that effect.'

'I don't see him doing any navigating at the moment. But very well. A small one.'

McKinnon poured and handed him a glass of Scotch: the expression on Sister Morrison's face was indication enough she and the Bo'sun placed different interpretations on the word 'small'.

'Come on, George,' McKinnon said. 'This is no place for us.'

Sister Morrison looked faintly surprised. 'You don't have to go.'

'We can't stand the sight of blood. Or suffering, come to that.'

Ulbricht lowered his glass. 'You would leave us to the mercy of Flannelfoot?'

'George, if you wait outside I'll go and give Trent a spell on the wheel. When you're ready to go back, Sister, you'll know where to find me.'

McKinnon would have expected that her ministrations might have taken ten minutes, fifteen at the most. Instead, almost forty minutes elapsed before she put in an appearance on the bridge. McKinnon looked at her sympathetically.

'More trouble than you expected, Sister? He wasn't just joking when he said he felt pretty low?'

'There's very little the matter with him. Especially not with his tongue. How that man can talk!'

'He wasn't talking to an empty bulkhead, was he?'

'What do you mean?'

'Well,' McKinnon said reasonably, 'he wouldn't have kept on talking if you hadn't kept on listening.'

Sister Morrison seemed to be in no hurry to depart. She was silent for some time, then said with a slight trace of a smile: 'I find this – well, not infuriating but annoying. Most people would be interested in what we were saying.'

'I am interested. I'm just not inquisitive. If you wanted to tell me, then you'd tell me. If I asked you to tell me and you didn't want to, then you wouldn't tell me. But, fine, I'd like you to tell me.'

'I don't know whether that's infuriating or not.' She paused. 'Why did you tell Lieutenant Ulbricht that I'm half German?'

'It's not a secret, is it?'

'No.'

'And you're not ashamed of it. You told me so yourself. So why – ah! Why didn't I tell you that I'd told him? That's what you're asking. Just never occurred to me.'

'You might at least have told me that *he* was half English.'

'That didn't occur to me either. It's unimportant. I don't care what nationality a person is. I told you about my brother-in-law. Like the Lieutenant, he's a pilot. He's also a lieutenant. If he thought it his duty to drop a bomb on me, he'd do it like a shot. But you couldn't meet a finer man.'

'You're a very forgiving man, Mr McKinnon.'

'Forgiving?' He looked at her in surprise. 'I've nothing to forgive. I mean, he hasn't dropped a bomb on me yet.'

'I didn't mean that. Even if he did, it wouldn't make any difference.'

'How do you know?'

'I know.'

McKinnon didn't pursue the matter. 'Doesn't sound like a very interesting conversation to me. Not forty minutes' worth, anyway.'

'He also took great pleasure in pointing out that he's more British than I am. From the point of view of blood, I mean. Fifty per cent British to start with plus two more British pints yesterday.'

McKinnon was polite. 'Indeed.'

'All right, so statistics aren't interesting either. He also says that his father knows mine.'

'Ah. That *is* interesting. Wait a minute. He mentioned that his father had been an attaché at the German Embassy in London. He didn't mention whether he was a commercial or cultural attaché or whatever. He didn't just happen to mention to you that his father had been the naval attaché there?'

'He was.'

'Don't tell me that his old man is a captain in the German Navy.'

'He is.'

'That makes you practically blood brothers. Or brother and sister. Mark my words, Sister,' McKinnon said solemnly, 'I see the hand of fate here. Something pre-ordained, you might say?'

'Pfui!'

'Are they both on active service?'

'Yes.' She sounded forlorn.

'Don't you find it funny that your respective parents should be prowling the high seas figuring out ways of doing each other in?'

'I don't find it at all funny.'

'I didn't mean funny in that sense.' If anyone had ever suggested to McKinnon that Margaret Morrison would one day strike him as a woebegone figure he would have questioned his sanity: but not any longer. He found her sudden dejection inexplicable. 'Not to worry, lassie. It'll never happen.' He wasn't at all sure what he meant by that.

'Of course not.' Her voice carried a total lack of conviction. She made to speak, hesitated, looked down at the deck, then slowly lifted her head. Her face was in shadow but he felt almost certain that he saw the sheen of tears. 'I heard things about you, today.'

'Oh. Nothing to my credit, I'm sure. You can't believe a word anyone says these days. What things, Sister?'

'I wish you wouldn't call me that.' The irritation was as unaccustomed as the dejection.

McKinnon raised a polite eyebrow. 'Sister? But you are a sister.'

'Not the way you make it sound. Sorry, I didn't mean that, you don't make it sound different from anyone else. It's like those cheap American films where the man with the gun goes around calling everyone "sister".'

He smiled. 'I wouldn't like you to confuse me with a hoodlum. Miss Morrison?'

'You know my name.'

'Yes. I also know that you started out to say something, changed your mind and are trying to stall.'

'No. Yes. Well, not really. It's difficult, I'm not very good at those things. I heard about your family this morning. Just before we came up. I'm sorry, I am terribly sorry.'

'Janet?'

'Yes.'

'It's no secret.'

180

'It was a German bomber pilot who killed them.' She looked at him for a long moment, then shook her head. 'Along comes another German bomber pilot, again attacking innocent civilians, and you're the first person to come to his defence.'

'Don't go pinning any haloes or wings on me. Besides, I'm not so sure that's a compliment. What did you expect me to do? Lash out in revenge at an innocent man?'

'You? Don't be silly. Well, no, maybe I was silly to say it, but you know very well what I mean. I also heard Petty Officer McKinnon, BEM, DSM and goodness knows what else was in a Malta hospital with a broken back when he heard the news. An Italian Air Force bomber got your submarine. You seem to have an affinity for enemy bombers.'

'Janet didn't know that.'

She smiled. 'Captain Bowen and I have become quite friendly.'

'Captain Bowen,' McKinnon said without heat, 'is a gossipy old woman.'

'Captain Bowen is a gossipy old woman. Mr Kennet is a gossipy old woman. Mr Patterson is a gossipy old woman. Mr Jamieson is a gossipy old woman. They're all gossipy old women.'

'Goodness me! That's a very serious allegation, Sister. Sorry. Margaret.'

'Gossipy old women speak in low voices or whispers. Whenever any two of them or three of them or indeed all four are together they speak in low voices or whispers. You can feel the tension, almost smell the fear – well, no, that's the wrong word, apprehension, I should say. Why do they whisper?'

'Maybe they've got secrets.'

'I deserve better than that.'

'We've got saboteurs aboard.'

'I know that. We all know that. The whisperers know that we all know that.' She gave him a long, steady look. 'I still deserve better than that. Don't you trust me?'

'I trust you. We're being hunted. Somebody aboard the *San Andreas* has a transmitter radio that is sending out a continuous location signal. The Luftwaffe, the U-boats know exactly where we are. Somebody wants us. Somebody wants to take over the *San Andreas*.'

For long moments she looked at his eyes as if searching for an answer to a question she couldn't formulate. McKinnon shook his head and said: 'I'm sorry. That's all I know. You must believe me.'

'I do believe you. Who could be sending out this signal?'

'Anybody. My guess is that it is a member of our own crew. Could be a survivor from the *Argos*. Could be any of the sick men we picked up in Murmansk. Each idea is quite ridiculous but one has to be less ridiculous than the others. Which, I have no idea.'

'Why would anyone want us?'

'If I knew that, I'd know the answer to a lot of things. Once again, I have no idea.'

'How would they take us over?'

'Submarine. U-boat. No other way. They have no surface ships and an aircraft is out of the question. Praying, that's what your whisperers are probably at – praying. Praying that the snow will never end. Our only hope lies in concealment. Praying, as the old divines used to say, that we will not be abandoned by fortune.'

'And if we are?'

'Then that's it.'

'You're not going to *do* anything?' She seemed more than faintly incredulous. 'You're not even going to try to do anything?'

It was quite some hours since McKinnon had made up his mind where his course of action would lie but it seemed hardly the time or the place to elaborate on his decision. 'What on earth do you expect me to do? Send them to the bottom with a salvo of stale bread and old potatoes? You forget this is a hospital ship. Sick, wounded and all civilians.'

'Surely there's *something* you can do.' There was a strange note in her voice, one almost of desperation. She went on bitterly: 'The much-bemedalled Petty Officer McKinnon.'

'The much-bemedalled Petty Officer McKinnon,' he said mildly, 'would live to fight another day.'

'Fight them now!' Her voice had a break in it. 'Fight them! Fight them! Fight them!' She buried her face in her hands.

McKinnon put his arm round her shaking shoulders and regarded her with total astonishment. A man of almost infinite resource and more than capable of dealing with anything that came his way, he was at an utter loss to account for her weird conduct. He sought for words of comfort and consolation but as he didn't know what he was supposed to be comforting or consoling about he found none. Nor did repeating phrases like 'Now, now, then' seem to meet the case either, so he finally contented himself with saying: 'I'll get Trent up and take you below.'

When they had arrived below, after a particularly harrowing trip across the upper deck between superstructure and hospital – they had to battle their way against the great wind and the driving blizzard – he led her to the little lounge and went in search of Janet Magnusson. When he found her he said: 'I think you'd better go and see your pal, Maggie. She's very upset.' He raised a hand. 'No, Janet, not guilty. I did not upset her.'

She said accusingly: 'But you were with her when she became upset.'

'She's disappointed with me, that's all.'

'Disappointed?'

'She wants me to commit suicide. I don't see it her way.'

She tapped her head. 'One of you is touched. I don't much doubt who it is.' McKinnon sat down on a stool by a mess table while she went into the lounge. She emerged some five minutes later and sat down opposite him. Her face was troubled.

'Sorry, Archie. Not guilty. And neither of you is touched. She's got this ambivalent feeling towards the Germans.'

'Ambi what?'

'Mixed up. It doesn't help that her mother is German. She's had rather a bad time. A very rough time. Oh, I know you have, too, but you're different.'

'Of course I'm different. I have no finer feelings.'

'Oh, do be quiet. You weren't to know – in fact, I think I'm the only person who does know. About five months ago she lost both her only brother and her fiancé. Both died over Hamburg. Not in the same plane, not even in the same raid. But within weeks of each other.'

'Oh Jesus.' McKinnon shook his head slowly and was silent for some moments. 'Poor bloody kid. Explains a lot.' He rose, crossed to Dr Singh's private source of supplies and returned with a glass. 'The legendary McKinnon willpower. You were with Maggie when this happened, Janet?'

'Yes.'

'You knew her before then?'

'Of course. We've been friends for years.'

'So you must have known those two boys?' She said nothing. 'Known them well, I mean?' Still she said nothing, just sat there with her flaxen head bowed, apparently gazing down at her clasped hands on the table. As much in exasperation as anything McKinnon reached out, took one of her wrists and shook it gently. 'Janet.'

She looked up. 'Yes, Archie?' Her eyes were bright with unshed tears.

'Oh dear, oh dear.' McKinnon sighed. 'You, too.' Again he shook his head, again he remained silent for some time. 'Look, Janet, those boys knew what they were doing. They knew the risks. They knew that, if they could at all, the German anti-aircraft batteries and night-fighter pilots would shoot them down. And so they did and so they had every right to do. And I would remind you that those were no mere pinpoint raids – it was saturation bombing and you know what that means. So while you and Maggie are crying for yourselves, you might as well cry for the relatives of all the thousands of innocent dead that the RAF left behind in Hamburg. You might as well cry for all mankind.'

Two tears trickled down her cheeks. 'You, McKinnon, are a heartless fiend.'

'I'm all that.' He rose. 'If anyone wants me I'll be on the bridge.'

Noon came and went and as the day lengthened the wind strengthened until it reached the screaming intensity commonly found in the hurricanes and typhoons of the more tropical parts of the world. By two o'clock in the afternoon when the light, which at best had never been more than a grey half-light, was beginning to fade, what little could be seen of the mountainous seas abeam and ahead of the *San Andreas* – the blizzard made it quite impossible to see anything abaft of the bridge – were as white as the driving snow itself, the shapeless troughs between the towering walls of water big enough to drown a suburban house or, to the more apprehensive eye, big enough to drown a suburban church including a fair part of its steeple. The *San Andreas* was in trouble. At 9,300 tons it was not a small vessel and the Bo'sun had had engine revolutions reduced until the ship had barely steerage way on, but still she was in trouble and the causes for this lay neither in the size of the ship, nor the size of the seas, for normally the *San Andreas* could have ridden out the storm without much difficulty. The two main reasons for concern lay elsewhere.

The first of these was ice. A ship in a seaway can be said to be either stiff or tender. If it is stiff, it is resistant to roll, and, when it does roll, recovers sharply: when it is tender it rolls easily and recovers slowly and reluctantly. Tenderness arises when a vessel becomes top-heavy, raising the centre of gravity. The prime cause of this is ice. As the thickness of ice on the upper decks increases, so does the degree of tenderness: when the ice becomes sufficiently thick the vessel will fail to recover from its roll, turn turtle and founder. Even splendidly seaworthy ocean-going trawlers, specially built for Arctic operations, have succumbed to the stealthily insidious and deadly onslaught of ice: and for aircraft carriers operating in the far north, ice on their vast areas of open upper decks provided a constant threat to stability.

McKinnon was deeply worried by the accumulation of ice on the decks of the *San Andreas*. Compacted snow from the blizzard had formed a certain thickness of ice but not much, for apart from the area abaft of the superstructure, most of the snow had simply been blown away by the powerful wind: but for hours now, according to the ever-changing direction of the constantly shifting masses of water, the *San Andreas* had been shipping copious amounts of water and spray, water and spray that turned to ice even before it hit the decks. The vessel occasionally rode on an even keel but more and more frequently it lurched into a sudden roll and each time recovered from it more and more slowly. The critical limit, he was well aware, was still some time away: but without some amelioration in the conditions, it would inevitably be reached. There was nothing that could be done: sledgehammers and crowbars would have had but a minimal effect and the chances were high that people wielding those would have ended up, in very short order, over the side: on those lurching ice-rink decks footing would have been impossible to maintain. For once, McKinnon regretted that he was aboard an American-built oil-burning ship instead of a British-built coal-burning one: boiler ashes spread on the deck would have given a reasonably secure footing and helped considerably towards melting the ice. There was nothing that one could do with diesel oil.

Of even more immediate worry was the superstructure. Except when on even keel the over-stressed metal, shaking and shuddering, creaked and groaned its protesting torture and, when it fell into the depths of a trough, the entire structure shifted quite perceptibly. At the highest point, the bridge on which he was standing, McKinnon estimated the lateral movement to be between four and six inches at a time. It was an acutely uncomfortable sensation and a thought-provoking one: how much of a drop and how acute an angle would be required before the shear factor came into operation and the superstructure parted company with the *San Andreas*? With this in mind McKinnon went below to see Lieutenant Ulbricht.

Ulbricht, who had lunched on sandwiches and Scotch and slept a couple of hours thereafter, was propped up in the Captain's bunk and was in a reasonably philosophical mood.

'Whoever named this ship the *San Andreas*,' he said, 'named it well. You know, of course, that the San Andreas is a famous – or notorious – earthquake-fault.' He grabbed the side of his bunk as the ship fell into a trough and juddered in a most alarming fashion. 'At the present moment I feel I'm living through an earthquake.'

'It was Mr Kennet's idea. Mr Kennet has, at times, a rather peculiar sense of humour. A week ago this was still the *Ocean Belle*. When we changed our paint from grey to the Red Cross colours of white, green and red, Mr Kennet thought we should change the name too. This ship was built in Richmond, California. Richmond is on the Hayward's Fault which is a branch of the San Andreas. He was of the opinion that *San Andreas* was much more of a romantic name than *Hayward's Fault*. He also thought it was an amusing idea to name it after a potential disaster area.' McKinnon smiled. 'I wonder if he still thinks it was an amusing idea.'

'Well, he's had plenty of time for reflection since I dropped those bombs on him yesterday morning. I should rather think he's had second thoughts on the matter.' Ulbricht tightened his grip on the side of his bunk as the *San Andreas* fell heavily into another trough. 'The weather does not improve, Mr McKinnon?'

'The weather does not improve. That's what I came to talk about, Lieutenant. Force twelve wind. With the darkness and the blizzard – it's as strong as ever – visibility is absolutely zero. Not a chance of a starsight for hours. I think you'd be far better off in the hospital.'

'Certainly not. I'd have to fight my way against a hurricane, not to say a blizzard, to reach the hospital. A man in my weakened condition? Not to be thought of.'

'It's warmer down there, Lieutenant. More comfortable. And the motion, naturally, is much less.'

'Dear me, Mr McKinnon, how could you overlook the most important inducement – all those pretty nurses. No, thank you. I prefer the Captain's cabin, not to mention the Captain's Scotch. The truth of the matter is, of course, that you suspect that the superstructure may go over the side at any moment and that you want me out of here before that happens. Isn't that so?'

'Well.' McKinnon touched the outer bulkhead. 'It is a bit unstable.'

'While you remain, of course.'

'I have a job to do.'

'Unthinkable. The honour of the Luftwaffe is at stake. You stay, I stay.'

McKinnon didn't argue. If anything, he felt obscurely pleased by Ulbricht's decision. He tapped the barometer and lifted an eyebrow. 'Three millibars?'

'Up?'

'Up.'

'Help is at hand. There's hope yet.'

'Take hours for the weather to moderate – if it does. Superstructure could still go at any time. Even if it doesn't, our only real hope lies with the snow.'

'And when the snow goes?'

'Then your U-boats come.'

'You're convinced of that?'

'Yes. Aren't you?'

'I'm afraid I am, rather.'

Three hours later, shortly after five o'clock in the afternoon and quite some time before McKinnon had expected it, the weather began to moderate, almost imperceptibly at first, then with increasing speed. The wind speed dropped to a relatively benign Force six, the broken and confused seas of the early afternoon resolved themselves, once again, into a recognizable wave pattern, the *San Andreas* rode on a comparatively even keel, the sheeted ice on the decks no longer offered a threat and the superstructure had quite ceased its creaking and groaning. But best of all, from McKinnon's point of view, the snow, though driving much less horizontally than it had earlier on, still fell as heavily as ever. He was reasonably certain that when an attack did come it would come during the brief hours of daylight but was well aware that a determined U-boat captain would not hesitate to press home an attack in moonlight. In his experience most U-boat captains were very determined indeed – and there would be a moon later that night. Snow would avail them nothing in daytime but during the hours of darkness it was a virtual guarantee of safety.

He went to the Captain's cabin where he found Lieutenant Ulbricht smoking an expensive Havana – Captain Bowen, a pipe man, permitted himself one cigar a day – and sipping an equally expensive malt, both of which no doubt helped to contribute to his comparatively relaxed mood.

'Ah, Mr McKinnon. This is more like it. The weather, I mean. Moderating by the minute. Still snowing?'

'Heavily. A mixed blessing, I suppose. No chance of starsights but at least it keeps your friends out of our hair.'

'Friends? Yes. I spend quite some time wondering who my friends are.' He waved a dismissive hand which was no easy thing to do with a glass of malt in one and a cigar in the other. 'Is Sister Morrison ill?'

'I shouldn't think so.'

'I'm supposed to be her patient. One could almost term this savage neglect. A man could easily bleed to death.'

'We can't have that.' McKinnon smiled. 'I'll get her for you.'

He phoned the hospital and, by the time he arrived there, Sister Morrison was ready. She said: 'Something wrong? Is he unwell?'

'He feels cruelly neglected and says something about bleeding to death. He is, in fact, in good spirits, smoking a cigar, drinking malt whisky and appears to be in excellent health. He's just bored or lonely or both and wants to talk to someone.'

'He can always talk to you.'

'When I said someone, I didn't mean anyone. I am not Margaret Morrison. Crafty, those Luftwaffe pilots. He can always have you up for dereliction of duty.'

He took her to the Captain's cabin, told her to call him at the hospital when she was through, took the crew lists from the Captain's desk, left and went in search of Jamieson. Together they spent almost half an hour going over the papers of every member of the deck and engine-room crews, trying to recall every detail they knew of their past histories and what other members of the crew had said about any particular individual. When they had finished consulting both the lists and their memories, Jamieson pushed away the lists, leaned back in his chair and sighed.

'What do you make of it, Bo'sun?'

'Same as you do, sir. Nothing. I wouldn't even begin to know where to point the finger of suspicion. Not only are there no suitable candidates for the role of saboteur, there's nobody who's even remotely likely. I think we'd both go into court and testify as character witnesses for the lot of them. But if we accept Lieutenant Ulbricht's theory – and you, Mr Patterson, Naseby and I do accept it – that it must have been one of the original crew that set off that charge in the ballast room when we were alongside that corvette, then it must have been one of them. Or, failing them, one of the hospital staff.'

'The hospital staff?' Jamieson shook his head. 'The hospital staff. Sister Morrison as a seagoing

Mata Hari? I have as much imagination as the next man, Bo'sun, but not that kind of imagination.'

'Neither have I. We'd both go to court for them, too. But it *has* to be someone who was aboard this ship when we left Halifax. When we retire, Mr Jamieson, I think we'd better not be applying for a job with Scotland Yard's CID. Then there's the possibility that whoever it is may be in cahoots with someone from the *Argos* or one of the nine invalids we picked up in Murmansk.'

'About all of whom we know absolutely nothing, which is a great help.'

'As far as the crew of the *Argos* is concerned, that's true. As for the invalids, we have, of course, their names, ranks and numbers. One of the TB cases, man by the name of Hartley, is an ERA – Engine-Room Artificer. He would know about electrics. Another, Simons, a mental breakdown case, or an alleged mental breakdown case, is an LTO – Leading Torpedo Operator. He would know about explosives.'

'Too obvious, Bo'sun.'

'Far too obvious. Maybe we're meant to overlook the far too obvious.'

'Have you seen those two? Spoken to them, I mean?'

'Yes. I should imagine you also have. They're the two with the red hair.'

'Ah. Those two. Bluff, honest sailormen. Don't look like criminal types at all. But then, I suppose, the best criminals never do. Look that way, I mean.' He sighed. 'I agree, with you, Bo'sun. The CID are in no danger from us.'

'No, indeed.' McKinnon rose. 'I think I'll go and rescue Sister Morrison from Lieutenant Ulbricht's clutches.'

Sister Morrison was not in the Lieutenant's clutches nor did she show any signs of wanting to be rescued. 'Time to go?' she said.

'Of course not. Just to let you know I'll be on the bridge when you want me.' He looked at Ulbricht, then at Sister Morrison. 'You managed to save him, then?'

Compared to what it had been only a few hours previously the starboard wing of the bridge was now almost a haven of peace and quiet. The wind had dropped to not more than Force four and the seas, while far from being a millpond, had quietened to the extent that the *San Andreas* rarely rolled more than a few degrees when it did at all. That was on the credit side. On the debit side was the fact that the snow had thinned to the extent that McKinnon had no difficulty in making out the arc-lit shape of the red cross on the foredeck reflecting palely under its sheathing of ice. He went back inside the bridge and called up Patterson in the engine-room.

'Bo'sun here, sir. Snow's lightening. Looks as if it's going to stop altogether pretty soon. I'd like permission to switch off all exterior lights. Seas are

196

still too high for any U-boat to see us from periscope depth, but if it's on the surface, if the snow has stopped and we still have the Red Cross lights on, we can be seen miles away from its conning-tower.'

'We wouldn't want that, would we. No lights.'

'One other thing. Could you have some men clear a pathway – sledges, crowbars, whatever – in the ice between the hospital and the superstructure. Two feet should be wide enough.'

'Consider it done.'

Fifteen minutes later, still without any sign of Margaret Morrison, the Bo'sun moved out on the wing again. The snow had stopped completely. There were isolated patches of clear sky above and some stars shone, although the Pole Star was hidden. The darkness was still pretty complete, McKinnon couldn't even see as far as the fo'c's'le with the deck lights extinguished. He returned inside and went below to the Captain's cabin.

'The snow's stopped, Lieutenant, and there are a few stars around, not many, and certainly not at the moment the Pole, but a few. I don't know how long those conditions might last so I thought you might like to have a look now. I assume that Sister Morrison has staunched the flow of blood.'

'There never was any flow of blood,' she said. 'As you know perfectly well, Mr McKinnon.'

'Yes, Sister.'

She winced, then smiled. 'Archie McKinnon.'

'Wind's dropped a lot,' McKinnon said. He helped Ul-bricht on with outer clothing. 'But those are just as necessary as they were before. The temperature is still below zero.'

'Fahrenheit?'

'Sorry. You don't use that. It's about twenty degrees below, Centigrade.'

'May his nurse come with him? After all, Dr Sinclair went with him last time.'

'Of course. Wouldn't advise you to come on the wing bridge, though.' McKinnon gathered up sextant and chronometer and accompanied them up to the bridge. This time Ulbricht made it unaided. He went out on both wing bridges in turn and chose the starboard from which to make his observations. It took him longer than it had on the previous occasion, for he found it necessary to take more sights, presumably because the Pole Star was hidden. He came back inside, worked on the chart for some time and finally looked up.

'Satisfactory. In the circumstances, very satisfactory. Not my navigation. The course we've been holding. No idea if we've been holding it all the time, of course, and that doesn't matter. We're south of the Arctic Circle now, near enough 66.20 north, 4.20 east. Course 213, which seems to indicate that the wind's backed only five degrees in the past twelve hours. We're fine as we are, Mr McKinnon. Keeping the sea and the wind to the stern should see us through the night and even if we do wander off course we're not going to bump into anything. This time tomorrow morning we'll lay off a more southerly course.'

'Thank you very much, Lieutenant,' McKinnon said. 'As the saying goes, you've earned your supper. Incidentally, I'll have that sent up inside half an hour. You've also earned a good night's sleep – I won't be troubling you any more tonight.'

'Haven't I earned something else, too? It was mighty cold out there, Mr McKinnon.'

'I'm sure the Captain would approve. As he said, so long as you're navigating.' He turned to the girl. 'You coming below?'

'Yes, yes, of course she must,' Ulbricht said. 'I've been most remiss, most.' If remorse were gnawing it didn't show too much. 'All your other patients –'

'All my other patients are fine. Sister Maria is looking after them. I'm off duty.'

'Off duty! That makes me feel even worse. You should be resting, my dear girl, that or sleeping.'

'I'm wide awake, thank you. Are *you* coming below? It's no trouble now, ship's like a rock and you've just been told you won't be required any more tonight.'

'Well, now.' Ulbricht paused judiciously. 'On balance, I think I should remain. Unforeseeable emergencies, you understand.'

'Luftwaffe officers shouldn't tell fibs. Of course I understand. I understand that the only foreseeable emergency is that you run short of supplies and the only reason you're not coming below is that we don't serve malt whisky with ward dinners.'

The Lieutenant shook his head in sadness. 'I am deeply wounded.'

'Wounded!' she said. They had returned to the hospital mess-deck. 'Wounded.'

'I think he is.' McKinnon looked at her in speculative amusement. 'And you, too.'

'Me? Oh, really!'

'Yes. Really. You're hurt because you think he prefers Scotch to your company. Isn't that so?' She made no reply. 'If you believe that, then you've got a very low opinion of both yourself and the Lieutenant. You were with him for about an hour tonight. What did he drink in that time?'

'Nothing.' Her voice was quiet.

'Nothing. He's not a drinker and he's a sensitive lad. He's sensitive because he's an enemy, because he's a captive, a prisoner of war and, of course, he's sensitive above all because he's now got to live all his life with the knowledge that he killed fifteen innocent people. You asked him if he was coming down. He didn't want to be asked "if". He wanted to be persuaded, even ordered. "If" implies indifference and the way he's feeling it could be taken for a rejection. So what happens? The ward sister tells her feminine sympathy and intuition to take a holiday and delivers herself of some cutting remarks that Margaret Morrison would never have made. A mistake, but easy enough to put right.'

'How?' The question was a tacit admission that a mistake had indeed been made.

'Ninny. You take his hand and say sorry. Or are you too proud?'

'Too proud?' She seemed uncertain, confused. 'I don't know.'

'Too proud because he's a German? Look, I know about your fiancé and brother and I'm terribly sorry but that doesn't –'

'Janet shouldn't have told you.'

'Don't be daft. You didn't object to her telling you about my family.'

'And that's not all.' She sounded almost angry. 'You said they went around killing thousands of innocent people and that –'

'Those were not my words. Janet did not say that. You're doing what you accused the Lieutenant of doing – fibbing. Also, you're dodging the issue. Okay, so the nasty Germans killed two people you knew and loved. I wonder how many thousands *they* killed before *they* were shot down. But that doesn't matter really, does it? You never knew them or their names. How can you weep over people you've never met, husbands and wives, sweethearts and children, without faces or names? It's quite ridiculous, isn't it, and statistics are so boring. Tell me, did your brother ever tell you how he felt when he went out in his Lancaster bomber and slaughtered his mother's fellow countrymen? But, of course, he'd never met them so that made it all right, didn't it?'

She said in a whisper: 'I think you're horrible.'

'You think I'm horrible. Janet thinks I'm a heartless fiend. *I* think you're a pair of splendid hypocrites.'

'Hypocrites?'

'You know – Dr Jekyll and Mr Hyde. The ward sister and Margaret Morrison. Janet's just as bad. At least I don't deal in double standards.' McKinnon made to leave but she caught him by the arm and indulged, not for the first time, in the rather disconcerting practice of examining each of his eyes in turn.

'You didn't really mean that, did you? About Janet and myself being hypocrites?'

'No.'

'You *are* devious. All right, all right, I'll make it right with him.'

'I knew you would. Margaret Morrison.'

'Not Ward Sister Morrison?'

'You don't look like Mrs Hyde.' He paused. 'When were you to have been married?'

'Last September.'

'Janet. Janet and your brother. They were pretty friendly, weren't they?'

'Yes. She told you that?'

'No. She didn't have to.'

'Yes, they were pretty friendly.' She was silent for a few moments. 'It was to have been a double wedding.'

'Oh hell,' McKinnon said and walked away. He checked all the scuttles in the hospital area – even from the relatively low altitude of a submarine conning-tower the light from an uncovered porthole can be seen for several miles – went down to the engine-room, spoke briefly to Patterson, returned to the mess-deck, had dinner, then went into the wards. Janet Magnusson, in Ward B, watched his approach without enthusiasm.

'So you've been at it again.'

'Yes.'

'Do you know what I'm talking about?'

'No. I don't know and I don't care. I suppose you're talking about your friend Maggie – and yourself. Of course I'm sorry for you both, terribly sorry, and maybe tomorrow or when we get to Aberdeen I'll break my heart for yesterday. But not now, Janet. Now I have one or two more important things on my mind such as, say, *getting* to Aberdeen.'

'Archie.' She put a hand on his arm. 'I won't even say sorry. I'm just whistling in the dark, don't you know that, you clown? I don't want to think about tomorrow.' She gave a shiver, which could have been mock or not. 'I feel funny. I've been talking to Maggie. It's going to happen tomorrow, isn't it, Archie?'

'If by tomorrow you mean when daylight comes, then, yes. Could even be tonight, if the moon breaks through.'

'Maggie says it has to be a submarine. So you said.'

'Has to be.'

'How do you fancy being taken a prisoner?'

'I don't fancy it at all.'

'But you will be, won't you?'

'I hope not.'

'How can you hope not? Maggie says you're going to surrender. She didn't say so outright because she knows we're friends – we *are* friends, Mr McKinnon?'

'We are friends, Miss Magnusson.'

'Well, she didn't say so, but I think she thinks you're a bit of a coward, really.'

'A very – what's the word, perspicacious? – a very perspicacious girl is our Maggie.'

'She's not as perspicacious as I am. You really think there's a chance we'll reach Aberdeen?'

'There's a chance.'

'And after that?'

'Aha! Clever, clever Janet Magnusson. If I haven't got any plans for the future then I don't see any future. Isn't that it? Well, I do see a future and I do have plans. I'm going to take my first break since nineteen thirty-nine and have a couple of weeks back home in the Shetlands. When were you last back home in the Shetlands?'

'Not for years.'

'Will you come with me, Janet?'

'Of course.'

McKinnon went into Ward A and passed up the aisle to where Sister Morrison was sitting at her table. 'How's the Captain?'

'Well enough, I suppose. Bit dull and quiet. But why ask me? Ask him.'

'I have to ask the ward sister's permission to take him out of the ward.'

'Take him out – whatever for?'

'I want to talk to him.'

'You can talk to him here.'

'I can just see the nasty suspicious looks I'd be getting from you if we started whispering together and the nasty suspicious questions I'd be getting afterwards. My dear Margaret, we have matters of state to discuss.'

'You don't trust me, is that it?'

'That's the second time you've asked me that silly question. Same answer. I do trust you. Totally. I trust Mr Kennet there. But there are five others I don't know whether to trust or not.'

McKinnon took the Captain from the ward and returned with him inside two minutes. After she'd tucked him back in bed, Margaret Morrison said: 'That must rank as the shortest state conference in history.'

'We are men of few words.'

'And that's the only communiqué I'll be getting?'

'Well, that's the way high-level diplomacy is conducted. Secrecy is the watchword.'

As he entered Ward B he was stopped by Janet Magnusson. 'What was all that about, then? You and Captain Bowen, I mean.'

'I have not had a private talk with the Captain in order to tell all the patients in Ward B about it. I am under an oath of silence.'

Margaret Morrison came in, looked from one to the other, then said: 'Well, Janet, has he been more forthcoming with you than with me?'

'Forthcoming? Under an oath of silence, he claims. His own oath, I have no doubt.'

'No doubt. What *have* you been doing to the Captain?'

'Doing? I've been doing nothing.'

'Saying, then. He's changed since he came back. Seems positively cheerful.'

'Cheerful? How can you tell. With all those bandages, you can't see a square inch of his face.'

'There are more ways than one of telling. He's sitting up in bed, rubbing his hands from time to time and twice he's said "Aha".'

'I'm not surprised. It takes a special kind of talent to reach the hearts and minds of the ill and depressed. It's a gift. Some of us have it.' He looked at each in turn. 'And some of us haven't.'

He left them looking at each other.

McKinnon was woken by Trent at 2.0 a.m. 'The moon's out, Bo'sun.'

The moon, as McKinnon bleakly appreciated when he arrived on the port wing of the bridge, was very much out, a three-quarter moon and preternaturally bright – or so it seemed to him. At least half the sky was clear. The visibility out over the now almost calm seas was remarkable, so much so that he had no difficulty in picking out the line of the horizon: and if he could see the horizon, the Bo'sun all too clearly realized, then a submarine could pick them up ten miles away, especially if the *San Andreas* were silhouetted against the light of the moon. McKinnon felt naked and very vulnerable. He went below, roused Curran, told him to take up lookout on the starboard wing of the bridge, found Naseby, asked him to check that the falls and davits of the motor lifeboats were clear of ice and working freely and then returned to the port wing where, every minute or two, he swept the horizon with his binoculars. But the sea between the *San Andreas* and the horizon remained providentially empty.

The *San Andreas* itself was a remarkable sight. Wholly covered in ice and snow, it glittered and shone and sparkled in the bright moonlight except for a narrow central area abaft of the superstructure where wisping smoke from the shattered funnel had laid a brown smear all the way to the stern post. The fore and aft derricks were huge glistening Christmas trees, festooned with thick-ribbed woolly halliards and stays, and the anchor chains on the fo'c's'le had been transformed into great fluffy ropes of the softest cotton wool. It was a strange and beautiful world with an almost magical quality about it, ethereal almost: but one had only to think of the lethal dangers that lay under the surrounding waters and the beauty and the magic ceased to exist.

An hour passed by and everything remained quiet and peaceful. Another hour came and went, nothing untoward happened and McKinnon could scarcely believe their great good fortune. And before the third uneventful hour was up the clouds had covered the moon and it had begun to snow again, a gentle snowfall only, but enough, with the hidden moon, to shroud them in blessed anonymity again. Telling Ferguson, who now had the watch, to shake him if the snow stopped, he went below in search of some more sleep.

It was nine o'clock when he awoke. It was an unusually late awakening for him but he wasn't unduly perturbed – dawn was still an hour distant. As he crossed the upper deck he noted that the conditions were just as they had been four hours previously – moderate seas, a wind no stronger than Force three and still the same gently falling snow. McKinnon had no belief in the second sight but he felt in his bones that this peace and calm would have gone before the morning was out.

Down below he talked in turn with Jones, McGuigan, Stephen and Johnny Holbrook. They had taken it in turn, and in pairs, to monitor the comings and goings of everybody in the hospital. All four swore that nobody had stirred aboard during the night and that, most certainly, no one had at any time left the hospital area.

He had breakfast with Dr Singh, Dr Sinclair, Patterson and Jamieson – Dr Singh, he thought, looked unusually tired and strained – then went to Ward B where he found Janet Magnusson. She looked pale and there were shadows under her eyes.

McKinnon looked at her with concern.

'What's wrong, Janet?'

'I couldn't sleep. I didn't sleep a wink last night. It's all your fault.'

'Of course. It's always my fault. Cardinal rule number one – when anything goes wrong blame the Bo'sun. What am I supposed to have done this time?'

'You said the submarine, the U-boat, would attack if the moon broke through.'

'I said it could, not would.'

'Same thing. I spent most of the night looking out through the porthole – no, Mr McKinnon, I did *not* have my cabin light switched on – and when the moon came out at about two o'clock I was sure the attack must come any time. And when the moon went I was sure it would come again. Moon. U-boat. Your fault.'

'A certain logic, I must admit. Twisted logic, of course, but not more than one would expect of the feminine mind. Still, I'm sorry.'

'But *you're* looking fine. Fresh. Relaxed. *And* you're very late on the road this morning. Our trusty guardian sleeping on the job.'

'Your trusty guardian lost a little sleep himself, last night,' McKinnon said. 'Back shortly. Must see the Captain.'

It was Sister Maria, not Sister Morrison, who was in charge in A Ward. McKinnon spoke briefly with both the Captain and First Officer, then said to Bowen: 'Still sure, sir?'

'More sure than ever, Archie. When's dawn?'

'Fifteen minutes.'

'I wish you well.'

'I think you better wish us all well.'

He returned to Ward B and said to Janet: 'Where's your pal?'

'Visiting the sick. She's with Lieutenant Ulbricht.'

'She shouldn't have gone alone.'

'She didn't. You were asleep so your friend George Naseby came for her.'

McKinnon looked at her with suspicion. 'You find something amusing.'

'That's her second time up there this morning.'

'Is he dying or something?'

'I hardly think she would smile so much if a patient was slipping away.'

'Ah! Mending fences, you would say?'

'She called him "Karl" twice.' She smiled. 'I'd call that mending fences, wouldn't you?'

'Good lord! Karl. That well-known filthy Nazi murderer.'

210

'Well, she said you asked her to make it right. No, you told her. So now you'll be taking all the credit, I suppose.'

'Credit where credit is due,' McKinnon said absently. 'But she must come below at once. It's too exposed up there.'

'Dawn.' Her voice had gone very quiet. 'This time you're sure, Archie?'

'This time I'm sure. The U-boat will come at dawn.'

The U-boat came at dawn.

SEVEN

It was little more than half-light when the U-boat, in broken camouflage paint of various shades of grey and at a distance of less than half a mile, suddenly appeared from behind a passing snow-squall. It was running fully on the surface with three figures clearly distinguishable on the conning-tower and another three manning the deck gun just for'ard of that. The submarine was on a course exactly parallelling that of the *San Andreas* and could well have been for many hours. The U-boat was on their starboard hand so that the *San Andreas* lay between it and the gradually lightening sky to the south. Both bridge wing doors were latched back in the fully open position. McKinnon reached for the phone, called the engine-room for full power, nudged the wheel to starboard and began to edge imperceptibly closer to the U-boat.

He and Naseby were alone on the bridge. They were, in fact, the only two people left in the superstructure because McKinnon had ordered everyone, including a bitterly protesting Lieutenant Ulbricht, to go below to the hospital only ten minutes previously. Naseby he required and for two reasons. Naseby, unlike himself, was an adept Morse signaller and had a signalling lamp ready at hand: more importantly, McKinnon was more than reasonably certain that the bridge would be coming under attack in a very short space of time indeed and he wanted a competent helmsman to hand in case he himself were incapacitated.

'Keep out of sight, George,' McKinnon said. 'But try to keep an eye on them. They're bound to start sending any minute now.'

'They can see you,' Naseby said.

'Maybe they can see my head and shoulders over the wing of the bridge. Maybe not. It doesn't matter. The point is that they will believe I can't see them. Don't forget that they're in the dark quadrant of the sea and have no reason to think that we're expecting trouble. Besides, a helmsman's job is to keep an eye on the compass and look ahead – no reason on earth why I should be scanning the seas around.' He felt the superstructure begin to shudder as Patterson increased the engine revolutions, gave the wheel another nudge to starboard, picked up a tin mug from the shattered binnacle and pretended to drink from it. 'It's like a law of nature, George. Nothing more reassuring than the sight of an unsuspecting innocent enjoying a morning cup of tea.'

For a full minute, which seemed like a large number of full minutes, nothing happened. The superstructure was beginning to vibrate quite strongly now and McKinnon knew that the *San Andreas* was under maximum power. They were now at least a hundred yards closer to the U-boat than they had been when it had first been sighted but the U-boat captain gave no indication that he was aware of this. Had McKinnon maintained his earlier speed his acute angling in towards the U-boat would have caused him to drop slightly astern of the submarine, but the increase in speed had enabled him to maintain his relative position. The U-boat captain had no cause to be suspicious – and no one in his right mind was going to harbour suspicions about a harmless and defenceless hospital ship.

'He's sending, George,' McKinnon said.

'I see him. "Stop," he says. "Stop engines or I will sink you." What do I send, Archie?'

'Nothing.' McKinnon edged the *San Andreas* another three degrees to starboard, reached again for his tin mug and pretended to drink from it. 'Ignore him.'

'Ignore him!' Naseby sounded aggrieved. 'You heard what the man said. He's going to sink us.'

'He's lying. He hasn't stalked us all this way just to send us to the bottom. He wants us alive. Not only is he not going to torpedo us, he can't, not unless they've invented torpedoes that can turn corners. So how else is he going to stop us? With

214

that little itsy-bitsy gun he's got on the foredeck? It's not all that much bigger than a pom-pom.'

'I have to warn you, Archie, the man's going to get very annoyed.'

'He's got nothing to be annoyed about. We haven't seen his signal.'

Naseby lowered his binoculars. 'I also have to warn you that he's about to use that little itsy-bitsy gun.'

'Sure he is. The classic warning shot over the bows to attract our attention. If he *really* wants to attract our attention, it may be into the bows for all I know.'

The two shells, when they came, entered the sea just yards ahead of the *San Andreas*, one disappearing silently below the waves, the other exploding on impact. The sound of the explosion and the sharp flat crack of the U-boat's gun made it impossible any longer to ignore the submarine's existence.

'Show yourself, George,' McKinnon said. 'Tell him to stop firing and ask him what he wants.'

Naseby moved out on the starboard wing and transmitted the message: the reply came immediately.

'He has a one-track mind,' Naseby said. 'Message reads: "Stop or be sunk".'

'One of those laconic characters. Tell him we're a hospital ship.'

'You think he's blind, perhaps?'

'It's still only half-light and the starboard side is our dark side. Maybe he'll think that we think he can't see. Tell him we're a neutral, mention the Geneva Convention. Maybe he's got a better side to his nature.'

Naseby clacked out his message, waited for the reply, then turned gloomily to McKinnon. 'He hasn't got a better side to his nature.'

'Not many U-boat captains have. What does he say?'

'Geneva Conventions do not apply in the Norwegian Sea.'

'There's little decency left on the high seas these days. Let's try for his sense of patriotism. Tell him we have German survivors aboard.'

While Naseby sent the message McKinnon rang down for slow ahead. Naseby turned in the doorway and shook his head sadly.

'His patriotism is on a par with his decency. He says: "Will check nationals when we board. We commence firing in twenty seconds".'

'Send: "No need to fire. We are stopping. Check wake".'

Naseby sent the message, then said: 'Well, he got that all right. He's already got his glasses trained on our stern. You know, I do believe he's angling in towards us. Very little, mind you, but it's there.'

'I do believe you're right.' McKinnon gave the wheel another slight nudge to starboard. 'If he notices anything he'll probably think it's because he's closing in on us and not vice versa. Is he still examining our wake?'

'Yes.'

'Turbulence aft must have died away quite a lot by this time. That should make him happy.'

'He's lowered his glasses,' Naseby said. 'Message coming.'

The message didn't say whether the U-boat captain was happy or not but it did hold a certain degree of satisfaction. 'Man says we are very wise,' Naseby said. 'Also orders us to lower our gangway immediately.'

'Acknowledge. Tell Ferguson to start lowering the gangway immediately but to stop it about, say, eight feet above the water. Then tell Curran and Trent to swing out the lifeboat and lower it to the same height.'

Naseby relayed both messages, then said: 'You think we're going to need the lifeboat?'

'I quite honestly have no idea. But if we do, we're going to need it in a hurry.' He called the engine-room and asked for Patterson.

'Chief? Bo'sun here. We're slowing a bit, as you know, but that's only for the moment. The U-boat is closing in on us. We're lowering both the gangway and the lifeboat, the gangway on the U-boat's instructions, the lifeboat on mine . . . No, they can't see the lifeboat – it's on our port side, their blind side. As soon as they are in position I'm going to ask for full power. A request, sir. If I do have to use the boat I'd appreciate it if you'd permit Mr Jamieson to come with me. With your gun.' He listened for a few moments while the receiver crackled in his ear, then said: 'Two things, sir. I want Mr Jamieson because apart from yourself and Naseby he's the only member of the crew I can trust. Show him where the safety-catch is. And no, sir, you know damn well you can't come along instead of Mr Jamieson. You're the officer commanding and you can't leave the *San Andreas.*' McKinnon replaced the receiver and Naseby said, plaintive reproach in his voice: 'You might have asked me.'

McKinnon looked at him coldly. 'And who's going to steer this damned ship when I'm gone?'

Naseby sighed. 'There's that, of course, there's that. They seem to be preparing some kind of boarding party across there, Archie. Three more men on the conning-tower now. They're armed with sub-machine-guns or machine-pistols or whatever you call those things. Something nasty, anyway.'

'We didn't expect roses. How's Ferguson coming along? If that gangway doesn't start moving soon the U-boat captain is going to start getting suspicious. Worse, he's going to start getting impatient.'

'I don't think so. At least, not yet awhile. I can see Ferguson so I'm certain the U-boat captain can too. Ferguson's having difficulty of some kind, he's banging away at the lowering drum with a hammer. Icing trouble for a certainty.'

'See how the boat's getting on, will you?'

Naseby crossed the bridge, moved out on to the port wing and was back in seconds. 'It's down.

About eight feet above the water, as you asked.'
He crossed to the starboard wing, examining the
U-boat through his binoculars, lowered them and
turned back to McKinnon.

'That's bloody funny. All those characters seem
to be wearing some kind of gas-masks.'

'Gas-masks? Are you all right?'

'Certainly I'm all right. They're all wearing a
horseshoe-shaped kind of life-jacket around their
necks with a corrugated hose attached to the top.
They're not wearing it at the moment, it's dangling down in front, but there's a mouthpiece and
goggles attached to the end of the tube. When did
German submariners start using gas?'

'They don't. What good on earth would gas be
to a U-boat?' He took Naseby's binoculars, examined the U-boat briefly and handed the glasses
back. 'Tauchretter, George, Tauchretter. Otherwise
known as the Dräger Lung. It's fitted with an oxygen cylinder and a carbon dioxide canister and its
sole purpose is to help people escape from a
sunken submarine.'

'No gas?' Naseby sounded vaguely disappointed.

'No gas.'

'That doesn't look like a sunken submarine
to me.'

'Some U-boat commanders make their crews
wear them all the time they're submerged. Bit
pointless in these waters, I would have thought. At
least six hundred feet deep here, maybe a thousand.

There's no way you can escape from those depths, Dräger set or not. How's Ferguson coming along?'

'As far as I can tell, he's not. Still hammering away. No, wait a minute, wait a minute. He's put the hammer down and is trying the release lever. It's moving, Archie. It's coming down.'

'Ah!' McKinnon rang for full power.

Some seconds passed, then Naseby said: 'Half way.' A similar length of time elapsed, then Naseby said in the same matter-of-fact voice: 'It's down, Archie. Eight feet, give or take. Ferguson's secured it.'

McKinnon nodded and spun the wheel to starboard until he had maximum rudder on. Slowly, ponderously at first, then with increasing speed, the *San Andreas* began to come round.

'Do you want to get your head blown off, George?'

'Well, no.' Naseby stepped inside, closed the wing door behind him and peered out through the little window in the door. The *San Andreas*, no longer riding with the sea, was beginning to corkscrew, although only gently so: but the entire superstructure was beginning to vibrate in a rather alarming fashion as the engines built up to maximum power.

'And don't you think you ought to lie down?'

'In a minute, Archie, in a minute. Do you think they've gone to sleep aboard that U-boat?'

'Some trouble with their eyes, that's for sure. I think they're rubbing them and not believing what they're seeing.'

Except that there was no actual eye-rubbing going on aboard the U-boat, McKinnon's guess was very close to the mark. The reactions of both the submarine commander and his crew were extraordinarily slow. Extraordinarily, but in the circumstances, understandably. The U-boat's crew had made both the forgivable and unforgivable mistake of relaxing, of lowering their guard at the precise moment when their alertness and sense of danger should have been honed to its keenest edge. But the sight of the gangway being lowered in strict compliance with their orders must have convinced them that there was no thought or possibility of any resistance being offered and that the taking over of the *San Andreas* was no more than a token formality. Besides, no one in the history of warfare had ever heard of a hospital ship being used as an offensive weapon. It was unthinkable. It takes time to rethink the unthinkable.

The *San Andreas* was so far round now that the U-boat was no more than 45° off the starboard bow. Naseby moved from the starboard wing door to the nearest small window let into the front of the bridge.

'They're lining up what it pleases you to call that little itsy-bitsy gun, Archie.'

'Then maybe we'd both better be getting down.'

'No. They're not lining up on the bridge, they're lining up on the hull aft. I don't know what they intend to –' He broke off and shouted: 'No! No! Get down, get down!' and flung himself at McKinnon, bringing both men crashing heavily to the deck of the bridge. Even as they landed, hundreds of bullets, to the accompaniment of the staccato chattering of several machine-guns, smashed into the fore end and starboard side of the bridge. None of the bullets succeeded in penetrating the metal but all four windows were smashed. The fusillade lasted no more than three seconds and had no sooner ceased when the U-boat's deck gun fired three times in rapid succession, on each occasion causing the *San Andreas* to shudder as the shells exploded somewhere in the after hull.

McKinnon hauled himself to his feet and took the wheel. 'If I'd been standing there I'd have been very much the late Archie McKinnon. I'll thank you tomorrow.' He looked at the central window before him. It was holed, cracked, starred, abraded and completely opaque. 'George?'

But Naseby needed no telling. Fire-extinguisher in hand, he smashed away the entire window in just two blows. He hitched a cautious eye over the bottom of where the window had been, saw that the *San Andreas* was arrowing in on the bows of the U-boat, then abruptly straightened in the instinctive reaction of a man who realizes that all danger is past.

'Conning-tower's empty, Archie. They've all gone. Bloody funny, isn't it?'

'Nothing funny about it.' The Bo'sun's tone was dry; if he was in any way moved or shaken by the narrowness of his recent escape he showed no signs of it. 'It's customary, George, to go below and pull down the hatch after you when you're going to dive. In this case, crash dive.'

'Crash dive?'

'Captain has no option. He knows he hasn't the firepower to stop us and he can't possibly bring his torpedoes to bear. Right now he's blowing all main ballast. See those bubbles? That's water being blown from the ballast tanks by high pressure air – something like three thousand pounds per square inch.'

'But – but he's left his gun crew on deck.'

'Indeed he has. Again, no option. A U-boat is much more valuable than the lives of three men. See those valves they're twisting on the right-hand side of their suits? Oxygen valves. They're turning their Dräger lungs into life jackets. Much good it will do them if they run into a propeller. Will you go out on the wings, George, and see if there's any flame or smoke aft.'

'You could phone.'

McKinnon pointed to the phone in front of the wheel, a phone that had been shattered by a machine gun bullet. Naseby nodded and went out on both wings in turn.

'Nothing. Nothing you can see from the outside.' He looked ahead towards the U-boat, not much more than a hundred yards distant. 'She's

223

going down, Archie. Fore and aft decks are awash.'

'I can see that.'

'And she's turning away to her starboard.'

'I can see that, too. Counsel of desperation. He's hoping that if he can turn his sub at an acute enough angle to us he'll be struck only a glancing blow. A glancing blow he could survive. I think.'

'Hull's submerged now. Is he going to make it?'

'He's left it too late.' McKinnon rang down for full astern and eased the wheel slightly to port. Five seconds later, with the top of the conning tower barely awash, the forefoot of the *San Andreas* tore into the hull of the U-boat some thirty feet for'ard of the conning tower. The *San Andreas* juddered throughout its length but the overall effect of the impact was curiously small. For a period of not more than three seconds they felt rather than heard the sensation of steel grinding over steel, then all contact was abruptly lost.

'Well,' Naseby said, 'so that's how it's done, is it?' He paused. 'There's going to be a lot of jagged metal on that U-boat. If a prop hits that –'

'No chance. The U-boat's been driven down, deep down – and they'll still be blowing main ballast. Let's just hope we haven't damaged ourselves too badly.'

'You said the U-boat captain had no option. We didn't either. You think there'll be any survivors?'

'I don't know. If there are any, we'll find out soon enough. I question very much whether they would even have had time to close watertight doors. If they didn't, then that U-boat is on its way to the bottom. If anyone is going to escape, they're going to have to do it before it reaches the two-hundred-and-fifty-foot mark – I've never heard of anyone escaping from a submarine at a depth greater than that.'

'They'd have to use the conning-tower?'

'I suppose. There is a for'ard escape hatch – it's really an access hatch to the deck gun. But the chances are high that the fore part of the U-boat is completely flooded, so that's useless. There may be an after escape hatch, I don't know. The conning-tower is probably their best bet, or would have been if we hadn't rammed their vessel.'

'We didn't hit anywhere near the conning-tower.'

'We didn't have to. The compressive power of something like ten thousand tons dead weight has to be pretty fierce. The conning-tower hatch may have been jammed solid. Whether it would be possible to ease it or not I wouldn't know. Worse still, it may have sprung open and with a hundred gallons of water a second pouring down into the control room there is no way anyone is going to get out, they'd probably be battered unconscious in the first few seconds. I'm going down on deck now. Keep going round to starboard and keep her astern till you stop, then heave to. I'll take the motorboat out as soon as you've lost enough way.'

'What's the point in taking the boat out if there are going to be no survivors?'

McKinnon led him out on to the port wing and astern to where three men were floundering about in the water. 'Those three characters. The gun crew. As far as I could tell they were only wearing overalls and oilskins. Maybe the odd jersey or two, but that would make no difference. Leave them out there another ten, fifteen minutes and they'll just freeze to death.'

'Let them. Those three bastards hit us aft three times. For all we can tell, some of those shells may have exploded inside the hospital.'

'I know, George, I know. But I dare say there's something in the Geneva Convention about it.' McKinnon clapped him lightly on the shoulder and went below.

Just outside the deck entrance to the hospital McKinnon found half a dozen people waiting for him – Patterson, Jamieson, Curran, Trent, McCrimmon and Stephen. Patterson said: 'I believe we've been in some sort of collision, Bo'sun.'

'Yes, sir. U-boat.'

'And?'

McKinnon pointed downwards. 'I just hope we don't go the same way. For'ard watertight bulkheads, sir?'

'Of course. At once.' He looked at McCrimmon and Stephen, who left without a word. 'And next, Bo'sun?'

'We were hit three times aft, sir. Any damage in the hospital?'

'Some. All three hit the hospital area. One appears to have exploded when it passed through the bulkhead between A and B wards. Some injuries, no fatalities. Dr Sinclair is attending to them.'

'Not Dr Singh?'

'He was in the recovery room with the two injured seamen from the *Argos*. Door's jammed and we can't get inside.'

'Shell explode in there?'

'Nobody seems to know.'

'Nobody seems – but that's the next compartment to A ward. Are they all deaf in there?'

'They were. It was the first shell that exploded between the two wards. That deafened them all right.'

'Ah. Well, the recovery room will just have to wait. What happened to the third shell?'

'Didn't explode.'

'Where is it?'

'In the dining area. Rolling about quite a bit.'

'Rolling about quite a bit,' McKinnon repeated slowly. 'That's handy. Just because it didn't go off on impact –' He broke off and said to Curran: 'A couple of heaving lines in the motorboat. Don't forget your knives.' He went inside and reappeared within twenty seconds, carrying a very small, very innocuous-looking shell, threw it over the side and said to Jamieson: 'You have your gun, sir?'

'I have my gun. What do you want the heaving lines for, Bo'sun?'

'Same reason as your gun, sir. To discourage people. Tie them up if we have to. If there are any survivors, they're not going to feel very kindly disposed because of what we've done to their boat and their shipmates.'

'But those people aren't armed. They're submariners.'

'Don't you believe it, sir. Many officers carry hand guns. Petty officers, too, for all I know.'

'Even if they had guns, what could they do?'

'Take us hostage, that's what they could do. And if they could take us hostage they could still take over the ship.'

Jamieson said, almost admiringly: 'You don't trust many people, do you?'

'Some. I just don't believe in taking chances.'

The motorboat was less than fifty yards away from the spot where the U-boat's gun crew were still floundering about in the water when Jamieson touched McKinnon on the arm and pointed out over the starboard side.

'Bubbles. Lots of little bubbles.'

'I see them. Could be there's someone coming up.'

'I thought they always came up in a great big air bubble.'

'Never. Big air bubble when they leave the submarine, perhaps. But that collapses at once.'

McKinnon eased back on the throttle as he approached the group in the water.

'Someone's just broken the surface,' Jamieson said. 'No, by God, two of them.'

'Yes. They've got inflatable life jackets on. They'll keep.' McKinnon stopped the engines and waited while Curran, Trent and Jamieson literally hauled the gun crew aboard – they seemed incapable of helping themselves. The trio were young, hardly more than boys, teeth chattering, shivering violently and trying hard not to look terrified.

'We search this lot?' Jamieson said. 'Tie them up?'

'Good lord, no. Look at their hands – they're blue and frozen stiff. If they couldn't even hang on to the gunwale, and they couldn't, how could they press the trigger of a gun even if they could unbutton their oilskins, which they can't?'

McKinnon opened the throttle and headed for the two men who had surfaced from the submarine. As he did, a third figure bobbed to the surface some two hundred yards beyond.

The two men they hauled aboard seemed well enough. One of them was a dark-haired, dark-eyed man in his late twenties: his face was lean, intelligent and watchful. The other was very young, very blond and very apprehensive. McKinnon addressed the older man in German.

'What is your name and rank?'

'Obersteuermann Doenitz.'

'Doenitz? Very appropriate.' Admiral Doenitz was the brilliant C-in-C of the German submarine fleet. 'Do you have a gun, Doenitz? If you say you haven't and I find one I shall have to shoot you because you are not to be trusted. Do you have a gun?'

Doenitz shrugged, reached under his blouse and produced a rubber-wrapped pistol.

'Your friend here?'

'Young Hans is an assistant cook.' Doenitz spoke in fluent English. He sighed. 'Hans is not to be trusted with a frying-pan, far less a gun.'

McKinnon believed him and headed for the third survivor. As they approached McKinnon could see that the man was at least unconscious for his neck was bent forward and he was face down in the water. The reason for this was not far to seek. His Dräger apparatus was only partially inflated and the excess oxygen had gone to the highest point of the bag at the back of the neck, forcing his head down. McKinnon drew alongside, caught the man by his life jacket, put his hand under his chin and lifted the head from the water.

He studied the face for only a second or two, then said to Doenitz: 'You know him, of course.'

'Heissmann, our First Lieutenant.'

McKinnon let the face fall back into the water. Doenitz looked at him with a mixture of astonishment and anger.

'Aren't you going to bring him aboard? He may just be unconscious, just half-drowned perhaps.'

'Your First Lieutenant is dead.' McKinnon's voice carried total conviction. 'His mouth is full of blood. Ruptured lungs. He forgot to breathe out oxygen on the way up.'

Doenitz nodded. 'Perhaps he didn't know that he had to do that. I didn't know. I'm afraid we don't have much time for escape training these days.' He looked curiously at McKinnon. 'How did you know? You're not a submariner.'

'I was. Twelve years.'

Curran called from the bows: 'There's one more, Bo'sun. Just surfaced. Dead ahead.'

McKinnon had the motorboat alongside the struggling man in less than a minute and had him brought aboard and laid on the thwarts. He lay there in a peculiar position, knees against his chest, his hands hugging both knees and trying to roll from side to side. He was obviously in considerable pain. McKinnon forced open the mouth, glanced briefly inside, then gently closed it again.

'Well, this man knew enough to exhale oxygen on the way up.' He looked at Doenitz. 'You know this man, of course.'

'Of course. Oberleutnant Klaussen.'

'Your captain?' Doenitz nodded. 'Well, he's obviously in considerable pain but I wouldn't think he's in any danger. You can see he's been cut on the forehead – possibly banged his head on the escape hatch on the way out. But that's not enough to account for his condition, for he must have been conscious all the way up or he wouldn't have got rid of the oxygen in his lungs. Were you travelling underwater or on the surface during the night?'

'On the surface. All the time.'

'That rules out carbon dioxide, which can be poisonous; but you can't build up carbon dioxide when the conning-tower is open. From the way he's holding his chest and legs it would seem to be caisson disease; for that's where the effects hurt most, but it can't be that either.'

'Caisson disease?'

'Diver's bends. When there's too rapid a build-up of nitrogen bubbles in the blood when you're making a very fast ascent.' McKinnon, with the motor boat under full throttle, was heading directly for the *San Andreas*, which was stopped in the water at not much more than half a mile's distance. 'But for that you have to be breathing in a high pressure atmosphere for quite some time and your captain certainly wasn't below long enough for that. Perhaps he escaped from a very great depth, perhaps a greater depth than anyone has ever escaped from a submarine and then I wouldn't know what the effects might be. We have a doctor aboard. I don't suppose he'll know either – the average doctor can spend a lifetime and not come across a case like this. But at least he can stop the pain.'

The motor boat passed close by the bows of the *San Andreas* which, remarkably, appeared to be quite undamaged. But that damage had been done was unquestionable – the *San Andreas* was at least three feet down by the head, which was no more than was to be expected if the for'ard compartments had been flooded, as, inevitably, they must have been.

McKinnon secured alongside and half-helped, half-carried the semi-conscious U-boat captain to the head of the gangway. Patterson was waiting for him there, as was Dr Sinclair and three other members of the engine-room staff.

'This is the U-boat captain,' McKinnon said to Dr Sinclair. 'He may be suffering from the bends – you know, nitrogen poisoning.'

'Alas, Bo'sun, we have no decompression chamber aboard.'

'I know, sir. He may just be suffering from the effects of having surfaced from a great depth. I don't know, all I know is he's suffering pretty badly. The rest are well enough, all they need is dry clothing.' He turned to Jamieson who had just joined him on deck. 'Perhaps, sir, you would be kind enough to supervise their change of clothing?'

'You mean to make sure that they're not carrying anything they shouldn't be carrying?'

McKinnon smiled and turned to Patterson. 'How are the for'ard watertight bulkheads, sir?'

'Holding. I've had a look myself. Bent and buckled but holding.'

'With your permission, sir, I'll get a diving suit and have a look.'

'Now? Couldn't that wait a bit?'

'I'm afraid waiting is the one thing we can't afford. We can be reasonably certain that the U-boat was in contact with Trondheim right up to the moment that he signalled us to stop – I think it would be very silly of us to assume otherwise. Flannelfoot is still with us. The Germans know exactly where we are. Till now, for reasons best known to themselves, they have been treating us with kid gloves. Maybe now they'll be feeling like taking those gloves off, I shouldn't imagine that Admiral Doenitz will take too kindly to the idea of one of his U-boats having been sunk by a hospital ship. I think it behoves us, sir, to get out of here and with all speed. Trouble is, we've got to make up our minds whether to go full speed ahead or full speed astern.'

'Ah. Yes. I see. You have a point.'

'Yes, sir. If the hole in our bows is big enough, then if we make any speed at all I don't see the watertight bulkheads standing up to the pressure for very long. In that case we'd have to go astern. I don't much fancy that. It not only slows us down but it makes steering damn difficult. But it can be done. I knew of a tanker that hit a German U-boat about seven hundred miles from its port of destination. It made it – going astern all the way. But I don't much care for the idea of going stern first all the way to Aberdeen, especially if the weather breaks up.'

'You make me feel downright nervous, Bo'sun. With all speed, Bo'sun, as you say, with all speed. How long will this take?'

'Just as long as it takes me to collect a rubber suit, mask and torch, then get there and back again. At the most, twenty minutes.'

McKinnon was back in fifteen minutes. Mask in one hand, torch in the other, he climbed up the gangway to where Patterson was awaiting him at the top.

'We can go ahead, sir,' McKinnon said. 'Full ahead, I should think.'

'Good, good, good. Damage relatively slight, I take it. How small is the hole?'

'It's not a small hole. It's a bloody great hole, big as a barn door. There's a ragged piece of that U-boat, about eight foot by six, embedded in our bows. Seems to be forming a pretty secure plug and I should imagine that the faster we go the more securely it will be lodged.'

'And if we stop, or have to go astern, or run into heavy weather – I mean, what if the plug falls off?'

'I'd be glad, sir, if you didn't talk about such things.'

EIGHT

'And what are you doing there?' McKinnon looked down on the recumbent form of Janet Magnusson who, her face very pale, was lying on, not in, the bed nearest the desk where she normally sat.

'I normally have a rest at this time of the morning.' She tried to inject an acid tone into her voice but her heart wasn't in it and she smiled, albeit wanly. 'I have been badly wounded, Archie McKinnon. Thanks to you.'

'Oh dear.' McKinnon sat on her bedside and put his hand on her shoulder. 'I am sorry. How –'

'Not there.' She pushed his hand away. 'That's where I've been wounded.'

'Sorry again.' He looked up at Dr Sinclair. 'How bad is badly?'

'Nurse Magnusson has a very slight graze on her right shoulder. Piece of shrapnel.' Sinclair pointed to a jagged hole in the bulkhead about six feet above deck level, then indicated the scarred and pock-marked deckhead. 'That's where the rest of the shrapnel appears to have gone. But Nurse Magnusson was standing at the time and caught quite a bit of the blast effect. She was thrown across the bed she's on now – it was, providentially, empty at the time – and it took us ten minutes to bring her round. Shock, that's all.'

'Layabout.' McKinnon stood. 'I'll be back. Anybody else hurt here, Doctor?'

'Two. At the far end of the ward. Seamen from the *Argos*. One in the chest, the other in the leg. Shrapnel ricocheting from the ceiling and pretty spent shrapnel at that. Didn't even have to dig it out. Not even bandages – cotton wool and plaster.'

McKinnon looked at the man, restless and muttering, in the bed opposite. 'Oberleutnant Klaussen – the U-boat commander. How is he?'

'Delirious, as you can see. The trouble with him – I've no idea. I tend to go along with your suggestion that he must have come up from a very great depth. If that's the case, I'm dealing with the unknown. Sorry and all that.'

'I hardly think there's any need to be sorry, sir. Every other doctor would be in the same boat. I don't think anyone has ever escaped from a depth greater than two hundred and fifty feet before. If Klaussen did – well, it's uncharted territory. There simply can't be any literature on it.'

'Archie.'

McKinnon turned round. Janet Magnusson was propped up on an elbow.

'You're supposed to be resting.'

'I'm getting up. What are you doing with that sledgehammer and chisel in your hand?'

'I'm going to try to open a jammed door.'

'I see.' She was silent for some moments while she bit her lower lip. 'The recovery room, isn't it?'

'Yes.'

'Dr Singh and the two men from the *Argos* – the one with the multiple burns and the other with the fractured pelvis – they're in there, aren't they?'

'So I'm told.'

'Well, why don't you go to them?' She sounded almost angry. 'Why stand around here blethering and doing nothing?'

'I hardly think that's quite fair, Nurse Magnusson.' Jamieson, who was accompanying McKinnon and Sinclair, spoke in tones of gentle reproof. 'Doing nothing? The Bo'sun does more than the whole lot of us put together.'

'I'm thinking perhaps there's no great hurry, Janet,' McKinnon said. 'People have been banging on that door for the past fifteen minutes and there's been no reply. Could mean anything or nothing. Point is, there was no point in trying to force that door till there was a doctor at hand and Dr Sinclair has just finished in the wards.'

'What you mean – what you really mean, Archie – is that you don't think the people inside the recovery room will be requiring the services of a doctor.'

'I hope I'm wrong but, yes, that's what I'm afraid of.'

She sank back in her bed. 'As Mr Jamieson didn't say, I was talking out of turn. I'm sorry.'

'There's really nothing to be sorry about.' McKinnon turned away and went into Ward A. The first person to catch his attention was Margaret Morrison. Even paler than Janet Magnusson had been, she was sitting in her chair behind her desk while Sister Maria carefully tied a bandage around her head. McKinnon didn't immediately go to her but went to the far right-hand side of the ward where Lieutenant Ulbricht was sitting up in his bed while Bowen and Kennet lay flat in theirs.

'Three more victims,' Sinclair said. 'Well, unfortunates, I should say. While the blast in Ward B went upwards I'm afraid it was slightly downwards here . . .'

McKinnon looked at Ulbricht. 'What's the matter with you?' Ulbricht had a thick bandage round his neck.

'I'll tell you what's the matter with him,' Sinclair said. 'Luck. The devil's own luck. A piece of shrapnel – it must have been as sharp as a razor – sliced through the side of his neck. Another quarter-inch to the right and it would have sliced through the carotid artery as well and then he'd have been very much the late Lieutenant Ulbricht.'

Ulbricht looked at McKinnon with little in the way of expression on his face. 'I thought you sent us down here for our own safety.'

'That's what I thought, too. I was certain they'd concentrate their fire on the bridge. I'm making no excuses but I don't think I miscalculated. I think the U-boat's gun crew panicked. I'm sure that Klaussen gave no instructions to fire into the hull.'

'Klaussen?'

'Oberleutnant. The captain. He survived. He seems fairly ill.'

'How many survivors altogether?'

'Six.'

'And the rest you sent to the bottom.'

'I'm the guilty party, if that's what you mean. I don't feel particularly guilty. But I'm responsible, yes.'

'I suppose that makes two of us. Responsible but not guilty.' Ulbricht shrugged and seemed disinclined to continue the conversation. McKinnon moved to the Captain's bed.

'Sorry to hear you've been hurt again, sir.'

'Me and Kennet. Left thighs. Both of us. Dr Sinclair tells me it's only a scratch and as I can't see it I have to take his word for it. Doesn't feel like a scratch, I can tell you. Well, Archie my boy, you've done it. I knew you would. If it weren't for those damned bandages I'd shake hands with you. Congratulations. You must feel pretty good about this.'

'I don't feel good at all, sir. If there were any survivors and if they managed to find a sealed compartment they'll be gasping out their lives – now – on the floor of the Norwegian Sea.'

'There's that, of course, there's that. But not to reproach yourself, Archie. Them or us. Unpleasant, but still well done.' Bowen adroitly switched the subject. 'Building up speed, aren't we? Limited damage up front, I take it.'

'Far from limited, sir. We're badly holed. But there's a large chunk of the U-boat's casing embedded in that hole. Let's just hope it stays there.'

'We can but pray, Bo'sun, we can but pray. And regardless of how you feel, every person aboard this boat is deeply in your debt.'

'I'll see you later, sir.'

He turned away, looked at Margaret Morrison, then at Dr Sinclair. 'Is she hurt? Badly, I mean.'

'She's the worst of the lot but nothing dangerous, you understand. She was sitting by Captain Bowen's bedside at the time and was hit twice. Nasty gash on the upper right arm and a minor scalp wound – that's the one Sister Maria has just finished bandaging.'

'Shouldn't she be in bed?'

'Yes. I tried to insist on it but I can tell you I won't be doing it again. How about you trying?'

'No, thank you.' McKinnon approached the girl, who looked at him with reproachful brown eyes that were slightly dulled with pain.

'This is all your fault, Archie McKinnon.'

McKinnon sighed. 'Exactly what Janet said to me. It's difficult to please everybody. I'm very, very sorry.'

241

'And so you should be. Not for this, though. The physical pain, I can tell you, is nothing compared to the mental hurt. You deceived me. Our greatly respected Bo'sun is exactly what he accused me of being – a fibber.'

'Oh dear. Long-suffering Bo'sun back in court again. What am I supposed to have done wrong now?'

'Not only that but you've made me feel very, very foolish.'

'I have? I would never do that.'

'You did. Remember on the bridge you suggested – in jest, of course – that you might fight the U-boat with a fusillade of stale bread and old potatoes. Well, something like that.'

'Ah!'

'Yes, ah! Remember that emotional scene on the bridge – well, emotional on my part, I cringe when I think about it – when I begged you to fight them and fight them and fight them. You remember, don't you?'

'Yes, I think I do.'

'He thinks he does! You had already made up your mind to fight them, hadn't you?'

'Well, yes.'

'Well, yes,' she mimicked. 'You had already made up your mind to ram that U-boat.'

'Yes.'

'Why didn't you tell me, Archie?'

'Because you might have casually mentioned it to somebody who might have casually mentioned it – unknowingly, of course – to Flannelfoot who would far from casually have mentioned it to the U-boat captain who would have made damn certain that he would never put himself in a position where he could be rammed. You might even – again unknowingly – have mentioned it directly to Flannelfoot.'

She made no attempt to conceal the hurt in her eyes. 'So you don't trust me. You said you did.'

'I trust you absolutely. I did say that.'

'Then why –'

'It was one of those then-and-now things. Then you were Sister Morrison. I didn't know there was a Margaret Morrison. I know now.'

'Ah!' She pursed her lips, then smiled, clearly mollified. 'I see.'

McKinnon left her, joined Dr Sinclair and Jamieson, and together they went to the door of the recovery room. Jamieson was carrying with him an electric drill, a hammer and some tapered wooden pegs. Jamieson said: 'You saw the entry hole made by the shell when you went up to examine the bows?'

'Yes. Just on – well, an inch or two above – the waterline. Could be water inside. Or not. It's impossible to say.'

'How high up?'

'Eighteen inches, say. Anybody's guess.'

Jamieson plugged in his drill and pressed the trigger. The tungsten carbide bit sank easily into the heavy steel of the door. Sinclair said: 'What happens if there's water behind?'

'Tap in one of those wooden pegs, then try higher up.'

'Through,' Jamieson said. He withdrew the bit. 'Clear.'

McKinnon struck the steel handle twice with the sledge. The handle did not even budge a fraction of an inch. On the third blow it sheared off and fell to the deck.

'Pity,' McKinnon said. 'But we have to find out.'

Jamieson shrugged. 'No option. Torch?'

'Please.' Jamieson left and was back in two minutes with the torch, followed by McCrimmon carrying the gas cylinder and a lamp on the end of a wandering lead. Jamieson lit the oxy-acetylene flame and began to carve a semi-circle round the space where the handle had been: McCrimmon plugged in the wandering lead and the wire-caged lamp burned brightly.

Jamieson said from behind his plastic face-shield: 'We're only assuming that this is where the door is jammed.'

'If we're wrong we'll cut away round the hinges. I don't think we'll have to. The door isn't buckled in any way. It's nearly always the lock or latch that's jammed.'

The compartment was filled with stinging acrid smoke when Jamieson finally straightened. He gave the lock a couple of blows with the side of his fist, then desisted.

'I'm sure I've cut through but the damn thing doesn't seem to want to fall away.'

'The latch is still in its socket.' McKinnon tapped the door with his sledge, not heavily, and the semi-circular piece of metal fell away inside. He hit the door again, heavily this time, and it gave an inch. With a second blow it gave several more inches. He laid aside the sledge and pushed against the door until, squeaking and protesting, it was almost wide open. He took the wandering lead from McCrimmon and went inside.

There was water on the deck, not much, perhaps two inches. Bulkheads and deckhead had been heavily starred and pock-marked by shrapnel from the exploding shell. The entrance hole formed by the shell in the outer bulkhead was a jagged circle not more than a foot above the deck.

The two men from the *Argos* were still lying in their beds while Dr Singh, head bowed to his chest, was sitting in a small armchair. All three men seemed unharmed, unmarked. The Bo'sun brought the light closer to Dr Singh's face. Whatever shrapnel may have been embedded in his body, none had touched his face. The only sign of anything untoward were tiny trickles of blood from his ears and nose. McKinnon handed the lamp to Dr Sinclair, who stooped over his dead colleague.

'Good God! Dr Singh.' He examined him for a few seconds, then straightened. 'That this should happen to a fine doctor, a fine man like this.'

'You didn't really expect to find anything else, did you, Doctor?'

'No. Not really. Had to be this or something like this.' He examined, briefly, the two men lying in their beds, shook his head and turned away. 'Still comes as a bit of a shock.' It was obvious that he was referring to Dr Singh.

McKinnon nodded. 'I know. I don't want to sound callous, Doctor, I know it might sound that way, but – you won't be needing those men any more? I mean, no postmortems, nothing of that kind.'

'Good lord, no. Death must have been instantaneous. Concussion. If it's any consolation, they died without knowing.' He paused. 'You might look through their clothing, Bo'sun. Or maybe it's in their effects or perhaps Captain Andropolous has the details.'

'You mean names, birth-dates, things like that, sir?'

'Yes. I have to fill out the death certificates.'

'I'll attend to that.'

'Thank you, Bo'sun.' Sinclair essayed a smile but it could hardly have been rated as a success. 'As usual, I'll leave the grisly part to you.' With that he was gone, a man glad to be gone. The Bo'sun turned to Jamieson.

'Could I borrow McCrimmon, sir?'

'Of course.'

'McCrimmon, go and find Curran and Trent, will you? Tell them what's happened. Curran will know what size of canvases to bring.'

'Needles and thread, Bo'sun?'

'Curran is a sailmaker. Just leave it to him. And you could tell him that it's a clean job this time.'

McCrimmon left and Jamieson said: 'A clean job? It's a lousy job. You always get the dirty end of the stick, McKinnon. I honestly don't know how you keep on doing it. If there's anything nasty or unpleasant to be done, you're number one on everybody's list.'

'Not this time I'm not. This time, sir, you're number one on my list. Someone has to tell the Captain. Someone has to tell Mr Patterson. Worst of all – much the worst of all – someone has to tell the nursing staff. That last is not a job I'd care for at all.'

'The girls. God, I hadn't thought of that. I don't care for it either. Don't you think, Bo'sun – seeing you know them so well, I mean –'

'No, I don't think, sir.' McKinnon half smiled. 'Surely as an officer, you wouldn't think of delegating to an underling something you wouldn't do yourself?'

'Underling! God, that's rich. Very well, never let it be said that I shirked my duty but as from now I feel one degree less sorry for you.'

'Yes, sir. One other thing: when this place is clear, would you have a couple of your men weld a patch over this hole in the bulkhead? Heaven knows they've had enough practice in welding patches recently.'

'Of course. Just let's hope it's the last patch.'

Jamieson left and McKinnon looked idly around him. His attention was caught by a fairly large wooden box in one corner and that only because its lid had been slightly sprung by the shock of the explosion. McKinnon, not without some effort, lifted the lid and peered for some seconds at the contents. He replaced the lid, retrieved his sledge and tapped the lid securely back into place. Stamped on the lid in big red letters were the words CARDIAC ARREST.

McKinnon, rather wearily, sat down at the table in the dining area. The injured sister and nurse, both looking as if they should have been in bed – they had been relieved by Sister Maria and Nurse Irene – were sitting there, as was, inevitably, Lieutenant Ulbricht, who not only gave the impression of having completely forgotten his narrow brush with death but was sufficiently back on balance to have found himself a seat between the two girls. Sinclair, Patterson and Jamieson were clustered round one end of the table. McKinnon looked consideringly at Ulbricht, then addressed himself to Dr Sinclair.

'Not calling your professional competence into question, sir, but is the Lieutenant fit to be up and around?'

'My professional competence is irrelevant.' One could see that Dr Sinclair had not yet recovered from the shock of the death of his colleague. 'The Lieutenant, like Sister Morrison and Nurse Magnusson, is uncooperative, intransigent and downright disobedient. The three of them would probably call it having minds of their own. Lieutenant Ulbricht, as it so happens, is in no danger. The injury to his neck couldn't even be described as a flesh wound. Torn skin, more like.'

'Then perhaps, Lieutenant, you would be prepared to take another fix? We haven't had one since last night.'

'At your disposal, Bo'sun.' If the Lieutenant harboured any ill will towards the Bo'sun for the deaths of his fellow countrymen, he was at pains to conceal it. 'Any time. I suggest just on noon.'

Patterson said: 'You finished through in the recovery room, Bo'sun?' McKinnon nodded. 'Well, one gets tired of keeping on saying thank-you so I'll spare you that. When do we bury them?'

'Your decision, sir.'

'Early afternoon, before it starts to get dark.' Patterson laughed without humour. 'My decision. Chief Engineer Patterson is your man when it comes to making decisions on matters that are of no importance. I don't recall making the decision to attack that submarine.'

'I did consult with Captain Bowen, sir.'

'Ah!' It was Margaret Morrison. 'So *that* was what that two-minute conference was about.'

'Of course. He approved.'

249

Janet said: 'And if he hadn't? Would you still have rammed that U-boat?'

McKinnon said patiently: 'He not only approved, he was enthusiastic. Very enthusiastic. With all respect to Lieutenant Ulbricht here, the Captain wasn't feeling too kindly disposed towards the Germans. Not at that moment of time, anyway.'

'You're being evasive, Archie McKinnon. Answer my question. If he *had* disapproved would you still have attacked?'

'Yes. No need to mention that to the Captain, though.'

'Nurse Magnusson.' Patterson smiled at Janet to rob his words of any offence. 'I hardly think Mr McKinnon deserves either interrogation or disapproval. I think he deserves congratulations for a magnificent job well done.' He rose, went to the cupboard where Dr Singh had kept his private supplies and returned with a bottle of Scotch and some glasses, poured a measure for McKinnon and set it before him. 'I think Dr Singh would have approved of this.'

'Thank you, sir.' McKinnon looked down at the glass on the table. 'He won't be needing this any more.'

There was silence round the table. Predictably, it was broken by Janet.

'I think, Archie, that that was less than a gracious remark.'

'You think so now. Maybe. Maybe not.' There was no hint of apology in his voice. He raised his glass and sipped from it. 'Knew his Scotch, did Dr Singh.'

The silence was longer this time, longer and strained. It was Sinclair, embarrassed by the silence, who broke it.

'I'm sure we all echo Mr Patterson's sentiments, Mr McKinnon. A splendid job. But – to quote yourself, I'm not questioning your professional competence – you did take a bit of a chance, didn't you?'

'You mean I endangered the lives of all aboard?'

'I didn't say that.' His look of discomfiture made it evident that he had thought it, if not said it.

'It was a calculated risk,' McKinnon said, 'but not all that calculated. The odds were on my side, quite heavily, I believe. I am quite certain that the U-boat was under orders that we were to be seized, not sunk, which is why I am equally certain that the gun crew fired into the *San Andreas* without orders.

'The U-boat captain, Oberleutnant Klaussen, was the wrong man in the wrong place at the wrong time. He was tired or immature or inexperienced or incompetent or over-confident – he may have been all those things at the same time. What is certain is that an experienced U-boat commander would never have put himself in a position where he was running parallel to us and less than a half a mile away. He should have stayed at a couple of miles' distance – which in

251

an emergency would have given him plenty of time to crash dive – ordered us to send across a boat, loaded it up with a half-dozen men with machine pistols and sent them back to take over the *San Andreas*. We could have done nothing to stop them. Even better, he should have closed up from astern, a position that would have made ramming impossible, then eased up alongside the gangway.

'And of course, he was too confident, too sure of himself, too relaxed by half. When he saw us lowering the gangway, he was convinced the game was over. It never even occurred to him that a hospital ship could be used as a man-o'-war. And he was either so blind or so stupid that he never even noticed that we were steadily closing in on him all the time we were in contact. In short, he made every mistake in the book. It would have been difficult to pick a worse man for the job.'

There was a long and rather uncomfortable silence. Mario, unobtrusive and efficient as ever, had filled all the glasses on the table but no one, with the exception of the Bo'sun, had as yet touched theirs.

Sinclair said: 'On the basis of what you say, the U-boat captain was indeed the wrong man for the job. And, of course, you wholly out-manoeuvered him. But surely the danger still existed. In the actual collision, I mean. The U-boat could have sunk us and not vice versa. We are only made of thin sheet plating: the hull of the submarine is immensely strong.'

'I would not presume to lecture you on medical matters, Dr Sinclair.'

Sinclair smiled. 'Meaning I should not presume to advise you on matters maritime. But, Mr McKinnon, you're a bo'sun on a merchant vessel.'

'Today, yes. Before that I spent twelve years in the submarine service.'

'Oh no.' Sinclair shook his head. 'Too much, just too much. This is definitely not Dr Sinclair's day.'

'I've known a good number of cases of collisions between merchant vessels and submarines. In nearly all cases those collisions were between friend and friend or, in peacetime, between a submarine and a harmless foreign vessel. The results were always the same. The surface vessel came off best.

'It doesn't seem logical but it does make sense. Take a hollow glass sphere with walls, say, of a third of an inch in diameter, submerge it to a very considerable depth – I'm talking of hundreds of feet – and it still won't implode. Bring it to the surface, give it a light tap with a hammer and it will shatter into a hundred pieces. Same with the pressure hull of a submarine. It can resist pressure at great depths but on the surface a short sharp blow, as from the bows of a merchant ship, will cause it to rupture. Admittedly, the chances of the submarine are not improved by the fact that the merchant ship may displace many thousands of tons and be travelling at a fair speed. On the other hand, even a vessel as small as a trawler can sink a submarine. Point is, Dr Sinclair, it wasn't all that dangerous: I hadn't much doubt as to what the outcome would be.'

'Point taken, Mr McKinnon. You see before you a rueful cobbler who will stick to his last from now on.'

Patterson said: 'This ever happen to you?'

'No. If it had, the chances are very high that I wouldn't be here now. I know plenty of instances. When I was in the service, the trade as we called it, we had a maxim which said, in effect, never mind the enemy, just watch out for your friends. Back in the Twenties, a British submarine – the MI it was – was accidentally struck by a merchant ship off the Devon coast. All died. Not long afterwards the American SI was overrun by the Italian passenger liner *City of Rome*. All died. Some time later, another American submarine was overrun by a coastguard destroyer off Cape Cod. All died. The *Poseidon*, British, was sent to the bottom by a Japanese ship. Accident. It was off the north China coast. A good number of survivors, but some died from the diver's bends. In the early years of the war, the *Surcouf*, crewed by the Free French and the biggest submarine in the world – so big that it was called a submarine cruiser – was sunk in the Caribbean by a ship in a convoy she was escorting. The *Surcouf* had a crew of a hundred and fifty: all died.' McKinnon passed a hand across his eyes. 'There were others. I forgot most of them. Ah, yes, there was the *Umpire*. Forty-one, I think. It took only a trawler, and not a very big one, to destroy her.'

Patterson said: 'You've made your point, as Dr Sinclair says, you've more than made your point. I accept that the element of risk was not high. You'll just have to bear with us, Mr McKinnon. Amateurs all. We didn't know. You did. The fact that the U-boat is at the bottom of the sea is testimony enough to that.' He paused. 'I have to say, Bo'sun, that your achievement doesn't appear to have given you any great satisfaction.'

'It hasn't.'

Patterson nodded. 'I understand. To have been responsible for the deaths of so many men – well, it's hardly a cheerful thought.'

McKinnon looked at him in mild surprise. 'What's done is done. So the U-boat's gone and its crew with it. It's no matter for celebration but it's no matter for recrimination either. The next Allied merchant ship to have appeared on the cross hairs of Klaussen's periscope sight would surely have gone to where Klaussen's U-boat is now. The only good U-boat is a U-boat with a ruptured pressure hull at the bottom of the ocean.'

'Then why – ' Patterson broke off, plainly at a loss for both thought and words, then said: 'The hell with the pros and cons, it was still a splendid job. I didn't fancy a prison camp any more than you. Well, I don't feel as modest about your accomplishments as you do.' He looked around the table. 'A toast to our Bo'sun here – and to the memory of Dr Singh.'

'I'm not nearly as modest as you think I am. I haven't the slightest objection to drinking a toast to myself.' McKinnon looked slowly around the other six. 'But I draw the line at drinking a toast to the memory of Flannelfoot.'

McKinnon was becoming very expert at causing silences. This, the fourth such silence, was much longer and much more uncomfortable than the ones that had preceded it. The other six stared at him, looked at each other with questioning, frowning glances, then returned their exclusive attention to McKinnon. Again, it was Janet who broke the silence.

'You do know what you're saying, Archie? At least I hope you do.'

'I'm afraid I do. Dr Sinclair, you had a cardiac arrest unit in the recovery room. Did you have another similar unit elsewhere?'

'Yes. In the dispensary.'

'And you were under strict instructions that, in an emergency, the dispensary unit was the one that was to be used first.'

'That is so.' Sinclair looked at him without understanding. 'How on earth do *you* know that?'

'Because I'm clever.' The normally calm and unemotional Bo'sun made no attempt to conceal his bitterness. 'After the event, I'm very clever.'

He shook his head. 'There's no point in you listening to me telling you how clever I haven't been. I suggest you go – I suggest you all go – and have a look at the recovery room cardiac unit. The unit's not there any more – it's in Ward A, by the Sister's desk. The lid is closed but the lock has been damaged as has the seal. You can wrench the lid open easily enough.'

All six looked at each other, then rose, left and were back within a minute. They sat in silence and remained in silence: they were either stunned by what they had seen or could not find the words to express their emotions.

'Nice, is it not?' McKinnon said. 'A high-powered radio transceiver. Tell me, Dr Sinclair, did Dr Singh ever lock himself up in the recovery room?'

'I couldn't say.' Sinclair shook his head quite violently, as if to clear it of disbelief. 'May well have done for all anyone would know.'

'But he did frequently go into that room alone?'

'Yes. Alone. Quite often. He insisted on looking after the two injured men personally. Perfectly within his rights, of course – he was the man who had operated on them.'

'Of course. After I'd found the radio – I still don't know what made me open up that damned cardiac unit – I examined the lock, the keyhole part that Mr Jamieson had burnt away with his torch, and the latch. Both were heavily oiled. When Dr Singh turned that key you would have

257

heard no sound of metal against metal or even the faintest click, not even if you were listening outside a couple of feet away – not that anyone could have had any conceivable reason for lurking outside a couple of feet away. After locking the door and checking that his two patients were under sedation – and if they weren't he would make sure they very quickly were – he could use his radio to his heart's content. Not, I should imagine, that he used it very often: the primary purpose, the essential purpose, of the radio was that it kept on sending out a continual homing location signal.'

'I still can't understand it or bring myself to believe it.' Patterson spoke slowly, a man still trying to struggle free of a trance. 'Of course it's true, it has to be true, but that doesn't make it any more credible. He was such a good man, such a kind man – and a fine doctor, was he not, Dr Sinclair?'

'He was an excellent doctor. No question. And a brilliant surgeon.'

'So was Dr Crippen for all I know,' McKinnon said. 'I find it as baffling as you do, Mr Patterson. I have no idea what his motives could have been and I should imagine that we'll never find out. He was a very clever man, a very careful man who never took a chance, a man who totally covered his tracks – if it weren't for a trigger-happy U-boat gun crew we'd never have found out who Flannelfoot was. His treachery may have had something to do with his background – although he spoke of Pakistani descent he was, of course, an Indian, and I believe that educated Indians have little reason to love the British Raj. May have had something to do with religion, if he had Pakistani roots he was probably a Muslim. The connection – I have no idea. There are a dozen other reasons apart from nationality and politics and religion that make a man a traitor. Where did those cardiac arrest units come from, Dr Sinclair?'

'They were loaded aboard at Halifax, Nova Scotia.'

'I know that. But do you know where they came from?'

'I have no idea. Does it matter?'

'It could. Point is, we don't know whether Dr Singh installed the radio transceiver after the unit came aboard or whether the unit was supplied with the transceiver already installed. I would take long odds that the transceiver had already been installed. Very tricky thing to do aboard a boat. Difficult to smuggle the transceiver aboard, equally difficult to get rid of the cardiac unit that was inside the box.'

Sinclair said: 'When I said I didn't know where that unit came from, that's quite true. But I know the country of origin. Britain.'

'How can you tell?'

'Stencil marks.'

'Would there be many firms in Britain that make those things?'

'Again, no idea. Not a question that comes up. A cardiac unit is a cardiac unit. Very few, I should imagine.'

'Should be easy enough to trace the source – and I don't for a moment imagine that the unit left the factory already equipped with the transceiver.' He looked at Patterson. 'Naval Intelligence should be very interested in finding out what route that cardiac unit took between the factory and the *San Andreas* and what stopovers it made en route.'

'They should indeed. And it should take them no time at all to find out where it changed hands and who made the switch. Seems damned careless of our saboteur friends to have left themselves so wide open.'

'Not really, sir. They simply never expected to be found out.'

'I suppose. Tell me, Bo'sun, why did you take so long in getting around to telling us about Dr Singh?'

'Because I had the same reaction as you – I had to work damned hard to convince myself of the evidence of my own eyes. Besides, you all held Dr Singh in very high regard – no one likes to be the bearer of bad news.' He looked at Jamieson. 'How long would it take, sir, to fix up a push button on Sister's desk in Ward A so that it would ring a buzzer in, say, here, the bridge and the engine-room?'

'No time at all.' Jamieson paused briefly. 'I know you must have an excellent reason for this – what shall we call it? – alarm system. May we know what it is?'

'Of course – so that the sister or nurse in charge of Ward A can let us know if any unauthorized person comes into the ward. That unauthorized person will be in the same state of ignorance as we are at the moment – he will not know whether that transceiver is in working order or not. He *has* to assume that it is, he has to assume that we may be in a position to send out an SOS to the Royal Navy. It's obviously all-important to the Germans that such a signal be not sent and that we remain alone and unprotected. They want us and they want us alive so the intruder will do everything in his power to destroy the set.'

'Wait a minute, wait a minute,' Patterson said. 'Intruder? Unauthorized person? What unauthorized person. Dr Singh is dead.'

'I've no idea who he is. All that I'm certain of is that he exists. You may remember that I said earlier that I thought we had more than one Flannelfoot aboard. Now I'm certain. Dr Sinclair, during the entire hour before Lieutenant Ulbricht and his Focke-Wulf made their appearance – and indeed for some time afterwards – you and Dr Singh were operating on the two wounded sailors – now the two dead sailors – from the *Argos*. That is correct?'

'That's so.' Sinclair looked and sounded puzzled.

'Did he leave the surgery at any time?'

'Not once.'

'And it was during this period that some unknown was busy tinkering with junction boxes and fuses. So, Flannelfoot number two.'

There was a brief silence, then Jamieson said: 'We're not very bright, are we? Of course you're right. We should have worked that out for ourselves.'

'You would have. Finding Dr Singh's dead body and then finding out what he was is enough to put any other thought out of your mind. It's only just now occurred to me. More time to get over the shock, I suppose.'

'Objection,' Patterson said. 'Query, rather. If that set is smashed the Germans have no means of tracking us.'

'They're not tracking us now,' McKinnon said patiently. 'Battery leads are disconnected. Even if they weren't, smashing the transceiver would be far the lesser of two evils. The last thing that Flannelfoot number two wants to see is the Royal Navy steaming over the horizon. They may have another transmitter cached away somewhere, although I very much doubt it. Dr Sinclair, would you please check the other cardiac unit in the dispensary, although I'm sure you'll find it okay.'

'Well,' Sinclair said, 'there's at least some satisfaction in knowing that they've lost us.'

'I wouldn't bet on that, Doctor. In fact, I'd bet against it. A submarine can't use its radio underwater but you have to remember that this lad was trailing us on the surface and was almost certainly in constant contact with its shore base. They'll know exactly our position and course at the time of the sinking of the submarine. I wouldn't even be surprised if there's another U-boat tagging along behind us – for some damned reason we seem to be very important to the Germans. And you mustn't forget that the further south-west we steam, the more hours of daylight we have. The sky's pretty clear and the chances are good that a Focke-Wulf or some such will pick us up during the day.'

Patterson looked at him morosely. 'You make a splendid Job's comforter, Bo'sun.'

McKinnon smiled. 'Sorry about that, sir. Just reckoning the odds, that's all.'

'The odds,' Janet said. 'You're betting against our chances of getting to Aberdeen, aren't you, Archie?'

McKinnon turned his hands palms upwards. 'I'm not a gambler and there are too many unknowns. Any of your opinions is just as good as mine. I'm not betting against our chances, Janet. I think we have a fair chance of making it.' He paused. 'Three things. I'll go and see Captain Andropolous and his men. I should think that "radio" is a pretty universal word. If not, sign language should work. Most of the crew of the *Argos* survived so the chances are good that there is a radio officer among them. He can have a look at this machine and see if we can transmit with it.

263

Lieutenant Ulbricht, I'd be grateful if you could come up to the bridge when it's time and take a noon sight. Third thing – if the lights in Ward A fail at any time, whoever is in charge is to press the panic button immediately.'

McKinnon made to rise, stopped and looked at his untouched drink.

'Well, perhaps after all, a toast to the departed. An old Gaelic curse, rather. Dr Singh. May his shade walk on the dark side of hell tonight.' He raised his glass. 'To Flannelfoot.'

McKinnon drank his toast alone.

NINE

Less than ten minutes after McKinnon's arrival on the bridge the phone rang.

'Jamieson here,' the voice said. 'Things do keep happening aboard this damned ship. There's been another accident.'

'Accident?'

'Accident on purpose. Incident, I should have said. Your pal Limassol.'

'Limassol' was the name that McKinnon had given to the man whom he had discovered to be the radio operator of the *Argos*. Apart from this discovery, the only other thing that the Bo'sun had been able to discover about him was that he was a Greek Cypriot from Limassol.

'What's happened to my pal Limassol?'

'He's been clobbered.'

'Ah.' McKinnon was not a man much given to exclamatory outbursts. 'Inevitably. Who clobbered him?'

'You should know better than to ask that question, Bo'sun. How the hell should I know who clobbered him? Nobody ever knows who does anything aboard the *San Andreas*. The Chief Officer was more prophetic than he knew when he gave this ship its new name. It's a bloody disaster area. I can only give you the facts as I know them. Sister Maria was on duty when Limassol sat down to have a look at the transceiver. After a while he stood and made the motion of screwing his forefinger against the palm of his other hand. She guessed, correctly, that he wanted tools and sent for Wayland Day to take him down to the engine-room. I was there and gave him the tools he wanted. He also took a bridge-megger with him. Gave every impression of a man who knew what he was doing. On his way back, in the passageway leading to the mess-deck, he was clobbered. Something hard and heavy.'

'How hard, how heavy?'

'If you'll just hang on for a moment. We have him down here in a bed in A Ward. Dr Sinclair is attending to him. He can tell you better than I can.'

There was a brief silence, then Sinclair was on the phone. 'Bo'sun? Well, damn it, confirmation of the existence of Flannelfoot number two – not that any confirmation was needed, but I didn't expect such quick and violent proof. This lad doesn't hang around, does he? Dangerous, violent, acts on his own initiative and his mind's working on the same wavelength as ours.'

'Limassol?'

'Pretty poorly, to say the least. Some metallic object, no question, could easily have been a crowbar. I would guess that the attacker's intent was to kill him. With most people he might well have succeeded but this Limassol seems to have a skull like an elephant. Fractured, of course. I'll have an X-ray. Routine and quite superfluous but mandatory. No signs of any brain damage, which is not to say that there isn't any. But no obvious damage, not, at least, at this stage. Two things I'm pretty certain about, Mr McKinnon. He'll live but he's not going to be of much use to you – or anyone – for some time to come.'

'As Dr Singh said about Lieutenant Cunningham – two hours, two days, two weeks, two months?'

'Something like that. I've simply no idea. All I know is that if he does recover rapidly he'll be of no possible use to you for days to come, so you can rule him out of any plans you may have.'

'I'm fresh out of plans, Doctor.'

'Indeed. We seem to be running out of options. Mr Jamieson would like to have another word with you.'

Jamieson came back on the phone. 'Maybe this could have been my fault, Bo'sun. Maybe if I'd been thinking a bit more clearly and a bit quicker this wouldn't have happened.'

'How on earth were you to know that Limassol was going to be attacked?'

'True. But I should have gone with him; not for his protection, but to watch him to see what he did to make the set work. That way I might have picked up enough to have some knowledge – rudimentary, but some – so that we wouldn't have to rely entirely on one man.'

'Flannelfoot would probably have clobbered you too. No point, sir, in trying to place the blame where none exists. The milk's spilt and you didn't spill it. Just give me enough time and I'll find out it was all McKinnon's fault.'

He hung up and related the gist of his conversation to Naseby, who had the wheel, and to Lieutenant Ulbricht, who had declared himself as feeling so fit that he no longer qualified as a bed patient.

'Disturbing,' Ulbricht said. 'Our friend seems to be resourceful, very quick-thinking and very much a man of decision and action. I say "disturbing" because it has just occurred to me that *he* may have been Flannelfoot number one and not Dr Singh, in which case we can expect a great deal more unpleasantness. In any event, it seems to rule out the crew of the *Argos* – none of them speaks English so they couldn't have known about the fake cardiac unit being in A Ward.'

McKinnon looked morose. 'The fact that none of them appears to understand a word of English – they're very good with their blank stares when you address them in that language – doesn't mean that one or two of them don't speak better English than I do. It doesn't rule out the crew of the *Argos*. And, of course, it doesn't rule out our own crew or the nine invalids we picked up in Murmansk.'

'And how would they have known that the tampered cardiac unit had been transferred from the recovery room to Ward A? Only – let me see – only seven people knew about the transfer. The seven at the table this morning. One of us could have talked, perhaps?'

'No.' McKinnon was very definite.

'Inadvertently?'

'No.'

'You trust us that much?' Ulbricht smiled but there was no humour in it. 'Or is it that you *have* to trust somebody?'

'I trust you all right.' McKinnon sounded a little weary. 'Point is, it wasn't necessary for anyone to talk. Everybody knows that Dr Singh and the two injured crewmen from the *Argos* are dead.' McKinnon made a dismissive little gesture with his hand. 'After all, we're going to bury them inside the half-hour. Everybody knows that they were killed by an explosive blast inside the recovery room and our newest Flannelfoot must have known that the transceiver was there and may have guessed, or suspected, that the case of the cardiac unit had been damaged sufficiently to reveal the existence of the transmitter. It had not, in fact, but that was pure luck on my part.'

'How do you explain the attack on the radio officer?'

'Easily.' McKinnon looked and sounded bitter. 'Flannelfoot didn't have to know where the radio was, all he had to know was that we had developed a certain interest in radio. Mr Jamieson tried to take some of the blame for the attack. Totally unnecessary when Mastermind McKinnon is around. My fault. My fault entirely. When I went down to find a radio officer the crew of the *Argos* were, as usual, in a corner by themselves. They weren't alone in the mess-deck – some of the injured men we picked up in Murmansk and some of our crew were there – but not close enough to hear us talking. Not that there was any talking. I just said the word "radio" several times, low enough not to be overheard, and this lad from Limassol looked at me. Then I made a motion of tapping my forefinger as if sending a signal in Morse. After that, I spun the handle of an imaginary electrical generator. None of this could have been seen except by the crew of the *Argos*. Then I made my stupid mistake. I cupped my hand to my ear as if listening to something. By this time Limassol had got the message and was on his feet. But our new Flannelfoot had got the message too. Just one little movement of my hand and he got it. He's not only violent and dangerous but very smart too. An unpleasant combination.'

'Indeed it is,' Ulbricht said. 'You have it right, you must have, and I can't see any reason for self-reproach. I used the right word back there – disturbing.'

Naseby said: 'Do you by any chance remember who exactly was in the mess-deck when you were there?'

'I do. Every crew member who wasn't on watch. On the deckside, only two were on watch – you and Trent down in the Captain's cabin there keeping an eye on the sextant and chronometer. All the off-duty engine-room staff. Two cooks and Mario. Seven of the seventeen invalids we picked up in Murmansk – the three who were supposed to be tubercular cases, the three who are supposed to be suffering from nervous breakdowns, and one of the exposure cases. He's so wrapped in bandages that he can barely walk so he doesn't come into consideration. A couple of nurses – they don't come into consideration either. And there's no doubt you're right, Lieutenant – the crew of the *Argos* has to be in the clear.'

'Well, that's something,' Ulbricht said. 'A moment ago you were expressing reservations against them which I found rather puzzling, as in that long talk in the Captain's cabin we had more or less agreed that the crew of the *Argos* was in the clear. The original suggestion, you may remember, came from you.'

'I remember. Next thing you know I'll be looking into the mirror and saying "and I don't trust you, either". Yes, I know I made the suggestion, but I still had this tiny doubt. At the time I more than suspected that we had another Flannelfoot aboard but I wasn't certain until less than half an hour ago.

It's impossible to believe that it wasn't our new Flannelfoot who blew the hole in the for'ard ballast room when we were alongside that sinking corvette. And it's unthinkable – and for me this is the clincher – that a member of the *Argos* crew would deliberately set out to murder a person who was not only a crewmate but a fellow countryman.'

'At least it's something,' Naseby said. 'Brings it down to our own crew, doesn't it?'

'Yes, our crew – and at least six allegedly physical and mentally disturbed cripples from Murmansk.'

Naseby shook his head sorrowfully. 'Archie, this trip is going to be the ruination of you. Never known you to be so terribly suspicious of everybody – and you've just said you could find yourself not even trusting yourself.'

'If a nasty suspicious mind is any kind of hope for survival, George, then I'm going to keep on having just that kind of mind. You will remember that we had to leave Halifax in a tearing hurry, in a cargo ship little more than half converted to a hospital. Why? To get to Archangel and that with all possible speed. Then, after that little accident when we were alongside that corvette it became equally essential that we be diverted to Murmansk. Why?'

'Well, we were listing a bit and down by the head.'

'We had stopped making water, weather conditions were fair, we could have reached the White

272

Sea, crossed it, and made Archangel without much trouble. But no, it was Murmansk or nothing. Again, why?'

'So that the Russians could place that explosive charge in the ballast room.' Ulbricht smiled. 'I recall your words – our gallant allies.'

'I recall them too. I wish I didn't. We all make mistakes, I'm certainly no exception, and that was one of my biggest. The Russians didn't place that charge – your people did.'

'The Germans? Impossible!'

'Lieutenant, if you imagine Murmansk and Archangel aren't hotching with German spies and agents, you're living in Alice's never-never Wonderland.'

'It's possible, it's possible. But to infiltrate a Russian naval working party – that's impossible.'

'It's not impossible but it doesn't even have to be necessary. People are capable of being suborned, and while it may not be true that every man has his price, there are always those who have.'

'A Russian traitor, you suggest?'

'Why not? You have your traitors. We have our traitors. Every country has its traitors.'

'Why should we – the Germans – want to place a charge in the *San Andreas*?'

'I simply have no idea. In the same way as I have simply no idea why the Germans have attacked, harassed and pursued us – but not tried to sink us – ever since we rounded the North

Cape. What I'm suggesting is, it's very likely that the same German agent or agents suborned one or more of the invalids we picked up in Murmansk. An alleged psychiatric case or mental breakdown patient, who is sick of both the war and the sea, would make an ideal choice for the traitor's part and I shouldn't even imagine that the price would have to be very high.'

'Objection, Mr McKinnon. It was a last-minute decision to detach the *San Andreas* from the convoy. You can't suborn a man overnight.'

'True. At the most, highly unlikely. Maybe they knew a week or two ago that we would be detached to Murmansk.'

'How on earth could they have known that?'

'I don't know. The same way I don't know why someone in Halifax knew quite a long time ago that Dr Singh would be in need of a transceiver.'

'And you don't think it extraordinary that the Russians, if they were not responsible for placing that charge, should have brought the *San Andreas* into Murmansk apparently for the sole benefit of your mysterious German agents?'

'They're not my agents but they're mysterious all right. The answer again is that I simply don't know. The truth appears to be that I just don't know anything about anything.' He sighed. 'Ah, well. Close to noon, Lieutenant. I'll go get the sextant and chronometer.'

* * *

Lieutenant Ulbricht straightened from the chart. 'Still, remarkably, holding the same course – 213. Precisely 64° North. Ideally, we should steer due south now but we're near enough to Trondheim as we are now, and that would only bring us closer. I suggest we maintain this course for the present, then turn due south some time during the night, midnight or thereabouts. That should bring us down the east coast of your native islands tomorrow, Mr McKinnon. I'll work it out.'

'You're the navigator,' McKinnon said agreeably.

In marked contrast to the conditions that had existed exactly forty-eight hours previously when the mass burial had taken place, the weather was now almost benign. The wind was no more than Force three, the sea calm enough to keep the *San Andreas* on an all but steady keel, and the cloud cover consisted of no more than a wide band of white, fleecy, mackerel sky against the pale blue beyond. McKinnon, standing by the starboard rail of the *San Andreas*, derived no pleasure whatsoever from the improvement: he would greatly have preferred the blanketing white blizzard of the previous burial.

Besides, the Bo'sun, the only other attendants or witnesses – by no stretch of the imagination could they have been called mourners – at the burial were Patterson, Jamieson, Sinclair and the two stokers and two seamen who had brought up the bodies. No one else had asked to come. For obvious reasons no one was going to mourn Dr Singh, and only Sinclair had known the two dead crewmen from the *Argos* and even then as no more than two unconscious bodies on operating tables.

Dr Singh was unceremoniously tipped over the side – not for him the well-wishing for his journey into the hereafter. Patterson, who would obviously never have made it as a clergyman, quickly read the liturgy from the prayer-book over the two dead Greek seamen and then they, too, were gone.

Patterson closed the prayer-book. 'Twice of that lot is twice too often. Let's hope there's not going to be a third time.' He looked at McKinnon. 'I suppose we just plod on on our far from merry way?'

'All we can do, sir. Lieutenant Ulbricht suggests that we alter course by and by to due south. That'll take us on a more direct route to Aberdeen. He knows what he's about. But that will be approximately twelve hours yet.'

'Whatever's best.' Patterson gazed around the empty horizon. 'Doesn't it strike you as rather odd, Bo'sun, that we've been left unmolested, or at least not located, for the better part of three hours? Since all communication from the U-boat has ceased in that time they must be very dense if they're not aware that something is far wrong with it.'

'I should imagine that Admiral Doenitz's U-boat fleet commander in Trondheim is very far from dense. I've the feeling they know exactly where we are. I understand that some of the latest U-boats are quite quick under water and one could easily be trailing us by Asdic without our knowing anything about it.' Like Patterson, only much more slowly, he looked around the horizon, then stood facing the port quarter. 'We are being tailed.'

'What? What's that?'

'Can't you hear it?'

Patterson cocked his head, then nodded slowly, 'I think I can. Yes, I can.'

'Condor,' McKinnon said. 'Focke-Wulf.' He pointed, 'I can see it now. It's coming straight out of the east and Trondheim is about due east of us now. The pilot of that plane knows exactly where we are. He's been told, probably via Trondheim, by the U-boat that's trailing us.'

'I thought a submarine had to surface to transmit?'

'No. All it has to do is to raise its transmitting aerial above the water. It could do that a couple of miles away and we wouldn't see it. Anyway, it's probably a good deal further distant than that.'

'One wonders what the Condor's intentions are.'

'Your guess, sir. We're not, unfortunately, inside the minds of the U-boat and Luftwaffe commanders in Trondheim. *My* guess is that they're not going to try to finish us off and that's not because they've been at great pains not to sink us so far. If they wanted to sink us, one torpedo from the U-boat I'm sure is out there would do the job nicely. Or, if they wanted to sink us from the air, they wouldn't use a Condor which is really a reconnaissance plane: Heinkels, Heinkel III's or Stukas with long-range tanks could do the job much more efficiently – and Trondheim is only about two hundred miles from here.'

'What's he after, then?' The Condor was two miles distant now and losing height rapidly.

'Information.' McKinnon looked up at the bridge and caught sight of Naseby out on the port wing looking aft towards the approaching Condor. He cupped his hands and shouted: 'George!' Naseby swung round.

'Get down, get down!' McKinnon made the appropriate gesture with his hand. Naseby raised an arm in acknowledgement and disappeared inside the bridge. 'Mr Patterson, let's get inside the superstructure. Now.'

Patterson knew when to ask questions and when not to. He led the way and within ten seconds they were all in shelter except the Bo'sun, who remained in the shattered doorway.

'Information,' Patterson said. 'What information?'

'One moment.' He moved quickly to the side of the ship, looked aft for no more than two seconds, then returned to shelter.

'Half a mile,' McKinnon said. 'Very slow, very low, about fifty feet. Information? Shell-holes, say, on the sides or superstructure, something to indicate that we had been in a fight with some vessel. He won't see any holes on the port side.'

Patterson made to speak but whatever he had to say was lost in the sudden clamour of close-range fire by machine-guns, in the cacophonous fury of hundreds of bullets striking the super-structure and side in the space of seconds, and in the abrupt crescendo of sound as giant aero engines swept by not more than fifty yards away. Another few seconds and all was relatively quiet again.

Jamieson said: 'Well, yes, I can see now why you told Naseby to get his head down.'

'Information.' Patterson sounded aggrieved, al-most plaintive. 'Bloody funny way they set about getting information. And I thought you said they weren't going to attack us.'

'I said they wouldn't sink us. Knocking a few of the crew off would be all grist to their mill. The more of us they can kill, the more they think they'll have us at their mercy.'

'You think they got the information they wanted?'

'I'm certain of it. You can be sure that every eye on that Condor was examining us very closely indeed as they passed by fifty yards away. They won't have seen the damage to our bows because it's underwater but they can't have helped seeing something else that's underwater up for'ard – our load-line. Unless they're completely myopic they're bound to have seen that we're down by

279

the head. And unless they're equally dense they're bound to realize that we've either hit something or been hit by something. It couldn't have been a mine or torpedo or we'd be at the bottom now. They'll have known at once that we must have rammed something and there won't be much guessing about what that was.'

'Dear, oh dear,' Jamieson said, 'I don't think I like this one little bit, Bo'sun.'

'Nor me, sir. Changes things quite a bit, doesn't it? Question of the German high command's priorities, I suppose. A question of alive or dead. Is it more important to them that they take us more or less alive or do they take revenge for their lost U-boat?'

'Whichever they choose, there's damn-all we can do about it,' Patterson said. 'Let's go and have lunch.'

'I think we should wait a moment, sir.' McKinnon remained still and silent for a few moments, then said: 'It's coming back.'

And back it came, flying at the same near wave-top height. The second fly-past was a mirror image of the first: instead of flying stern to stem on the port side it flew stem to stern on the starboard side, again to the accompaniment of the same fusillade of machine-gun fire. Some ten seconds after the firing ceased McKinnon, followed by the others, left the shelter and went to the port rail.

The Condor was off the port quarter, climbing steadily and flying directly away from them.

'Well, well,' Jamieson said. 'We seem to have got off lightly. Bound to have seen those three shell-holes on the starboard side, weren't they, Bo'sun?'

'Couldn't have missed them, sir.'

'They could be gaining bombing altitude before turning back to settle accounts with us?'

'He could bomb us from a hundred feet without the slightest bit of danger to himself.'

'Or maybe he just isn't carrying any bombs?'

'No. He'll be carrying bombs all right. Only the Focke-Wulfs on the big half-circle from Trondheim to Lorient in France round the British Isles, or the ones who patrol as far out as the Denmark Strait don't carry bombs. They carry extra fuel tanks instead. The ones on shorter patrols always carry bombs – 250-kilo bombs, usually, not the smaller ones that Lieutenant Ulbricht used. The pilot of the Condor is, of course, in direct radio communication with Trondheim, has told them why they're not hearing from the U-boat any more, but still has been told to lay off us. For the meantime, anyway.'

'You're right,' Patterson said. 'He's not coming back. Funny. He could have spent all day – till nightfall at least – circling us and reporting our position. But no, he's off. I wonder why.'

'No need to wonder, sir. The Condor's exit is all the proof we require that we are being tailed by a U-boat. No point in having a U-boat and a plane tailing us at the same time.'

'Isn't there anything we can do about that damned U-boat?'

'Well, we can't ram him because we don't know where he is and we can be certain that there's no chance that he'll surface because he's bound to have heard by now – or will hear very soon – what happened to the other U-boat. We can, just possibly, shake him off but not at this moment. Sure, by shutting off our engines and generators we could make him lose contact but that wouldn't be for very long – he'd just raise his periscope, traverse the horizon and nail us again.'

'Not at this moment – you mean, after it gets dark?'

'Yes, I thought we might try then. We lie doggo for half an hour, then steam away on a new course at very low engine revolutions – the less racket we make the less chance there is of our being picked up. Might take us the better part of an hour to reach full speed. At the best, it's only a gamble and even if we do win that gamble it's still no guarantee that we're free and clear. The U-boat will just radio Trondheim that they've lost us. They still know approximately where we are and a Condor with a few dozen flares can cover an awfully big area in a very short time.'

'You do my morale a power of good,' Jamieson said. 'Their tactics puzzle me. Why do they have a Condor fly out here, fly back again and then, as you suggest, fly out here at dusk? Why doesn't it stay out here all the time and have another Condor relieve it. It doesn't make sense to me.'

'It does to me. Although we're still a long way from Aberdeen the German brass-hats in Norway may well be making a decision as to whether or not to try to stop us again. My feeling – it's no more than that – says they will. No way a Condor can stop us without sinking or crippling us. It's become quite clear that they have no wish to sink us or cripple us to the extent that we can no longer proceed under our own steam. The U-boat can surface about a mile off, watch carefully for even a couple of degrees deviation in our course – and they'll be watching for that very, very carefully – then proceed to pump shell after shell into the superstructure and hospital zone until we run up the little white flag.'

'You're a great comfort to me, Bo'sun.'

As McKinnon entered the bridge, Naseby handed him a pair of binoculars.

'Starboard door, Archie. No need to go outside. A bit for'ard of midships. Near enough west, I would say.'

McKinnon took the glasses, studied the area indicated for about ten seconds, then handed the glasses back.

'Mile and a half, I would say. Looks like a mirror only, of course, it's not a mirror, it's a U-boat's periscope reflecting the sun. We, George, are being subjected to psychological warfare.'

'Is that what you call it?'

'Meant to see it, of course. By accident, of course. Carelessness, of course. Slowly, very slowly, George, round to port until we're heading more or less due east, then keep it on that bearing. While you're doing that I'll call up the Chief Engineer and ask his permission.'

He located Patterson in the mess-deck, told him the situation and asked for permission to head east.

'Whatever you say, Bo'sun. Doesn't exactly get us nearer home, does it?'

'That's what will make the Germans happy, sir. It's also what makes me happy. As long as we're heading for Norway, which is where they want us anyway, and not to Scotland, they're hardly likely to clobber us for doing exactly what they want us to do. Come darkness, of course, it's heigh-ho for Scotland again.'

'Satisfactory, Bo'sun, very satisfactory indeed. Do we make the news public?'

'I suggest you tell Mr Jamieson and Lieutenant Ulbricht, sir. As for the rest, any more talk about U-boats would only put them off their lunch.'

TEN

'Have I the ward sister's permission to have a few words with the Captain?'

'The Captain is only two beds away.' Margaret Morrison eyed the Bo'sun speculatively. 'Or do you have another secret session in mind?'

'Well, yes, it is rather private.'

'More U-boat ramming, is it?'

'I never want to see another U-boat in my life.' McKinnon spoke with some feeling. 'The only thing that heroics will get us is an early and watery grave.' He nodded towards the bed where Oberleutnant Klaussen was lying, moving restlessly and mumbling to himself in a barely audible monologue. 'Is he like this all the time?'

'All the time. Never stops rambling on.'

'Does any of what he says make sense?'

'Nothing. Nothing at all.'

McKinnon guided the Captain into a chair in the small lounge off the crew's mess.

'Mr Patterson and Mr Jamieson are here, sir. I wanted them to hear what I have in mind and to have your permission to – perhaps – carry out certain things I have in mind. I have three suggestions to make.

'The first concerns our destination. Are we absolutely committed to Aberdeen, sir? I mean, how ironclad are the Admiralty orders?'

Captain Bowen made a few pointed but unprintable observations about the Admiralty, then said: 'The safety of the *San Andreas* and of all aboard her are of paramount importance. If I consider this safety to be in any way endangered I'll take the *San Andreas* to any safe port in the world and the hell with the Admiralty. We're here, the Admiralty is not. We are in the gravest danger: the biggest peril facing the Admiralty is falling off their chairs in Whitehall.'

'Yes, sir.' The Bo'sun half-smiled, 'I did think those questions rather unnecessary but I had to ask them.'

'Why?'

'Because I'm convinced there's a German espionage network in Murmansk.' He outlined the reasons he had given to Lieutenant Ulbricht less than an hour previously, 'If the Germans know so much about us and our movements, then it's nearer a certainty than a possibility that they also know that our destination is Aberdeen. Maintaining any kind of course for Aberdeen is like handing the Germans a gift from the gods.

'Even more important, from my way of thinking, anyway, is *why* the Germans are so very interested in us. We probably won't know until we arrive in some safe port and even then it might take some time to find out. But if this unknown factor is so very valuable to the Germans, might it not be even more valuable to us? It is my belief – I can't give any solid grounds for this belief – that the Germans would rather lose this valuable prize than let us have it. I have the uncomfortable feeling that if we got anywhere near Aberdeen the Germans would have a submarine, maybe two, loitering somewhere off Peterhead – that's about twenty-five miles nor'-nor'-east of Aberdeen – with orders not to let us move any further south. That could mean only one thing – torpedoes.'

'Say no more, Bo'sun,' Jamieson said. 'You've got me convinced. Here's one passenger who wants Aberdeen struck right off our cruise itinerary.'

'I have a feeling you're right,' Bowen said. 'Maybe one hundred per cent. Even if the chances were only ten per cent we wouldn't be justified in taking the risk. I have a complaint to make against myself, Bo'sun. I'm supposed to be the captain. Why didn't *I* think of that?'

'Because you had other things on your mind, sir.'

'And where does that leave me?' Patterson said.

'I've only just thought of it myself, sir. I'm sure that when Mr Kennet and I were ashore in Murmansk we missed something. We must have. What I still don't understand is why the Russians pulled us into Murmansk, why they were so prompt and efficient in repairing the hole in the hull and completing the hospital. If I had the key to answer that question I'd know the answer to everything, including the answer to why the Russians were so helpful and cooperative, in marked contrast to their standard behaviour which usually ranges from unfriendliness to downright hostility. But I don't have that key.'

'We can only speculate,' Bowen said, 'If you've had time to consider this, Bo'sun, you've obviously had time to consider alternative ports. Safe ports. Bolt-holes, if you like.'

'Yes, sir. Iceland or the Orkneys – that is, Reykjavík or Scapa Flow. Reykjavík has the disadvantage of being half as far away again as Scapa: on the other hand, the further west we go the more we steam out of the reach of the Heinkels and Stukas. Heading for Scapa, we should be within easy reach, practically all the way, of the Heinkels and Stukas based in Bergen and there's the other disadvantage that ever since Oberleutnant Prien sank the *Royal Oak* up there, the mine defences make entry impossible. But it has the advantage that both the Navy and the RAF have bases there. I don't know for certain but I should think it very likely that they maintain frequent air patrols round the Orkneys – after all, it is the base of the Home Fleet. I have no idea how far out those patrols range, fifty miles, a hundred, I don't know. I think there's a good chance that we would be picked up long before we're even near Scapa.'

'Tantamount to being home and dry, is that it, Bo'sun?'

'I wouldn't quite say that, sir. There are always the U-boats.' McKinnon paused and considered. 'As I see it, sir, four things. No British pilot is going to attack a British hospital ship. We'd probably be picked up by a patrol plane like a Blenheim which wouldn't waste much time in calling up fighter support and no German bomber pilot in his senses is going to risk meeting up with Hurricanes or Spitfires. The patrol plane would also certainly radio Scapa to have them open a minefield passage for us. Lastly, they'd probably send out a destroyer or frigate or sloop – something fast, anyway, with enough depth-charges to discourage any U-boat that might be around.'

'Not a very enviable choice,' Bowen said. 'Three days to Scapa, you would say?'

'If we manage to shake off this U-boat which I'm pretty sure is following us. Five days to Reykjavík.'

'What if we don't manage to shake off our shadower? Aren't they going to become very suspicious indeed when they see us altering course for Scapa Flow?'

'If they do succeed in following us, they won't notice any course alteration for a couple of days or more. During that time we'll be on a direct course to Aberdeen. Once we get south of the latitude of

Fair Isle we'll alter course south-west or west-south-west or whatever for Scapa.'

'It's a chance. It's a chance. You have any preference, Mr Patterson?'

'I think I'll leave my preference to the Bo'sun.'

'I second that,' Jamieson said.

'Well?'

'I'd feel happier in Scapa, sir.'

'I think we all would. Well, Bo'sun, suggestion number one dealt with. Number two?'

'There are six exits from the hospital area, sir, three for'ard and three aft. Don't you think it would be wiser, sir, if we had *everybody* confined to the hospital area, except, of course, for those on watch in the engine-room and on the bridge? We know our latest Flannelfoot is still with us and it seems a good idea to confine his sphere of operations – if he has any left, which we don't know – to as limited an area as possible. I suggest we seal up four of those doors, two aft, two for'ard and post guards at the other two doors.'

'Weld them up, you mean?' Jamieson said.

'No. A bomb *might* hit the hospital. The two doors not sealed off *might* buckle and jam. Everyone would be trapped. We just close the doors in the usual way and give them a couple of moderate taps with a sledge.'

Patterson said: 'And maybe Flannelfoot has access to his own private sledgehammer.'

'He'd never dare use it. First metallic clang and he'd have the whole ship's company on his back.'

'True, true.' Patterson sighed, 'I grow old. You had a third point?'

'Yes, sir. Involves you, if you will. I don't think it would do any harm if you were to assemble everybody and tell them what's going on – not that you can get across to Captain Andropolous and his crew – because I'm sure most have no idea what's going on. Tell them about Dr Singh, the transceiver and what happened to Limassol. Tell them that another Flannelfoot is at large and that's why we've closed all four doors so as to limit his movements. Please tell them that although it's not a very nice thing, they are to watch each other like hawks – it is, after all, in their own survival interests – and to report any suspicious behaviour. It might just cramp Flannelfoot's style and it will at least give them something to do.'

Bowen said: 'You really think, Bo'sun, that this – the sealing off of the doors and the warning to the ship's company – will keep Flannelfoot in check?'

'On the basis of our performance to date,' McKinnon said gloomily, 'I very much doubt it.'

The afternoon and the early evening – and even although they were now more than three hundred miles south of the Arctic Circle early evening in those latitudes was still very early indeed – passed away as peacefully as McKinnon had expected. There was no sign of the U-boat but he had been certain that the U-boat would not show itself. There was no sign of any reconnaissance

Condor, which only served to confirm his belief in the enemy concealed below, nor did any Heinkels or Stukas appear over the eastern horizon, for the hour of the *coup de grâce* had not yet come.

Half an hour after sunset the night was as dark as it was likely to become on the Norwegian Sea. Cloud cover was patchy and the rest of the sky hazy although a few pale stars could be seen.

'Time, I think, George,' McKinnon said to Naseby. 'I'm going below. When the engines stop – that should be in seven or eight minutes' time – bring her round 180° till we're heading back the way we came. You should be able to pick up our wash even though it is dark. After that – well, we can only hope that you'll pick up a star. I should be back in about ten minutes or so.'

On his way down he passed the Captain's cabin. There was no longer anyone there to guard the sextant and chronometer: with two of the for'ard exits from the hospital area closed off and the third under guard it was impossible for anyone to reach the upper deck and so the bridge. On the deck it was so dark, the Bo'sun was pleased to note, that he had to use the guideline to find his way to the hospital. Stephen, the young stoker, was there, acting the part of sentry: McKinnon told him to join the others on the mess-decks. When they got there McKinnon found Patterson waiting for him.

'Everybody here, sir?'

'Everybody. Not forgetting Curran and Ferguson.' Those two had been holed up in the

292

carpenter's shop in the bows. 'Riot Act duly read. Anybody making the slightest sound after we stop – after the engines have stopped, rather – inadvertently or not, will be silenced. Talking only in whispers. Tell me, Bo'sun, is it really true that you can pick up the sound of a knife and fork on a plate?'

'I don't really know. I don't know how sensitive the listening devices on a modern U-boat are. I do know that the sound of a spanner being dropped on a steel deck is easily detectable. No chances.'

He went into the two wards, checked that everybody had been told of the need for absolute silence, switched on the emergency lamps and went down to the engine-room. Only Jamieson and McCrimmon were there. Jamieson looked at him and switched on an emergency lamp.

'Now, I take it?'

'It's as dark as it's going to get, sir.'

Even by the time McKinnon had reached the mess-decks the engine revolutions had fallen away. He sat down at a mess table next to Patterson and waited in silence until the engines had stopped and the sound of the generator had died away. With the complete silence and only the feeble light from the emergency lamps to illuminate the area, the atmosphere held the elements of both the eerie and the sinister.

Patterson whispered: 'No chance that the U-boat will think that their listening apparatus has failed?'

'No, sir. You wouldn't have to be a very efficient Asdic operator to know when engine revolutions are falling, then dying away.'

Jamieson and McCrimmon appeared, each carrying an emergency lamp. Jamieson sat beside McKinnon.

'All we need now, Bo'sun, is a ship's chaplain.'

'A few prayers wouldn't come amiss, sir. Especially a prayer that Flannelfoot hasn't got a bug sending out a location signal.'

'Please. Don't even talk about such things.' He was silent for some moments, then said: 'We're heeling, aren't we?'

'We are, yes. Naseby is making a 180° turn, heading back the way we came.'

'Ah!' Jamieson looked thoughtful. 'So that he will over-shoot us. Turning back on our tracks. But won't he do the same? I mean, wouldn't that be the first thing that would occur to him?'

'Quite honestly, I don't and wouldn't have the faintest idea as to what his first, second or tenth thoughts are. His first thought might be that our reversing course is so obvious a ploy that he's not even going to consider it. He might even think that we're carrying straight on for the Norwegian coast, which is so ludicrous a possibility that he may even be considering it. Or we might be heading back north-east again for the Barents Sea. Only a madman would do that, of course, but he'll have to consider the fact, whether we think he thinks we're mad – or not. Alternatively – and there are a lot of alternatives – he may figure that once *we* figure we're clear of his Asdic clutches we'll just continue on our course to Aberdeen. Or some place in north Scotland. Or the Orkneys. Or the Shetlands. There are an awful lot of options open to us and the chances are that he will pick the wrong one.'

'I see,' Jamieson said. 'I say this in admiration, Bo'sun, and not in reproof: you have a very devious mind.'

'Let's just hope the Oberleutnant in charge of that U-boat out there hasn't an even more devious mind.' He turned to Patterson. 'I'm going up top to join Naseby and see if there's any sign of life around.'

'Sign of life? You mean you think the U-boat may have surfaced and is looking for us.'

'May have done.'

'But it's dark, you said.'

'He'll have a searchlight. Two of them, for all I know.'

Jamieson said: 'And you think he'll be using them?'

'It's a possibility. Not a probability. He's bound to know by this time what happened to his fellow U-boat this morning.'

Patterson touched his arm. 'You wouldn't – ah – be considering another possibility – another collision?'

'Heavens, no. I don't really think the *San Andreas* could survive another bump like that. Not, of course, that the captain of that submarine is to know that. He may well be convinced that we're desperate enough for anything.'

'And we're not?'

'It's a long way down to the bottom of the Norwegian Sea.' McKinnon paused reflectively. 'What we really need now is a nice little old blizzard.'

'Still the Condor, still the flares. Is that it, Bo'sun?'

'It's not a thought that goes away easily.' He turned to Jamieson. 'Under way in half an hour, sir?'

'Half an hour it is. But gently, gently?'

'If you would, sir.'

McKinnon examined the sea from both sides of the upper deck but all was dark and quiet and still. He climbed to the bridge and went out on the wings, but even from this higher perspective there was nothing to be seen, no sweeping finger of a searchlight, nothing.

'Well, George, this makes a change. All is quiet, all is peaceful.'

'Is that a good sign or a bad one?'

'Take your pick. Still quite a bit under way, aren't we?'

'Yes. I've just picked up our wake. And I've just located a couple of stars, one off the port bow, the other off the starboard. No idea what they are, of course, but it should keep us heading more or less west until we come to a halt.'

'Which should take quite a while yet.'

*   *   *

In just under fifteen minutes the *San Andreas* was dead in the water and fifteen minutes after that she came to life again, albeit very, very slowly. From the bridge any sounds from the engine-room were quite inaudible, the only indication that they were under way came from the very faint vibration of the superstructure. After a few minutes McKinnon said: 'Any steerage way yet, George?'

'Barely. We're about ten degrees off course right now. To the south. A couple of minutes and we'll be heading west again. I wonder, I wonder.'

'You wonder, I wonder, we all wonder – are we alone in the Norwegian Sea or do we have company, company that has no intention of making its presence known? I just guess and hope that we're alone. Beyond a certain distance a submarine is not very good at picking up a very slow-turning engine and prop. What it can pick up is a generator – which is why there will be no lights down below for another fifteen minutes yet.'

Just under half an hour after McKinnon had arrived on the bridge the telephone bell shrilled. Naseby answered and handed the phone to the Bo'sun.

'Bo'sun? This is Ward A. Sinclair speaking. I think you had better come down.' Sinclair sounded weary or dispirited, or both. 'Flannelfoot has struck again. There's been an accident. No need to break your neck, though – nobody's been hurt.'

'We've been far too long without an accident.'
The Bo'sun felt as weary as Sinclair. 'What happened?'

'Transceiver's wrecked.'

'That's just splendid. I'm on my way – at a leisurely pace.' He replaced the phone. 'Flannelfoot's at it again, George. It seems that the transceiver in Ward A is not quite what it was.'

'Oh Jesus.' It wasn't an exclamation of shock, horror or anger, just a sign of resignation. 'Why wasn't the alarm buzzer pressed.'

'I shall no doubt find that out when I get there. I'll send Trent to relieve you. I suggest you broach Captain Bowen's supplies. Life aboard the *San Andreas*, George, is like life everywhere, just one damned thing after another.'

The first thing that took McKinnon's eye in Ward A was not the transceiver in the Cardiac Arrest box but the sight of Margaret Morrison, eyes closed, lying on a bed with Janet Magnusson bending over her. The Bo'sun looked at Dr Sinclair, who was sitting disconsolately in the chair that was normally occupied by the ward sister.

'I thought you said nobody had been hurt.'

'Not hurt in the medical sense, although Sister Morrison might take issue with me on that matter. She's been chloroformed but will be fine in a few minutes.'

'Chloroformed? Flannelfoot doesn't seem to have a very original turn of mind.'

'He's a callous bastard. This girl has just been wounded, once quite nastily, but this character seems to have been missing when they handed out humanitarian instincts.'

'You expect delicacy and a tenderness of feeling from a criminal who tries to murder a man with a crowbar?' McKinnon walked to the side of the table and looked down at the mangled remains of the transceiver. 'I'll spare you the obvious remarks. Naturally, of course, no one knows what happened because of course there were no eye-witnesses.'

'That's about it. If it's any use, Nurse Magnusson here was the person to discover this.'

McKinnon looked at her. 'Why did you come through? Did you hear a noise?'

She straightened from the bed and looked at him with some disfavour.

'You *are* a cold-blooded fish, Archie McKinnon. This poor, poor girl lying here, the radio smashed and you don't even look upset or annoyed, far less furious. *I* am furious.'

'I can see that. But Margaret will be all right and the set is a total ruin. I see no point in getting angry about things I can do nothing about and what passes for my mind has other things to worry about. Did you hear anything?'

'You're hopeless. No, I heard nothing. I just came in to talk to her. She was crumpled over her table. I ran for Dr Sinclair and we lifted her into this bed here.'

'Surely *someone* saw *something*. They couldn't all have been asleep.'

'No. The Captain and the Chief Officer were awake.' She smiled sweetly. 'You may have noticed, Mr McKinnon, that the eyes of both Captain Bowen and Chief Officer Kennet are heavily bandaged.'

'You just wait,' McKinnon said *sotto voce*, 'until I get you to the Shetlands. They think a lot of me in Lerwick.' She made a *moue* and the Bo'sun looked across to Bowen. 'Did you hear anything, Captain?'

'I heard something that sounded like the tinkling of glass. Wasn't much, though.'

'You, Mr Kennet?'

'Same, Bo'sun. Again it wasn't much.'

'It didn't have to be. You don't require a sledgehammer to crush a few valves. A little pressure from the sole of the foot would be enough.' He turned to Janet again. 'But Margaret wouldn't have been asleep. She'd have been bound – no, he couldn't have come that way. He'd have had to pass through your ward. I'm not being very bright today, am I?'

'No, you're not.' She smiled again but this time without malice. 'Not our usual hawk-eyed selves this evening, are we?'

McKinnon turned and looked past the Sister's table. The door to the recovery room was about an inch ajar. McKinnon nodded.

'It figures. Why should he bother to close it when it would be obvious to anyone with half an eye – he must have forgotten about me – that there was no

300

other way he could have entered. Mess-deck, side passage, operating room, recovery room, Ward A – simple as that. Every door unlocked, of course. Why should they have been otherwise? Well, we don't bother locking them now. When did this happen, anyone know – sometime between engine start-up and the lights coming back on again?'

'I think it had to be that,' Sinclair said. 'It would have been the ideal time and opportunity. About ten minutes after start-up but five minutes before the generator came on Mr Patterson gave permission for people to talk normally and move around as long as they didn't make any loud noise. The emergency lights are pretty feeble at the best of times, everyone was talking excitedly – relief of tension I suppose, hopes that we had slipped the submarine, thankfulness that we were still in one piece, that sort of thing – and lots of people moving around. It would have been childishly simple for anyone to disappear unnoticed and return again after a minute, still unnoticed.'

'Had to be that,' the Bo'sun said. 'Anyone of the crew, or that lot from Murmansk – in fact, anyone who was out there. Still no nearer the identity of the man with the key to the dispensary. Captain, Mr Kennet, I am wondering why you didn't call Sister Morrison. Surely you must have smelled the chloroform?'

Janet said: 'Oh, come on Archie, you can see that their noses are bandaged up. Could you smell anything with a handkerchief to your nose?'

'You're just half right, Nurse,' Bowen said. 'I did smell it but it was very faint. The trouble is that there are so many medical and antiseptic smells in a ward that I paid no attention to it.'

'Well, he wouldn't have gone back to the mess-deck with a sponge reeking of chloroform. Hands too, for that matter. Back in a moment.'

The Bo'sun unhooked an emergency light, went into the recovery room, looked around briefly, then passed into the operating theatre where he switched on the lights. Almost immediately, in a bucket in a corner, he found what he was looking for and returned to Ward A.

'A sponge – duly reeking of chloroform – a smashed ampoule and a pair of rubber gloves. Quite useless.'

'Not to Flannelfoot, they weren't,' Sinclair said.

'Useless to us. Useless as evidence. Gets us nowhere.' McKinnon perched on the Sister's table and looked in slight irritation at Oberleutnant Klaussen who was muttering away to himself, unintelligibly, incessantly.

'Is he still like this? Always like this?'

Sinclair nodded. 'Goes on non-stop.'

'Must be damned annoying. To the other patients and to the sister or nurse in charge. Why isn't his bed wheeled into the recovery room?'

'Because the sister in charge – that's Margaret, remember? – doesn't want him removed.' Janet was being cool and patient. 'He's her patient, she wants to keep a close eye on him and she doesn't mind. Any more questions, Archie?'

'You mean why don't I be on my way or keep quiet or go and do something. Do what? Do some detecting?' He looked gloomy. 'There's nothing to detect. I'm just waiting till Margaret comes round.'

'Signs of grace at last.'

'I want to ask her some questions.'

'I might have known. What questions? It's as certain as can be that the assailant crept up behind her unseen and had her unconscious before she knew anything about it. Otherwise she'd have reached for the button or called for help. She did neither. There are no questions you can ask her that we can't answer.'

'As I'm not a gambler I won't take your money away from you. Question number one. How did Flannelfoot know – and he *must* have known – that, apart from Captain Bowen and Mr Kennet who are effectively blind at the moment, everyone else in Ward A was asleep? He would never have dared to do what he did if there was even a remote possibility of someone being awake. So how did he know? Answer, please.'

'I – I don't know.' She was obviously taken aback. 'That had never occurred to me before. But I don't think it occurred to anyone else either.'

'Understandable. Such questions occur only to stupid old bo'suns. You're just being defensive, Janet. Question number two. *Who* told him?'

'I don't know that either.'

'But maybe Maggie does. Number three. What solicitous member of the crew or passengers made solicitous enquiries about the state of health of the patients in Ward A?'

'How should I know?'

'Maggie might know, mightn't she? After all, she would be the obvious choice to be asked that question, wouldn't she? And you said you could answer any questions that she could. Bosh! Question number four.'

'Archie, you're beginning to sound like a prosecuting counsel. I'm not guilty of anything.'

'Don't be daft. You're not in dock. Fourth question and the most important of all. Flannelfoot, as we all know to our cost, is no fool. He must have taken into account the possibility that someone would ask the question of Maggie: with whom, Sister Morrison, did you discuss the state of health of your patients? He *had* to assume that Maggie was in the position to put the finger on him. So my question is why, to protect his anonymity, did he not, after rendering her unconscious, slit her throat? A nice sharp knife is just as silent as a chloroform sponge. It would have been the logical thing to do, wouldn't it, Janet? But he didn't. Why didn't he murder her?'

Janet had gone very pale and when she spoke her voice was barely above a whisper.

'Horrible,' she said. 'Horrible, horrible.'

'Are you referring to me again? Goes well, I must say with what you last called me – a heartless fiend.'

'Not you, not you.' Her voice was still unsteady. 'It's the question. The thought. The possibility. It – it could have happened that way, couldn't it, Archie?'

'I'm more than mildly astonished that it didn't. But I think we'll find the answer when Maggie wakes up.'

The silence that fell upon the ward was broken by Bowen.

'Very gallant of you, Bo'sun, very gallant indeed. Not to have reproached the young lady for being unable, as she had claimed she could, to answer the questions you asked. If it's any consolation to your friend Janet, not one of those questions occurred to me either.'

'Thank you, sir,' she said. 'That was very kind of you. Makes me feel more than halfway better already. See, Archie, I can't be all that stupid.'

'Nobody ever suggested you were. How long will it take her to come round, Dr Sinclair?'

'Five minutes, fifteen, twenty-five? Impossible to say. People vary so much in their recovery times. And even when she does come out of it she'll be fuzzy for some time, not mentally clear enough to remember and answer what might be difficult questions.'

'When she is, call me, please. I'll be on the bridge.'

ELEVEN

Half an hour later McKinnon joined Margaret Morrison in the small lounge off the mess-deck. She was pale and unsmiling but looked composed enough. He sat down opposite her.

'How do you feel now?'

'Bit sick. Bit nauseated.' She half-smiled. 'Dr Sinclair seemed to be more concerned about the state of my mind. I think that's well enough.'

'Fine. Well, not fine, it was a damnable thing to happen to you, but I feel less like commiserating with you than congratulating you.'

'I know. Janet told me. I'm not one for mock shudders, Archie – but, well, he could have done, couldn't he? I mean, cut my throat.'

'He could have done. He should have done.'

'Archie!'

'Oh God, that wasn't very well put, was it? I meant that for his own sake he should have done. He may just possibly have given away enough rope to hang himself.'

'I don't understand what you mean.' She smiled to rob her words of offence. 'I don't think anyone understands quite what you mean. Janet says you're a very devious character.'

'Be you white as snow, etcetera. Only the truly honest get maligned in this fashion. A cross one has to bear.'

'I have difficulty in seeing you in the role of martyr. Janet said you had lots of questions to ask me.'

'Not lots. Just one. Well, a few, but all the same question. Where were you this afternoon before we stopped?'

'In the mess-deck. Out there. Then I went to relieve Irene just before the lights went out.'

'Anyone enquire about the health of the patients in Ward A when you were out there?'

'Well, yes.' She seemed faintly surprised. 'I often get asked about the patients. Natural, isn't it?'

'This late afternoon, I meant.'

'Yes. I told them. Also natural, isn't it?'

'Did they ask if anyone was asleep?'

'No. Come to think of it, they didn't have to. I remember telling them that only the Captain and First Officer were awake. It was some sort of joke.' She broke off, touched her lips with her hand and looked thoroughly chagrined. 'I see. It wasn't really such a joke, was it – it let me in for half-an-hour's involuntary sleep, didn't it?'

'I'm afraid it did. Who asked the question?'

'Wayland Day.'

'Ah! Our pantry boy – ex-pantry boy, I should say, and now your faithful shadow and worshipper from afar.'

'Not always as far away as you might think, gets a little embarrassing at times.' She smiled and then was suddenly serious. 'You're barking up the wrong tree, Archie. He may be a bit of a pest, but he's only a boy and a very nice boy. It's unthinkable.'

'I don't see a tree in sight. Agree, unthinkable. Our Wayland would never be a party to anything that might harm you. Who were the others at your table? Within hearing distance, I mean.'

'How do you know there was anyone else at my table?'

'Margaret Morrison is too clever to be stupid.'

'That *was* stupid. Maria was there –'

'Sister Maria?' She nodded. 'She's out. Who else?'

'Stephen. The Polish boy. Can't pronounce his surname – no one can. Then there were Jones and McGuigan, who are nearly always with Wayland Day – I suppose because they are the three youngest members of the crew. Two seamen by the name of Curran and Ferguson – I hardly know them because I hardly ever see them. And, yes, I seem to remember there were two of the sick men we picked up in Murmansk. I don't know their names.'

'You *seem* to remember?'

308

'No. I do. It's because I don't know their names, I suppose. I'm sure one's a TB case, the other a nervous breakdown.'

'You could identify them again?'

'Easily. Both had red hair.'

'E.R.A. Hartley and L.T.O. Simons.' McKinnon opened the lounge door. 'Wayland!'

Wayland Day appeared within seconds and stood at respectful attention. 'Sir.'

'Go and find Mr Patterson and Mr Jamieson. Oh yes, and Lieutenant Ulbricht. My compliments to them and ask them if they would please come here.'

'Yes, sir. Right away, sir.'

Margaret Morrison looked at the Bo'sun in amusement. 'How did you know that Wayland was so close?'

'Ever tried to lose your shadow on a sunny day? I can prophesy things – nothing to do with the second sight – such as that Lieutenant Ulbricht will be the first along.'

'Oh, do be quiet. Has this been of any good to you? Another stupid question. Must have been or you wouldn't have sent for those three.'

'Indeed it has. Another little complication but I think we can manage it. Ah, Lieutenant Ulbricht. That was very quick. Please sit down.' Ulbricht took his seat by the side of Margaret Morrison while McKinnon contemplated the ceiling.

She said in a vexed voice: 'There's no need for that.'

Ulbricht looked at her. 'What do you mean, Margaret?'

'The Bo'sun has a warped sense of humour.'

'Not at all. She just doesn't like me being right.' He looked round, greeted Patterson and Jamieson then rose and closed the door with a firm hand.

'As serious as that, is it?' Patterson said.

'I'd rather we weren't overheard, sir.' He gave them a brief résumé of the talks he'd had with Janet Magnusson and Margaret Morrison, then said: 'One of those nine people within hearing distance of Sister Morrison knew that Captain Bowen and Mr Kennet were the only two patients in Ward A who were awake and made the fullest use of that information. Agreed?'

No one disagreed.

'We can rule out Sister Maria. No hard reason, except that it's inconceivable.'

'Inconceivable.' Both Patterson and Jamieson spoke at the same time.

'Stephen? No. He's pro-British enough to make us all feel ashamed and he'll never forget that it was the Royal Navy that saved his life in the North Sea.'

Margaret Morrison looked up in surprise. 'I didn't know that.'

'Neither did we, Sister, even although he is in the engine-room department. Not till the Bo'sun told us. His agents are in every nook and cranny.' Patterson seemed slightly aggrieved.

'Wayland Day, Jones and McGuigan. No. They're hardly out of kindergarten and haven't lived enough or been steeped enough in sin to make apprentice counter-espionage agents, junior grade. That leaves us with four suspects.'

'Curran and Ferguson are out. I know them. They are shirkers and malingerers of the first order and haven't the energy, interest or intelligence to make the grade. That apart, they spend all their spare time holed up in the carpenter's shop in the bows and leave it so seldom that they can hardly know what's going on in the rest of the ship. Final proof, of course, is that though they may not be very bright they're hardly stupid enough to set off an explosive charge in the ballast room while they are sleeping in the carpenter's shop directly above. That leaves Simons and Hartley, two of the sick men – or allegedly sick men – that we picked up in Murmansk. Don't you think we should have them up here, Mr Patterson?'

'I do indeed, Bo'sun. This is becoming interesting.'

McKinnon opened the door. 'Wayland!'

If possible, Wayland Day made it in even less time than the previous occasion. McKinnon gave him his instructions, then added: 'Have them here in five minutes. Tell them to bring their pay-books.' He closed the door and looked at Margaret Morrison.

'Wouldn't you like to leave now?'

311

'No, I wouldn't. Why should I? I'm as inter-ested and involved in this as any of you.' In a wholly unconscious gesture, she touched her throat. 'More, I would say.'

'You might not like it.'

'A Gestapo-type interrogation, is that it?'

'How they are treated depends entirely on Mr Patterson. I'm only venturing an opinion, but I wouldn't think that Mr Patterson goes in very much for thumbscrews and racks. Not standard engine-room equipment.'

She looked at him coldly. 'Facetiousness does not become you.'

'Very little does, it seems.'

'Hartley and Simons,' Jamieson said. 'We had them on our list of suspects. Well, more or less. Remember, Bo'sun?'

'I remember. I also remember that we agreed that the CID were in no danger of a takeover from us.'

'Something I have to say,' Ulbricht said. 'Discouraging, but I have to say it. I was here from the time the generator lights went out until they came on again. With their red heads, those two men are unmistakable. Neither of them left their seats in that time.'

'Well, now.' Margaret Morrison had an air of satisfaction about her. 'Rather puts a damper on your theory doesn't it, Mr McKinnon?'

'Sad, Sister, very sad. You really would like to prove me wrong, wouldn't you? I have the odd feeling that I will have been proved wrong before this trip is over. Not by you, though.' He shook his head. 'It's still sad.'

Sister Morrison could be very persistent. She put on her best ward sister's face and said: 'You heard what the Lieutenant said – neither of those two men left their seats during the crucial period.'

'I should be astonished if they had done.' Margaret Morrison's prim frown gave way to perplexity which in turn yielded to a certain wariness. McKinnon looked at Ulbricht. 'Lieutenant, we are not just dealing with Flannelfoot number two: we are dealing with Flannelfeet numbers two and three. We have established that it was number two, a crew member, who blew the hole in the ballast room when we were alongside that sinking corvette. But no crew member under suspicion was within hearing range of Sister Morrison. So the finger points at Hartley or Simons. Maybe both. It was clever. There was no way we could reasonably associate them with the misfortune of the *San Andreas*, for at the time the first hole was blown in the ballast they were still in hospital in Murmansk, where one or both had been suborned. Of course neither was going to leave his seat during the time of the attack. That could have been too obvious.'

Ulbricht tapped his head. 'The only thing that is obvious to me is that Lieutenant Ulbricht is not at his brightest and best today. Hit me over the head with a two-by-four long enough and I'll see the point as fast as any man. Of course you have the right of it. Obvious.' He looked at Margaret Morrison. 'Don't you agree?'

There was a distinct tinge of red in the normally pale face. 'I suppose so.'

'There's no supposing.' The Bo'sun sounded slightly weary. 'What happened was that the information was passed on before – well before – the engines stopped. How long before the engines stopped did Wayland Day ask you the question about Ward A?'

'I don't know. I'm not sure.'

'Come on, Margaret. Can't you see it's important?'

'Fifteen minutes?' she said uncertainly. 'Maybe twenty. I'm really not sure.'

'Of course you're not. People don't check their watches every five minutes. But during those fifteen or twenty minutes one of those two men left his seat and returned?'

'Yes.' Her voice was very low.

'Which one?'

'I don't know. I really don't. Please believe me. I know I said earlier that I could easily identify them –'

'Please, Margaret. I believe you. What you meant is that you could identify them as a pair, not individually. Both look uncommonly alike, both have red hair and you didn't even know their names.'

She smiled at him, a grateful little smile, but said nothing.

'You do have the right of it, Bo'sun. Apart from that, I'm convinced of it because there's no other explanation.' Patterson rubbed his chin. 'This inter-rogation business. Like Mr Jamieson and yourself, I don't really think I'm CID material. How do we set about it?'

'I suggest we first try to establish their bona fides – if any – to see if they are what they say they are. Hartley claims to be an Engine-Room Artificer. I'll leave him to you. Simons says he's a Leading Torpedo Operator. I'll speak to him.' He looked at his watch. 'The five minutes are up.'

Patterson didn't invite either man to sit. For some seconds he looked at them coolly and thought-fully, then said: 'My name is Chief Engineer Patterson. I am in temporary command of this vessel and have some questions to ask. The rea-sons for the questioning can wait. Which of you is E.R.A. Hartley?'

'I am, sir.' Hartley was slightly taller, slightly more heavily built than Simons, but otherwise the resemblance was remarkable: Margaret Morrison's confusion over the pair was more than under-standable.

'You claim to be an E.R.A. Can you prove it?'

'Prove it?' Hartley was taken aback. 'What do you mean – "prove it", sir? I don't have any cer-tificates on me if that's what you're after.'

'You could pass a practical test?'

'A practical test?' Hartley's face cleared. 'Of course, sir. I've never been in your engine-room but that's no matter. An E.R.A. is an E.R.A. Take me to your engine-room and I'll identify any piece of equipment you have. I can do that blindfold – all I have to do is touch. I'll tell you the purpose of that or any piece of equipment and I can strip it down and put it together again.'

'Hm.' Patterson looked at Jamieson. 'What do you think?'

'I wouldn't waste our time, sir.'

'Neither would I.' He nodded to the Bo'sun, who looked at Simons.

'You L.T.O. Simons?'

'Yeah. And who are you?' McKinnon looked at the thin arrogant face and thought it unlikely that they would ever be blood-brothers. 'You're not an officer.'

'I'm a seaman.'

'I don't answer questions from a Merchant Navy seaman.'

'You will, you know,' Patterson said. 'Mr McKinnon is hardly the equivalent of the Royal Navy's ordinary seaman. The senior seaman aboard, the equivalent of your warrant officer. Not that it matters to you what he is. He's acting under my orders and if you defy him you defy me. You understand?'

'No.'

McKinnon said in a mild voice: ' "No, *sir*," when you're talking to a senior officer.'

Simons sneered, there was a blur of movement and Simons was doubled over, making retching sounds and gasping for breath. McKinnon looked at him unemotionally as he gradually straightened and said to Patterson: 'May I have an option as regards this man, sir? He's an obvious suspect.'

'He is. You may.'

'Either irons, bread and water till we reach port or a private interrogation with me.'

'Irons!' Simons' voice was a wheeze, a McKinnon jab to the solar plexus was not something from which one made an instant recovery. 'You can't do that to me.'

'I can and if necessary will.' Patterson's tone was chillingly indifferent, 'I am in command of this ship. If I choose, I can have you over the side. Alternatively, if I have proof that you are a spy, I can have you shot as a spy. Wartime regulations say so.' Wartime regulations, in fact, said nothing of the kind but it was most unlikely that Simons knew this.

'I'll settle for the private interrogation,' McKinnon said.

A horrified Margaret Morrison said: 'Archie, you can't –'

'Be quiet.' Patterson's voice was cold, 'I suggest, Simons, that you will be well advised to answer a few simple questions.' Simons scowled and said nothing.

McKinnon said: 'You an L.T.O?'

''Course I am.'

'Can you prove it?'

'Like Hartley here, I haven't any certificates with me. And *you* don't have any torpedoes to test me with. Not that you would know one end of a torpedo from another.'

'What's your barracks?'

'Portsmouth.'

'Where did you qualify L.T.O.?'

'Portsmouth, of course.'

'When?'

'Early 'forty-three.'

'Let me see your pay-book.' McKinnon examined it briefly, then looked up at Simons. 'Very new and very clean.'

'Some people look after their things.'

'You didn't make a very good job of looking after your old one, did you?'

'What the hell do you mean?'

'This is either a new one, a stolen one or a forged one.'

'God's sake, I don't know what you're talking about!'

'You know all right.' The Bo'sun tossed the pay-book on the table. 'That's a forgery, you're a liar and you're not an L.T.O. Unfortunately for you, Simons, I was a Torpedo Gunner's Mate in the Navy. No L.T.O's qualified in Portsmouth in early nineteen forty-three, or indeed for some considerable time before and after that. They qualified at Roedean College near Brighton – used to be the leading girls' school in Britain before the war.

You're a fraud and a spy, Simons. What's the name of your accomplice aboard the *San Andreas*?'

'I don't know what you're talking about.'

'Amnesia.' McKinnon stood and looked at Patterson. 'Permission to lock him up, sir?'

'Permission granted.'

'Nobody's going to bloody well lock me up,' Simons shouted. 'I demand – ' His voice broke off in a scream as McKinnon twisted his forearm high up behind his back.

'You'll stay here, sir?' McKinnon said. Patterson nodded. 'I won't be long. Five, ten minutes. We won't be needing E.R.A. Hartley any more?'

'Of course not. Sorry about that, E.R.A. But we had to know.'

'I understand, sir.' It was quite apparent that he did not understand.

'You don't. But we'll explain later.' Hartley left, followed by McKinnon and Simons, the latter with his right wrist still somewhere up in the vicinity of his left shoulder-blade.

'Ten minutes,' Margaret Morrison said. 'It takes ten minutes to lock up a man.'

'Sister Morrison,' Patterson said. She looked at him. 'I admire you as a nurse. I like you as a person. But don't interfere in things or presume to pass judgement on things you know nothing about. The Bo'sun may only be a bo'sun but he operates at a level you know nothing about. If it weren't for him you'd be either a prisoner or dead. Instead of constantly sniping at him you'd be

319

better occupied in giving thanks for a world where there's still a few Archie McKinnons around.' He broke off and cursed in silent self-reproach as he saw tears trickling down the lowered head.

McKinnon pushed Simons inside an empty cabin, locked the door, pocketed the key, turned and hit Simons in exactly the same spot as previously although with considerably more force. Simons staggered backwards across the corticene, smashed heavily into the bulkhead and slid to the deck. McKinnon picked him up, held his right arm against the bulkhead and struck his right biceps with maximum power. Simons screamed, tried to move his right arm and found it impossible: it was completely paralysed. The Bo'sun repeated the process on the left arm and let him slide down again.

'I am prepared to keep this up indefinitely,' McKinnon's voice was conversational, almost pleasant. 'I'm going to keep on hitting you, and if necessary, kicking you anywhere between your shoulders and toes. There won't be a mark on your face. I don't like spies, I don't like traitors and I don't care too much for people with innocent blood on their hands.'

McKinnon returned to the lounge and resumed his seat. Ulbricht looked at his watch and said: 'Four minutes. My word, you do keep *your* word, Mr McKinnon.'

'A little dispatch, that's all.' He looked at Margaret Morrison and the still visible tear stains. 'What's wrong?'

'Nothing. It's just this whole horrible ugly business.'

'It's not nice.' He looked at her for a speculative moment, made as if to say something, then changed his mind. 'Simons has come all over cooperative and volunteered some information.'

'Cooperative?' Margaret said incredulously. 'Volunteered?'

'Never judge a man by his appearances. There are hidden depths in all of us. His name is not Simons, it's Braun, "au", not "ow".'

'German, surely,' Patterson said.

'Sounds that way but he *is* RN. His passport is a forgery – someone in Murmansk gave it to him. He couldn't be more specific than that, I assume it must have been a member of what *must* now be that espionage ring up there. He's not an L.T.O., he's an S.B.A., a Sick Bay Attendant, which ties in rather nicely with the chloroform used twice and the drugging of Captain Andropolous.' He tossed two keys on the table. 'I'm sure Dr Sinclair will confirm that those are the dispensary keys.'

'Goodness me,' jamieson said. 'You have not been idle, Bo'sun, and that's a fact. He – Braun – must have been most communicative.'

'He was indeed. He even gave me the identity of Flannelfoot number two.'

'What!'

'Remember, Margaret, that I said to you only a few minutes ago that I would be proved wrong about something before the trip was over. Well, it hasn't taken long for me to prove I was right about that. It's McCrimmon.'

'McCrimmon!' Jamieson was half out of his seat. 'McCrimmon. That bloody young bastard!'

'You are sitting – well, more or less – next to a young lady.' McKinnon's tone of reproof was mild.

'Ah! Yes. So I am. Sorry, Sister.' Jamieson sat again. 'But – McCrimmon!'

'I think the fault is mainly mine, sir. I've been on record as saying that although he was a criminal, I regarded him as a trustworthy criminal. Serious flaw in judgement. But I was half right.'

'I can accept that it was McCrimmon.' Patterson's tone was calm and if he was upset it wasn't showing. 'Never liked him. Truculent, offensive, foul-mouthed. Two terms in Barlinnie, the maximum security prison outside Glasgow. Both for street violence. I should imagine that the feel of an iron crowbar in his hand is nothing new to that man. The Royal Navy would never have accepted a man with his record. One can only assume that we have lower standards.' He paused and considered. 'We pull him in?'

'I wonder. I'd love to have a little chat with him. Point is, Mr Patterson, I don't think we'd get any useful information out of him. Men who hired him would be far too clever to tell a character like McCrimmon any more than he needed to know. They certainly wouldn't tell him what their plans, their end was. It would be a case of "just do so-and-so and here's your cash". Also, sir, if we leave him loose, we can watch every move he makes without his knowing that we are watching. It's quite possible he has something more up his sleeve and if we can watch him in the act of what he's doing it might give us some very valuable information indeed. What, I can't imagine, but I have the feeling that we should give him that little more rope.'

'I agree. If he's bent on hanging himself, just that little more rope.'

Lieutenant Ulbricht had found them a star to steer themselves by. He was on the bridge with McKinnon as the San Andreas headed due west at full speed, Curran at the wheel. Cloud cover was patchy, the wind light and the sea relatively calm. Ulbricht had just caught a brief but sufficient glance of the Pole Star and had established that they were in almost exactly the same place as they had been at noon that morning. He had remained on the bridge where he seemed to prefer to spend his time except, the Bo'sun couldn't help noticing, during those periods when Margaret Morrison was off duty.

'Think we've shaken him now, Mr McKinnon? Three and a half hours, maybe four, since we *may* have shaken him.'

'Nor hide nor hair of him and that's a fact. But because we can't see him, as I keep on saying, doesn't mean that he's not there. But, yes, I do have this odd feeling that we may have slipped him.'

'I have a certain regard for your so-called odd feelings.'

'I only said "may". We won't know for certain until the first Condor comes along with its flares.'

'I wish you wouldn't talk about such things. Anyway, it's possible that we may have lost him *and* that the Focke-Wulf may fail to find us. How long do you intend to maintain this course?'

'The longer the better, I should think. *If* they have lost us, then they'll probably reason that we're heading back on a course to Aberdeen – as far as we know, they have no reason to believe that we have reason to believe that they know we're heading for Aberdeen and would therefore opt for some place else. So they may still think that we're on a roughly south-south-west course instead of due west. I have heard it said, Lieutenant Ulbricht, I can't remember who it was, that some Germans at some times have one-track minds.'

'Nonsense. Look at our poets and playwrights, our composers and philosophers.' Ulbricht was silent for some moments and McKinnon could imagine him smiling to himself in the darkness. 'Well, yes, maybe now and again. I sincerely hope that this is one of those times. The longer they keep combing the area in the direction of Aberdeen and the longer we keep heading west the less chance they will have of locating us. So we keep this course for an hour or two more?'

'Yes. Longer. I propose that we maintain this course throughout the night, then, shortly before dawn, lay off a course directly for Scapa Flow.'

'Sounds fair enough to me. That'll mean leaving the Shetlands on our port hand. May even have a glimpse of your islands. Pity you couldn't drop in in passing.'

'There'll come a day. Dinner-time, Lieutenant.'

'So soon? Mustn't miss that. Coming?'

'May as well. Curran, get on the phone and ask Ferguson to come up here. Tell him to keep a constant look-out on both wings. 360 degrees, you understand.'

'I'll do that. What's he supposed to be looking out for, Bo'sun?'

'Flares.'

McKinnon met Jamieson just after they'd entered the mess-deck and drew him to one side.

'Our traitorous friend been up to anything he should not have been up to, sir?'

'No. Guaranteed. Chief Patterson and I had a discussion and we decided to take all the engine-room staff into our confidence – well, all except one, Reilly, who seems to be the only person who talks to him. Reilly apart, McCrimmon would win any unpopularity contest without trying, he's the most cordially detested person in the engine-room. So we spoke to each man individually, told them the score, and told them not to discuss the matter with any other member of the crew. So he'll be under constant supervision, both in the engine-room and in the mess-decks.' He looked closely at McKinnon. 'We thought it a good idea. You don't seem quite sure?'

'Whatever you and Mr Patterson decide is okay by me.'

'Dammit.' Jamieson spoke with some feeling. 'I suggested to the Chief that we talk to you but he was sure you'd think it a good idea.'

'I really don't know, sir.' McKinnon was doubt-ful. 'It *seems* a good idea. But – well, McCrimmon may be a villain but he's a clever villain. Don't for-get that he's gone completely undetected and unsuspected so far and would have kept on that way but for a lucky accident. Being a crude, vio-lent and detestable person with a penchant for crowbars doesn't mean that he can't be sensitive to atmosphere, to people being over-casual on the one hand and too furtively watchful on the other. Also, if Reilly is on speaking terms with him shouldn't he be under observation too?'

'It's not all that bad, Bo'sun. Even if he does suspect he's under observation, isn't that a guar-antee for his good behaviour?'

'Either that or a guarantee that when – if – he does something he shouldn't be doing he's going to make damn sure that there's no one around when he does it, which is the last thing we wanted. If he believed he was still in the clear he might have betrayed himself. Now he never will.' McKinnon looked at their table. 'Where's Mr Patterson?'

Jamieson looked uncomfortable. 'Keeping an eye on things.'

'Keeping an eye on things? Keeping an eye on McCrimmon, you mean. Mr Patterson has never missed dinner since joining this ship. You know that, I know that – and you can be sure McCrimmon knows that. If he has the slightest suspicion that we have the slightest suspicion I can just hear those alarm bells clanging in his head.'

'It *is* possible,' Jamieson said slowly, 'that it may not have been such a good idea after all.'

Patterson wasn't the only absentee at the table that night. Janet Magnusson was on duty and both Sister Maria and Dr Sinclair were engaged in the ticklish and rather painful task of re-bandaging Captain Bowen's head. Captain Bowen, it was reported, was making a considerable amount of noise.

Jamieson said: 'Does Dr Sinclair think he'll be able to see again?' Jamieson, like the three others at the table, was nursing a glass of wine while waiting for the first course to be served.

'He's pretty sure,' Margaret Morrison said. 'So am I. Some days yet, though. The eyelids are badly blistered.'

'And the rest of the ward sound asleep as usual?' She winced and shook her head and Jamieson said hastily: 'Sorry, that wasn't a very tactful question, was it?'

She smiled. 'It's all right. It's just that it'll take me a day or two to get Simons and McCrimmon out of my head. As usual, only Mr Kennet is awake. Perhaps Oberleutnant Klaussen is too – it's hard to say. Never still, keeps rambling on.'

'And making as little sense as ever?' McKinnon said.

'None. All in German, of course, except for one word in English which he keeps repeating over and over again as if he was haunted by it. It's odd, the theme of Scotland keeps cropping up all the time.' She looked at Ulbricht. 'You know Scotland well. We're headed for Scotland. I'm half-Scots. Archie and Janet, although they claim to be Shetlanders, are really Scots.'

McKinnon said: 'And don't forget the lad with the chloroform pad.'

She grimaced. 'I wish you hadn't said that.'

'Sorry. Stupid. And what's the Scots connection with Klaussen?'

'It's the word he keeps repeating. Edinburgh.'

'Ah! Edinburgh. The Athens of the North!' Ulbricht sounded very enthusiastic. 'Know it well, very well. Better than most Scots, I dare say. Edinburgh Castle. Holyrood Palace. The shrine. The Gardens. Princes Street, the most beautiful of all – ' His voice trailed off, then he said in a sharp tone: 'Mr McKinnon! What's the matter?'

The other two looked at the Bo'sun. His eyes were those of a man who was seeing things at a great distance and the knuckles of the big hand around the glass were showing white. Suddenly the glass shattered and the red wine flowed over the table.

'Archie!' The girl reached across the table and caught his wrist. 'Archie! What is it!'

'Well, now that was a damn stupid thing to do, wasn't it?' The voice was calm, without emotion, the Bo'sun back on balance again. He wiped away the blood with a paper napkin. 'Sorry about that.'

She twisted his wrist until the palm showed. 'You've cut yourself. Quite badly.'

'It doesn't matter. Edinburgh, is it? He's haunted by it. That's what you said, Margaret. Haunted. So he damn well ought to be. And I should be haunted, too. All my life. For being so blind, so bloody well eternally stupid.'

'How can you say such a thing? If you see something that we can't see, then we're all more stupid than you are.'

'No. Because I know something that you don't know.'

'What is it, then?' There was curiosity in her voice, but it was overlaid by a deeper apprehension. 'What is it?'

McKinnon smiled. 'Margaret, I would have thought that you of all people would have learnt the dangers of talking in public. Would you please bring Captain Bowen to the lounge.'

'I can't. He's having his head bandaged.'

'I rather think, Margaret, you should do what the Bo'sun suggests.' It was the first time that Ulbricht had used her Christian name in company. 'Something tells me that the Captain will need no second invitation.'

'And bring your pal,' McKinnon said. 'What I have to say may well be of interest to her.'

She looked at him for a long and thought-ful moment, then nodded and left without a word. McKinnon watched her go, an equally thoughtful expression on his face, then turned to Jamieson. 'I think you should ask one of your men to request Mr Patterson to come to the lounge also.'

Captain Bowen came into the lounge accompa-nied by Dr Sinclair, who had no alternative but to come for he was still only half way through re-bandaging Bowen's head.

'It looks as if we'll have to change our minds again about our plans,' McKinnon said. He had a certain air of resignation about him, due not to the change in plans but to the fact that Janet was firmly bandaging his cut palm. 'It's certain now that the Germans, if they can't take us, will send us to the bottom. The *San Andreas* is no longer a hospital ship, it's more of a treasure ship. We are carrying a fortune in gold. I don't know how much but I would guess at something between twenty and thirty million pounds sterling.'

Nobody said anything. There wasn't much one could make in the way of comment about such a preposterous statement and the Bo'sun's relaxed certainty didn't encourage what might have been the expected exclamatory chorus of surprise, doubt or disbelief.

'It is, of course, Russian gold, almost certainly in exchange for lend-lease. The Germans would love to get their hands on it, for I suppose gold is gold no matter what the country of origin, but if they can't get it they're going to make damned sure that Britain doesn't get it either, and this is not out of spite or frustration, although I suppose that that would play some part. But what matters is this. The British Government is bound to know that we're carrying this gold – you've only got to think about it for a moment to see that this must have been a joint planned operation between the Soviet and British Governments.'

'Using a hospital ship as a gold transport?' Jamieson's disbelief was total. 'The British Government would never be guilty of such a pernicious act.'

'I am in no position to comment on that, sir. I can imagine that our Government can be as perfidious as any other and there are plenty of perfidious governments around. Ethics, I should think, take very much a back seat in war – if there are any ethics in war. All I want to say about the Government is that they are going to be damned suspicious of the Russians and would put the worst possible interpretation on our disappearance – they may well arrive at the conclusion that the Russians intercepted the ship after it had sailed, got rid of the crew, sailed the *San Andreas* to any port in northern Russia, unloaded the gold and scuttled the ship. Alternatively, they might well believe the Russians didn't even bother to load any gold at all but just lay in wait for the *San Andreas*. The Russians do have a submarine fleet, small as it is, in Murmansk and Archangel.

'Whichever option the Government prefers to believe, and I can imagine it highly likely that they will believe one or the other, the result will be the same and one that would delight the hearts of the Germans. The British Government is going to believe that the Russians welshed on the deal and will be extremely suspicious not only of this but of any future deal. They'll never be able to prove anything but there is something they *can* do – reduce or even stop all future lend-lease to Russia. This could be a more effective way of stopping Allied supplies to Russia than all the U-boats in the North Atlantic and Arctic.'

There was quite a long silence, then Bowen said: 'It's a very plausible scenario, Bo'sun, attractive – if one may use that word – even convincing. But it does rather depend on one thing: why do you think we have this gold aboard?'

'I don't think, sir. I know. Only a few minutes ago, just after we had sat down to dinner, Sister Morrison here happened to mention Oberleutnant Klaussen's constant delirious ramblings. In his delirium one word kept recurring – Edinburgh. Sister says he seemed to be haunted by that word. I should damn well think he was. It was not so very long ago that a U-boat sent the cruiser *Edinburgh* to the bottom on her way back from Russia. The *Edinburgh* was carrying at least twenty million pounds of gold bullion in her holds.'

'Good God!' Bowen's voice was no more than a whisper: 'Good God above! You have the right of it, Archie, by heaven you have the right of it.'

'It all ties in too damn nicely, sir. It had been dunned into Klaussen that he was not to repeat the exploits of his illustrious predecessor who had dispatched the *Edinburgh*. It also accounts – the sinking of the *Edinburgh*, I mean – for the rather underhanded decision to use the *San Andreas*. Any cruiser, any destroyer can be sunk. By the Geneva Convention, hospital ships are inviolate.'

'I only wish I had told you sooner,' Margaret Morrison said. 'He'd been muttering about Edinburgh ever since he was brought aboard. I should have realized that it must have meant something.'

'You've nothing to reproach yourself with,' McKinnon said. 'Why should the word have had any significance for you? Delirious men rave on about anything. It wouldn't have made the slightest difference if we had found out earlier. What does matter is that we have found out before it's too late. At least, I hope it's not too late. If there are any reproaches going they should come in my direction. At least I *knew* about the *Edinburgh* – I don't think anyone else did – and shouldn't have had to be reminded of it. Spilt milk.'

'It does all mesh together, doesn't it?' Jamieson said. 'Explains why they wouldn't let you and Mr Rennet see what was going on behind that tarpaulin when they were repairing the hole in the ship's side. They didn't want you to see that they were replacing that ballast they'd taken out to lighten ship by a different sort of ballast altogether. I suppose you knew what the original ballast looked like?'

'As a matter of fact, I didn't. I'm sure Mr Kennet didn't know either.'

'The Russians weren't to know that and took no chances. Oh, I'm sure they'd have painted the bullion grey or whatever the colour of the ballast was: the size and shape of the blocks and bars of the gold would almost certainly have been different. Hence the "No Entry" sign at the tarpaulin. Everything that has happened since can be explained by the presence of that gold.' Jamieson paused, seemed to hesitate then nodded as if he had made up his mind. 'Doesn't it strike you, Bo'sun, that McCrimmon poses a bit of a problem?'

'Not really. He's a double agent.'

334

'Damn it!' Jamieson was more than a little chagrined. 'I'd hoped, for once, that I might be the first to come up with the solution to a problem.'

'A close run thing,' McKinnon said. 'The same question had occurred to me at the same time. It's the only answer, isn't it? Espionage history – or so I am led to believe – is full of accounts of double agents. McCrimmon's just another. His primary employer – his only really true employer – is, of course, Germany. We may find out, we may not, how the Germans managed to infiltrate him into the service of the Russians but infiltrate him they did. Sure, it was the Russians who instructed him to blow that hole in the ballast room, but that was even more in the Germans' interest than the Russians'. Both had compelling reasons to find an excuse to divert the *San Andreas* to Murmansk, the Russians to load the gold, the Germans to load Simons and that charge in the ballast room.'

'A tangled story,' Bowen said, 'but not so tangled when you take the threads apart. This alters things more than a little, doesn't it, Bo'sun?'

'I rather think it does, sir.'

'Any idea of the best course – I use that word in both its senses – to take for the future?'

'I'm open to suggestions.'

'You'll get none from me. With all respect to Dr Sinclair, his ministrations have just about closed down a mind that wasn't working all that well in the first place.'

'Mr Patterson?' McKinnon said. 'Mr Jamieson?'

'Oh no,' Jamieson said. 'I have no intention of being caught out in that way again. It does my morale no good to have it quietly explained to me why my brilliant scheme won't work and why it would be much better to do it your way. Besides, I'm an engineer. What do you have in mind?'

'On your own heads. I have in mind to continue on this course, which is due west, until about midnight. This will help to take us even further away from the Heinkels and Stukas. I'm not particularly worried about them, they rarely attack after dark and if we're right in our assumption that we've slipped that U-boat, then they don't know where to look for us and the absence of any flares from a Condor would suggest that, if they are looking, they are looking in the wrong place.

'At midnight, I'll ask the Lieutenant to lay off a course for Aberdeen. We must hope that there will be a few helpful stars around. That would take us pretty close to the east coast of the Shetlands, Lieutenant?'

'Very close indeed, I should say. Hailing distance. You'll be able to wave a last farewell to your homeland, Mr McKinnon.'

'Mr McKinnon isn't going to wave farewell to any place.' The voice was Janet Magnusson's and it was pretty positive. 'He needs a holiday, he tells me, he's homesick and Lerwick is his home. Right, Archie?'

'You have the second sight, Janet.' If McKinnon was chagrined at having his thunder stolen he showed no signs of it. 'I thought it might be a good idea, Captain, to stop off a bit in Lerwick and have a look at what we have up front. This has two advantages, I think. We're certain now that the Germans will sink us sooner than permit our safe arrival in any British port and the further south we go the greater the likelihood of being clobbered, so we make as little southing as possible. Secondly, if we are found by either plane or U-boat, they'll be able to confirm that we're still on a direct course to Aberdeen and so have plenty of time in hand. At the appropriate moment we'll turn west, round a place called Bard Head, then north-west and north to Lerwick. From the time we alter course till the time we reach harbour shouldn't be much more than an hour and it would take rather longer than that for the German bombers to scramble from Bergen and reach there.'

'Sounds pretty good to me,' Jamieson said.

'I wish I could say the same. It's far too easy, too cut and dried, and there's always the possibility of the Germans figuring out that that's exactly what we will do. Probability would be more like. It's too close to a counsel of desperation, but it's the least of all the evils I can imagine and we have to make a break for it some time.'

'As I keep on saying, Bo'sun,' Jamieson said, 'it's a great comfort having you around.'

TWELVE

The time wore on to midnight and still the Condors kept away. Apart from two men on watch in the engine-room, Naseby and Trent on the bridge and Lieutenant Ulbricht and McKinnon in the Captain's cabin, two hospital look-outs and two night nurses, everyone was asleep, or appeared to be asleep, or should have been asleep. The wind, backing to the north, had freshened to Force four and there was a moderate sea running, enough to make the *San Andreas* roll as she headed steadily west but not enough to inconvenience one.

In the Captain's cabin Lieutenant Ulbricht looked up from the chart he had been studying, then glanced at his watch.

'Ten minutes to midnight. Not that the precise time matters – we'll be making course alterations as we go along. I suggest we take a last sight, then head for the Shetlands.'

*   *   *

338

Dawn came, a cold and grey and blustery dawn, and still the Condors stayed away. At ten o'clock, a rather weary McKinnon – he'd been on the wheel since 4.0 a.m. – went below in search of breakfast. He found Jamieson having a cup of coffee.

'A peaceful night, Bo'sun. Does look as if we've shaken them off, doesn't it?'

'So it would seem.'

'Seem? Only "seem"?' Jamieson looked at him speculatively. 'Do I detect a note of something less than cheerful confidence? A whole night long without a sign of the enemy. Surely we should be happy with our present circumstances?'

'Sure, I am. The present's just fine. What I'm not so happy about is the future. It's not only quiet and peaceful at the moment, it's too damn quiet and peaceful. As the old saying goes, it's the lull before the storm, the present the lull, the future the storm. Don't you feel it, sir?'

'No, I don't!' Jamieson looked away and frowned slightly. 'Well, I didn't, not until you came along and disturbed the quiet and even tenor of my way. Any moment now and you'll be telling me I'm living in a fool's paradise.'

'That would be stretching it a bit, sir.'

'Too quiet, too peaceful? Maybe it is at that. Cat and mouse, again – with us, of course, in the role of mouse? They have us pinned and are just waiting for a convenient moment – convenient for them, that is – to strike?'

'Yes. I've just spent six hours on the wheel and I've had plenty of time to think about it – two minutes should have been enough. If there's anybody living in a fool's paradise it's been me. How many Focke-Wulf Condors do you think they have in the Trondheim and Bergen airfields, sir?'

'I don't know. Too damn many for my liking, I'm sure.'

'And for mine. Three or four of them acting in concert could cover ten thousand square miles in a couple of hours, all depending upon how high they are and what the visibility is. Bound to locate us – us, the most valuable prize on the Norwegian Sea. But they haven't, they haven't even bothered to try. Why?'

'Because they know where we are. Because we didn't manage to slip that submarine after sunset.'

McKinnon nodded and propped his chin on his hands. His breakfast lay untouched before him.

'You did your best, Bo'sun. There was never any guarantee. You can't reproach yourself.'

'Oh yes I can. It's a thing I'm getting pretty good at – reproaching myself, I mean. But in this case, not for the reason you think. Given only the slightest degree of luck we should have shaken him yesterday evening. We didn't. We forgot the Factor X.'

'You sound like an advertisement, Bo'sun. Factor X, the secret ingredient in the latest ladies' cosmetics.'

'What I mean, sir, is that even if we slipped him – moved out of his Asdic listening range – he could still have found us, Asdic or not, Condors or not. A good archer always carries a second string for his bow.'

'A second string?' Jamieson put his cup down very carefully. 'You mean we have a second of those damned location transmitter bugs aboard?'

'Can you think of any other solution, sir? Luck has made us too smug, too self-confident, to the extent that we have been guilty of gravely under-estimating the ungodly. Singh or McCrimmon or Simons – all three of them, for all I know – have been smarter than us, smart enough, anyway, to gamble on the likelihood of our missing the glar-ingly obvious, just because it was too obvious. Chances are high that this won't be a transceiver, just a simple transmitter no bigger than a lady's handbag.'

'But we've already searched, Bo'sun. Very thoroughly indeed. If there wasn't anything there then, there won't be anything now. I mean, transmitters just don't materialize out of thin air.'

'No. But there could have been one before we made our search. It could have been transferred elsewhere before that – it's entirely possible that any or all of the three Flannelfeet may have antic-ipated just such a search. Sure we combed the area of the hospital, cabins, store-rooms, galleys, everything – but that's all we did search.'

'Yes, but where else – ' Jamieson broke off and looked thoughtful.

'Yes, sir, the same thought had occurred to me. The superstructure is no more than an uninhabited warren at the moment.'

'Isn't it just?' Jamieson put down his cup and rose. 'Well, heigh-ho for the superstructure. I'll take a couple of my boys with me.'

'Would they recognize a bug if they saw one? I don't think I would.'

'I would. All they've got to do is to bring me any piece of equipment that has no place aboard a ship.'

After he had gone McKinnon reflected that Jamieson, in addition to his engineering qualifications, was also an A.M.I.E.E. and, as such, probably able to identify a bug.

Not more than ten minutes later Jamieson returned, smiling widely and in evident satisfaction.

'The unfailing instinct of your true bug-hunter, Bo'sun. Got it first time. Unerring, you might say.'

'Where?'

'Cunning devils. Suppose they thought it would be ironic and the last place we would look. What more fitting place for a radio device than a wrecked radio room? Not only had they used one of the few undamaged batteries there to power it, they'd even rigged up a makeshift aerial. Not that

342

you would ever know that it was an aerial of any kind, not just to look at it.'

'Congratulations, sir. That was well done. Is it still in place?'

'Yes. First instincts, of course, were to rip the damn thing out. But then, wiser counsels, if I can use that term about myself, prevailed. If they have us on that transmitter, then they have us on their Asdic.'

'Of course. And if we'd dismantled our set and stopped the engine and generator, they'd just have poked their periscope above the surface and located us in nothing flat. There'll be a better time and better place to dismantle that bug.'

'During the night, you mean, Bo'sun – if we're still afloat by nightfall?'

'I'm not rightly sure, sir. As you infer, it all depends upon what condition we're in come the dark.'

Jamieson looked at him in what could have been a faintly disbelieving speculation, but said nothing.

McKinnon, in an empty cabin next to that of Captain Andropolous, was sound asleep when Johnny Holbrook shook him half an hour after noon.

'Mr Naseby is on the phone, sir.'

McKinnon sat up in his bunk, rubbed his eyes and looked with something less than favour at the teenage ward orderly who, like Wayland Day, walked in awe of the Bo'sun.

'Couldn't somebody else have spoken to him?'

'Sorry, sir. Specially asked for you.'

McKinnon moved out into the mess-deck where people were already gathering for lunch. Patterson was there with Jamieson and Sinclair, together with Margaret Morrison and Nurse Irene. He picked up the phone.

'George, I was in a better world right now.'

'Sorry about that, Archie. Thought you'd better know. We have company.' Naseby could have been talking about the weather.

'Ah!'

'Starboard. About two miles. A bit under, perhaps. Says to stop or he will fire.'

'Oh.'

'Also says that if we try to alter course he will sink us.'

'Is that so?'

'So he says. May even mean it. Shall I turn into him?'

'Yes.'

'Full power?'

'I'll ask for it. Up in a minute.' He replaced the phone.

'My word,' Margaret Morrison said. 'That was an intriguing conversation. Full of information, if I may say so.'

'We bo'suns are men of few words. Mr Patterson, could we have full power?' Patterson nodded heavily, rose without speaking and crossed to the telephone.

Jamieson said in a resigned voice: 'No need to ask, I suppose?'

'No, sir. Sorry about your lunch.'

'The usual – ah – direct tactics?' Sinclair said.

'No option. Man says he's going to sink us.'

'He's going to say more than that when he sees us altering course towards him,' Jamieson said. 'He's going to say that the *San Andreas* is crewed by a bunch of unreconstructed lunatics.'

'If he does, he could well be right.' As he turned to go Ulbricht put out a restraining hand.

'I'm coming too.'

'Please not, Lieutenant. I don't believe our new acquaintance is going to sink us but he's sure as hell going to try to stop us. The primary target will be the bridge, I'm sure. You want to undo all the good work Dr Sinclair and the nursing staff have already done, the stitching and bandaging all over again? Selfish. Margaret!'

'You stay where you are, Karl Ulbricht.'

Ulbricht scowled, shrugged, smiled and stayed where he was.

When McKinnon reached the bridge the *San Andreas*, under maximum helm, was already beginning to slew round to starboard. Naseby looked round as McKinnon entered.

'Take the wheel, Archie. He's sending.'

Naseby moved out on the starboard wing. Someone on the conning-tower of the U-boat was indeed using an Aldis lamp but transmitting very slowly – almost certainly, McKinnon guessed, because a non-English-speaking operator was sending letter by given letter. For'ard of the conning-tower three men were crouched around the deck-gun which, as far as the bo'sun could judge at that distance, was pointed directly at them. The signalling ceased.

'What does he say, George?'

' "Regain course. Stop or I fire".'

'Send him that bit about a hospital ship and the Geneva Convention.'

'He won't pay a blind bit of attention.'

'Send it anyway. Distract him. Give us time. The rules say you don't shoot a man when you're having a conversation with him.'

Naseby started transmitting but almost immediately jumped back inside the bridge. The puff of smoke from the gun was unmistakable, as was the shock and sound of a shell exploding inside the superstructure almost immediately afterwards. Naseby gave McKinnon a reproachful look.

'They're not playing by your rules, Archie.'

'So it would seem. Can you see where we've been hit?'

Naseby went out on the starboard wing and looked below and aft.

'Crew's mess-deck,' he said. 'Well, what was the crew's mess-deck. Nobody there now, of course.'

'Not what they were aiming for, you can be sure of that. A Force four is nothing to us but it makes for a very unstable gun-platform on a submarine. I don't like that very much, George, they're liable to hit anywhere except where they're aiming for. We can only hope that the next one is as high above the bridge as that one was below it.'

The next one came straight through the bridge. It shattered the starboard for'ard window – one of those that had been replaced after Klaussen's machine-gunners had destroyed them – penetrated the thin sheet-metal that separated the bridge from what had been the wireless office and exploded just beyond. The sliding wooden door, now in a hundred jagged fragments, blew forward into the bridge and the concussive blast of the explosion sent both men staggering, McKinnon against the wheel, Naseby against a small chart table: but the razor-sharp shards of the shell casing had flown in the other direction and both men were unhurt.

Naseby recovered some of the air that had been driven from his lungs. 'They're improving, Archie.'

'Fluke.' The *San Andreas*, its superstructure beginning to vibrate quite badly as engine revolutions built up, was now bearing down directly on the conning-tower of the U-boat which, however, was still considerably more than a mile distant. 'Next one will miss the bridge by a mile.'

The next one, in fact, missed the ship completely and went into the sea a hundred yards astern of the *San Andreas*. It did not detonate on impact.

The following shell struck somewhere in the vicinity of the bows. Where it had exploded was impossible to tell from the bridge, for there was no visible uplifting or buckling of the fo'c's'le deck, but that it had done its damage was beyond doubt: the furious rattling of chain as one of the fore anchors plunged down to the floor of the Norwegian Sea could be heard a mile away. The rattling ceased as abruptly as it had begun, the fastening doubtless torn from the floor of the chain locker.

'No loss,' Naseby said. 'Who's ever anchored in a thousand feet or whatever?'

'Who cares about the anchor? Point is, are we open to the sea?'

Yet another shell buried itself in the bows and this time there was no doubt where it had landed for a small area of the fo'c's'le deck, port side, lifted upwards almost a foot.

'Open to the sea or not,' Naseby said, 'this hardly seems to be the time to investigate. Not as long as they are zeroing in on the bows, which is what they appear to be doing. We're all that closer now so they're getting all the more accurate. They seem to be going for the waterline. It can't be that they want to sink us. And don't they know the gold is there?'

'I don't know what they know. Probably know there's gold aboard: no reason why they should know where. Not that a little shrapnel lowers the value of gold. Anyway, I suppose we should be grateful for small mercies: at this angle of approach it's impossible that they can hit the hospital area.'

A third shell struck and exploded in the bows in almost the same position as the previous one – the already uplifted section of the fo'c's'le had heaved up almost another foot.

'That's where the paint and carpenter's shops are,' Naseby said absently.

'That's what I've been thinking.'

'Were Ferguson and Curran in the mess-deck when you left?'

'That's why I've been thinking. Can't remember seeing them, although that's not to say they weren't there. They're such an idle couple they might well have passed up lunch for an hour's kip. I should have warned them.'

'There wasn't time for you to warn anyone.'

'I could have sent someone. I did think they'd concentrate their fire on the bridge but I should still have sent someone. My fault. Slipping, as I told Jamieson.' He paused, narrowed his eyes in concentration and said: 'I think they're turning away, George.'

Naseby had the glasses to his eyes. 'They are. And there's someone on the bridge, captain or whoever, using a loud-hailer. Ah! The gun crew are working on their gun and – yes – they're aligning it fore-and-aft. This mean what I think it means, Archie?'

'Well, the conning-tower's empty and the gun crew are going down the hatch so it must mean what you think. See any bubbles coming up?'

'No. Wait a minute. Yes. Yes, lots.'

'Blowing main ballast.'

'But we're still a mile away from them.'

'Captain's taking no chances and I don't blame him. He's not a clown like Klaussen.'

They watched for some moments in silence. The U-boat was now at a 45° angle, the decks barely awash and vanishing quickly.

'Take the wheel, George. Give the Chief Engineer a ring, will you, tell him what's happened and ask him to drop down to normal speed. Then back on the course we were on. I'm going to check on any flooding for'ard.'

Naseby watched him go and knew that flooding was secondary in the Bo'sun's mind. He was going to find out whether, indeed, Curran and Ferguson had elected to miss lunch.

McKinnon was back in about ten minutes. He had a bottle of Scotch in his hand and two glasses and no smile on his face.

Naseby said: 'Their luck run out?'

'Abandoned by fortune, George. Abandoned by McKinnon.'

*   *   *

350

'Archie, you must stop it. Please stop blaming yourself. What's done is done.' Janet had intercepted him as he had entered the mess-deck – he had come down with Naseby and left Trent on the wheel with Jones and McGuigan as look-outs – and pulled him into a corner. 'Oh, I know that's trite, meaningless, if you want. And if you want another trite and meaningless remark, you can't bring back the dead.'

'True, true.' The Bo'sun smiled without humour. 'And speaking of the dead – and one should speak no ill of the dead – they were a couple of moderately useless characters. But both were married, both had two daughters. What would *they* think if they knew that the gallant bo'sun, in his anxiety to get at a U-boat, completely forgot them?'

'The best thing would be if *you* forgot them. Sounds cruel, I know, but let the dead bury their dead. *We* are alive: when I say "we" I'm not talking about you, I'm talking about every other person aboard, including myself. Your duty is to the living. Don't you know that every single person on this ship, from the Captain and Mr Patterson down, depends on you? We're depending on you to take us home.'

'Do be quiet, woman.'

'You'll take *me* home, Archie?'

'Scalloway? Hop, skip and jump. Of course I will.'

She stood back at arm's length, hands on his shoulders, searched his eyes, then smiled.

351

'You know, Archie, I really believe you will.'

He smiled in return. 'I'm glad of that.' He didn't for a moment believe it himself but there was no point in spreading undue gloom and despondency.

They joined Patterson, Jamieson and Ulbricht at the table. Patterson pushed a glass in front of him. 'I would say that you have earned that, Bo'sun. A splendid job.'

'Not so splendid, sir. I had no option but to do what I did. Can't say I feel sorry for a U-boat captain but he's really up against a nearly impossible problem, faced with a hiding to nothing. He's under orders not to sink us so the best he can do is to try to incapacitate us as much as possible. We run at him and he hides. Simple as that.'

'The way you put it, yes. I hear you had a very narrow escape on the bridge.'

'If the shell had passed through metal and exploded in the bridge, that would have been it. But it passed through the glass instead. Luck.'

'And up front?'

'Three holes. All above the waterline. What with those and the damage that the U-boat did to us – rather, the damage we inflicted on ourselves – there's going to be a fair old job for the ship repairers when we get into dry dock. The watertight bulkheads seem sound enough. That's the good part. The bad part – and I'm afraid this is all my fault – is that –'

'Archie!' Janet's voice was sharp.

'Oh, all right. You'll have heard – Ferguson and Curran are dead.'

'I know and I'm sorry. Damnable. That makes twenty now.' Patterson thought for a few moments. 'You reckon this situation will continue for some time?'

'What situation, sir?'

'That they keep on trying to stop us instead of sinking us.'

McKinnon shrugged. 'It is much more important to the Germans that they discredit the Russians with our Government than that they get the gold. As things stand at the moment they want both to have their cake and eat it. Factor of greed, really.'

'So as long as they remain greedy we're relatively safe?'

'Safe from sinking, yes. But not safe from being taken over.'

'But you just said –'

'All they have to do is to bring up another U-boat and they'll have us cold. With two U-boats we have no chance. If we go after one the other will parallel our course and pump shells into us at their leisure. Not the engine-room, of course, they want to take us under our own steam to Norway. The hospital area. First shell in there and the white flag flies – if we've any sense we'd fly it before the first shot. Next time I go up to the bridge I'll take a nice big bedsheet with me.'

'There are times, Bo'sun,' Jamieson said, 'when I wish you'd keep your thoughts to yourself.'

'Merely answering a question, sir. And I have another thought, another question, if you like. Only a tiny handful of people would have known of this operation, the plan to use the *San Andreas* as a bullion carrier. A cabinet minister or two, an admiral or two. No more. I wonder who the traitor is who sold us down the river. *If* we get back and *if* some famous and prominent person unaccountably commits suicide, then we'll know.' He rose. 'If you'll excuse me, I have some work to do.'

'What work, Archie?' It was Janet. 'Haven't you done enough for one day?'

'A bo'sun's work is never done. Routine, Janet, just routine.' He left the mess-deck.

'Routine,' Janet said. 'What routine?'

'Curran's dead.'

She looked puzzled. 'I know that.'

'Curran was the sailmaker. It's the sailmaker's job to sew up the dead.'

Janet rose hastily and left the table. Patterson gave Jamieson a sour look.

'There are times, Second, when I wish *you* would keep your thoughts to yourself. You do have half an eye, I take it.'

'True, true. Delicacy? A water buffalo could have done it better.'

THIRTEEN

Patterson finished speaking – by this time he was getting quite professional at reading burial services – planks tilted and the shrouded forms of Curran and Ferguson slid down into the icy wastes of the Norwegian Sea. It was then that the engine-room noise faded away and the *San Andreas* began to slow.

Nearly all the crew were on deck – the dead men had been an amiable enough couple and well liked. The cooks and stewards were below, as were the nursing staff and three stokers. Trent and Jones were on the bridge.

Jamieson was the first to move. 'It looks,' he said, 'as if we have made a mistake.' He walked away, not quickly, with the air of a man who knew that this was not a moment that called for any particular urgency.

Patterson and McKinnon followed more slowly. Patterson said: 'What did he mean by that? That we've made a mistake, I mean?'

'He was being kind, sir. What he meant was that the all-wise bo'sun has made another blunder. Who was on watch down below?'

'Just young Stephen. You know, the Polish boy.'

'Let's hope he's not the next to go over the side.'

Patterson stopped and caught McKinnon by the arm. 'What do you mean by that? And what do you mean – "blunder"?'

'The one thing ties up with the other.' McKinnon's voice sounded dull. 'Maybe I'm tired. Maybe I'm not thinking too well. Did you notice who *wasn't* at the funeral, sir?'

Patterson looked at him for a few silent moments, then said: 'The nursing staff. Kitchen staff. Stewards. Men on the bridge.' His grip tightened on the Bo'sun's arm. 'And McCrimmon.'

'Indeed. And whose brilliant idea was it to let McCrimmon roam around on the loose?'

'It just worked out the wrong way. You can't think of everything. No man can. He's a slippery customer, this McCrimmon. Do you think we'll be able to pin anything on him?'

'I'm certain we won't. Nevertheless, sir, I'd like your permission to lock him up.' McKinnon shook his head, his face bitter. 'There's nothing like locking the door when the horse has bolted.'

Stephen was lying on the steel plates, covered with oil still gushing from a severed fuel line. There was a rapidly forming bruise, bleeding slightly, behind his right ear. Sinclair finished examining his head and straightened.

'I'll have him taken to hospital. X-ray, but I don't think it necessary. I should think he'll waken up with nothing more than a sore head.' He looked at the two steel objects lying on the deck-plates beside Stephen. 'You know who did this, Bo'sun?'

'Yes.'

'The Stilson wrench that laid him out and the fire-axe that slashed the fuel line. There could be fingerprints.'

'No.' With his toe McKinnon touched a clump of engine-room waste. 'He used that and there'll be no prints on that. He looked at Patterson. 'This line can be replaced, sir?'

'It can. How long, Second?'

'Couple of hours,' Jamieson said. 'Give or take.'

McKinnon said: 'Would you come along with me, Mr Patterson?'

'It will be a pleasure, Bo'sun.'

'You could have killed him, you know,' McKinnon said conversationally.

From his bench seat in the mess-deck McCrimmon looked up with an insolent stare.

'What the bloody hell are you talking about?'

'Stephen.'

'Stephen? What about Stephen?'

'His broken head.'

'I still don't know what you're talking about. Broken head? How did he get a broken head?'

357

'Because you went down to the engine-room and did it. And cut open a fuel line.'

'You're crazy. I haven't left this seat in the past quarter of an hour.'

'Then you must have seen whoever went down to the engine-room. You're a stoker, McCrimmon. An engine stops and you don't go down to investigate?'

McCrimmon chewed some gum. 'This is a frame-up. What proof do you have?'

'Enough,' Patterson said. 'I am putting you under arrest, McCrimmon, and in close confinement. When we get back to Britain, you'll be tried for murder, high treason, convicted and certainly shot.'

'This is absolute rubbish.' He prefaced the word 'rubbish' with a few choice but unprintable adjectives. 'I've done nothing and you can't prove a thing.' But his normally pasty face had gone even pastier.

'We don't have to,' McKinnon said. 'Your friend Simons or Braun or whatever his name is – has been, well, as the Americans say, been singing like a canary. He's willing to turn King's evidence on you in the hope of getting less than life.'

'The bastard!' McCrimmon was on his feet, lips drawn back over his teeth, his right hand reaching under his overalls.

'Don't,' Patterson said. 'Whatever it is, don't touch it. You've got no place to run, McCrimmon – and the Bo'sun could kill you with one hand.'

'Let me have it,' McKinnon said. He stretched out his hand and McCrimmon, very slowly, very carefully, placed the knife, hilt first, in the Bo'sun's palm.

'You haven't won.' His face was both scared and vicious at the same time. 'It's the person who laughs last that wins.'

'Could be.' McKinnon looked at him consideringly. 'You know something that we don't?'

'As you say, could be.'

'Such as the existence of a transmitting bug concealed in the wireless office?'

McCrimmon leapt forward and screamed, briefly, before collapsing to the deck. His nose had broken against the Bo'sun's fist.

Patterson looked down at the unconscious man and then at McKinnon. 'That give you a certain kind of satisfaction?'

'I suppose I shouldn't have done it but – well, yes, it did give a certain kind of satisfaction.'

'Me, too,' Patterson said.

What seemed, but wasn't, a long day wore on into the evening and then darkness, and still the Germans stayed away. The *San Andreas*, under power again, was still on a direct course to Aberdeen. Stephen had regained consciousness and, as Dr Sinclair had predicted, was suffering from no more than a moderate headache. Sinclair had carried out what were no better than temporary repairs to McCrimmon's broken face but it was really a job for a plastic surgeon and Sinclair was no plastic surgeon.

Lieutenant Ulbricht, a chart spread out on the table before him, rubbed his chin thoughtfully and looked at McKinnon who was seated opposite him in the Captain's cabin.

'We've been lucky so far. Lucky? Never thought I'd say that aboard a British ship. Why are we being left alone?'

'Because we're just that. Lucky. They didn't have a spare U-boat around and our friend who's trailing us wasn't going to try it on his own again. Also, we're still on a direct course to Aberdeen. They know where we are and have no reason to believe that we still aren't going where we're supposed to be going. They have no means of knowing what's happened aboard this ship.'

'Reasonable, I suppose.' Ulbricht looked at the chart and tapped his teeth. 'If something doesn't happen to us during the night something is going to happen to us tomorrow. That's what I think. At least, that's what I feel.'

'I know.'

'What do you know?'

'Tomorrow. Your countrymen aren't clowns. We'll be passing very close to the Shetlands tomorrow. They'll suspect that there is a possibility that we might make a break for Lerwick or some such place and will act on that possibility.'

'Planes? Condors?'

'It's possible.'

'Does the RAF have fighters there?'

'I should imagine so. But I don't know. Haven't been there for years.'

'The Luftwaffe will know. If there are Hurricanes or Spitfires there, the Luftwaffe would never risk a Condor against them.'

'They could send some long-range Messerschmitts as escort.'

'If not, it could be a torpedo?'

'That's not something I care to think about.'

'Nor me. There's something very final about a torpedo. You know, it's not necessary to sail south round Bressay and turn round Bard Head. We could use the north channel. Maryfield is the name of the village, isn't it?'

'I was born there.'

'That was stupid. Stupid of me, I mean. We make a sharp turn for the north channel and it's a torpedo for sure?'

'Yes.'

'And if we steam steadily south past Bressay they may well think that we're keeping on course to Aberdeen?'

'We can only hope, Lieutenant. A guarantee is out of the question. There's nothing else we can do.'

'Nothing?'

'Well, there's something. We can go down below and have dinner.'

'Our last, perhaps?'

McKinnon crossed his fingers, smiled and said nothing.

Dinner, understandably, was a rather solemn affair. Patterson was in a particularly pensive mood.

'Has it ever occurred to you, Bo'sun, that we might outrun this U-boat? Without bursting a few steam valves, we could get two or three knots more out of this tub.'

'Yes, sir. I'm sure we could.' The tension in the air was almost palpable. 'I'm also sure that the U-boat would pick up the increased revolutions immediately. He would know that we were on to him, know that we know that he's following us. He would just surface – that would increase his speed – and finish us off. He's probably carrying a dozen torpedoes. How many do you think would miss us?'

'The first one would be enough.' Patterson sighed. 'Rather desperate men make rather desperate suggestions. You could sound more encouraging, Bo'sun.'

'Rest after toil,' Jamieson said. 'Port after stormy seas. There's going to be no rest for us, Bo'sun. No safe harbour. Is that it?'

'Has to be, sir.' He pointed at Janet Magnusson. 'You heard me promise to take this lady back home.'

Janet smiled at him. 'You're very kind, Archie McKinnon. Also, you're lying in your teeth.'

McKinnon smiled back at her. 'Ye of little faith.'

Ulbricht was the first to sense a change in the atmosphere. 'Something has occurred to you, Mr McKinnon?'

'Yes. At least, I hope it has.' He looked at Margaret Morrison. 'I wonder if you would be so kind as to ask Captain Bowen to come to the lounge?'

'*Another* secret conference? I thought there were no more spies or criminals or traitors left aboard.'

'I don't think so. But no chances.' He looked around the table. 'I would like it if you all joined us.'

Just after dawn the next morning – still a very late dawn in those latitudes – Lieutenant Ulbricht gazed out through the starboard wing doorway at low-lying land that could be intermittently seen through squalls of sleety snow.

'So that's Unst, is it?'

'That's Unst.' Although McKinnon had been up most of the night he seemed fresh, relaxed and almost cheerful.

'And that – *that* is what you Shetlanders break your hearts over?'

'Yes, indeed.'

'I don't want to give any offence, Mr McKinnon, but that's probably the most bare, bleak, barren and inhospitable island I've ever had the misfortune to clap my eyes on.'

'Home sweet home,' McKinnon said placidly. 'Beauty, Lieutenant, is in the eye of the beholder. Besides, no place would look its sparkling best in weather conditions like this.'

'And that's another thing. Is the Shetland weather always as awful as this?'

McKinnon regarded the slate-grey seas, the heavy cloud and the falling snow with considerable satisfaction. 'I think the weather is just lovely.'

'As you say, the eye of the beholder. I doubt whether a Condor pilot would share your point of view.'

'It's unlikely.' McKinnon pointed ahead. 'Fine off the starboard now. That's Fetlar.'

'Ah!' Ulbricht consulted the chart. 'Within a mile – or two at the most – or where we ought to be. We haven't done too badly, Mr McKinnon.'

'We? You, you mean. A splendid piece of navigation, Lieutenant. The Admiralty should give you a medal for your services.'

Ulbricht smiled. 'I doubt whether Admiral Doenitz would quite approve of that. Speaking of services, you will now, I take it, be finished with mine. As a navigator, I mean.'

'My father was a fisherman, a professional. My first four years at sea I spent with him around those islands. It would be difficult for me to get lost.'

'I should imagine.' Ulbricht went out on the starboard wing, looked aft for a few seconds, then hastily returned, shivering and dusting snow off his coat.

'The sky – or what I can see of the sky – is getting pretty black up north. Wind's freshening a bit. Looks as if this awful weather – or, if you like, wonderful weather – is going to continue for quite some time. This never entered your calculations.'

'I'm not a magician. Nor am I a fortune-teller. Reading the future is not one of my specialities.'

'Well, just let's call it a well-timed stroke of luck.'

'Luck we could use. A little, anyway.'

Fetlar was on the starboard beam when Naseby came up to take over the wheel. McKinnon went out on the starboard wing to assess the weather. As the *San Andreas* was heading just a degree or two west of south and the wind was from the north it was almost directly abaft. The clouds in that direction were dark and ominous but they did not hold his attention for long: he had become aware, very faintly at first but then more positively, of something a great deal more ominous. He went back inside and looked at Ulbricht.

'Remember we were talking about luck a little while back?' Ulbricht nodded. 'Well, our little luck has just run out. We have company. There's a Condor out there.'

Ulbricht said nothing, just went outside on the wing and listened. He returned after a few moments.

'I can hear nothing.'

'Variation in wind force or direction. Something like that. I heard it all right. Up in a north-easterly direction. I'm quite sure that the pilot didn't intend that we should hear him. Some passing freak of wind. They're being either very careful or very suspicious or maybe both. They have to consider the possibility that we might make a break for some port in the Shetlands. So the U-boat surfaces before dawn and calls up the Focke-Wulf. Pilot's doubtless been told to stay out of sight and hearing. He'll do that until he hears from the U-boat that we've suddenly changed direction. Then he'll come calling.'

'To finish us off,' Naseby said.

'They won't be dropping any rose petals, that's for sure.'

Ulbricht said: 'You no longer think that it will be torpedo-bombers or glider-bombers or Stukas that will come and do the job?'

'No. They wouldn't get here in time and they can't come earlier and hang around waiting. They haven't the range. But that big lad out there can hang around all day if need be. Of course, I'm only assuming there's only one Condor out there. Could be two or three of them. Don't forget we're a very, very important target.'

'It's a gift not given to many.' Ulbricht was gloomy. 'This ability to cheer up people and lighten their hearts.'

'I second that.' Naseby didn't sound any happier than Ulbricht. 'I wish to hell you hadn't gone out on that wing.'

'You wouldn't like me to keep the burden of my secrets alone, would you? No need to tell anyone else. Why spread gloom and despondency unnecessarily, especially when there's damn-all we can do about it.'

'Blissful ignorance, is that it?' Naseby said. McKinnon nodded. 'I could do with some of that.'

Shortly after noon, when they were off a small and dimly seen group of islands which McKinnon called the Skerries, he and Ulbricht went below, leaving Naseby and McGuigan on the bridge. The snow, which was now really more sleet than snow, had eased but not stopped. The wind, too, had eased. The visibility, if that was the word for it, varied intermittently between two and four miles. Cloud cover was about two thousand feet and somewhere above that the unseen Condor lurked. McKinnon had not heard it again but he didn't for a moment doubt that it was still there.

The Captain and Rennet were sitting up in bed and the Bo'sun passed the time of day with them and Margaret Morrison. Everybody was being elaborately calm but the tension and expectancy in the air were unmistakable and considerable. It would have been even more considerable, McKinnon reflected, if they had known of the Condor patrolling above the clouds.

He found Patterson and Sinclair in the mess-deck. Sinclair said: 'Singularly free from alarms and excursions this morning, aren't we, Bo'sun?'

'Long may it continue that way.' He wondered if Sinclair would consider the accompanying Condor an alarm or an excursion. 'The weather is rather on our side. Snowing, poor visibility – not fog but not good – and low cloud cover.'

'Sounds promising. May yet be that we shall touch the Happy Isles.'

'We hope. Speaking of the Happy Isles, have you made preparations for off-loading our wounded cripples when we reach the Isles?'

'Yes. No problem. Rafferty is a stretcher case. So are four of the men we picked up in Murmansk – two with leg wounds, two frostbite cases. Five in all. Easy.'

'Sounds good. Mr Patterson, those two rogues, McCrimmon and Simons or whatever his name is. We'll have to tie them up – at least tie their hands behind their backs – before we take them ashore.'

'If we get the chance to take them ashore. Have to leave it to the last minute – double-dyed criminals they may be but we can't have a couple of men go down in a sinking ship.'

'Please don't talk about such things,' Sinclair said.

'Of course, sir. Have they been fed? Not that I really care.'

'No.' It was Sinclair. 'I saw them. Simons says he's lost his appetite and McCrimmon's face is too painful to let him eat. I believe him, he can hardly move his lips to speak. It looks, Bo'sun, as if you hit him with a sledgehammer.'

'No tears for either.'

McKinnon had a quick lunch and rose to go. 'Have to go to relieve Naseby.'

McKinnon said: 'Two hours or so. Perhaps earlier if I can see a convenient bank of low cloud or snow or even fog – anything we can disappear into. You or Mr Jamieson will be in the engine-room about then?'

'Both, probably.' Patterson sighed. 'We can only hope it works, Bo'sun.'

'That's all we can do, sir.'

Shortly after three o'clock in the afternoon, on the bridge with Naseby and Ulbricht, McKinnon made his decision to go. He said to Ulbricht: 'We can't see it but we're near enough opposite the south tip of Bressay?'

'I would say so. Due west of us.'

'Well, no point in putting off the inevitable.' He lifted the phone and called the engine-room. 'Mr Patterson? Now, if you please. George, hard a-starboard. Due west.'

'And how am I to know where west is?'

McKinnon went to the starboard wing door and latched it open. 'Going to be a bit chilly – and damp – but if you keep the wind fair and square on your right cheek that should be it, near

369

enough.' He went into the wrecked radio room, disconnected the transmitting bug, returned to the bridge and went out on the port wing.

The weather had changed very little. Grey skies, grey seas, moderate sleet and a patchy visibility extending to not more than two miles. He returned to the bridge again, leaving the door open so that the north wind had a clear passage through the bridge.

'One wonders,' Ulbricht said, 'what thoughts are passing through the mind of the U-boat captain at this moment.'

'Probably not very pleasant ones. All depends whether he was depending on the transmitting bug or the Asdic or both to keep tabs on us. *If* it was the bug, then he might trail us at a prudent distance so that he could have his aerial raised to pick up the transmitting signal without being seen. In that case he might have been out of Asdic listening range. And if *that* is the case he might well believe that the transmitter has failed. He has, after all, no reason to believe that we might have stumbled on the bug and that we know of McCrimmon's shenanigans.'

The *San Andreas*, silent now, was heading approximately west, still with a good turn of speed on.

'So he's in a quandary,' McKinnon said. 'Not a position I would like to be in. So what decision does he make? Does he increase speed on the same course we've been following in the hope of catching us up or does he think we might be running for shelter and go off on an interception course for Bard Head in the hope of locating us? All depends how crafty he is.'

'I just don't know,' Ulbricht said.

'I know,' Naseby said. 'We're just assuming that he hasn't been tracking us on Asdic. If he's as crafty as you are, Archie, he'll set off on an interception course – *and* he'll ask the Condor to come down and look for us.'

'I was afraid you'd say that.'

Fifteen minutes passed in an increasingly eerie silence, then McKinnon went out on the port wing. He didn't remain there long.

'You were right, George.' The Bo'sun sounded resigned. 'He's out there, searching for us. I can hear the Condor's engines quite clearly but he hasn't seen us yet. But he will, though, he will. He's only got to quarter the area long enough – and that won't be long – and he'll nail us. Then a signal to the U-boat, a cluster of bombs for us and the U-boat comes to finish us off.'

'That's a very depressing thought,' Naseby said.

Ulbricht went out on to the port wing and returned almost immediately. He said nothing, just nodded his head.

McKinnon picked up the engine-room phone. 'Mr Patterson? Would you start up, please? And please don't bother working her up slowly. Quickly, if you would, and to maximum power.

The Condor is down searching for us and it can only be a matter of minutes before he finds us. I'd like to make tracks out of here with all speed.'

'You're not as fast as a Condor,' Naseby said.

'I'm sadly aware of that, George. But I don't intend to remain here like a sitting duck while he comes and clobbers us. We can always try a little evasive action.'

'He can also turn and twist a damn sight faster than we can. You'd be better off trying a few prayers.'

The Condor took another twenty minutes to find them but find them he did and wasted no time in making his presence felt as well as heard. In the classic fashion he approached from astern, flying low as Naseby had predicted he would, certainly at not more than three hundred feet. Naseby gave the rudder maximum helm to port but it was a wasted effort: as Naseby had also said, the Condor could turn and twist much faster than they could.

The bomb, certainly not the size of a 500-pounder, struck the deck some sixty feet for'ard of the superstructure, penetrated and exploded in a flash of flame and a large jet of oily black water.

'That was odd,' Naseby said.

The Bo'sun shook his head. 'Not odd. Greed.'

'Greed?' Ulbricht looked at him, then nodded. 'Gold.'

'They haven't given up hope yet. How far would you say it was to Bard Head?'

'Four miles?'

'About that. If they don't get us – stop us, I mean – by that point, then they're going to sink us.'

'And if they stop us?'

'They wait till the U-boat comes up and takes us over.'

'It's a sad thing,' Naseby said. 'Very sad. This love of money, I mean.'

'I think,' McKinnon said, 'that they'll be back in a minute or so to show us some more love.'

And, indeed, the Condor was executing a very tight turn and heading back to pass the *San Andreas* on the port side.

'Some of you Condor pilots,' McKinnon said to Ulbricht, 'have very determined and one-track minds.'

'There are times when one wishes they hadn't.'

The second attack was an exact replica of the first. The pilot – or his navigator – was evidently a precision bombardier of some note for the second bomb landed in exactly the same place with precisely the same results.

'These are not very big bombs,' McKinnon said, 'but it's for sure we can't take much more of this. Another one like that and I think we'll call it a day.'

'The white bedsheet, is that it?'

'That's it. I have it up here. I wasn't kidding. Listen! I hear an aero engine!'

'So did I,' Ulbricht said. 'All made in Germany.'

'Not this one, it's not. Different note altogether. It's a fighter plane. My God, how stupid can I be! Come to that, how stupid can you be? Or the pilot of that Condor? Of course they've got radar on the island. Place is probably hotching with the stuff. Of course they've picked us up, of course they've picked the Condor up. So they've sent out someone to investigate. No. Not someone. I hear two.' McKinnon reached out and flooded the decks and side of the *San Andreas* with its Red Cross lights. 'We had better not be mistaken for the *Tirpitz*.'

'I can see them now,' Ulbricht said. His voice was without expression.

'Me, too.' McKinnon looked at Ulbricht and managed to keep the elation out of his voice. 'Do you recognize them?'

'Yes. Hurricanes.'

'I'm sorry, Lieutenant.' The regret in the Bo'sun's voice was genuine. 'But you know what this means?'

'I'm afraid I do.'

It was no contest. The Hurricanes rapidly over-hauled the Condor from the rear and fired simul-taneously, one from above, the other from below. The Focke-Wulf didn't blow up or disintegrate or burst into flames or anything dramatic of that nature. Trailing clouds of smoke, it crashed steeply into the sea and vanished at once below the waves. Lieutenant Ulbricht's face still remained empty of all expression.

The two fighter planes returned to the *San Andreas* and began to circle it, one close in, the other at the distance of about a mile. Although it was difficult to see what they could do against a submarine about to launch a torpedo except blow its periscope off, their presence was immensely comforting and reassuring.

McKinnon stepped out on the port wing and waved at one of the planes, the one making a close circuit of the ship. The Hurricane waggled its wings.

Jamieson answered the telephone when McKinnon called. 'I think you can reduce to normal speed now, sir. The Condor's gone.'

'Gone where?' There was, as there might well have been, bafflement in Jamieson's voice.

'Under the sea. A couple of Hurricanes shot him down.'

The Hurricanes remained with them until they were within a mile of Bard Head when a lean, purposeful frigate approached out of the gathering dusk and slid effortlessly alongside. The Bo'sun was on the deck.

A man aboard the frigate – presumably the captain – used a loud-hailer.

'Are you in need of care and protection, friend?'

'Not now we're not.'

'Are you badly damaged?'

'Some. A few shells and bombs. But we're a going concern. There's a nasty old U-boat hanging around.'

'Not now he won't be. He'll be all to hell and gone. What's that you see on my poop?'

'Ah! Depth charges.'

'Well, well.' The bearded naval Commodore shook his head in wonderment and looked at the others gathered in the small lounge of the hotel. 'The story is impossible, of course, but on the evidence of my eyes – well, I've just got to believe you. Your crew and passengers all taken care of, Mr Patterson?'

'Yes, sir. Here and in nearby houses. We have everything we want.'

'And there's somebody very high up in either the Cabinet or Admiralty who's been telling tales. Shouldn't take too long to root him out. Bo'sun, you're quite, quite sure about this gold?'

'Your pension against mine, sir. I should imagine there's a considerable difference.' He rose, took Janet Magnusson's arm and helped her to her feet. 'If you will excuse me, everybody. I promised to take this lady back home.'